The County

By

T.A. Novak

Lou,
Work the County with Jake.
T. Novak 9/2/2018

This book is a work of fiction. Places, events and situations in this story are purely fictional. Any resemblance to actual persons, living or dead, is coincidental.

ISBN: 978-0-9885051-1-7 (Paperback)

Library of Congress Control Number: 2014922939

This book is printed on acid free paper in the United States of America.

Cover art by
Lori Villarreal

Alley Cop Publishing-Est. 02/08

Dedication

This book is dedicated to the past and present members of Michigan's Oakland County Sheriff's Department and the police officers throughout the United States of America—men and women who daily risk their lives for the citizens of this country.

I would especially like to humbly dedicate this work to the two NYC Police Officers, Rafael Ramos and Wenjian Liu, who were ambushed and killed for just being police officers.

The names of the victims of the Oakland Child Killer were purposely withheld within this novel out of respect for the four children murdered, their parents and surviving relatives.

Requiescat In Pace.

Acknowledgements

I don't believe any author can claim that their work was the result of their efforts alone. I am indebted to the Lake Havasu City Writers Group and especially my wife, Edie, for the critiques and encouragement over the years.

The cover is the creation of a great artist, Lori Villarreal, and the total package would not be what it is without the help and dedication of Paul Bailey and his Easytime Publishing.

I am also indebted to those who contributed by sharing their inside knowledge about the Oakland County Sheriff's Department, or questions I had concerning the mental health field. Any errors are my own as I tried to weave their input into my novel.

My words of gratitude cannot thank Lieutenant Thomas Parker, OCSD (Retired) and Faye Shannon enough. Without their help and encouragement, the final product would not be what it is—something I can be proud of.

Chapter One

Jake sat behind the wheel of his 1975 Pontiac Bonneville with its four-barrel carb feeding the 250 horses that were rumbling under the hood. He was positioned on the Baldwin Road down ramp watching the approaching headlights of the intermittent nighttime traffic on I-75 that weaved south toward Pontiac and Detroit.

He wasn't looking for anyone breaking the speed limit. He had a purpose. Five minutes before, a radio broadcast had said two men in a white Buick were involved in a gas station robbery on Miller Road in Flint. Jake had jotted down the physical descriptions of the two black men and their car before taking up his position. Now it was just a waiting game—maybe even a complete waste of time—hoping a car fitting that description would be heading toward either city. Jake settled in to watch and wait anyway.

If the robbers were heading south, he knew he had just a short window of opportunity. Miller Road was about fifty miles north of where he waited. If he was right, he had about forty minutes or a bit more, depending on how fast they were driving. Jake figured he could afford to spend an hour of his midnight shift playing a hunch. He was glad to be on his own after nearly a month of working with a senior deputy. Some other guy might not want to take the time, but he liked the hunt. A cop was never sure about what he might run across while on duty—day or night.

He was watching the southbound traffic while his mind wandered. He had written two speeders when he first hit the road and that brought a smile to his face. Yes, he was writing traffic tickets. He thought about the time in Detroit that Lieutenant Orth chewed him out for only writing one ticket in 1967. Nine years later writing tickets was part of his job on the Oakland County Sheriff's Department. But now, as he straddled the shoulder of the down ramp, he was back doing what he liked most about wearing a badge—hunting bad guys.

The interior of his car, Three Seventeen, was not all that different from the Detroit-issued patrol cars he had driven, though his Pontiac had a bit more under the hood than the Plymouths and Fords. He was happy having a light bar overhead and a radio under the dash, even if his car was now painted black and white and had a six-point star on the door. Colors or the type of car made no difference to Jake. The main thing was: he was still a cop.

One other major change, beside the color of his uniform, was instead of a partner he had a Mossberg Model 590 riot gun with a twenty inch barrel locked in a rack next to him. Jake reflected on some of the partners he'd had in Detroit and smiled. The shotgun, even locked in the rack, was better than a few of them. Some were just like working a one-man unit. Then too, he missed great partners like Remington Southworth, Gunny Wynn, and Jesse Scott. Jake chuckled to himself as Jesse came to mind. He'd get about as much conversation out of the Mossberg as he did Jess.

Jake's life as a deputy was drastically different from Detroit. For one, his road patrol duties in the county could take him anywhere within its 908 square miles, though the deputies mainly policed the northern end of the county. Most of the smaller communities like Troy and Oak Park had their own departments. The city of Detroit totaled only 143 square miles and Jake was mostly assigned to patrol only a portion of it—like his last job in the Fifth Precinct that covered about 11 square miles. Then too, in Detroit, if you looked hard enough, the bad guys were everywhere. Now, after a month, he realized that working in Oakland County meant there weren't so many bad guys and a lot of his time would be spent looking for an occasional runaway horse or pranksters who were knocking over mailboxes.

Jake's thoughts were interrupted by a light-colored GM product streaking south on the Interstate and he slammed his foot down on the accelerator. The 250 horses sprung to life as he flicked on his headlights. In a minute he was doing ninety as he closed the distance between his unit and the car that caught his eye. He hadn't yet turned on his overhead light bar. If anything, he wanted to look like any other car speeding down the freeway in the middle of the night. It took him three miles to close the gap enough to recognize that the car in front of him was a Chevrolet.

Still curious, Jake slowly passed the Chevy to get a glimpse of the occupants. *White factory workers heading home* registered in Jake's mind. Neither looked his way. A car with a star on its door was not a welcome sight at one thirty in the morning, especially when the Chevy was doing about ten over and the two guys inside probably had the odor of beer on their breath.

Jake took the next off-ramp to head back to his hiding place. He had burned up twenty minutes checking out the Chevy. His window of opportunity was closing.

Occasional static on the radio broke the silence. Unit Three Thirty-four reported two cows loose on Pontiac Trail and was looking for back-up. Jake heard another road-patrol car respond as he slid back into his spot on the down ramp. He didn't feel like chasing cows just yet.

He knew it was just a wild stab in the dark that a car wanted for a hold-up in Flint would be going all the way to Detroit or maybe to Pontiac, but that's how he operated, imagining the possibilities. And there was a slim possibility.

Jake's eyes latched onto another light-colored GM engineered car heading south. He put his unit in Drive, turned on his headlights and stomped on the accelerator.

Two miles later, he knew it was a Buick. He eased up on the gas to pace the car and get a rough read on its speed. The car was doing a nice, safe 55—the posted limit.

He closed the gap so he could read the plate and grabbed the mic. "Station Three, this is Three Seventeen. Can you get me a larceny check and registration on Mary Boy four-two-seven-six?"

Jake didn't need an answer. In less than ten seconds, the driver of the 1973 white Buick decided he didn't want to be driving the speed limit with a cop on his tail.

"Three Seventeen's in pursuit of…" Jake was shouting into the mic. The chase was on. He flipped on his overhead red and blue lights and started calling out the exit numbers as they flashed by. At the same time, he was hearing other cars from other departments that were using the same radio frequency, converging on southbound I-75.

Three-Twenty, another county unit, joined a Troy department car, then cars from Sterling Heights and Birmingham were heard over the radio slipping in ahead of the Buick that was now topping ninety-five miles-per-hour.

Jake smiled to himself. *You're not going to outrun my radio.* That's when he saw the flashers of the other police units ahead as the freeway took the bend under Big Beaver Road. In the blink of an eye, the white Buick was skidding sideways and rolling. Sparks and glass flew and he caught a glimpse of what looked like a rag doll ejecting from where the Buick's passenger door had been a second before. A concrete abutment under Livernois stopped the Buick. Jake stood on the brakes and went from a near hundred miles-per-hour to nothing in just a few heartbeats. He knew his own heart rate had to be maxed. A chase would do that.

He picked up the mic that was hanging over his right thigh. "Station Three, can you send a couple of ambulances to…" Jake looked for a mile post for a reference point. There'd be no hurry. The Buick was unrecognizable, and if anyone remained in it, they'd be dead. The body that looked like a rag doll flying through the air would be too.

Corporal Mel Williams was picking a speck of lint off of his dark brown Stetson *Lawman* hat as he asked, "So what makes a cop leave the crime-laden streets of Detroit to start anew, patrolling the woods and waters of Oakland County?" Mel drew the short straw and was breaking Jake in. "You've been with me more than a week now and have to be bored to death."

Mel and Jake were taking a break at the Ram's Horn on Rochester Road after writing two traffic tickets and taking one accident report. Every shift, the same question came up, either from his partner or other deputies. A waitress came by and poured some coffee. "Menus?" she asked. Mel told her they'd be back later for lunch.

Jake's usual response to Mel's question was that it made his wife happy, but that did not stop the questions. It was as if he left the Catholic Church, shaved his head and became a Buddhist. A cop here or in Detroit was still a cop. They didn't seem to understand that. He watched his partner fidget with his hatband, then reshape the brim.

"It's the hat," Jake said. "I always wanted to wear a cowboy hat." Jake paused for a beat. "I even think I may have been a town marshal in my previous life." Jake smiled. "You believe in reincarnation Mel?"

"You serious?"

"Yeah. You know I can't sit with my back to any door. There's got to be a reason, right? Maybe I took a bullet in the back?"

"Reincarnation. You are serious." Mel stirred a little cream in his coffee while Jake measured out a bit of sugar and added it to his.

Mel barely met the five-ten height requirement for the county and maybe weighed 200 pounds. A thin mustache over his lip gave him something of a Clark Gable look, that, along with his constant smile. Jake was just a smidgen taller than Mel and his normal weight was 205.

Jake continued the conversation. "The woods and lakes beat the hell out of the jungles of Detroit. I'll adjust to the cows and horses." Jake picked up his own Stetson and twirled it on his finger. He still wore his normal close-cut flat top and though weighing about the same as Mel, was Marine Corps fit. He kept in shape by using his basement gym every other day. Jake was not bulging with muscles, just fit. He took a sip from his mug. "What about you? How'd you end up becoming a deputy?"

Mel just smiled. "I like guns." The deputy carried a Smith and Wesson model 19 blue steel .357 Magnum with an eight inch barrel in a holster that hung low. The pistol, along with the thin reddish-brown mustache he sported, and the way he wore his hat, canted to the left, gave Jake the impression that Mel might have been a western gunslinger in his previous life; if he really believed the reincarnation bullshit he had been throwing Mel's way.

Mel checked his watch. "Time to get back on the road," pushing his empty cup to the middle of the table. He let the door slam behind him before Jake could catch up. They were working Three Twenty in Avon Township. Mel was saddled with Jake for two weeks to a month break-in. Jake was hoping that there was more to do than tickets and accident reports as he slid in behind the wheel. Mel had him drive everywhere. "Best way to learn the roads," he had said.

Jake inherited two sons when he and Edie tied the knot the past November. He had lost his first wife and four children three years, five months and seven days before he remarried. His family perished in a fiery crash on I-80 just outside of Omaha.

Now he was a dad and a husband again, as well as a rookie deputy sheriff after spending nearly ten years working the streets of Detroit. He loved the recent changes in his life—his wife, the boys and the move to the Oakland County Sheriff's Department—mainly because he was still wearing a badge.

His step-sons, Hank and Sam, were eleven and nine. Jake soon learned that they were two peas from opposite ends of the same pod. He had met Edie and her sons at a Halloween party two and a half years before they got married.

Hank was the older brother who mainly went with the flow in life, while Sam seemed destined to be just the opposite—either by choice or predestination.

Edie had said that when Sam was about six, he questioned why his eight-year old brother was bigger than him. They lived in the same house, ate the same food, had the same parents, yet Hank was three inches taller. She said that didn't sit too well with her younger son. He wanted to be bigger and stronger—right now. Sam's competitive spirit became an obsession.

Jake saw a little bit of this one-way competition between Sam and his older brother when he had started helping to coach their Little League team. After Jake married the boys' mother, he realized that Sam was pretty serious about catching up to Hank. If Hank drank a glass of milk, Sam would drink two. If Hank ate one portion of meat, he'd eat one and a half. When it came to vegetables, Sam hated them, but if Hank ate four Brussels sprouts, Sam was going to choke down five. Sam had a goal and he stuck to it like he'd never make his next birthday if he didn't. Jake just thought Sam was pretty comical.

Hank never thought too much about the competiveness his kid brother had. What he thought was fun wrestling matches with Sam were really major big-time "wrassling" bouts in his younger brother's eyes. Edie had confided in Jake that one time, when Hank was about ten, Hank let Sam win one match while playing in a pile of leaves they'd helped their mom gather. That night, just before mom scooted them off to bed, Sam looked up at his big brother and said, "Don't worry, Hank, if the guys at school start pickin' on you, I'll kick their ass." He even gave Hank a little hug seconds before Edie fed him a bite of Dial soap. Edie said that Hank just laughed at Sam's bubbly mouth and went off to bed.

Jake remembered that story, thinking no one could have that much competitiveness. Now, he was witnessing it first-hand. Jake had no problem at all jumping back into the father role. He had a wife who loved him and two boys who were now 10 and 12 and called him Dad.

Hank and Sam had latched onto Jake shortly after he started seeing their mom. It was the boys who asked him to help coach their baseball team. Their real dad, Gary Douglas, blew town with a girlfriend when the boys were four and two. They never saw him again. Hank barely remembered his dad and Sam didn't at all.

Edie brought Jake up to speed on the boys once things looked like he'd be the man in their lives. She told him about two trips to school over Sam's behavior. True to his word, if anyone messed with Hank, there was this little bumble bee of a kid brother that'd be on some bully's back wailing away at someone always bigger than him.

Jake tried to slowly mentor the boys about playground fights, but had a hard time trying to convince them as he remembered his own grade-school days and a fight or two he'd had.

Hank never let anyone bully Sam, but he was a bit more subtle. The word quickly spread by the time Jake married Edie that no one messed with the Douglas brothers—neither of them. What Jake had said to them about fighting didn't matter at all. The boys were the ones who drew the line in the sand and no one crossed it. But neither Jake nor Edie ever had to make another trip to the school after they got married.

Jake felt a twinge of disgust as he read a report he sought

out after seeing a TV newscast the previous night. The story about a young boy found dead piqued his interest because he now had Hank and Sam in his life.

The copies of the report that he had gotten from the detectives stated that in the southern part of the county a 12-year-old boy from Ferndale was last seen leaving an American Legion Hall on Sunday afternoon, February 15, 1976. The boy had told his mother he was going home to watch television. His body was found on February 19, neatly laid out in a snow bank in the parking lot of an office building at Ten Mile Road and Greenfield in Southfield. He had been strangled and sexually assaulted. Rope marks were seen on his wrists. He was wearing the same clothes he had on when last seen alive. There wasn't any more information available beyond the report. No one reported seeing the boy once he left the legion hall or anything prior to the body being found.

The Pontiac Mall opened its doors at precisely 10 a.m. Ron Peck took off his tan windbreaker that he wore to fend off the light spring drizzle. He folded it neatly, then draped it over the back of the bench before he sat. His view was unobstructed, except for the occasional shopper who wandered by. The interruption was always short. Ladies shopping on a Saturday morning didn't waste much time in front of the arcade. A boy was squirming in front of the first pinball machine just inside the archway, trying to will the little silver ball onto one of the flippers he was ready to manipulate. That's what caught Ron's eye.

The man watching the kid wasn't interested in the bells ringing, or the horse's loud whinny on the game called "Ghost Town Hero" coming from the arcade. He was interested in the boy's tight Levi's and the way he moved his hips as he played. Ron liked little boy's asses. That is why he was there on a drizzly April morning in 1976.

Chapter Two

It was not uncommon for shoppers at the mall to see men sitting while the missus went between Montgomery Ward and Hudson's, and hitting all the small shops in between. Ron fit right in with the normal clientele. He was handsome, well groomed, pushing forty, naturally wavy light brown hair with blue eyes. He had a smile that would charm any lady looking his way. If one were to look for distinguishing characteristics, there were none, except maybe for his left eye. It had a lighter hue to the blue—almost gray. It was only noticeable during a long conversation that included eye-to-eye contact.

Saturday mornings were best for Ronald to be hanging around the Pontiac Mall. He had a favorite place to sit—the bench next to the small fountain and goldfish pond, directly across from the arcade. The main entrance was within sight of where he sat. From there he could watch moms or dads drop off their kids while they parked the car, or, more than likely, went somewhere else. The mall was a good babysitter for pre-teens and high school aged kids. The girls who came in giggling didn't get a second glance from Ronald. He was only interested in the younger boys who came to play at the arcade.

None of the residents of Pontiac, Michigan, nor Oakland

County, were aware of just who Ronald Peck was. He had just moved to the state. He'd been a power company lineman, working for Pennsylvania Power and Light from 1960 until he went to work for Virginia Electric in 1971. He was now working on a crew for Detroit Edison, servicing Oakland and Macomb Counties.

During his career, he had moved often, and about six months earlier had to hurriedly leave town to avoid the Virginia Beach authorities. A little indiscretion on his part at the Mirror Maze Fun House on the beach had them looking for a well-dressed middle-aged white male with brown wavy hair, wearing a black tee shirt and beige pants. He had attempted to molest an 11-year old boy in the restroom, and had narrowly eluded the boy's father only because the dad was hanging onto a younger daughter as Ron banged out the restroom door, and jumped a turnstile as the boy began screaming.

The December issue of the Electrical Workers Union's paper had full-page ads that had said there were jobs available in Michigan. Working in Michigan had never crossed his mind until he was packing to leave town within a couple of hours after the little miscue at the fun house. He had loaded everything he owned into his new 1976 Dodge van and left the apartment he had leased for a year just three months before. The pre-paid rent wasn't worth any hesitation; his priority was avoiding incarceration. With his work experience, he was sure he'd land a job within a week.

Two days of travel had him in Pontiac, Michigan, and three days later he had an apartment and a job. Linemen were hard to come by, especially experienced ones. Ronald knew the trade and didn't mind the work. It paid well.

The only real problem that he encountered was the new Dodge van. He was now living in a General Motors town. The guys in his new crew let him know right off they didn't like his set of wheels. He told them he'd trade up once he got settled. No one knew Ronald's big secret—a penchant for young boys.

And now he was sitting in the mall, not giving a flip about the goldfish swimming next to him, but fixing his eyes on one boy in jeans playing a pinball machine.

———

Aside from the silent competitiveness that still was within Sam, the boys got along great. Not only did they play sports together, they spent a lot of time just being boys—like rafting on a nearby pond, or taking their bikes to go fishing on the Clinton River. During the winter they shared a toboggan, coaxing their mom or Jake to take them to some snow-covered hill.

One of the favorite things they liked to do was go to the penny arcade at the new Pontiac Mall. Edie or Jake would take them there, each with a fistful of change, and let them knock themselves out for a couple of hours one or two Saturday mornings a month.

At the arcade, there were bowling games and pinball machines, but both of them liked the shooting games the best. Their favorite was the Texas Ranger Gatling Gun. Maybe they liked it because their stepdad was a cop. On the Ranger Gatling Gun, Sam was an equal match with Hank and he liked to pretend they were cops. Then too, a hundred shots were only a dime. With two dollars of change each, they had a lot of fun seeing who could get the top rating of Ranger while the other had to settle for the lesser levels like Sheriff, Cowboy, or in the beginning, the lowly Scout.

Most boys their age liked playing cowboys and Indians or cops and robbers. Hank and Sam were no different, and the Arcade let them do that. It was a fun place to be on a Saturday morning.

———

Jake had dropped the boys off at the Mall. Edie wanted them gone while she tidied up the house. Jake had planned on going to the range in the basement at his department's headquarters. "I'll pick you guys up around noon and take you to lunch somewhere."

He heard Hank call out "Burgerland" as he drove off. Jake still liked to shoot twice a week just as he did when he worked in Detroit, and he figured the boys could take care of themselves.

———

Movement to Ron's left caught his eye. Two more boys with wide smiles heading straight for the arcade came into view. One was about twelve, the other, maybe a year younger. Both, just the age Ron preferred. It was a beautiful morning at the Pontiac Mall in his fantasy-filled mind. He was hoping to score. One of the three boys, or maybe another would succumb to his offers of coins to play the games, free candy, or maybe a suggestion to take in a movie.

———

It was near 12:30 p.m. when Jake swung by the mall to get Hank and Sam. He knew they'd be just about out of cash. He planned it that way. They'd find a burger joint, have lunch, then go home to rake the yard since the rain had stopped an hour earlier. It was the end of April and time to get the yard in shape. Winter had run its course and the willow tree out back had shed its normal trash. That was the deal he made with the boys. The money for the arcade was "payment in advance" for help with the yard work.

Jake spotted them waiting outside the main door to the Pontiac Mall as he pulled into the lot. Sam jumped in the passenger's side first, scooting in the middle and Hank followed. Jake's Ford pickup was just right for hauling around the boys. Before Hank could even get his door closed, Sam started. "Dad, there was this weird guy hanging around the arcade."

"Sam, I think you're weird. He was just friendly," Hank said.

"That's 'cause he was slipping dimes into your gun game."

"He was just being nice..."

"No! He was weird. Did'you see that one eye of his? He's a weirdo."

"Whoa, whoa, boys," Jake interrupted. "We're goin' for burgers. Slow down and you can tell me all about it on the way there." He started driving away from the mall entrance.

Hank leaned forward so he could talk past his brother. "Sam pretends he's a cop. He's always imagining things."

"I didn't imagine anything a half hour ago when that creep led that other kid out of the arcade," Sam shouted.

"I heard the guy say they were going to get some popcorn." Hank was shaking his head as he said it. "Sam, you're the weird one."

"Oh yeah? But while you were taking your turn on the Gatling gun, I followed them. They went right out the mall door."

"See dad. He's playing detective again." Hank bounced against the back of the seat. "A real junior Sam Spade. Humph!"

"Who's Sam Spade?" Sam asked.

"A lot you know, little brother. He's a story-book detective."

Jake had already took his foot off the gas, remembering a young boy was killed somewhere in the county right after he started with the department. The boy had been sexually assaulted with an object before he was killed. Jake's mind was working as the boys continued their bantering.

"Dad, the guy's weird. A creep. He led the kid out to his truck. An ugly green van." As Sam talked, his head pivoted past Jake, "That one right there." His hand flicked across Jake's nose, pointing out a green Dodge van among the row of cars parked near the entrance to the mall. "You need to check him out, Dad."

"Yeah, you need to," laughed Hank.

Jake caught sight of the van Sam was pointing at and

made a wide swing around the lot, parking two rows away from it. “Okay partner,” he said to Sam. “I’ll check your guy out. Then, we’re off to Burgerland.”

“Dad, I’m hungry,” Hank said.

“Me too. Be back in a sec.”

Jake left the boys in his idling Ford and slipped between the cars heading for the van. He approached it from the rear, peeking in one of the windows on the back door. No one was in the driver’s seat, or on the passenger’s side. He paused long enough to hear a sobbing and a boy’s trembling voice. “No mister. I don’t want you to do that.” The voice took Jake’s eyes downward into the back of the van. In the mid-day light he could barely make out a young boy, nude from his waist down and a man holding the kid’s arm.

Jake didn’t need to see the man’s erect cock to know what was going on, and knew the van’s doors had to be locked. He looked left, then right, and saw a crumbled piece of parking lot curbing about the size of a loaf of bread. The side of the van had double doors on the passenger side. Jake eyes went from lock to lock just inside of the windows, then threw the concrete chunk through the window, followed by his arm through the new hole, flicking the lock and opening the door. Jake was moving behind his right hand that was holding his off-duty pistol, a .38 Colt Detective Special. The first thing he saw was wide eyes and a gaping mouth on the man kneeling behind the bent over boy. Jake’s pistol was firmly aimed between the man’s eyes. “You twitch, asshole, you’re dead.”

Fifteen seconds later, the boy had his Levi’s back on and was climbing onto the passenger’s seat, sobbing. The man, with his pants bunched around his ankles, was lying on the back floor of the van with his hands locked behind his head. Jake eyed up the back of the van. The back seat had been removed and a plush, black, fake-fur rug lined the entire rear of the van all the way up and on the roof. Jake spoke quietly. “Son, you okay?”

Two sobs later he heard, “I, I think so,” then the voice of

Sam, "You got 'im, Dad." He turned and saw both of his boys outside and behind him.

"Hank, go into the mall and get the security officer to call the sheriff's office. Get them here. Sam, take our young friend here to my truck." He looked at the kid. His eyes were swollen from crying. "Boy, what's your name?"

"Frankie," came out between sobs.

"Frankie, go with my son. I need you to stay with us until the police come." The boy stumbled out of the van. "Am I in trouble?"

"No, but this guy is. Now go with Sam." He looked at his young son. "Good job, Sam."

When the boys were gone, the bare-assed man spoke. "C-Can I pull up my pants?"

"It'd be smarter for me to have you leave them right where they are. Less chance of you running." Jake paused for a few seconds. "Go ahead and pull them up. I want you to run. Then I could blow your fuckin' brains all over this parking lot."

"I'm not running," the guy answered as he rolled over and started pulling up his jockey shorts and pants.

"I want you to run," Jake said in a whisper. "On second thought, I'd shoot you in the balls first and let you bleed to death."

"You wouldn't..."

"I would." Jake's voice interrupted.

Five minutes later Ronald Peck, white male, age 38 was handcuffed and in the custody of the Deputy John Kaminski. The 11-year old Frankie was in another unit. Walt Goodness, a corporal, had all of Jake's information. "Want to follow us in to make a report?"

"I'll be a little behind you. I promised the boys a burger, and I need some time alone with them."

The cop nodded. He knew Jake had to talk to his boys about what just went down. He had already radioed in to have Frankie's parents meet them at the station. "Take your time." The two OCSD cars drove off and Jake and his boys headed for his truck.

"Tol' you the guy was a weirdo, Hank." With a bounce in his step, Sam continued. "And did you see Dad bust out that window? I'm going to be a policeman, too. You just wait and see."

"For sure, you're the hero here today," Jake smiled, patting his son on the back. "Hank, I think he'll make a good cop, too, don't you?"

Hank just shrugged and put his arm over this brother's shoulder. "I don't know how I'm going to be able to live with a little brother who's a hero."

Sam jumped in the truck. "Forget the little brother shit…"

Jake poked Sam with a finger, "You remember how Dial soap tasted?"

Sam's eyes drooped. "Mom tol' you that story, eh?"

"Your mom and I have no secrets."

The three of them were in Jake's Ford pickup and headed for Burgerland. Burgers, fries and malts were in their future, then the trip to headquarters. The detectives would need a statement from Hank and Sam too.

On the way home, Sam spoke up. "We shouldn't tell Mom about this. She won't let us go to the arcade anymore."

Jake just smiled. "As I said, your mom and I have no secrets. Then too, you both learned a little about life today. It's full of bad guys."

He paused, thinking*: Maybe this guy's the one who killed that boy in February.*

"I think Hank and you'll be able to pick out the bad guys. She'll let you go—if I keep an eye on you two."

"We don't need a babysitter," Sam quickly said.

"I know that, but moms need to know you're safe. Nobody will know I'm watching." Jake smiled. "You won't either."

Chapter Three

As was the plan, the boys helped Jake rake the yard to clean up the small limbs their tree shed every winter. He had asked the boys not to say anything to their mom about what happened at the mall. "Some things have to be discussed at the right time," he had said. Jake was thinking about talking to Edie after the boys went to bed.

Sam just couldn't contain himself. At the supper table, it all came out before the dishes were cleared. Jake saw tears forming in his wife's eyes as Sam was saying, "An' you should have seen dad bust out the window with a piece of concrete…"

When her son got to the part about the boy's pants being down, the mother bear side of Edie came out. "What was it, just a month or two ago where a boy was killed?" she blurted out. "And when were you going to tell me about this?" She looked directly at Jake as streams of tears flowed down her cheeks. "The boy that was killed, wasn't he about the same age as Hank and Sam?"

Jake nodded, telling the boys to go and see what was on TV. He knew that he had no answers that would appease his wife. He led the boys into the living room, knowing that they had been involved in too much serious stuff already, and Edie wanted a serious conversation.

Within seconds, Sam found a rerun of *Adam-12*, but Jake said it was Hank's turn to choose. *Happy Days* was Hank's choice. He liked Richie Cunningham. Naturally, Fonzie was Sam's favorite. The boys took up their regular places on the floor with their backs against the couch. They were laughing when Jake went back to help his wife with the dishes.

Edie broke the silence. "Jake, how'd we let our boys get exposed to a pervert at the mall?"

"It was nothing we did or didn't do. Sam did the right thing, telling me about the guy."

"I don't want our boys involved in stuff like this. They're too young."

"Edie, Hank and Sam just happened to be there…"

Edie interrupted, "We're not dropping them off at the mall again. My sons will not be put in any danger." With those words, the conversation ended.

Later, after the boys went to bed, Jake said, "We need to talk." He tried to ease into what he had to tell her.

That didn't work as Edie screamed, "What do you mean? Hank and Sam will have to go to court?"

"The boys will no doubt be subpoenaed for the guy's trial..." Tears interrupted him. He pulled her into his arms squeezing her tight, knowing that for years she was all the boys had for protection. "Hon, there's bad things going on everywhere. It's the way it is." He lifted her chin to look in her eyes. "Between you and me we'll protect them from as much as we can. They are my sons too."

"Your honor, my client pleads not guilty," said attorney Robert Bauman when the charges were read. It was the following Monday morning. Jake took the stand and related how he ended up checking out Peck's green van, what he saw and the actions he took. The hearing was to see if there was enough evidence to hold Ronald Peck for trial. Corporal Joseph Goodness was also in court to introduce the statement taken from the victim. The session took less than twenty minutes. Judge Wilson Bradley bound Ronald Peck over for trial on the charges of "Indecency with a minor" and "Attempted Sodomy," setting the bond at $50,000. The prosecutor quickly asked the judge to increase the bond, citing two other warrants from out of state that just came to light, and the possibility of flight. The judge agreed, raising Peck's bond to $200,000 cash.

After the hearing Corporal Goodness told Jake that the county prosecutor had tried to tie Peck in with the February Ferndale murder. "Peck said he was living in Virginia Beach and had never been in Michigan until recently." Goodness smiled. "His story holds up, but it turns out that the guy's prints matched those found at the scene on a child molestation case back there." The cop laughed. "That snowballed into another open case in Bethlehem, Pennsylvania. Warrants are being issued by both of those departments. Peck is going to jail for a long time."

Jake filled Edie in on what happened in court that day. He didn't want to, but finally said, "The boys will be subpoenaed after a court date is set."

"I don't want them going to court and seeing that creep again," taking the tissue Jake had offered. "I think they've been exposed to too much already."

Jake hesitated. He didn't have an answer that would satisfy her. "Eed, the boys will do fine. Their testimony will make sure Peck will be put in jail." He let her sob on his shoulder for a while before he told her about the two other warrants. He kept the rest of his thoughts to himself. He knew a conviction in Michigan would put those other crimes on the back burner, never to be prosecuted. Virginia and Pennsylvania probably wouldn't extradite. It would cost too much.

The Oakland County Jail was a very secure and well-run facility. Three weeks after the arrest of Ronald Peck, the *Oakland Press* carried a short article on page three beneath the fold. The article's headline simply read: County Jail Inmate Stabbed. The story that followed stated that a man, being held on sex offenses at the jail, was stabbed three times and was a police prisoner at St. Joseph Mercy Hospital.

Jake was glancing at the paper over coffee while waiting for on-duty roll call. He called the jail. "Yes, it was Ronald Peck who was stabbed. And no, Deputy Bush, he did not make it. He's dead." Jake hung up the phone and a little smile crossed his lips. *Edie won't have to worry about the boys going to court now.*

On the way to his car, Jake stopped in to see the detectives. There he found out there was a note shoved in Pecks' shirt pocket. It just read: For the Ferndale kid. They didn't seem too concerned about who killed the guy. Jake wasn't surprised either. It was a fact that child molesters didn't fare too well behind bars. He called Edie and told her about Peck. He wanted to make sure she'd stop worrying about the boys testifying in court.

During his first two weeks working for the county, Jake had heard his training officer refer to him as "Deputy Spit and Polish." He didn't care. Mel hadn't been in the Marines. He wasn't about to explain to his partner that the drill instructors at Marine Corps Recruit Depot in San Diego had you do 100 pushups on the grinder because your button line was not even with the zipper line on your trousers. If you didn't learn from that, for the second infraction you and your squad did 200 pushups. If the squad got punished for something you did, you'd probably be the recipient of a blanket party after lights were out. Jake was smart enough to learn from his first 100 pushups.

Then too, as an MP at Naval Air Station Moffet Field, you not only lined up the button line with the zipper line, your uniform was always neatly pressed, and Shinola wax and Brasso were always close at hand. You polished all your metal and spit-shined your shoes and holster. A Marine, especially an MP, had to look sharp. Looking sharp in uniform became a habit.

Jake carried this mindset with him to Detroit. His shoes were spit-shined, so was his holster and Sam Browne. A drop of *Brasso* and a rag had the badge finger-print free along with any metal buckles on his gear.

The uniform in Oakland County may have differed in color from Detroit's, but Jake took the same kind of care with his uniform, shoes and equipment. The Marines had taught him that when you were in uniform, you wore it with pride. And Jake was proud to wear a uniform.

It had been raining for two hours before Jake reported for work. Over time he had learned that the afternoon shifts were usually slow, so he'd go out to his assigned area and see if he could find a mover or two before the traffic dwindled down to nothing. Jake was filling in on the Highland Township car, Three Thirty-two. Dan Daniels had called in sick.

His radio came alive: "Station Three to Three Thirty-two, 4811 Fish Lake Road, at the farm. See the man for a complaint." Jake acknowledged the run and checked his map. There were a lot of roads that he hadn't a clue as to where they were, but the AAA maps worked fine at finding where he needed to go. From the map he could see that he'd be in the middle of nowhere on a gravel road—good gravel if he was lucky.

The Bonneville's tires slipped a time or two while Jake watched for mailboxes and a number. The first number he caught told him he had to drive a mile or two north to get to the address. The rain was not letting up, keeping at a steady pace and making his wipers work overtime. He could feel the mud caking on the sides of his car. There was a lot of clay mixed in with the gravel. Soon, he spotted a six by eight foot sign on his left. The address was in an oval at the top, in white lettering over a dark green background. Chiseled into the wood below was one word: “Nußbaumhain” in about five-inch letters. Beneath that the sign read: Walnut Grove Golden Retrievers Est. 1960 Herr and Frau Zemens proprietors.

A house sat a couple of hundred yards off the road up a two-track driveway. Jake eased his unit to a stop with the house on his right. To his left, a fenced yard with stairs leading to a platform stood in the middle of a well-worn grassy area littered with plastic toys and balls. It was obviously an exercise run for the big dogs that were out romping in the rain playing with one another. There were six dogs and they all came up, nosing the two-by-four welded wire fencing next to the sheriff department’s black and white unit.

Jake climbed out, reaching around to grab his raincoat from the back seat, hoping to stay as dry as the weather would allow. He already had the clear-plastic rain bonnet on his Stetson and turned when he heard a voice behind him. “Come into za building. I chust cleaning za kennel.” The man doing the talking was in his sixties with strands of long, wet, graying dark hair sticking out from under a ball cap bearing a Purina logo. He was wearing a three-quarter Barbour waxed-cotton coat and barn boots that reached his knees.

Jake was glad to get out of the rain and under some shelter, and happier when he felt the heat within the kennel building. “I chust put in new bedding for za puppies,” the man said. Beyond a short wall made of bales of straw Jake saw about seven balls of golden fur, all sleeping on fresh, loose straw bedding. Before Jake could introduce himself, the full-grown dogs that were romping in the rain head-butted their way in out of the weather through a dog door, all too willing to share their muddy paws and wet muzzles with him.

"Down Hilma!" The man snapped his finger and pointed at the dog. The trouble was that it wasn't just Hilma. All six dogs were pushing Jake into the wall behind him, some with their paws, some with their massive heads. All were wet and muddy. "Dis is my girls," the man said, rattling off six German-sounding names and pointing at each. "Wilda, Wiebke, Zelda, Velma and Benilda. You already met Hilma." Jake assumed they were females since the guy said they were his "girls."

"What's the complaint you called in?" Jake asked. The man had a reddish golden by the collar, as he looked at Jake with a question in his eyes.

"Come, I show you my farm," he said, pulling Jake by the arm while commanding "Back" to the girls as he closed the kennel building's door. "Come I show you my walnut trees." He was leading Jake into the steady rain and into the well-manicured yard behind the house and kennel.

"We haf eleven acres here. I plant za walnut trees. Come walk with me." He touched Jake's elbow and they walked into the steady rain. The man said there were 33 trees, transplanted from another farm, all evenly spaced with flower beds beneath. He said nothing is supposed to grow under walnut trees, "but my Frau and I are master gardeners." Near every tree was a small flat rock with a name etched on it. "All graves for my lost souls," he said. "This is Margaret—my favorite. She had ten litters of puppies for us."

As they walked, the rain-soaked ground was wicking up Jake's pants. His shoes were soaked and mud-splattered by the time they covered the first acre of their tour. Without taking a breath, the man went on and on about the flora on his farm, and the oddity of what was growing under the trees. "Nussing is supposed to grow under there," he repeated. He paused briefly and named all the dogs buried under each tree.

At the back end of the farm a pair of headstones marked the property line. The name Heide Zemens was etched with the date 1913-1972 under the name. The other headstone had the name Reinhold Zemens on it with 1912 and a blank spot next to the dash. "My Frau," the man said. He paused for a few minutes, whispering as his head was bent and his hat was over his heart. The rain pelting down on Jake's plastic-covered Stetson finally brought the man back out of his thoughts. "She loved the rain. Come, let us stay dry."

Jake followed a pace behind the man. "Mr. Zemens. The call I got said you had a complaint."

"What complaint?" He picked up his pace. "I haf no complaint. Who says I haf a complaint?"

"You didn't call the sheriff's office?"

"No. Why would I call?" The man shrugged his shoulders and banged in the door to the kennel building. "You'd better get out of the rain, sheriff. You catch cold."

Jake's trousers were wet up to his knees and his shoes soaked through to his socks as he slid into his unit, pitching his raincoat into the back seat. He tipped his hat upside down to drain on the floor of the passenger's side of the Bonneville, put on the heater, and turned the blower onto high. He backed out the driveway and waved to the dogs. They were back outside playing in the rain.

It was May and he was chilled, wet and dirty. At the road he paused to call in. "Station, Three Thirty-Two's back in service."

"Three Thirty-Two, meet the officer at 10100 Highland Road."

Jake knew Highland Road was M-59 and was back down the muddy road. He thought the number might be just into Livingston County. No matter. He was hoping for a chance to dry out a little.

The address turned out to be the Big Boy Restaurant, and around the back of it Jake saw a bunch of sheriff's department cars. As he parked, he noticed three were from Livingston County, the rest from Oakland.

A cop convention? Jake parked and went inside. He was already wet, so he left his raincoat behind.

The tables near the door were filled with what looked like the regular clientele. From the back he caught sight of Corporal Mel Williams waving at him with the same shit-eating grin he always wore. The tables in the rear were crammed with uniforms, except one. Dan Daniels was in civvies. Jake headed straight for Dan. "Thought you were sick?"

"Only enough to have you work my car."

"For?"

"The initiation." Daniels' eyes raked Jake from his shoe tops to his shoulders, then back down. "See you met the crazy German and his girls." The cops in uniform behind him started laughing. "So much for our spit-shined Marine," Daniels added.

Jake looked a question at Williams who smiled and shrugged his shoulders. "You're just hard to welcome aboard," Mel said.

"Explain," Jake demanded.

Williams went on to say that usually they'd steal a rookie's car, scaring the shit out of the guy, "but you always lock your fuckin' car."

"I'm from Detroit, remember? They'd steal a baby buggy for diapers if it was left unattended for more than ten seconds."

"That's why we had to resort to other means." Williams kept smiling. "Then when all this rain hit, I called Daniels, knowing the boss always has the low man covering his area."

"It usually doesn't take five months," Daniels chimed in. "Getting you dirty was my idea. I'd been to the nut farm once. What's a better way to welcome Mr. Spit and Polish?" The cops behind had been laughing quietly until then. They started roaring; obviously all were in on the joke.

"Someone get Jake a cup a coffee and a bowl of soup," Williams said over the laughter. "The damn guy's shivering."

A half hour later Jake was back at the station digging out a change of uniform from his locker, along with a dry pair of socks and another pair of spit-shined ankle-high Kangaroo-skin brogans. Both the Marines and Detroit taught him to have a backup.

Old habits never die.

Tickets, reports and chasing down a runaway horse or cow was a long way from the busy times that Jake had in Detroit, but that's what the change in uniforms brought him. He missed the action, but was enjoying his new job and family.

Chapter Four

Sometimes Jake shared his stories over dinner with Edie and the boys. Today he talked about getting wet on his visit with the German farmer and his golden retrievers. Edie and the kids laughed when he told them about the little prank played on him. He had to laugh too. In Detroit, there weren't too many things he could share with his family.

Some of the evenings on Jake's days off, the family went driving around Oakland County, looking at small farms and the countryside to the west of Pontiac. Edie was serious about wanting a horse or two. Jake didn't care either way. The boys were worrying about their baseball and football teams, so they weren't too enthused. They didn't want to leave their friends.

That soon changed when on the last Sunday in August Edie had the afternoon totally planned. It was a big secret, even to Jake. After church she announced that they had to change into jeans. She already had some chicken fried up, along with some of her special potato salad and plenty of fresh-picked tomatoes to go in the cooler. There were a dozen Pepsis iced down too. She had a bag full of the essentials: paper plates, napkins and silverware, a red and white checkerboard tablecloth and plenty of snacks. She gave Jake the address of a place near Highland in Oakland

County. “It’ll be fun. Just wait and see,” she said with a gleam in her eyes.

Jake just looked at the boys, “Your Mom’s orders are that we’re to have fun.” He put a fake smile on his face. The boys didn’t respond.

Hank asked as he climbed into the back seat, “Do they still have them amusement parks we heard Mom and you talk about?”

Edie’s eyebrows lifted as she turned to the back seat. “Have you boys been listening to what your dad and I talk about?” Jake loved being referred to as *Dad.*

“Yeah, I’d like to go to an amusement park,” Sam joined in. “I wanna go on a roller coaster. Jimmy Gross said he’s been on ‘em all at Cedar Point.”

Jake drove, telling the boys about Walled Lake and Jefferson Beach, old amusement parks he’d visited as a kid. “Then there was Bob-Lo, where you had to take a boat to get there.” Jake knew they were all closed and demolished. Maybe Bob-Lo wasn’t yet, but he knew downtown Detroit and the docks off of Fort Street were not where he’d like to take his wife and the boys, even if he packed a gun.

Jake made a mental note to talk to Edie about a trip to Ohio to visit Cedar Point. He’d been there once with his first family. There, Sam and Hank could ride all the roller coasters they wanted. Jake wouldn’t. He just didn’t like having the shit scared out of him for seventy-five seconds after waiting in line for an hour.

He vividly remembered timing the *Corkscrew* coaster he had been on when Deb dared him to ride it with her. He thought the guy manning the gate would turn him and his daughter away because she was not tall enough. *Wrong.* The guy let Jake and Deb pass. *I won’t make that mistake again. No, I’ll take all the excitement the job will give me. I don’t have to wait in line for that.*

Jake jumped back to the present. “Mind telling me where I’m going?” He glanced at Edie, as he headed up the gravel road she told him to turn on.

She smiled, saying, "You'll see."

The next thing Jake saw was a sign over the road with two tall posts holding it up. The sign read, *Henkell's Farm. Horses to rent.*

"Aha!" He glanced in the rearview mirror. The boys hadn't seen the sign, but he finally figured out what his wife was up to. He whispered to his wife, "Quite sneaky, my dear."

Edie just giggled.

The Sunday afternoon picnic and horseback adventure at Henkell's Farm turned out just as Edie had hoped. Sam was the most enthusiastic as soon as he was helped aboard his horse. Frank Henkell had put him on a tall gray roan named Lanky. The horse had Sam looking down on his older brother for the first time. Hank was sitting on Lazarus, a dingy white gelding that looked half asleep.

The farmer/horse wrangler had Jake and his family all saddled on safe trail-broke mounts. Edie had made all the plans by phone with Frank.

"Now guys, I put your mom on the lead horse, 'cause she's been on a horse before," Frank was saying. "Just follow her 'tween them two Birch trees yonder. Barky knows the way." With that Mr. Henkell gave Barky a gentle slap on his hindquarters.

Edie smiled, then clicked Barky on, leading her small posse for what was supposed to be a two-hour ride through the fields and woods at the nearby Highland Recreation Area. Jake took up the rear of the parade on a sway-back Palomino named Maisey.

Barkey was a tall black gelding that shuffled to the front, bringing a broad smile from Mom. She was the trail boss. It was Edie's taste of heaven. Two hours of it.

Within two hundred yards of the barn on the return trip, all four horses broke into a run. Edie wasn't the only one who had to grab a good hold of a saddle horn. Frank Henkell was leaning against the corral gate, chewing on a weed and smiling as the posse returned.

A half hour later, Mom was still in charge and all smiles as she dished up the chicken, potato salad, and tomatoes on the picnic table under a tall oak tree next to the Henkell house. Frank and Maude Henkell joined them. The weather was cooperating and Mrs. Henkell had made a cake and some home-made ice cream for dessert.

Sam was beaming as he handed a plate of food to his older brother. "Lanky sure showed you his heels on the way to the barn," he was saying to Hank.

"Did you notice the name of the horse I was on?" Hank looked toward Jake for support, and got nothing but a smile. "Mom probably fixed it so I'd be on the slower horse," Hank said. Edie, Jake and the Henkells just listened as the two boys bantered back and forth as to who was the best cowboy.

On the way home, as the boys slept leaning against one another in the back seat, Jake asked Edie one question, "Did you ever tell Mr. Henkell that the only experience you had was when your grandpa put you on the back of his big black Percheron when the plowing was done?"

"I just told him I rode before." She snuggled her head on Jake's shoulder as she answered.

"Devious plan you had here, getting the boys to take a liking to horses." Jake kissed his wife on the top of her head.

"First you say I am sneaky, now it's devious?" She looked up at Jake and smiled.

"Well?"

"I'd just say it was a well-planned afternoon."

"Does that mean we're going house hunting?"

"Maybe. But a house that has enough land…"

Jake cut his wife off in mid-sentence. "Yeah, I know. For a horse or two." He planted another kiss on her head. "I suppose you have the horse named already?"

"Thunder." She smiled, fluttering her eyes at Jake. "Don't you think that's a great name for a black Missouri Fox

Trotter?"

Late summer turned to fall, then all too fast into winter. Working the roads of Oakland County became quieter as the snow started to fall. Edie and the boys were planning for Christmas while Jake was dealing with a drunk driver that he stopped. The guy had been to a Christmas party.

Before all the holiday wrappings disappeared and the parties ceased another tragedy hit Oakland County. A body was found. As the report read, a 12-year-old girl from Royal Oak had filled a backpack and ran away from her home following an argument with her mother over dinner on Wednesday, December 22, 1976. The day after her disappearance, her bicycle was found behind a hobby store on Main Street in Royal Oak. Her body was found four days later along the side of Interstate 75 near Big Beaver Road in Troy. She was killed by a single shotgun blast to the face. She was fully clothed and still wearing her backpack. The body was placed within sight of the Troy police station, once again, laid out neatly in the snow. Police and the sheriff's departments were trying to see if there was a link between this murder and the one earlier in the year.

Another tragedy closely followed when a 10-year old girl from Berkley disappeared. She was last seen purchasing a magazine on Sunday, January 2, 1977, at 3:00 p.m. at a 7-Eleven store on Twelve Mile Road and Oakshire in Berkley. A little more than two weeks later a mail carrier spotted her fully clothed body on the side of a rural road in Franklin Village in Oakland County. She had been smothered. The body was laid within view of nearby homes, eyes closed and arms folded across the chest, once again in the snow.

After the discovery of this girl's body, authorities quickly realized they were dealing with evidence that linked the three cases. Reports were released publicly about the possibility that a serial killer was operating in the Oakland County area, but tangible evidence that would lead authorities to the killer was almost nonexistent.

The Michigan State Police led a group of law-enforcement officials from 13 communities in the formation of a task force, devoted solely to the investigation. Jake kept abreast of any information emanating from the task force and Edie stopped looking for a home in Oakland County.

Chapter Five

Edie wasn't the only one worried about what was happening in Oakland County. Fear and mass hysteria was sweeping southeastern Michigan as young people were inundated with information about the dangers of talking to strangers from their parents and school officials. Mothers and fathers began clogging the streets around schools dropping off and picking up their children. The few kids who did walk went in groups and under the watchful eyes of parents in "safe houses," where children could go and call home if for some reason they felt uncomfortable.

Jake and Edie spent a lot of time talking to the boys. More than once, Sam said, "Dad, we know, already." The daily newspapers, as well as the area's numerous radio and television stations, aggressively covered the case.

Nearly two months later, on March 16, 1977, an 11-year old boy borrowed 30 cents from his older sister and left his home in Birmingham with a skateboard in hand. He was going to buy some candy at a drugstore on nearby Maple Road. At about 8:30 p.m. he left the store by the rear entrance, which opened to a parking lot shared with a supermarket, and vanished. An intensive search was executed that covered the entire Detroit metropolitan area, adding to the already heavy media coverage of the previous three slayings.

In the late evening hours of March 22, 1977, two teenagers in a car spotted his body in a shallow ditch alongside Gill Road, about 300 feet south of Eight Mile Road in Livonia, just across the county line in Wayne County. His skateboard was placed next to his body. His clothing had been neatly pressed and washed. He had been suffocated and sexually assaulted.

Soon after this abduction, a composite drawing of the suspected kidnapper and his vehicle was released. A woman claimed she had seen a boy with a skateboard talking to a man in the drugstore parking lot the boy had told his parents he was going to. The car was reportedly a blue AMC Gremlin with a white side stripe.

Jake, along with the rest of the Oakland County Sheriff's Department, spent many hours stopping and questioning every Gremlin owner in Oakland County. Jake took his investigation a step further, stopping any small car that could be mistaken for an AMC Gremlin.

The task force checked out more than 18,000 tips, which resulted in about two dozen arrests on unrelated charges and the busting of a multi-state child pornography ring operating on an island in Lake Michigan. However, task force members were unable to make much headway in the investigation. From there, the case went cold. But Jake kept stopping cars. Inwardly, he was worried about Hank and Sam, though never saying anything to Edie.

The ice and blackened piles of snow from the winter were melting as spring approached. For some reason, the child killings just seemed to stop. Cows were back to breaking down fences, stories about small time crooks were back to making the papers and Elvis Presley was coming to town. He was the big news. He was doing a spring tour, doing shows in Toledo, Ohio, Kalamazoo, Ann Arbor and

Saginaw, Michigan.

The Hilton Hotel in Troy at Stevenson and Fifteen Mile Road became the base of operations for Elvis and his entourage while he performed over the four-day period.

The Oakland County Sheriff's Department was requested to provide the security while Elvis was staying at the hotel. This at first appeared odd, since the City of Troy had its own police department. Why things happened this way was never revealed. One possibility was that somebody with the Elvis group or from Hilton management knew someone at the top and asked for a favor. The security was deemed necessary because, although *The King* was on a rapid downhill slide with his weight and hinted drug problems, he still drew throngs of screaming groupies and fans, 99% of whom were women.

The Oakland County Sheriff's Department happened to have a deputy named Thomas Parker and Elvis Presley's manager was Colonel Thomas Parker. The 1977 Elvis Tour brought them together, as improbable as that may seem. Jake went along for the ride only because he was low man on the department's totem pole.

Four deputies who were on open assignment, those who did fill-in duty when guys were off, were assigned to work two 12-hour shifts to provide the hotel security. Sergeant Louie Brooks broke the news to Parker and Bush right after rollcall, a week before Elvis was due in town, that they drew the short straws and would be working the 6 p.m. to 6 a.m. shift.

The guys who worked the Elvis detail deduced the sheriff's department might have been chosen simply because Elvis liked the hats they wore.

Elvis had appeared in Pontiac, Michigan on New Year's Eve, 1975, and had a few pictures taken wearing one deputy's hat. Elvis was a "wanna-be cop."

Jake wondered what his sister-in-law, a shameless Elvis fan, would give for a one of those pictures.

Parker had two years on the job and Jake had just over a

year. Parker, although quite a bit younger than Jake, was essentially the senior man on the midnight shift—if that meant anything.

Parker dropped a comment over his shoulder as they headed out the door. "Jake, did you know that Elvis's manager is Colonel Thomas Parker?"

"No," Jake answered. "The only thing I remember about Elvis was our school piping in 'Heartbreak Hotel' to the cafeteria back around 1956."

"They piped music into your cafeteria? I thought you went to Notre Dame in Harper Woods."

"I did."

"Wasn't that a pretty strict Catholic school?"

"It still is, but we had Father Bryson—one hell of a rock and roll priest. He put on sock hops in the gym, too."

"Blasphemous." There was a doubtful tone in Tom Parker's voice.

"It's called being an entrepreneur. Catholics know how to make money. The Friday night sock hops brought it in. Father Bryson and the Marist Fathers weren't dumb."

That was the gist of their conversation until they showed up at the Hilton for duty fifteen minutes before their scheduled start time. They found Penny Knox, the Hilton manager, scurrying around as some of the tour's roadies were dumping their stuff on the floor reserved for the Elvis contingent. The main group, including Elvis, was heading straight to Toledo for that night's performance.

"Got any ideas what's expected of us?" Parker asked when they found the manager after missing her between elevators for the third time.

"Just keep them from totally trashing my hotel," she said with a stern face. "And kindly escort out those who don't belong out the door."

Jake let Parker do all the talking. After all, he was senior man. Deputy Thomas P. Parker stood about six foot two and kept his dark brown hair neatly trimmed. Jake thought he had the build of a rough-carpenter, a guy climbing between trusses and pounding nails. That just meant as a cop, he could hold his own in a bar fight, or in this case, fending off overzealous females who might want *The King* to autograph a pair of pink panties (while still being worn or after he removed them). Jake thought that his partner might even get a look or two from some of the groupies, then reconsidered: *No, they were in love with The King, chubby or not.* Tom's best bet would be to get to know the *Colonel*.

Any preconceived ideas Jake might have had about this assignment were tossed out the window fast. Other than the frantic manager, the hotel appeared to be doing business as usual when he and Tom arrived. Of course, with Elvis and his crew doing a 7 p.m. show in Toledo, it should have been fairly quiet. The entire top floor of the Hilton had been reserved for Elvis and company. That included six suites and fourteen other rooms. The manager had said that Colonel Tom Parker wanted to make sure they would not be interrupted when they returned from wherever they were playing each night. "The colonel said his people would need their rest," Penny added as she jumped into a downward elevator.

Parker and Bush surveyed the lay of the land. There were stairwells at each end of the floor with a bank of three elevators in the middle. The State Fire Marshall's Office required that no doors could be locked and all elevators be accessible to all the floors. There was no compromising these rules for Elvis or anyone else.

The deputies' plan was to casually walk the floor individually checking the stairwells and the elevators. After two hours Parker and Bush had only confronted three women, one at a time, presenting themselves as members of the Housekeeping Department after climbing sixteen flights of stairs to get to the eighth floor. Jake and Tom used their detecting skills in determining the Hilton housekeepers wouldn't use the stairway or wear something that was more suitable for someone playing a French maid in a porn flick. Each was escorted downstairs on one of the elevators.

"This job's going to be a piece of cake," Tom said to Jake once in passing in the hallway. It wasn't a half hour later when he had offers of whole cakes, platters of fried chicken, plates of cookies and vegetable trays complete with different dips, all compliments of the hordes of females riding elevators or climbing the stairs. All hell was breaking loose. Elvis was due back. There were claims of women being Elvis's cousins, sisters, and even one who said Elvis called her because he needed to get "laid" after a grueling performance in a hick town called Toledo. "There isn't an ounce of shame in any of them," Tom said to Jake as he put one back on an elevator and hit the down button.

"I can half understand teenagers," Jake said with a grin, "but some of these broads are pushing forty."

"Your age, Jake?"

Jake just smiled at that last remark. He had just turned thirty-seven. *Yeah, I'm pushing it.*

Jake had started to become overwhelmed with special perfumed packages addressed to Elvis Presley at the top of the stairs at either end, or sent up by elevators. Sometimes the packages were accompanied by a female or two, sometimes just arriving anonymously.

The closer to midnight it became, the heavier the traffic seemed to get. That first night, somewhere near 12:30 a.m., an Elvis impersonator rode up on an elevator. Jake knew he was a fake at first glance when he stood alone as the doors opened. If he was Elvis, he'd be surrounded by the women that jammed the hotel lobby and parking lot bearing gifts or baring their breasts— which some did.

"You need to hit the down button," Jake commanded. "This is a private floor fully reserved."

The man in the white sequined jump suit didn't take the hint. "Elvis expects me. I'm his stunt double. The colonel pays me well to take care of some of the ladies who are always pestering him."

Jake looked at the man. Elvis had gained a lot of weight, but he sure wasn't three hundred pounds, wearing an afro with long sideburns—and black. Jake turned the man around and hit the button for Elvis's double. "Next time I see you I'll arrest you for criminal trespass." Jake didn't know if he would, but sometimes a bit of bullshit went a long way. Jake didn't see the man again that night and Tom never said anything about seeing a black Elvis impersonator.

The reality was that Tom and Jake were kept quite busy sending women back down the stairs or the elevators. When the real Elvis did arrive, the party started. Nothing Jake had seen in Detroit could have prepared him for the near-orgy that developed on the top floor of the Hilton that night. Every one of Elvis's group had one or two women hanging on their arms as they got off the elevator. And for four nights in a row there was a repeat performance with different *friends* hanging on different arms, all invited guests of the Elvis entourage. When the day crew, Mike Dempsey and John Kaminski, arrived for their first morning shift, the party was still going. Jake knew their day shift wasn't going to be any easier.

Dempsey was the older of the two, but didn't look much like a cop. With red hair and freckles and weighing just over 160, he had to be in uniform to be recognized as a deputy. Kaminski was just the opposite. One look at him and you knew he was a cop—a big one. Jake knew him slightly as "Big John," the name the guys hung on him because it seemed like most of them were looking up at him.

Jake's parting words were, "Good luck, guys. I don't think sleep is on their agenda."

On one of the nights Jake was escorting six women down an elevator to make sure they were heading out the front door. He was tired of seeing them. As the door opened, there before him, along with at least twenty other screaming women, was his sister-in-law Faye. Her smile turned to a frown. "Jake, what are you doing here?"

"That's what I was going to ask you."

She paused for a second, turned and grabbed something

from the woman behind her. "Here, I brought a…" she lifted the tin foil "…a pecan pie for Elvis."

"Does your Jerry know where you're at?"

She smiled. "He fell asleep in his bean-bag chair while watching the Pistons. He won't miss me 'til morning."

"Sorry Sis. Can't let you go up."

"At least take the pie." She turned to the woman behind her, "You don't mind do you?" Before he heard an answer, Jake hit the *Close* button on the panel next to the door. He figured his partner was getting overrun with screaming women upstairs and might need his help.

After four nights, the party still going strong when their relief arrived, but finally the roadies were loading up their gear. Jake and Tom had enough. They were well fed, but tired of dealing with the Elvis crowd and their fans.

As they walked to their cars, Jake asked, "You ever get to talk to the *Colonel*?"

"He never gave the time of day, the arrogant bastard."

"Some colonels are like that…'specially the self-appointed ones."

"Well, at least we ate well," Tom said.

"Yeah, some of those women can fry up a good batch of chicken."

"Jake, most of it was probably re-packaged KFC."

"Fooled me." He unlocked his pickup.

As Parker got to his car, he called to Jake. "Do you know where my wife went last night?"

"Probably the same place as mine. To Saginaw to see Elvis." They both were laughing to themselves as they drove off.

A week later, Jake ran into Dempsey and Kaminski at headquarters. "How'd the day shift go with Elvis?"

Kaminski smiled and said, "If they slept, it had to be in shifts." Dempsey didn't answer. He just blushed.

Chapter Six

Another half a handful of popcorn landed somewhere near Lynn's mouth, the rest bounced off the ratty XXXL T-shirt she was wearing, some coming to rest on the pillows propped up around her on the couch. A few kernels hit the floor. Two mice quickly made off with those before they stopped bouncing. Mickey and Minnie loved watching Lynn take in her favorite soaps. She burped to make way for the rest of the tepid can of Blatz sitting on the end table as she settled in for Tuesday's segment of *Days of Our Lives.*

Across the room, Leo was lying in the same position on the orange bean-bag chair where he'd fallen asleep during the third quarter of a college basketball game more than twelve hours before. His mouth was agape and a rivulet of drool stretched from its left side to his grease-stained, stretched out blue polo shirt. The mice had already cleaned up the crust bits he'd left behind in the empty box from a Domino's delivery balanced on fifteen empty cans of his favorite—Stroh's.

An eighteen by twenty-four framed photo hung askew on the wall between them. In it, a blonde Mary Lynn, at least a hundred pounds trimmer, wearing a long white gown, carrying a delicate bouquet, was staring deeply into the dark eyes of Leonardo whose well-chiseled body filled a finely tailored tuxedo.

Three years after the wedding photo was taken, Lynn and Leo Franks existed in a 1970 Crossroads Park Model that was sitting on the very back lot at Upland Hills Estates near the town of Highland. Forget the fancy names, this was a run-down trailer in a rat-infested trailer park, something that they really couldn't afford since Leo lost his job at the Mills Stamping Plant on the south side of Flint, Michigan.

The park model was "just a place to start their heavenly wedded bliss" Leo told her when he carried her across the threshold in July, 1974. They had spent a three-day honeymoon at a cheap motel in St. Ignace, just across the Mackinac Bridge. He did take Lynn on what he called a romantic cruise —the ride to the famous Mackinac Island on a ferry boat—and splurged on a few pounds of fudge for her.

By their third anniversary, Leo had morphed into a common drunk. Holding a job was a lot harder than holding a beer can. For two months after he was fired, he tried his hand at driving a Schwan's truck delivering frozen foods. He was like a Fuller Brush man on wheels, only peddling tasty frozen treats.

He lost that job, not because he was drunk, but because he and his wife were eating on the company. They especially liked the lasagna. When Leo's inventory did not match his sales over his first two months, the area manager pulled his keys and tore up his time card.

Lynn was no better at making a living. She was a beautician by training, but had the charisma of the chair she was renting at "Cut and Curl," a small shop in the Pontiac Mall. The owner gave Lynn a month more than she should have before asking her to clear out her stuff. The sandpaper personality was causing the shop to "lose too many customers." Thus Lynn became a stay-at-home, soap-watching vegetable and grew into her near-new Salvation Army obtained extra-large clothes.

There was a steady rain tapping on the roof of Leo and Lynn's trailer, when Leo heard a loud pounding on their tattered screen door. He pushed himself away from a TV tray holding a plate of beans and franks and went to a window near the door. With one finger he moved aside the yellow stained shade on the window. *Shit, not him.* Leo slowly walked to the door. The rent was overdue two months and he expected to see the Highland Hills Estates manager for the past two weeks, and now, there he was. It took Leo fifteen seconds to tell the old, bent over, bald headed Wayne Simmons that he'd have the money owed and the next month's rent by the end of the day. "Lynn and I were just heading to the bank as you knocked," he lied.

The steady drizzle continued as Leo and Lynn piled into their '68 Plymouth clunker just to make it appear that they were in fact heading out to the bank. What the park manager didn't know was that the sum total of five dollars and thirty-eight cents remained in the Franks' bank account—four hundred and fifty dollars shy of what the Franks needed just to catch up on the lot rental.

"God damn it, Lynn. The needle's on empty. You were supposed to put some gas in it."

"Where in the hell do you think I got the money for the beans and franks?"

Lynn spotted a 7-Eleven as Leo was just driving around, trying to figure out how to come up with the rent money. "I've got two bucks, sweetheart, how 'bout we get a couple of Slurpees and some Cheetos?" she asked.

"Maybe a couple of candy bars too," Leo answered, "like you don't inhale enough calories."

"Look asshole, you're the one that's supposed to be the breadwinner…"

"Enough, bitch! I am tired of your nagging while you eat bonbons and watch soaps all day."

He wheeled into the quick-stop store, snatched the two bucks she was holding in her hand and went in the front door. The rain had him hunched over and he had his hands in his jacket pockets as he was mumbling, "I'd like to stick a gun to her head," as he walked briskly to the counter.

A teenage East Indian was behind the counter and heard

the words *stick a gun*, and immediately threw his hands up in the air. "Sir, please do not shoot. I give you the money." He dropped one hand, hitting the *No Sale* key and the cash drawer popped open. Three quick grabs and all the twenties, tens and fives were on the counter between a rack of Snickers and a stack of that day's *Oakland Press*.

Leo shrugged, whining, "I wanted a couple of Slurpees."

The teenager couldn't move fast enough. He had been robbed two weeks before and two cherry Slurpees quickly hit the counter next to the crumpled stack of bills. Leo shrugged again, stuffed the bills into his left jacket pocket and grabbed the two drinks and banged out the door.

The kid stood shaking with his hands up, remembering his father yelling at him the last time: "Just give them the money. Your mother would never forgive me when you're dead." He watched the old, banged up green Plymouth back away from the front of the store and turn onto the highway. He couldn't make out the plate number. A shiver ran down his spine. He'd forgotten to stash the excess cash in the floor safe slot the past two hours. *I'm in deep donkey dung!*

A half mile away, Leo took a pull on his cherry Slurpee. "I think I found a new line of work." Lynn just sucked on her drink, not wanting to stop long enough to ask what happened to the Cheetos. She was halfway through the Slurpee when Leo dug in his jacket pocket and tossed a wad of bills onto her lap. "Here, count it. See if we can pay the rent."

"What the hell?" She dropped the king-sized cardboard cup as she scrambled to grab the wad of money. "Where'd this come from?"

"A donation toward the rent," he said as a broad smile crossed his face. "Like I said, I found a new line of work."

"Such as?"

"Knocking over 7-Elevens." Leo looked over at Lynn as he spotted a familiar orange sign for Gulf gasoline and pulled in. "Is there enough in there to fill up the car and get a case of beer?"

Lynn was still counting the money as her spilled Slurpee

puddled around her feet. “Don’t interrupt. Now I gotta start over again.” She counted the big bills first, then said, “There’s plenty for gas and your Stroh’s and my Blatz.” She held out a couple of twenties for Leo.

———

The broadcast over the Oakland County frequency said that a dented up old green Plymouth was wanted in an armed robbery of a 7-Eleven store on the corner of Bullard Road and M-59. Jake pulled onto the shoulder of the gravel road he was on to jot down the information on the car and occupants: A white male, near thirty, unshaven with a pot belly, wearing a tan jacket. A passenger was seen in the car, described as a white female with a heap of disheveled blonde hair and wearing very large sunglasses. The man had his hand in his pocket as if armed.

Jake wrote down the information and started thinking where the best place would be to sit and watch for an old green Plymouth.

———

It cost Leo $12.53 to fill up their Plymouth Valiant and he mumbled at the cost of gasoline as he pulled into a Kroger’s for their beer. “Well, did you finish counting it yet?”

Lynn looked at Leo, “I told you not to interrupt. Go get the beer while I start over again, asshole!” Leo shuffled out of the car and grabbed a cart to haul the beer.

Leo put the two cases in the trunk after moving around an old blanket and a set of dishes Lynn had picked up at a yard sale. He looked over at his wife as he slid in behind the wheel “Well?”

“Six hundred and twenty five, not counting the change you should have in your pocket.” She leaned over and kissed Leo on his cheek. “I was just kidding with the asshole remark. Let’s go find another 7-Eleven.”

“Lynn, I was only shittin’ you about that. That kid was

just throwing money at me. It was pure luck, and now we can pay the rent. I'm not goin' to jail."

The sun broke through the clouds and Leo was driving home, happy to have a couple of bucks in his pocket.

Five minutes later Lynn spoke up. "You know, we could make a good living at this. We took in almost seven hundred dollars in less than ten minutes."

"No. I ran into some dumb kid from India and he just..."

"He gave you seven hundred dollars, asshole. More money than we'd seen in a couple of years. They want to give you the money, take it. Look at all these Arabs, Pakistanis and Indians taking over these stop and go stores."

"Lynn, we'll get caught. Let's quit while we're ahead."

Lynn was silently putting away the beer in the fridge at their park model home after Leo stopped and paid Wayne Simmons the lot rent. Leo turned on the TV to catch the local news. As he popped the top on a cold Stroh's, a video clip of the front of the 7-Eleven came up with a voice of Ted Bradfield, the local newsman from WXYZ out of Detroit, reporting about a robbery earlier in the day in Pontiac with a vague description of the man and woman wanted. He ended the clip with "the police say the investigation is ongoing, which is cop-talk for no leads."

Lynn was opening her own beer, leaning against the archway into the kitchen. "See Leo, they haven't got shit." She sat down on the couch with her husband and ran her free hand across his thigh. "Y'see honey, we could do something like this once in a while and live like kings."

"You say we, but it is me they're looking for."

"Shh, shh," she put a finger to his mouth. "Let's go to the Chop House and have a steak tonight. Celebrate a little."

It had been a while, months, maybe a year, since Leo had a steak. His mouth watered. "I'll put on a fresh shirt." Leo found a nearly clean T-shirt, combed his hair with his fingers and told Lynn that he was ready. A thick steak sounded good to him.

"Here, take this." It was Lynn, prodding her husband as he poured a cup of coffee at the kitchen counter. He had to rinse one of the fifteen cups that were scattered among the heap of dirty dishes and silverware to his left. It had been three weeks since they went out for steaks.

"What's this?" he asked as he turned to look at the butt end of a little pistol showing from Lynn's extended hand.

"The key to a cashbox at any quick-stop store."

"Whoa, whoa. I'm not touching that thing." Leo threw his hands up and was backing away. He dropped the coffee cup and it broke, spilling its contents. "Where in the hell did you get that thing?"

"Had it. Daddy gave it to me for protection when I was going to beauty school in Pontiac."

"And what do you want me to do with it?"

"You're the breadwinner. It's time to go back to work."

"I told you I'm not doing that shit and ending up in jail."

"Well, I got news for you. We're broke and I'm not going back to beans and franks. It's time to get some money you damn sissy." Lynn tugged on Leo's arm, leading him toward the couch, gently sitting him on the one cushion that didn't have springs protruding.

As she paced the floor she told him how she'd checked out a store on Ormond just north of White Lake Road, reminding him how easy it was to come into nearly $700. "It's a bait and booze stop with a couple of gas pumps." She said it was far enough away from the 7-Eleven they'd already hit and a long way from home. "They do a hell of a business."

Leo just looked at his wife for a while. "You're serious?"

She plopped her ass on the side of the couch, putting her arm around Leo's neck, bending so he could get a good look at the cleavage that went with the hundred and some extra pounds she carried. "Honey, for once we had a couple of bucks in our pocket, all for a couple of minutes work." She smiled and teased his ear with her finger and leaned over, running her tongue into it.

Leo thought for a second, his hand settling on her left thigh. Robbery wasn't on his mind. "Can we talk about it after a good fuck?"

Lynn giggled, grabbed Leo's hand and led him off to the bedroom.

Jake's radio came to life. "Attention all units in Oakland County. Be on a lookout for a dark green Plymouth Valiant with two occupants, a white male and a white female. They were last seen leaving the scene of a shooting and attempted robbery at a convenience store on Ormond north of White Lake Road."

He heard Three thirty-three answer the call as he jotted down the information, then looked at his county maps. He still hadn't totally gotten the feel for the lay of the land in Oakland County. He found Ormond and White Lake Roads, trying to think where'd be a good place to sit and watch. The more he looked at the map, the more he realized how impossible it would be to pick a likely spot to watch for a dark green Plymouth Valiant—until he remembered a 7-Eleven hold up and a car matching that description. That hold up was near US-23 on Highland Road. His first thought was to sit on M-59, but chose otherwise. *They'd have to be smart enough to go wherever taking back roads.* He started heading from Keego Harbor toward the Highland Area.

"How in the fuck did you end up shooting the guy?" Lynn asked as she snaked east on Gale Road, pushing the gas pedal to the floor on the little Valiant.

"He grabbed the gun. I didn't even know it was loaded." Leo was panting, looking over one shoulder than the other.

"I tol' you we shouldn't be doin' shit like this."

"Sit your ass still, Leo. Someone sees your head spinning like a top; they'll know you're guilty of something." At Williams Lake Road, Lynn took a right. "Get some balls, will ya?"

"You're going the wrong way," Leo gasped.

"I'm not going straight home, stupid. They're probably watching the main roads."

"I just want to get home." Leo cranked down the window and tossed the little black gun toward the ditch.

"What the hell'd you do that for?" Lynn jammed on the brakes, the Valiant skidding sideways on the gravel. She threw the car in reverse and stopped. "Get your ass out there and find it," she ordered.

"I don't want to see another gun…"

"My daddy bought that gun. His name is on some record somewhere. Find the fuckin' gun or I'll leave your ass right here."

Fifteen minutes later, Lynn was going south on Williams Lake Road again. "And what are we going to do with the damn gun?" Leo asked.

"Toss it in one of the thousand lakes we'll pass on the way home." Lynn took a short jaunt across M-59 to pick up Williams Lake Road heading south again. "We'll toss it in Union Lake. It's deep and we'll go right by it." Lynn checked roads as she passed them. "Boy, you are a dumb fuck. You know, someone could find that gun in that ditch a year from now and they'd be tracking us down." Lynn took the turn at Cooley Lake Road to head west. She glanced in her rear-view mirror. "Oh-Oh!" A hundred yards behind her was a black and white.

Jake spotted a dark green car make the turn in front of him as he drove west, nearing Union Lake Road. *Luck. Just plain-assed luck!* He reached for his mic. "Station three from

Three thirty-four. I am behind a dark green Plymouth Valiant…"

"Quick, gimme the gun," Lynn said.

Leo looked back over his left shoulder. He didn't need to ask. There was a county sheriff's car on their tail. "Whacha going to do with it?" Leo's eyes went wide as he handled the .25 caliber Colt Automatic like it was on fire. He dropped it in his wife's lap. "I tol' you I didn't want it. Sure, get it outta that ditch, you said." He was screaming by the time the next two words came out. "Now what?"

"Shut up. I'm thinking."

"First, you make me take the gun. Then this dumb guy grabs it instead of giving me the money. He gets shot, we run. I toss the gun. You make me get it back…"

"Shut the fuck up! He's going to pull us over."

Jake eased out of his unit, leaving his door open for what little cover it offered. His .357 Smith was aimed at the rear window of the Valiant. He had heard Corporal Williams respond to Station Three's request of "any units in the vicinity of …"

"I want to see hands," Jake yelled. He saw some movement between the man and the woman. His eyes went first to the man, then to the woman. She had a heap of blonde hair and wearing sunglasses. "Now! Show your hands." Jake was in a combat stance, half-stepping toward the front of his car, his sight leveled at the back of the man's head in the passenger side.

"Don't shoot. We're not armed." It was the woman's voice. She started to open her door. Jake saw that she was large—very large, and struggling to get out from behind the wheel of the car.

"Slowly, lady," Jake shouted. "Mister. You freeze. One at

a time." Jake thought of times he had Jess or Remington covering his ass in Detroit. Now, it was just him and two people who may have shot someone twenty minutes before. *Where are you, Marshal Mel?*

Another black and white was kicking up dust from the west. Jake's eyes went to it a fraction of a second, just long enough to where his next mental picture was of a woman's right hand moving with something black and boxy. CRACK! The windshield on Jake's car shattered.

Williams was out of his unit while it still was moving. His gun coming up, both deputies' thoughts were the same: *Acquire the target and squeeze.*

Williams touched off two shots, both dead center in the mass standing next to the Plymouth. The woman with blonde hair was spinning left and falling.

Jake had paused to make sure Williams was out of his line of fire and squeezed off two rounds also. His first hit the glass in the open door behind the spinning woman, the second hit the target.

The .357 magnum loads did what they were designed to do; nullify the situation.

Jake's sight picture moved slightly to the right, stopping on the head frozen in the passenger's seat. Jake heard a wail coming from within the Plymouth, then outright shrieks. "I tol' her no guns. I tol' her we shouldn't…"

Jake was side-stepping across the front of his unit. "Hands! Show me some fuckin' hands!" The passenger turned, putting two empty hands out his open window.

Mel was moving to his right, his pistol aimed at the woman on the pavement. The woman's right foot twitched twice, then stopped. With his boot, he moved the small automatic further away from a still outstretched hand. The large sunglasses were twisted, half off of her head, its right stem resting atop a heap of blonde hair. The eye that he could see was wide open, but looking nowhere. "Jake, you okay?" Mel yelled.

"Yeah." Jake got to the passenger's door and opened it.

"Out. Very slow." The man tumbled out his door. "On the ground," Jake commanded.

The man fell to his knees, trembling, then to his belly. "This is all an accident. The other robbery—then today, the gun just went off. I didn't think it was even loaded." The man started crying while Jake knelt beside him, running his hands up and down the prone body, looking for a weapon. He was clean, but his pants were wet. He pissed himself. Leo cried out, "Lynn, I told you…" Big sobs stopped him in mid-sentence.

The county coroner showed up an hour after the shooting and hauled away the body of the woman tentatively identified as Mary Lynn Franks. He had to wait ten minutes while the Michigan State Police Crime Lab team finished with their photographs of the scene. It was good the three-man team was still there. The coroner needed help loading the body into his black wagon. Jake's unit, Three thirty-four, was towed back to headquarters. It had a shattered windshield. All that remained at the scene were where they had marked the area with little yellow cones. The State Police would be leading the investigation into the deputy-involved shooting.

Leonardo Franks, the husband, had already been transported to the Oakland County Jail. He had not stopped talking even after he had been read his rights.

"It's stupid, stupid. Two cop cars and she starts shooting? The gun musta just went off—like it did with me." Leo was going through one tissue after another, wiping tears and blowing his nose. Detective Don Yeaman had his tape recorder going as he jotted notes.

Jake sat in a small cubicle on the opposite side in the detective bureau typing a report. He stopped for a minute, and got up. He needed a drink. He passed Mel Williams who was pecking out his own report at another typewriter, and stopped in front of the clerk at the desk.

"Got any fresh coffee?"

The clerk looked up. "Is less than four hours fresh?"

"I guess it'll have to do." Jake poured two cups of the dark brew, put one down in front of Mel, and went to finish his report. There wasn't much to type. A car fitting the description of one wanted in a hold up turned in front of him while driving west on Cooley Lake Road. He stopped again. *Just about every road is named after a lake. Detroit was simpler.* Jake didn't even know how he ended up on Cooley Lake road. He was just cruising back roads away from the scene of the robbery. *Pure luck.*

Ten minutes later he pulled the report out of the Remington electric he was using, signed it and went to see the desk boss. He knew he'd be off the road for a while until the investigation was over. Mel Williams was waiting at the desk with two more coffees. "I made some fresh. I couldn't drink that mud you brought me."

Jake grabbed his coffee and retreated back to the report room. Mel joined him. "You okay with what went on?" Mel asked.

"Yeah." Jake took a swig. "Ugh! No sugar."

"Cowboys don't use sugar." Mel had his ever-present wide smile as he said it.

"Thanks for the assist back there," Jake said as he noticed Mel's smile disappear. Jake had never seen the guy without a smile. "You okay?" Jake saw Mel's cup shaking a bit as he took a sip.

"First time," Mel answered. He steadied the cup by putting his left hand under it. "And it had to be a woman." He tried to take another sip, but was shaking too much. "How 'bout you?"

"The state boys said there were four more rounds in the mag on that .25 Colt. If we didn't do something…" He stopped and looked at the senior deputy. "I'm glad you were there." Both drank silently. Jake stirred around, opening a couple of drawers on the table where he was sitting.

"What you lookin' for?" Mel asked.

"Sugar. I'm not a cowboy."

The smile came back. "Fuckin' city slicker." Williams thought for a minute, the serious look appearing again. "You been in any shootings?"

Jake just shrugged off the question. He'd never mentioned anything about the three times he had to use his pistol in Detroit. He always thought that those things were best buried. If someone wanted to pull his file, everything was there, but Jake didn't think things like that were for general conversation. Jake figured he was like his Uncle Ray, his mom's brother. Ray served in WWII and was wounded twice and never talked about it. Jake had remembered asking Uncle Ray about it a few times. Uncle Ray never answered Jake's questions.

Jake finally said, "Yeah" to Mel's shooting question. Jake found a pack of sugar in the fourth drawer he opened. Mel watched Jake pinch off part of the pack. "Two hundred ninety-two granules," he said. "Makes even *your* coffee palatable." Jake paused, slowly stirring the contents of his cup.

"You count the damn granules?"

"Always. Don't like it too sweet." Jake saw the smile back on Mel's face. Just like Uncle Ray, Jake had changed the subject.

A day later, Jake was having another coffee with Mel. "You know, Mel, they're going to line us up with some shrinks."

"I heard."

"Talk to them. Tell them everything that's on your mind."

"This the voice of experience talking?"

"Yeah." Jake offered no more.

Jake and Mel were off road patrol until the state police finished their investigation for the Oakland County

Prosecutor's Office. There wasn't any busy work as Jake had found in Detroit, so he and Mel burned up a few boxes of wad cutters down in the basement range. The recent incident turned their practice into something more serious. They also took care of their monthly qualification requirements, both shooting as if their life depended on it. As sometimes it does.

Chapter Seven

A week went by before the Oakland County Prosecutor ruled the shooting of Mary Lynn Franks as justified. Ballistics proved that Williams had hit her twice and Jake once. Williams' two hits were the fatal shots. They were back on the road, writing tickets, taking minor complaint calls, and doing generally nothing but being out there.

May turned into June, then June into July. It got hot and muggy. Like anywhere else, the day shift was spent working traffic. That meant writing tickets, which was rather easy to do. Someone was always late for work, for an appointment, or getting home. Jake got used to writing two to four a day. Tickets kept the bosses happy and gave him something to do. In one sense, he missed the crime-laden streets of Detroit, but then again, he was working in what was considered a much safer environment. The Lynn and Leo Franks crime spree was an abnormality. Working in Oakland County was a big step down from Detroit's daily hold-ups and murders. He just had to get used to the pace.

Yeah, getting used to the mostly-nothing-to-do daily routine was something that Jake had to work at, along with the cow or horse that walked right through a barbed wire fence that was barely attached to a rotted post probably erected in 1930 or so. A car hitting a wandering cow was a bit more damaging than the deer problems they often encountered on the rural roads in the county. Many times he'd heard the other deputies saying, "Wait 'til the fall and the start of their mating season. Car and deer collisions peak in November."

Jake could wait for fall. He was kept busy finding the owners of a horse or two and five separate cow incidents. There were times when he wished he was on a horse rather than in his Pontiac. Horses could maneuver and went through ditches with ease. Four wheels didn't, and he was tired of cleaning the mud and muck off of his shoes. *But then, I'd have to learn how to ride.* The thought had Jake smiling. *Edie would like that.*

With summer waning, Jake and the boys were done with baseball for another year. Edie had gone back to checking with real estate companies for a place with ten acres or more. The media frenzy over the "Oakland County Child Killings" had faded away, although the task force was still at work trying to solve the crimes. Jake made a point to keep abreast of the case. He had Hank and Sam to protect and wanted answers for any questions his wife might ask.

———

Working the road in Oakland County was much slower than Jake expected. He wasn't overwhelmed with radio runs which gave him the opportunity to get to know some of the characters he ran across. One such person was a guy called "Brown Bottle Billy."

Jake had come to know Billy when he pulled the guy out of a ditch on M-59 earlier in the spring when a car full of kids swerved purposely off the road to put a scare into the "bottle picking bum." At least that was the quote from one of the six cars of gawkers that had stopped before Jake happened on the scene. No one got a plate number off of the yellow Dodge Dart that caused the guy to tumble into the ditch, but they did say that it was definitely a 1973 Dart.

"The fancy one with the twin air scoops on the hood," one witness had said.

Jake put out a quick description of the car over the air, saying it was heading west from Bogie Lake Road. He didn't try to chase down the Dodge because he had a more urgent concern. Billy and his bike ended up in three feet of cold water in the ditch and Jake was the only one who'd brave the litter-laden waters to help rescue the man, his bike, and his cloth bag half full of long-neck beer bottles.

In 1977 the cash return on a beer bottle was only two cents, but Billy felt that those ditch castaways were one way for him to put some money in his pockets. Every day the man would hang his very old *Detroit Ne*ws carrier's cloth bag over his handlebars and push off on his dinged-up Huffy bicycle to cover his ditch route. The only days he wasn't on the road were when it was raining or in the dead of winter.

Jake got to find out all about Billy one cool September morning while working in Highland Township. Jake had seen Billy pedaling his way along the shoulder of Commerce Road, and, being curious as to how the man was doing, asked Billy to meet him at a nearby country café that was just up the road. "The owner makes some good soup, and today's for sure a soup day," Jake said to him. The deputy saw the question in the man's eyes and quickly added, "I'm buying."

When Jake said that, a smile broadened on Billy's face. He, like the last time Jake saw him, was unbathed, had shallow cheeks and wore a brown flap-eared leather aviator's hat, tattered pants and the same green flannel shirt. A new addition in his attire was a red plaid wool jacket with a broken zipper. Billy had it pinned shut in two places with diaper pins, the kind with the blue plastic heads.

At the café, between huge bowls of Mamie's chicken and dumpling soup, Billy summed up his life story for Jake.

He said he didn't really have a last name as far as he could remember, saying someone had given him the last name of Fenton because he was arrested in Fenton,

Michigan, a couple of years before. Billy said he was in jail for being drunk in a public place—an alley. He said he did not know how he got there and where he came from. "Truth be told, when I ended up in the hospital, the doctors said my brain had been fried from drugs and booze—though I don't know for sure." Billy tipped up the bowl and slurped up the remnants, asking Jake if he could have another. Jake called the waitress over while the man talked.

"The city of Fenton's where I got the bike. The chief of police had it in their property room for over a year and said I could have it when they were finally booting me out the door."

The second bowl came and Billy continued talking between each spoonful. "Nice guy, the Chief." He looked like he was pondering for a few seconds. "Don't even remember his name. I forget things now."

Billy said the chief told him that the standard fingerprint check came up blank. As far as the Fenton Police, the State of Michigan and the FBI knew he'd never been arrested before and never served in the armed forces. "I know I was born in 1943" he laughed, adding, "I've no way of proving it, but I just know."

A third bowl of soup was ordered and Billy kept on talking. He said he took on Fenton as his last name "because that's where my new life began." He polished off the third bowl, burped and wiped his mouth off with a napkin. "Some church people came to visit when I was in jail and gave me a Bible and Jesus became my savior." Billy then admitted that from that time on he'd have himself a bottle of Boone's Farm "just on occasion." He smiled, adding, "I do know that Jesus shared the fruit of the vine. It's in the Bible." He winked, "so I do indulge in a sip every now and then."

From the city of Fenton, Billy said he moved from shelter to shelter and from church to church, taking hand-outs from "whoever happened to have pity on me." When Jake asked where Billy was living now, the only response he got was, "Somewhere on the edge of Pontiac." Jake didn't press the issue.

Jake paid for lunch and walked back to his unit; he stuck two quarters to the back of his business card with a piece of Scotch tape. The front had a contact phone number at the county headquarters for Deputy John Anthony Bush. He gave the card to Billy. "Call me if you are ever in a fix," Jake said.

Billy read the card. "Who in the hell's this John Anthony Bush?"

"Me. Jake."

"Then write Jake across it, or I'll forget." He laughed, revealing three gaps where teeth were missing. "Talk about my name. You have more than I could ever remember."

Jake watched the young weather-beaten man push off on his bike, heading toward the next ditch. He had money to make.

Over two years before, on July 30, 1975, in the middle of the day, Jimmy Hoffa had been parked in his green 1974 Pontiac Grandville at the Machus Red Fox Restaurant in Bloomfield Township. The restaurant was in Oakland County. At about 2:45 p.m. that day a delivery driver saw Jimmy Hoffa leaving the parking lot in the back seat of a 1975 Mercury Marquis Brougham with someone sitting next to him.

No one had gotten another glimpse of Jimmy since that day, at least no one who would talk about it. Various tips had been received by the FBI and the Oakland County Sheriff's Department, but none proved fruitful in finding Mr. Hoffa, dead or alive.

Some of the thinking was that he had not been taken far, was killed and buried. Thus Jake Bush found himself spending the next three nights parked next to a sagging abandoned barn just off of I-75. He was there to protect the integrity of the site during the midnight shift. A tip came into the Detroit office of the FBI because there was a suspicious-looking overgrown mound of dirt that might be important in the Hoffa case. A forensic team was sifting dirt slowly during the daylight hours, looking for bones, possibly those of James Riddle Hoffa.

Jake was not too fond of this type of work and really did not give a rip about Jimmy Hoffa. The guy was convicted of jury tampering, had spent about five years in jail and had obvious mob ties. From what Jake had read, Hoffa was supposed to be meeting Anthony "Tony Jack" Giacalone and Anthony "Tony Pro" Provenzano, two heavyweights in the mob. Jake didn't think they'd ever see Jimmy Hoffa or his remains again.

Jake thought this was a bullshit job, but his nonetheless for as long as it took to determine if the tip was another in a long line of false information, wasted time and for sure, squandered taxpayer dollars.

This assignment came as a surprise at that night's roll call. Now, Jake was parked in his county car with darkness surrounding him and only stars to count, if it was a clear night—and it wasn't. It was November and it started to snow, with the flakes melting as they hit the ground. He knew a situation like this could lead to the inevitable—falling asleep. He had worked midnights before and his body just wasn't meant to sit still and stay awake in the dead of the night. Then too, he wasn't convinced the rest of the guys on his shift were done with their initiation process. They all knew where he'd be and if they'd tried to steal his car a couple of times and never succeeded, maybe they'd try to put a scare into him. The closest yard light was at least a half mile away to the east and I-75 was another half mile to the west.

Memories of a dead albatross found while driving a Military Police patrol truck at Moffett Field on a midnight shift came to mind. Jake and two of his companions removed the mattress off of a top bunk over a very superstitious and dead asleep Lenny Harris. Over the flat wire springs that remained above Harris, they stretched out the dead bird, its four-foot wing span going from side to side and its head hanging within inches of the sleeping Marine's face. Five minutes later the barracks' lights went on with the Corporal of the Guard screaming "Revelry! Revelry!" It was three in the morning.

After a week of sleepless nights, Harris found an empty top bunk to move to. *Boys will be boys.*

Jake decided to walk around the barn with his three-cell Maglite, partly because he was curious and mostly because he was determined to stay awake. Nobody was going to hang a dead albatross anywhere near him.

Being city-born, he hadn't the opportunity to browse around a barn, new or one sagging under decaying beams. On his second trip around the back of the barn, the toe of his brogans nudged something hard. Getting down on his haunches with the aid of his light he fingered off some dirt. It was a part of a wooden handle. Jake retrieved the lug wrench from the back of his Pontiac and used it to unearth an old wooden handled scythe. The blade was still intact, but dull and pitted from who knows how long it had been lying just beneath the dirt. Jake doubted it had anything to do with the forensic dig going on fifty feet away, but he leaned it against the barn for the team to find in the morning—maybe it was an omen of some sort.

It was around 2 a.m. as he came around the barn he saw the outline of someone sneaking up on his empty car. Jake wished he still had the scythe with him. He watched and waited. When the figure bent down to go around to the driver's side of Jake's car, Jake let out a screech and flicked on his three-cell under his chin.

A very startled Mel Williams, trying to run, but frozen in place let out an, "Oooh Shit!" He grabbed at his chest, bending over. "Jake, you fuckin' bastard. You trying to give me a heart attack?"

Jake was laughing so hard, his sides were hurting. He stifled his laugh long enough to ask, "And what are you doing here, Mel?"

"Bringing you some coffee."

"Thanks. Where is it?"

"Back in my car. About a hundred yards up the road." Jake gave Mel a ride back to his unit. They drank some coffee and laughed. *Boys will be boys.* Jake asked Mel to bring him back another coffee and a burger the next time. Mel did, two hours later, but this time he just drove up to make the delivery.

Between Mel's visits, the inside of the barn was tugging at Jake's curiosity. Again, he used the lug wrench to pry his way in, sliding the main door open just far enough to squeeze through. The first thing he did was to slowly scan the roof above with his light to make sure nothing would fall on him. The sudden beam of light had wings flapping and dust falling. Jake didn't know pigeons liked the tranquility of old barns. Five minutes later, he was satisfied he could check out the floor of the barn without anything tumbling down. The air was still and filled with the musty smell of old straw and wood. About fifteen bales of hay, most with the binder twine pulled loose, littered the floor. A few old road-apples remained in the one and only stall on the far wall. Jake's mind wandered, thinking he should have this FBI Forensic Team run a test on them to give him an age or a time span when they hit the ground. *History is good to know.* He was also wondering if Jimmy Hoffa had been in the Teamsters back when they had horses pulling the wagons. He laughed at that thought.

In the back corner under some loose straw he found the remnants of a roll of binder twine. A tag was still attached. It took a while, but he was able to piece together the wording on it: Binder Twine Plant, Michigan State Prison, Jackson, Michigan. *You learn something every day.* He wondered if there was still a binder twine plant at the state prison. *Nah, that'd be cruel and unusual punishment.* Jake knew the prison system had gotten too lax. He spent some time in the barn picking up pieces of shriveled leather, a hammer head, and some buckles, just to stay awake waiting for daylight.

The next two nights Jake brought a sack lunch and a thermos of coffee along with a book. It was time to get back into Joseph Wambaugh. He had a copy of the author's latest: *The Choir Boys.* He didn't think Mel or anyone else would be visiting—unless they came up with their headlights on.

After the third night, the dig was shut down. From what Jake had heard, the forensic team found the bones of a horse that had been buried about ten years before. Jake wondered if the road apples were from that horse. He laughed to himself again, thinking he should have left a couple in an evidence bag next to the scythe. And yes, the scythe was gone by the next night, probably in the hands of one of the team members, one who collected old farm tools, or played the Grim Reaper on Halloween. Jake thought again about his past three nights. It wasn't a bullshit job. It was a horseshit one that came with the badge he wore.

Chapter Eight

The Christmas season of that year had Jake and the boys join Edie in looking at three places that were for sale.

"In the snow?" Jake asked.

"Yes, in the snow. The book on house hunting says to look at a place under less than perfect conditions. If it looks good to you, then give it a second look later."

Jake just shrugged, knowing his wife was probably right. She knew how to shop, but he didn't know there was a book on it. He thought she was just born to shop—from clothes for the boys, things for the house, and now, for a different place to live that had room for a horse or two.

The first place they went to, the driveway wound through some woods. It was beautiful, but with only three inches of snow on the ground, it was a test for Edie's Chrysler Newport to make it up the driveway.

"We can't afford a house and two vehicles with four-wheel drive," Jake said as they pulled in behind a car that had the blue and white logo for *Real Estate One* on its doors.

"I know," Edie answered. "But can't we just look?"

"Look, but please don't fall in love. Deputies don't get paid that much and neither do surgical techs."

Beside the long driveway, the first house they looked at didn't deserve the five minutes of time that they had spent inside. The old cupboards and yellow appliances in the kitchen had Edie calling a halt to the showing before going into the next room. Jake was happy for that.

The next two houses would deserve another look in the spring. The first, a newer three-bedroom brick ranch that sat in front of ten acres with a small barn behind, had some potential. Jake could just imagine the fences that needed to be put up along with a bigger barn if they were going to have horses. The second was an older three-bedroom home on twenty acres of cleared land. Jake liked it because it had a two-car garage and a remodeled basement. *It'll need fences and a barn just like the other place has, but here we might be able to grow our own hay.* He laughed at the thought. Edie had him thinking about horses too—something that would never have crossed his mind a few months before. Both homes were located in northern Oakland County just south of the Genesee County line.

A few tickets and two accident reports kept Jake busy on most of his afternoon shift the month of January. Radio calls were infrequent as the country folk hibernated in the north end of the county. Jake had been temporarily assigned to Three Thirty-two when Deputy Dan Daniels transferred to the county jail complex. Daniels wanted an inside job. Beau Walker was next up for the assignment, but was off having a little back surgery. He fell off of a roof while building a new house. Junior men fill in wherever they're needed. Jake was still at the bottom of the seniority list.

The next two months Jake spent his time learning his new temporary area. On the day shift he stopped by to visit the small business owners that dotted Highland Township, first off, to meet them and to see if there were any needs or complaints that he could help them with. It was almost like his days of walking a beat in the Eleventh Precinct in Detroit, only now he was in a car and one business might be a mile or two from the other instead or right next door. He laughed to himself as he was doing the mental comparison. There were no bait shops on Joseph Campau and he had three on M-59 and four more on some of the bigger lakes in his area.

April brought Jake back around to the afternoon shift. It was staying light later and most of the snow had melted except for the deeply shadowed wooded areas or the graying piles left by the snow plows in the many church parking lots that dotted the countryside. He was heading for Green's Bait Shop on Duck Lake for a start of the shift for coffee with Jim and Judy Yates. They had told Jake that Wednesdays was a pie day, and Judy made the best apple pies in the county from their own apples they stored in a root cellar out back. Jake remembered Mel Williams laughing during his break in about Jake's lack of basic knowledge about terms like "root cellars," or "mucking out" a horse barn. Mel called Jake a "dumb city slicker" a time or two.

Around eight he planned to meet with a couple of other deputies, Mel Williams and John Kaminski, at Nick's, a local greasy spoon in Highland Township. They liked to get together about once a week just to shoot the bull. Jake hadn't planned on being too busy, being that it was a Wednesday and the department had a full crew on the road every Wednesday.

Jake's radio came alive. "Three Thirty-two, two men assaulting another at the strip mall, M-59 and Bogie Lake Road."

Jake answered, hung up his mic and made a U-turn. As he pulled in the driveway of the mall that consisted of a beauty shop, a dentist's office and a Shell gas station, he spotted Billy's bike overturned near the ditch. Twenty yards away on the ramp of the gas station was a yellow Dodge Dart with its doors open. One man was pushing Billy against the car's trunk; the other threw a punch that caught Billy in the side of the head. Both men were laughing as Jake jumped out, running toward the melee.

"Hold it!" Jake yelled, grabbing the man throwing the punch and pushing the second aside. "Up against the car," he commanded.

The man Jake had by the back of his jacket, turned swinging his right arm, yelling, "Get the fucker, Mark." Mark had bounced off the side of the Dodge and charged Jake. In the slit pocket on the back of his right leg, Jake had the only piece of equipment he carried from his days in Detroit—his twenty-four-ounce blackjack. It was an equalizer in any fight where the odds weren't in his favor.

Mark, a six-foot-three wide body, caught Jake's leather encased blackjack across the left side of his jaw. Two teeth that looked like Chiclets dribbled out with a gush of blood as Mark spun and fell to the ground. At the same time, Jake took two blows from the man to his left. A backswing with the blackjack caught the guy on his right ear. The fight was over. The two men had blood trickling through their fingers. Jake had a small lump on the side of his head from one of the punches he had taken.

"On your bellies," Jake ordered. He tugged a sleeve and pulled Billy upright. "Billy, you all right?" The man's aviator's cap was twisted on his head, one flap over his left eye. He appeared dazed from the punch he took to his jaw.

Billy shook his head, trying to straighten his cap. "I don't know why these guys are always picking on me. I don't bother them."

The man that Jake cracked over the ear tried to get up. Jake put his foot with a little of his weight behind it on the man. "Just stay down, Mister Bad Ass, or the next thing I'll do is split your forehead open."

Jake's typed report listed the arrest of Mark Sanborn,

white male, nineteen and his brother, Andrew, age twenty-two at an address in the village of Highland. A short trip had been made to the emergency room at St. Joseph Mercy Hospital to have them looked at and they were released to spend the rest of the night in jail. The brothers were being held for assault and battery.

Misdemeanors, such as theirs, were handled the following morning. The two troublemakers had said they were "only having a little fun with the old street bum." For their fun Mark had lost a couple of teeth and had a badly swollen jaw. The older brother Andrew had a split ear that took a couple of stiches and a very large lump on the side of his head.

Two hours later Jake was pulling Billy's bike out of his trunk. "I'll need you in court in the morning to testify."

"I don't have a different set of clothes to wear," Billy answered, his eyes cast downward.

"Meet me at quarter to eight next to the courthouse, I'll buy you breakfast. What you're wearing will be fine."

A smile crossed Billy's face. "Thanks for being my friend, Jake."

"My pleasure." He shook Billy's hand. "I'm guessing that these are the same guys who ran you into that ditch this past spring." Jake got out the man's cloth newspaper bag from the trunk, handing it to Billy.

"Yeah, it was them. I try to avoid them, but sometimes they just find me."

"Well, now that they've been on the receiving end of their type of fun, maybe they'll leave you alone."

"See you tomorrow." Billy shuffled next to his bike, looking back at Jake. "Can I have pancakes and sausage?"

"Sure. Why not?" Billy skipped twice, jumped onto the seat of his old Huffy bike and was riding away.

Jake had missed the pie and coffee at Green's Bait Shop and was late getting to Nick's, but Mel and John were still there. "You'll like the chili," John said as he got to their table. "It'll put hair on your chest."

"Sounds like what I need," Jake said as he took a seat. "Did I miss any good bullshit?"

———

The 50th District Court in Pontiac, Michigan, handled misdemeanors and preliminary examinations in felony cases. One of the three judges who sat on this bench was called "Little Miss Iron Panties," behind her back of course, by most of the attorneys who had appeared before her. They had said she was a no-nonsense magistrate who took her position very seriously and you'd better watch what you say in her court and how you say it.

"All rise. Oakland County Circuit Court is now in session, the honorable Judge Judith Lincoln presiding." Jake watched the judge climb the two steps to take her seat behind the bench and wondered how a woman of no more than five two and less than a hundred pounds could have picked up the name she had.

Two cases of drunk drivers were heard first. Their pleas and reassigning the cases to later dates took less than a half hour. "The people versus Andrew Sanborn and Mark Sanborn," the court clerk announced.

Jake stood and moved to the front of the court, motioning for Billy to join him. The man with disheveled hair, in an old ratty coat held closed by two diaper pins, holding a brown flap-eared leather aviator's cap in his hands shuffled toward the bench.

The judge had her glasses at the end of her nose, reading the report before her. She looked up. "Which one of you is Mark Sanborn?"

Mark raised his hand. A very fat lip accompanied the swollen jaw. When he tried to talk, his words came out as one word: "Thaphmeyorhonor."

"And you with the bandaged ear, you're Andrew?"

"Yeah."

"It's 'Yes Ma'am.' You're not talking to one of your bimbos, mister."

Andrew's face turned red. "Yeees Ma'aaam."

"I will not be mocked by some young punk who seems to delight in picking on less fortunate people." Her gavel went down. "Ninety days." She turned back to Mark. "You've been here before, and so has your brother. Neither of you seemed to have gotten the message. You can join him. Ninety days."

"Wait lady," Andrew yelled.

"One more word and it'll be another ninety for contempt." She turned to her left. "Get them out of here, bailiff." The Sanborns never said another word as they were led away.

Thankfully, Jake never had to say a word and now he knew where the judge picked up her nickname. She earned it.

Chapter Nine

A rust-riddled 1970 gray Ford sat at the curb kitty-corner across from Herrington Elementary on Bay Street in Pontiac, Michigan. Joan had been cruising around it and Owens Elementary for two weeks. It was a sunny May afternoon and there was only about another month of school left. She was on her third Marlboro as the last yellow bus pulled away from the front of the school. Two boys were wrestling on the front lawn, no doubt waiting for a parent to pick them up. Joan didn't want a boy. She was looking for a girl. Somewhere around seven, the age her Sophia would have been—had she lived.

A man driving a Chevy stopped and the two boys climbed in. Joan smiled. Dad was a little late. She lit up another cigarette and put her car in gear to leave just as a little girl walked around the corner of the building. The girl looked left, then right, balancing on one leg. She was looking for a ride home.

Joan pulled away from the curb and stopped alongside the little girl. She leaned over and cranked down the passenger window.

"Hi, sweetie. Your mom sent me over to get you."

The little girl looked left, then right. "I forgot if Mommy said I had to take the bus today." The girl looked back at the door to the school. "All the buses are gone," she moaned.

"That's why I'm here. Your momma asked me to come get you."

"You know my Mommy?" The little girl frowned. "Huscome I never saw you before?"

Joan popped the door handle on the little girl's side. "I live just down the road from you. Come on. Hop in."

The girl looked back at the school. "You sure Mommy sent you?"

"Yeah, and she gave me money to buy you an ice cream on the way home."

The little girl pulled on the half-open door and slid in the front seat. Joan pulled away from the curb, reaching over, patting the little girl on her hand. "What's your momma call you, little darlin'?"

"Brianna. Me and Missy were playing on the swings and I forgot if I was poseto take the bus." Brianna looked up at the woman driving. "Weren't we poseto turn there? Mommy always turns at that gas station."

"Sweetie, I know a special ice cream place down this road, that's why I didn't turn."

"I like chocolate," Brianna said as she sat back in her seat. "Can I have chocolate?"

Joan turned onto M-59 heading west. She thought she remembered seeing a 31 Flavors in Highland. "Sure, you can have chocolate. Even two scoops if you want."

Brianna smiled, "I'm glad Mommy sent you," her long brown curls bouncing as she turned her head, straining to look out the window.

The sun was still high as Joan drove west. The city of Pontiac was fading behind her. "How old are you, Brianna?"

"Seven an' a half. Almost eight. My birthday's in September."

How'd I get so lucky? Sophia would've been eight in October. Joan spotted a sign for a Dairy Queen up ahead. *That'll do.* She pulled in.

"You sit tight, Brianna. I'll be right out with your ice

cream." Joan slammed her door and skipped up a curb into the store.

A teenage girl with an acne problem smiled as Joan approached the counter. "Hi, welcome to Dairy Queen."

"A double scoop of chocolate, please."

"We don't have scoops, just soft ice cream."

Joan looked up at the menu posted on the wall behind the counter. "Then give me the medium cone. Make it chocolate."

Twenty minutes later, Joan, Brianna and the gray Ford Fairlane were bumping down a dirt road three miles northwest of Milford and miles from the Herrington Elementary School. Brianna, with chocolate spread past the dimples in her cheeks, was munching on the last of her cone. She looked out her window and watched the trees go by. "I don't live around here."

"I know, sweetie, we're staying at my place for the night. Your momma said she and your daddy were going somewhere tonight and asked me to take you home for the night."

Brianna took the back of her right hand and tried to wipe away some of the brown goo off her cheeks. "I don't have a daddy. He died in Vietnam." Brianna leaned up and looked down the wood-lined road to the front. " 'member you said you lived down the road from our house. We live in a city. Not in the woods."

Joan reached over and patted Brianna's hand. "You're a smart little girl, sweetie. Bet you even know your address."

Brianna nodded her head, her curls flopping up and down. "914 East Almond."

"I'm sorry I said your daddy. I meant your momma had a date. Did you get enough ice cream?"

"Yup. But Mommy said we were having pisgetti tonight."

"You hungry again?"

"Yup. An' I like pisgetti."

"We'll have spaghetti. Don't worry." Joan turned into a narrow lane, nestled between two 50-year old oak trees.

There wasn't a mailbox at the road, just a bent over faded post where one used to be. A small shack stood where the lane ended. A weathered rocking chair was the only thing on the wooden porch. Joan knew she had at least one can of Franco-American in the pantry. Sophia loved Franco-American spaghetti.

Sophia, lovely Sophia. You died so young.

Joan had kept the secret within from years before. Her baby suffocated in a hot car while Joan visited a Pontiac drug pad and getting high on cocaine. She didn't mean to hurt her Sophia, and didn't know anything was wrong until the next day when she staggered to her car. She found Sophia lying on the front seat. Her baby's lips were blue. She was dead.

Joan served three years of a five-year sentence at Women's Huron Valley Correctional Facility. The charge was Manslaughter, pled down to Involuntary Manslaughter. *Three whole years. Wasn't losing my baby enough?*

But now she had her Sophia back. In time, Brianna would forget that name. She'd be Sophia from now on.

"I thought the 'Child Killer' died or left town," Jake said as he took notes from the teletype with sketchy details on a kidnapping that happened earlier that day. Jake's shift had swung onto midnights. The corporal sitting to Jake's right just shrugged at the question as he checked the teletype machine. The corporal was Mel Williams. Mel had been on the Oakland County Sheriff's Department for nine years when he drew the short straw to "break in" the hot-shot cop from Detroit. For over two years Jake and Mel were on the same shift.

Mel poured a couple of cups of coffee. They had twenty minutes until they relieved the afternoon crew. He put a cup in front of Jake. "I don't think it's the same guy unless he's grabbing someone younger this time."

"God I hope not. This kid's only seven."

Jake heard the shift sergeant bang in the door. It was time to go to work. By the time Jake climbed in his unit, Mel was already off the ramp. Jake thought the guy was always in a hurry. "Marshal Mel of Avon Township" were the words on Jake's lips as he cranked the key on his Pontiac, then the thought of the kidnapping took over. He was praying the child killer had not returned. Jake prayed because he never had to deal with kids being snatched before. He could deal with stolen cars, robberies, even a murder every now and then, but kids murdered? *What kind of sick bastards are we dealing with?* And Hank and Sam then crossed his mind.

Jake mentally filed away the information on the teletype: A rust-riddled 1973 gray Ford being driven by a white woman. No, that wasn't a woman who killed those four children. He found comfort in that thought, and drove toward his area. This kidnapping happened in Pontiac, but that city was a part of Oakland County and Jake knew the woman in the gray Ford could be anywhere.

May turned to June and nothing was heard about the little girl or the woman in the gray Ford. No ransom demand. Nothing.

A heavy July rainstorm with its black clouds blotted out the sun, bringing an early darkness to Lone Tree Road near Milford. Jake was heading east in Three thirty-two working the Highland township area when he saw a car squatting near the ditch on the north side of the road. The rear tire on the driver's side was flat. He caught a glimpse of a head behind the wheel. It looked like a woman. The rain was beating down on the top of his unit, the wipers were working overtime, and, as much as he hated the thought of getting out in the rain, he slowed his unit down for the stop sign at Milford Road then made a U-turn, heading back for the disabled car. Jake canted the front of his black and white unit part way onto the roadway and flipped on his overhead light bar. If he was going to get out in the rain, he wanted to make sure his car would help him from becoming part of the pavement. He wasn't in a hurry. He was hoping that the downpour was one of those summer storms that came and went in ten minutes. Jake heard the clap of thunder seconds after the flash of lightning in the western sky. *Wrong. This'll last for a while.* If it could, the rain seemed to pick up intensity.

In the glove box was the clear plastic rain bonnet that fit over his summer, straw Stetson. Folded on the back seat was his long black rain slicker. He grabbed what the guys called *the condom*, slowly working the elastic band over the brim of his hat, and tapping down the excess plastic around the hatband. Jake was sure it would do the job and keep his head dry. He reached around, grabbed the slicker and leaned forward to get part of it on before he opened his door. He thought of the "Serve and Protect" motto he'd seen stenciled on some small town cop units and laughed to himself, thinking most probably wouldn't get out in a rain like this. He didn't like getting wet either, but someone needed help, and that was his job. As he went to open his door, he thought the rat-a-tat drumbeat of the rain slowed a bit, but knew he was still going to get his ass wet.

Jake sloshed up to the driver's window and tapped on it. The woman was looking away, talking to a child in the back seat. Jake tapped again. "Lady, do you have a spare?" yelling over the noise of the rain. He tipped his head to the side as he tried to get a look at the driver. The condom let a stream of water hit his left shoulder. Slowly the woman behind the wheel looked at Jake just for a second. Jake tapped on the window again, motioning for her to roll down her window. She didn't seem like she wanted to, but she did crack it about an inch. "Do you have a spare tire?" he repeated.

"I think so," she answered as she looked away and said something to the child in the back seat again.

"Give me your keys. I'll change your tire so you two can get out of this rain."

"No. We'll be all right."

"Lady, I'll change your tire for you and..." he bent down and took a better look in the back seat, "your daughter." Jake put out his right hand near the crack in the window. "I'll have you back on the road in ten minutes. Just give me the keys."

The window went down another inch and the woman dangled a set of keys from her left index finger. She didn't say a word, just offered the keys. Jake sloshed around to the back of her car. He knew the rounded key was for the trunk. All Fords were like that—the square one for the ignition, the round one for the trunk. He popped it open. Lying loose was a spare tire, almost bald, but it did have air in it. It would be better than the wheel sitting on the ground, half on blacktop, half on gravel. As he grabbed the tire, he saw a bumper jack and the standard handle/lug wrench next to it. Jake hated bumper jacks, but that's all he had. He didn't think the jack from his Pontiac would work on the Ford. Then too, he hadn't looked in his own trunk in a month or more.

It took Jake ten minutes just to get the weight off of the rear wheel and to start loosening the lug nuts. Jack handles that double as lug wrenches just don't give the torque needed. The rain continued, some sneaking by the condom-covered Stetson and down his neck. He had to kneel on the wet pavement to get a good tug on the wrench. Jake questioned his sanity a time or two as the water wicked from his knees up to his crotch. His ten minute estimate turned into more than thirty minutes before he was able to drop the rear tire back onto the ground. He could see that it needed about another ten pounds of air, but the woman was better off now than when he first stopped. She could drive to a gas station and get more air. There was no rear hub cap, so Jake dropped the flat and all the tools into the trunk and slammed it shut. The girl in the back seat was looking out the back window as Jake started to move. He thought she was mouthing a word. He smiled at her and went to give the girl's mother the keys.

She cranked down the window and he handed them to her. "Stop at the first gas station you come across and get some more air in that tire." The woman just grabbed the keys, nodded and cranked the window back up. The engine fired at the first turn on the ignition and she drove off.

"And thanks to you too," Jake said as the car faded out of sight. *Strange bitch.*

Jake went back to his black and white and tossed the slicker in the back seat. His tan shirt was wet all the way down his back; his brown pants were wet up to his ass. He tried to remember if he'd ever been wetter. *Yeah, the dog farm*. He climbed in behind the wheel and shook his hat off toward the floor on the other side of his shotgun rack. He pulled off the condom. *Well, at least my head and hat's dry.* He reached over and scratched a note on his log sheet. *Out of service on a humanitarian mission. A flat tire on a Ford. License FP...* Jake tried to think of the numbers. He took a stab at FP1722. He might have been a number off, but was sure he was close. It was time to go home.

Jake knew a hot shower would feel real good along with a dry bed. There was no sense in putting on dry clothes at the station. It'd be only a very wet half hour ride home. The meandering rivers and creeks that wound through Macomb County meant it would take him at least that long.

He hoped that maybe they'd find a nice house to the west of Pontiac. It would be easier getting to and from work. There was a lot of country there and room for a horse—the black one Edie always talked about. Jake thought about that for a minute. *That's when I'll learn to ride.*

Edie had a small ham sandwich made for him, along with a cup of tea. Hank and Sam would have been in bed by 9:30. They had ball practice the next morning at 10 a.m. Jake was still coaching the team and working afternoons fit right in with their practices. Games were at 7 p.m. and another dad ran the team when Jake didn't have the night off.

He glanced at the paper lying next to his sandwich. Edie was in the other room watching Johnny Carson and the

Tonight Show. The hot shower and warm robe had him in a relaxed mode. A small article on page three caught his eye. The headline read: *Police and FBI Baffled.* They were still looking for a little girl.

There was no sleeping that night. Jake's mind was on a Ford with a flat tire and a woman driving with a young girl in the back seat. Until now, he hadn't thought of the teletype from two months before.

Could it have been? The car was gray. And it was raining hard. Jake couldn't sleep because he might have fucked up. There was a seven-year old girl still missing.

Jake woke with a start. He saw the eyes of a young girl through rain-splattered glass, pleading as she mouthed one word. *HELP.* As he got the coffee going, he wondered if in fact that was the word the girl in the back seat of the Ford did mouth the night before.

He knew he couldn't take the boys to practice. He checked his list and found the name of a guy he knew worked afternoons. He'd see if someone else could run practice today. He had a little girl on his mind.

Edie came into the kitchen. "What got you up so early?" she asked. He told her about the night before, the flat tire on a Ford and helping a woman by changing it in a downpour. "Hope someone like you comes by if something like that happens to me." She smiled and poured two cups out of the pot and turned around, giving Jake a morning kiss.

"Yeah, I thought the rain was bad enough," he stirred in a bit of sugar, "until I looked in the paper last night."

"And…" she paused, stirring in her cream.

"And I saw the article on a girl that was kidnapped a couple of months ago. The case is still open and going nowhere."

"What's that got to do with you?"

"She might have been in that car with the flat tire." Jake told her the whole story, finishing by telling her he was going to get someone to run baseball practice that morning.

He wanted to check on some things with the Pontiac Police Department. “It can’t wait,” he said.

“I’ll call Marge, see if she can run the boys over to practice. Do what you have to do.”

Ten minutes later Jake was on the road heading to the Pontiac PD. In a half hour Jake was standing in front of the Lieutenant manning the desk in Pontiac. “What time do your Dicks get in?” he asked.

“And you are?”

“Sorry.” Jake flipped out his star. “With the County. I need to check on an old kidnapping report.”

“Just saw Morrow grabbing a coffee, so someone’s in there.” The lieutenant motioned with his chin off to his left.

In ten minutes Jake had the file on Brianna Richards, missing and presumed kidnapped since May 14, 1978. He had hoped otherwise, but inside the manila folder stapled to the inside flap, was a picture of a soon to be eight-year-old girl. Jake paused and closed his eyes. It looked like the girl Jake had seen the night before through the rear window of a rust-riddled, gray Ford Fairlane.

———

FBI Agent Allen Jenkins was in Detective George Morrow’s office within an hour, sitting across from Deputy John Anthony Bush, listening to Jake’s account of what happened the night before. Jenkins was scratching in his note pad. He looked up at Morrow. “Did you run that plate number?”

“Yes. It came back on a Dodge.”

Jenkins and Morrow looked at Jake.

“I could be off a number.” Jake stirred in his chair, letting the numbers run through his mind. “I’ll go to the Secretary of State’s Office and see what I can find.” He thought about the heavy rain and the mud-splattered plate. *No excuses* he told himself.

“One thing we can say for sure, if you saw the kidnapped

girl, she's still alive and in the area. And that's more than we've had since the day she went missing." Jenkins closed his notebook. "We weren't really sure about the gray Ford. A guy who picked up his boys thought he saw one in the neighborhood the day she disappeared. For once I have something to tell the mother. She's been calling the office every day. She said she was going nuts, not knowing anything, and I don't blame her. Now I can give her some hope." The agent started to leave. "I'll have my office start running some checks on different versions of the plate number and chase down the registration information. Now at least we have a starting point."

Jake waved off the offer of more coffee from Morrow. "Jenkins, please tell Mrs. Richards I am really sorry."

Jenkins shrugged. "Maybe it wasn't the girl."

"Maybe," Jake answered.

Morrow, who had been quiet most of the time, mumbled a remark as he gathered up his file. Jake caught the gist of it—Morrow thought he blew it.

Jake watched the FBI agent leave and looked at Morrow. "I know what you're thinking." Jake stood. "I've got some things that I can do." He left, closing Morrow's door behind him. He was heading to the local Secretary of State's office. He could have called, but wanted to do this in person. Morrow was right. He might have been within feet of a kidnapper and her victim.

Chapter Ten

Jake wrote down a few combinations of the license number he thought he saw the night before. Beth Ramsey, one of the clerks at the Secretary of State's Pontiac branch, offered to guide Jake through their files. He was generally good with numbers, or so he liked to think. He ended up with twelve combinations.

Beth took those twelve and checked their files. Out of the twelve, there were three Fords. Jake eliminated the one 1975 Ford; it was too new to have noticeable rust on it. A 1971 Ford Falcon was registered to a Norman Wells of 3435 Burns Road. Burns Road was in the area of where he changed the flat tire. The plate number was FP1732. A definite possibility. There was the third Ford with the plate number FB1722, registered to a Joan Chapman with a Keego Harbor address on a 1970 Ford Fairlane. He had two pretty good leads and both were in Oakland County.

Jake checked his watch. It was one in the afternoon and he was due to start his shift at four. He could swing by the Burns address when he hit the street that afternoon. He needed to go home, check on the boys, change into his uniform and get back to work. He thought about using his spare set of clothes at the station, but the kidnapping had him thinking of the boys. Edie was working. He jumped in his truck and headed for home. It was about 25 miles there, a good half hour trip, then the return trip. He didn't think about eating until just then. A piece of toast in the morning just wasn't enough to last all day. Jake was pissed at himself.

If I'd just been paying attention.

Then it started to rain again, a strong July afternoon rain. He wondered, if it hadn't been raining, would things have ended differently? He didn't have an answer.

At 4:15 p.m. Jake was knocking on the door at 3435 Burns. Norman Wells was not home, but his wife was and said he had the car. She was definitely not the woman Jake had seen the night before, but he wanted to see the car. Norman was working at a car dealership on M-59. Fifteen minutes later Jake met Norman Wells at the little country Ford dealership and crossed off that lead. It wasn't the car from the night before.

Keego Harbor was a bit out of his territory, but that was Jake's next stop. He had Joan Chapman's address. It turned out to be an abandoned double wide on Stennett Street. There hadn't been any life around it for a year or two. Across the road Jake saw a Buick in the driveway next to a white clapboard house. He hoped that a knock on the door across the street from the last known address for Joan Chapman would give him some leads.

"Yes, can I help you?" A balding man opened the screen door, half hanging out. His sleeveless undershirt was stained, his gray trousers wrinkled like he'd been sleeping in them. He was wearing an old pair of moccasins that his right toe had worn through.

"Sir, I'm Jake Bush. I was looking for someone who was living in that trailer across the street. It doesn't look like anyone's been there for a while."

"Nobody has." The man rubbed his chin. "Mabel said the woman who lived there got put in jail."

"Can I talk to Mabel?"

"She's dead. Two years June 30th." The man looked over his shoulder like Mabel might be behind him. "I think the woman who lived there was gone before Mabel passed."

"Did you happen to know the woman's name?"

"Only knew the family name. Chapman. Seen it on the mailbox. The box might be in the ditch. Haven't seen it in a while."

"Anything else you can tell me about who lived there?"

"Mabel could. She always knew what was going on up and down the road," the man smiled, then looked from right to left with a lost look in his eyes. "Mabel knew a lot just by sitting on the porch and watching." He paused. "She's been dead for over two years," he repeated, like his mind was drifting off.

"Can you describe the woman?" Jake asked.

The man shrugged. "She was white." Jake stood quietly, waiting. The man didn't say another word. A tear was slowly making its way down his right cheek. He came fully out onto the porch and plopped down on an old glider and slowly started to sway. It squeaked as he moved in a small arc back and forth. He was just looking past Jake, not saying another word.

"Thanks," Jake said as he left the porch and returned to his car. He wondered if he'd be that lost if his wife died. *Yes, I would.* He had been there.

Jake cranked the engine, thinking that the township office might have more information on the former resident.

Jake got to the township office at ten minutes after five. He wanted to check on the property at 1420 Stennett, the address on the registration for Joan Chapman. There were no cars in the parking lot and the doors were locked tight. He was ten minutes too late.

His next stop was at a pay phone. He dialed the desk at

headquarters. He heard the clerk pick up. "Bill, this is Bush. Can you get a record search on a woman for me? A Joan Chapman." He paused, listening to the clerk. "I don't have an address; just that she'd been in jail recently." Jake listened again. "Do what you can, Bill. Thanks." Deputy Bill Johnson had said it would at least be a day or so before he could get to it.

Jake found himself sitting in his car thinking about Bill Johnson. From what Jake had seen of him, the clerk was always bitching about one thing or another. It was just his nature. But Jake was told that Johnson always seemed to find whatever was asked of him. All Jake could do is hope and wait.

The next afternoon, the balding clerk, wearing his glasses on the tip of his nose, saw Jake coming through the door at headquarters. As usual, he had half of a cigar clenched between his teeth. He handed Jake a copy of Chapman's arrest records.

"You don't know what kinda shit I had to go through to get this.

"Thanks, Bill. I'll pick you up a cigar for your trouble."

"No cheap stuff like White Owls," Bill smiled.

Jake knew that Bill fancied R.G. Duns. They came in five packs and weren't that expensive.

"They're sending me a copy of her mug shot. Should see that tomorrow."

"Thanks. Maybe I'll get your two cigars."

Jake looked at his watch. He wanted to be in Keego Harbor well before five. A half hour later, he was asking about the status of the property at 1420 Stennett.

"Tax information is not readily available, but I can tell you this, that property is well into the forfeiture and foreclosure process. The taxes are in the arrears." The woman recommended Jake get in touch with the Oakland County Clerk. It would be closed before Jake could get there, so again, he had to wait for another day.

It was his day off before starting midnights, but Jake found himself thinking of the Chapman woman. He studied her record. She was a white female with a birth date of February 17, 1945, and had been twice arrested for violation of the state narcotics law. Jake surmised she was a user.

She also served three years of a five-year sentence at Women's Huron Valley Correctional Facility. The charge was manslaughter, pled down to "Involuntary Manslaughter."

A phone call later to Detective Morrow and a trip into Pontiac, Jake had a copy of Chapman's last arrest report in his hands. She had left her baby in a car while getting a fix at a Pontiac drug pad. The baby died. Morrow also said that a new arrest warrant had been issued for parole violation the past July—she had failed to make her monthly face-to-face meeting with her parole officer as of May. Jake rechecked the kidnapping report. Brianna Richards went missing on May 14.

This isn't a coincidence.

He had burned up most of the day and wanted to be heading west on Lone Tree Road, the place where he'd last seen the little girl and the woman he thought was Joan Chapman, but he had to get home. He felt helpless.

He had already checked with Morrow and the FBI agent. There was no progress. None. Even with the new license number Jake had given them.

He buzzed by headquarters before heading home to get the mug shot Johnson had promised him.

Shit! It was the woman in the Ford.

He headed for the Pontiac Police station and stuck his head into Morrow's office. "It's Joan Chapman."

"Whoa, guy. Who's Joan Chapman?"

"The woman I changed the tire for. I finally got her mug shot."

"You sure?"

"Positive. Older, but it's the same woman." He showed the picture to the detective.

Joan never left the house for five days after the cop changed her tire in a driving rain. That was too close for comfort. The only thing she could think of doing was staying home, hoping the old house she was living in was well hidden. She remembered running into her ex-husband once after she got out of jail. He hinted that he'd like to get back together and fix up their old place. She declined. She never went back to their home after Sophia died. Too many memories.

She laughed at the thought of Randy wanting to get back together. He was the one who got her involved with drugs in the first place in a round-about way. He was always gone, driving cross-country with his big red Peterbilt. Joan remembered the too many lonely nights that led to too many boyfriends, then to dabbling with drugs, and the accident with the baby. She blamed Randy for it all. And now that she had Sophia back again, she had no time for a man. She had a daughter to take care of.

The five days she spent hidden away with her little girl gave her a lot of time to think. She couldn't take the chance on the cop not remembering her car. She'd replace it as soon as she got some money, and money was the real problem. She knew she couldn't get ahead on food stamps and welfare. Getting a job meant leaving Sophia. She couldn't do that. The girl was still a handful. Joan's thoughts turned to school. *How am I going to send her to school?* She had a real dilemma on her hands.

There were a few things she learned during her stay at the Women's Huron Valley Correctional Facility. The main thing was how to take care of herself. She knew she had to make Joan Chapman disappear. The name had to go.

Through all the things that went on in Jake's life, the shooting a year ago and the missing girl, Edie was right there, listening to the baggage he brought home. The 11 o'clock news on WXYZ-TV beat Jake to the punch the day of the shooting. He remembered that night. She usually left a note for him and a snack, since she had to leave for work at the hospital by 6:30 in the morning.

That night she was there, making an egg salad sandwich when he walked into their home on Romeo Plank Road. They talked. He had a wife who wanted to be a part of his life, both the good and bad, and she was good to talk to. Edie was a comfort for a man who was just involved with a life and death situation, and was there when the missing girl took over his life.

The crazy hours Jake was working and the extra hours looking for Joan Chapman took a toll on him making Little League practice with the boys. Some of the other fathers took over and Jake just showed up when he could. The boys understood, or so Jake hoped. It was good that the trips to the gym were replaced by a set of weights and benches in the basement at home. A lot of times, when he had something really bothering him, he needed to pump some iron. He spent a lot of time in the basement.

Edie had told Jake that Sam was spending a lot of time downstairs with the weights too. She was thinking that Sam still hadn't outgrown the thing about Hank being bigger. Sam's hero status from the mall incident was long gone, and now he said his goal was to be tougher and get ready for football. Jake was happy that some of the friendly competition was still going on between the boys—well, the one-way competition anyway. They were too young for serious stuff.

Joan spent a lot of time in grocery stores or perusing the shops at the Pontiac Mall. She always had *her* little girl by the hand, aimlessly pushing a shopping cart, or walking at the mall. She didn't realize that finding someone whose life you could borrow would take so long. Joan was looking for a certain age, someone thirtyish and white. She could always change her hair color. Then too, the right woman would have to have her life available for Joan to borrow, like a purse left in a shopping cart at Kroger's, or one lying on the floor of a changing room at Hudson's or Montgomery Ward's. She knew the picture on a driver's license could be changed for a couple of bucks. *Well, maybe fifty.*

On her fourth day she found a bonanza. A woman her age was at Hudson's trying on clothes. Her purse was on the floor just inside the archway to the changing rooms. The teenage clerk was hanging onto two dresses while the customer was trying on a third. The clerk was listening to the customer grumbling about the mislabeled size.

"Honey, this can't be a twelve. I know I wear a twelve."

No one paid any attention to Joan as she was walking out the main door of the enclosed mall holding hands with a young girl. She was carrying two purses, one in a Hudson's bag. Five blocks away she used a credit card at a Mobil station to fill up her Ford. She bought *Sophia* an Eskimo Pie and got herself a Coke. The old man behind the counter wasn't paying any attention as Joan signed the name she saw on the front of the card—Nadine Wilson.

The next day Joan dropped off the driver's license at a basement apartment on Pontiac's west side. It took only a minute for a new picture to be taken.

"Come back in a couple hours," the grungy little man in wire-rimmed glasses said. "With sixty bucks, of course."

Joan just shrugged. Nadine had six twenties and a couple of singles in the purse. Joan was already getting used to the name. It was unique and had a special ring to it.

She climbed back in her Ford, checking the back seat. She smiled. *Sophia* was sleeping nicely. The sleeping pills did the job. She didn't have to worry about the girl running off when she had to leave her alone.

With a full tank of gas, she headed toward Flint. There was a fairly new mall, the Genesee Valley Center, and it was ripe for picking. She wanted to go car shopping and only needed a few hundred dollars more to find something to replace her old Fairlane. One used car lot on Eight Mile already said they'd give her $250 for it. They had a nice 73 Pontiac they said she could have for $600 and her car.

———

After pulling his first few midnight shifts, Jake found himself in the offices of the Oakland County Clerk. He was interested in the Register of Deeds office as well as where the divorce records were kept. Joan Chapman's files had shown her being divorced before she went to jail. He was thinking that maybe, through the ex-husband, he might find out where Joan lived. Then too, with her maiden name, maybe he could find a relative she might be living with. It was worth a try. The only thing he found was the name of her former husband.

Finding an address for Randolph Chapman came a lot easier than Jake expected. He ran a "wants and warrants" check on the man and found out he was currently being held at the Macomb County Jail awaiting trial on a burglary charge. After an uneventful midnight shift, Jake was heading toward Mt. Clemens and the Macomb County Jail. He had called the day before to make sure he could get in to see the prisoner.

"Must be something serious that she's done. You're the third cop asking about her."

"I am?" Jake asked.

"One Fed. Forgot his name. Then a detective, Tomorrow, or something like that." Randy was talking over a phone to the deputy on the other side of the thick plate glass window at the county jail's visitor's area.

"Recently?"

"Nah. They came to my house about a month or two ago."

Randy looked at the ceiling, then over each shoulder. "Before I found these luxurious accommodations." Chapman smiled. "The bitch rob a bank or something?"

"Might have snatched a kid." Jake watched Randy's eyes, looking for a tell.

There was a momentary blank stare. "Jezus Christ." Randy's eyes widened. Jake waited, wanting the man to do the talking. "She already killed a kid…" He looked away, turning his back on Jake. "She said it was mine, but I'm not so sure. Neighbors said there was a revolving door on our house while I was off driving across country."

"The place on Stennett in Keego Harbor?"

"Yeah. Besides everything else, she got that in the divorce."

"From the court records, your ex-wife said the kid dying was an accident." Jake kept talking, hoping to get Randy to open up. "Was it?"

"How in the fuck should I know? We split about a year before whatever happened." Randy spun a quarter turn on his stool. "She made me out the bad guy during the divorce. Said I abused Sophia, the lying bitch. The damn judge believed her. Not only did I lose the house and had to sell the damn truck, I couldn't even see my own kid..." Randy stood, shrugged his shoulders, adding, "…if it was mine."

"Do you have any idea where she might be living? Your old double-wide hasn't been lived in for a few years."

"What did you say your name was?"

"Jake Bush. Jake will do." Jake wanted to establish some rapport with the man. A first name was a start. Jake waited for a reply.

Randy was in no hurry. He lit a cigarette. "Jake, eh?" The man thought a while. "I remember running into her once at a gas station on Highland Road after she got out of jail. I just assumed she'd moved back into the place."

"Looks like she never did." Jake wanted to keep Randy talking. "She got any relatives she was close to? A sister, a cousin?"

Randy just shook his head. “You say she snatched a kid?”

“We’re pretty sure. She hasn’t seen her parole office since a girl was kidnapped. She was regular before then.”

Randy put the phone down on the table, appearing to end their conversation. He started to rise, then stopped and grabbed the phone again. “You know, she’s convinced that I was the one who started her on drugs. That’s a lie. I was the one that caught her snorting coke. With the coke and whatever, I think her brains are mush.” He sat back down and lit up another cigarette. “That one time I saw her, she looked like shit. I even offered to help her.” Randy looked through the thick glass that separated him from Jake. “Stupid as it sounds, I still loved her.”

“No clue as to where I can find her?”

“None.”

Jake was out of questions, except one. “How’d you go from truck driver to being in here?”

“You ever go through a divorce?”

Jake shook his head.

“Two words: Lawyers and lawyers. It cost a bunch. Lost my truck, my home, everything. I had to eat.” Randy paused for a minute, finally saying, “Stay single. That’s my advice.” He hung up the phone and started walking away. He stopped, came back and picked up the phone. “She had an uncle. Kinda a recluse. Lived in the woods. We went there once.”

“Do you remember where it was?”

“On a dead-end road.” Randy thought for a couple of minutes. “North of M-59. That’s all I remember.”

“You remember the uncle’s name?”

Randy shrugged. “She called him Uncle Leo.”

Jake left, knowing he hadn’t wasted his morning. As he drove home he was thinking of his next move. He had Joan’s maiden name from the county clerk’s office: Anderzech. And now he had another name to go with it—Leo Anderzech.

Jake was happy to hear that Jenkins and Morrow were following up leads and looking for Brianna too.

Chapter Eleven

Although working midnights, Jake spent a few mornings at the Oakland County Clerk and the Register of Deeds Office. He hadn't made any headway in finding a woman named Joan Chapman, but he wasn't about to quit.

He found himself back in the Register of Deeds Office at the county building. He was looking for a property that was under the name of Leo, Leonard or similar first names with the family name of Anderzech. The woman was heavy on his mind along with the little girl who he thought he saw on a rainy July night.

The lady behind the counter wasn't overly happy when Jake showed up in uniform, but neither was Jake. The midnight shift affects him that way most of the time. He felt like a bad start of the day had an effect on Margaret Collins too. That was the name on the tag over her left breast. "What was the name you were looking for?" she snapped. The Register of Deeds office was not swamped with people waiting in line, just one deputy from Oakland County.

"Anderzech. Leo, or maybe Leon."

"Well, which one? Leo or Leon?" She did not ask how the last name was spelled. In one flip of the page she answered. "Nope. No one by that name has property registered in this county." She slammed the binder shut and started to put it away.

“Ma’am. This is important. What was the name you were looking for?”

“Whatever you said.” She slipped the binder next to thirteen others, in the proper alphabetic order from what Jake could see.

“Can I look?” Jake asked.

“Sorry, employees only.” She turned her back on Jake, starting to walk away.

“Mrs. Collins, if you had a kid that was kidnapped, would you be so short with me?” The woman stopped in her tracks.

“There’s no Mrs. in front of my name. I’m not married.” Margaret’s chin was slightly elevated as she answered through pursed lips. She was a tall, thin woman wearing black slacks and a black sleeveless top. Her hair was wrapped tightly in a bun and because of that, the long earrings stood out like a cascade of bangles.

Jake surmised that she had been married at one time, and around forty-five years old. She was attractive enough, but seemed angry. Maybe, because her age had crept up on her, or had a husband at one-time who found something younger. Her attitude said she was pissed at the world and at men. He needed to change her attitude if he was going to get her help.

“Do you have any children?”

“Two. Grown and gone.”

“Grandchildren?”

“What difference does that make?”

“Because I have one mother and four grandparents praying for me to find a little girl named Brianna. And you’re not helping me answer their prayers.”

Margaret Collins said she had four grandchildren. She went back behind the counter and pulled a couple of binders out and turned them toward Jake. “What was the last name again?”

Jake had hit her soft spot: grandchildren.

She turned to the right page. The names starting with an A followed by an N. Jake saw she was right. No Anderzech.

She looked at Jake. “Any chance the name was changed?” She paused a beat. “Like Americanized?”

Jake smiled. “Maybe you’ve hit on something.” He thought for a while. “How about Andrews or something like that?”

“Or Anderson, a pretty common name around here,” Margaret added.

The directory files had fifteen Andrews listed as property owners and three times that many Andersons. Each last name had a few with a first name of Leo, Leon, Leonard or just with the letter L. There was even a Liutas Anderson. In all, Jake had twenty-two leads when he was done scribbling addresses in his note pad. He thanked Margaret and started to leave. He paused, then went back to the desk. “Ma’am, I just remembered something. The person I talked to about this Leo or Leon said the guy lived above M-59. Could I eliminate some of these names on my list with that information?”

“It’d help. That would narrow it down to about fifteen townships.” She got the binders out again mumbling under her breath. She crossed eight names off of Jake’s list.

While she was doing this, Jake thought of something else. Maybe Randy Chapman could narrow it down even more. “Can I use your phone?”

“For a local call?”

“Long distance. The Macomb County Jail.”

Margaret thought for a second. “I should call my boss.” She started to pick up the phone, but then pushed it toward Jake.

Jake thought Margaret at the Register of Deeds Office was hard to get information out of until he got ahold of a deputy at the Macomb County Jail. His badge number, name and the names of the FBI Agent and Pontiac PD detective got him nowhere. Strict phone/prisoner protocol said he needed to make another trip to Mount Clemens. He made an appointment with the Macomb County deputy to see Randy Chapman the next morning.

Jake smiled at Margaret Collins, "Thanks for your help. I'll need to check something in the morning and I hope to be able to cut that list down even more. So I'll be back." Jake didn't think it was in Margaret's nature to smile and say he'd be welcome anytime. She didn't.

———

Joan, alias Nadine Wilson, on one trip to the Genesee Valley Center came across five purses unattended in one way or another in an hour. They ended up in the large tote bag she carried. At the mall a Sears store was on one end with a J.L. Hudson's on the other, and about fifty shops in between. She never made it to Sears. She heard a woman behind her yelling at a clerk. "Somebody stole my purse." Her voice was more of a shriek. "Did you see anyone?"

Joan safely banged out the first exit she came to, went to her car and headed home. Although Joan was looking for cash, she hung onto any check books, driver's licenses, Social Security cards, and credit cards in the purses. Her friends at the Women's Huron Valley Correctional Facility said all were worth something. Joan had planned on using some of the checks.

A side trip to Pontiac a day later and talking to the right people got her another $500 in fifty dollar bills for those documents. That, along with the $678 in cash, was more than enough for the 1973 Pontiac that she hoped was still waiting for her at Nelson's Used Cars in Ferndale, her next stop.

It was. Joan almost slipped up when she was signing off on the title for her Ford. She started to write Nadine, but scribbled with the pen a little. "Didn't think the ink was coming out…" then signed the name Joan Chapman on the proper line. The owner, Ben Nelson, took care of transferring her plates to the Pontiac.

She had to help *her* little girl sleeping across the back seat of the Ford into her new car. She explained to Ben Nelson that her daughter was a little ill, a line she had used a few times already. Brianna, or as she called her, Sophia, still needed to be kept under the control of a pill or two while out in public.

The dark blue Pontiac LeMans, a no-frills version, replaced the gray Ford Fairlane she was sure the cops might be looking for. She was breathing a little easier as she turned into the lane leading to her little place in the woods. *Thank you Uncle Leo.* She felt safe at home.

Her uncle had let Joan move in with him when she first got out of jail. She said she couldn't bear to live in the place she shared with her Sophia. Leo was always sweet on his sister's only daughter. That was six months before he died. He had no children and had never been married, so the place was virtually hers. Now, she had her Sophia back. *If only the little brat would behave herself.*

Jake was back seeing Margaret Collins two hours after visiting the Macomb County Jail. Randolph Chapman had said Joan's Uncle Leo lived somewhere west of Keego Harbor. That took another three names off of Jake's list. Margaret said his search would be narrowed down to six townships. He had planned to knock on doors, but three of the properties listed had P.O. Box numbers for mailing addresses. He looked at the property descriptions on the tax rolls with none of them making sense, then, with pleading eyes back to Margaret.

A half hour later Jake had made notes on where to find these properties, coordinating Margaret's county map with his own. "Thanks again, Margaret," Jake said, truly grateful for all the help she'd given him.

"I didn't do anything for you. I did it for the little girl."

So much for making a friend. Jake smiled, thinking that he should line Mel Williams up with the Collins woman. It would be a good combination: Mel smiling all the damn time and Margaret never. *Maybe the marshal would get her to smile?* He planned on talking to Mel about a blind date.

Jake was rotating onto the day shift, giving him plenty of time to knock on doors. Mel said no to the blind date, but not right away.

"The way you describe her, she's over six feet tall."

"Long slender legs, pal," Jake matched Mel's smile. "And she's horny."

Mel thought for a second or two. "Hell, she's four inches taller than me." He paused a beat or two. "What makes you think she's horny?"

"She's ornery. Ornery women are horny women."

Mel was shaking his head, thinking. But in the end he still said no.

Jake did the next best thing; he had some flowers sent to Margaret Collins. Then he started on his list. Tickets could wait. Leo Andrews was first on the list. He lived in Holly Township.

By noon, around dispatched runs, Jake had checked three names off of his list, the last near one of the properties Collins had given him directions to. There was no mailing address, just a P.O number at the Highland Post Office. He turned onto Hickory Ridge Road, heading north, finding Shag Bark Lane past Clyde. A dark Pontiac was waiting at the stop sign as Jake turned in. A woman with red hair was behind the wheel. She drove off as Jake pulled onto the road.

Shag Bark Lane was a slow winding road that headed west. It ended in a little turn-around three quarters of a mile off of Hickory Ridge. Jake didn't see a sign saying it was a dead end, but it was. He hadn't seen any distinct driveways, so he drove slowly. The woman at the Register of Deeds said the property would be on the north side of the road. Jake spotted an overgrown two-track, nestled in between two old oak trees. There was no mailbox at the road, just an old bent over post. He turned in. A hundred yards in he came to a small clearing and a shack. A weathered rocking chair was the only thing on the wooden porch fronting the faded yellow clapboard house that was in need of a good scraping and a fresh coat of paint. He could see where a car had been parked next to the house, beating down the high grass. What little yard there was had never been mowed. He thought about the Pontiac that he had just passed five minutes before, wondering if that was the car that came from here. *Had to be.*

He parked his black and white and went to the door. After five minutes of pounding, he gave up. He circled the house looking in the yellowed windows. There were no blinds or shades on the windows. At the back door Jake looked into a hallway that emptied into the kitchen. He could see dishes stacked and drying next to the sink. On the light green linoleum hallway floor two pair of tennis shoes were lying on top of one another. One pair was kid size, both were a dirty white. Around the front of the house Jake looked into what appeared to be the living room. A small TV with rabbit ears sat on top of a cabinet. He could see the corner of an old couch off to his left. The house definitely looked lived in.

He cranked up his unit and left, driving slowly, looking for other hidden driveways on his way back to the main road. There were none. Jake knew the Pontiac had to come from the house he'd just left. It was the only one on the lane. At the stop sign he underlined the directions to L. Anderson's property. He'd return another day.

Jake was heading toward another place on his list. The radio interrupted him. "Three Thirty-three, property damage accident at Highland and Bogie Lake Road."

"Thirty-three on the way." Jake's detective work would have to wait.

Chapter Twelve

As junior man, Jake filled in where needed and he was now working in Avon Township, one of the east townships in the county. He laughed at that distinction—*junior man.* Most of the guys called him "gramps" because he was over thirty-five. His assignment put a damper on him checking more names off of his list and looking for Joan Chapman.

The department worked on a twenty-eight day rotation so he had time this month working the day shift. He had been working a lot on his days off, but knew he'd be more effective working in a black and white. The car and uniform got quicker results. After two days feeling marooned in Avon Township, Jake went to see his shift sergeant after off-duty roll call.

"Sarge, got a minute?"

His boss, John Garcia, was an imposing figure, six foot three and not an ounce of fat. He had started working on the Pontiac department and after a year moved to the sheriff's department. He made sergeant just after his fifth year on the job. He was a no-nonsense cop who earned his stripes. John's grandfather had come to Pontiac to work in the auto industry and his dad was an auto worker, too. John did not want to build cars. He wanted to be a cop since witnessing a robbery when he was ten.

A Pontiac officer bought him a carton of milk and some Oreo cookies just after the robbery because John stopped a police car and gave them a description of the get-away car. John Garcia was a hero in the eyes of his fellow fifth graders when he got a certificate from the mayor. Because of John, the robbers were caught within a mile of the store they robbed. John Garcia still had that certificate displayed on the inside of his locker door at headquarters. He was one of the two Hispanic officers on the department.

"You want to work where?" John asked.

"Any cars in the northwest. I am following up leads on that kidnapping last May."

"You talk to the Pontiac detective, Morrow, and the FBI?"

"Yeah. I gave then some ideas, but they aren't too sure about me."

"Someone said you might have changed a tire on a pretty good suspect and let her walk."

Jake just shrugged. "Maybe. It sure wasn't on purpose." He was tired of the innuendos behind his back. "A little time in Highland or any of the northwest townships and I'll know for sure."

The sergeant smiled, remembering how he had to prove himself to the *Spic* haters a few years before. He had heard some of the rumblings about this former Detroit cop. Some thought the hotshot *Polack* from the big city had to pay his dues. "I'll see what I can do."

Jake had Monday and Tuesday off. On Wednesday he found himself filling in on Three Thirty-five in Commerce Township. *Close enough.* He knocked two more names off of his list between radio calls. They both came up empty.

It was taking Jake some time to get used to the twenty-eight day rotations. No matter what shift he worked, one week he'd have a Monday and Tuesday off, the next he'd be off Thursday through Sunday. The latest rumors he'd heard were that they were going to go to straight shifts by fall. That'd mean midnights for him unless they had a bunch of volunteers, mainly guys moonlighting as farmers or whatever. He dreaded the thought of working straight midnights. He didn't like them in Detroit and surely wouldn't like them here.

Hank and Sam's Little League season was over, and with Edie working, that meant he'd be with the boys doing whatever on his days off. Jake liked to fish and so did the boys. When he hit his four-day-off stretch, they had plenty of family time and he enjoyed it, but he felt he was close to finding the Chapman woman and maybe a little girl.

It was August 11th, a Wednesday. Sergeant Garcia had a full complement of cars on the road. The only guys who were off were those sick or on vacation. Jake was working five straight days and Garcia had him working Three Thirty-seven, an extra car working the far northwest covering Holly, Rose, Groveland and Springfield Townships.

The county car turning onto her road the week before didn't go unnoticed by Joan. She was a bundle of nerves. Sure, she had a different car, but they transferred her plates from the Ford to the Pontiac. She was panicking. She didn't know if the cop who changed her flat had written down her plate number. *I'm fucked.*

A new name, a new hair color, a new car and she still worried. Surely the cop somehow found her house. She'd never seen a cop car on her road in two years. She needed to do something for her and Sophia. *Why don't they just leave me alone?* Joan put her head on the steering wheel, trying to think between sobs.

Then it came to her. Somehow she could lose her license plate. Three minutes with a screw driver and her old plate was off. She flung it as far as she could into the woods.

"Lady, what ya doing?" Brianna's voice scared Joan. She swung instinctively at the little girl, but missed.

Joan knelt down, hugging the girl. "Sophia, don't you go

sneaking up on me like that." Joan then ran her fingers through the girl's hair. "Quick, get in the car. I have an errand to run. Then we'll get some ice cream."

" 'member you said you were going to call my mother. She should be back from vacation."

"Sophia, I'm your mother now. It's time to get that straight. Your mom doesn't want you."

"I'm Brianna. And my mommy loves me. She wouldn't…"

A slap silenced Brianna. That wasn't the first time she'd been slapped. Her only defense was to pretend a lot, mostly, that her mom would one day find her. Then too, she missed school, the playground and her friends. She climbed in the back seat of the new car and drifted off into her pretend world. There, a doll with one leg was her only friend.

Two hours later the Pontiac LeMans was pulling back up the lane to their house. Brianna had just finished the last of her waffle cone. It cost Joan five dollars for a replacement plate at the Secretary of State's office. It cost another twenty-five at the house where she had her license doctored up to get the name taken off the new registration and the name Nadine Wilson typed in its place.

———

Jake had knocked all but two names off of his list. He was heading back to Shag Bark Lane to see if someone was home at the little house in the middle of nowhere. The radio called his number. At Clyde Road and Hickory Ridge there was another fender bender. A nervous teenager, driving with her father, had cut a corner too close and caught their back bumper on the stop sign. He was penciling in a sketch in the small box on the pre-printed accident report when a dark blue Pontiac passed, kicking up some dust and gravel. The driver had red hair. Jake had enough for the report as he quickly returned the girl's learner's permit.

The car had come from the north. *Too many coincidences.*

Red hair, dark Pontiac. He had to check it out. Two miles down Hickory Ridge road he had his light bar on and was motioning the woman over to the side. He was looking for someone named Chapman or maybe Anderson.

"Ma'am, can I see your license and registration please?" Jake tilted his head to get a better look at the driver.

"I wasn't speeding. Why are you stopping me?"

"I'm looking for a woman." He didn't want to give a name or a reason.

"Humph!" The woman pushed her license and the registration out the open window, mumbling, "Asshole."

Jake saw the young girl lying on the back seat in the Pontiac. "You always talk like that around your daughter?" He didn't get an answer. "Is she all right?"

"That's why I don't like getting stopped. I'm going to get some medicine for her."

Jake scanned the woman's papers. Nadine Wilson appeared on both. "Sorry to have troubled you, ma'am," handing her back the license and registration. Not an Anderson or Chapman, as he had hoped. Jake watched as the woman drove off. Something wasn't right. The red hair was obviously a dye job, and he had seen those eyes before. There was a scared look in them a few seconds ago *and maybe another time on a rainy July night*.

On the back of the Pontiac's trunk was one of those stenciled decals that car dealers like to put on their cars. It was free advertising. It simply read, *Nelson's Autos-Ferndale.* Ferndale was a half hour drive.

A portly man was sitting behind a desk leaning back in his chair, feet up and puffing on a cigarette when Jake pulled into the used car lot. The big windows on the small building on Eight Mile Road were typical for the car lots that dotted the border between Detroit and whatever city or town ran along the north side of the automobile capital of the world. Colored pendants and lights were hung from posts and signs posted on the building advertising "Cash for Cars" or, as in this case: “Ben’s Dealing. Stop for a quote.”

As Jake pulled next to the building, the man, wearing an orange tie and matching suspenders over a short sleeved white shirt jumped out of his chair. He snuffed out the cigarette and bumped open the screen door on the small sales hut. “Howdy sheriff. You come to the right place. I give police discounts. Ten percent over what the vehicle cost me.”

Jake paused at a gray Ford Fairlane in the front row. It had a bit of rust around the wheel wells, typical of older cars that wintered in Michigan. “If you’re looking for a second car for your kid, I just took it in. Nice ride. Needs tires, but it’s cheap.”

“Are you Ben?” Jake asked, remembering the rust on the back wheel well.

“The one and only. Ben Nelson’s the name. Home of the best buys on Eight Mile.”

“How long ago did you take this car in trade?” Jake’s chin pointed at the Ford.

“If you want it, I’m dealing.” Ben pulled out another cigarette from his shirt pocket. “Mind if I light up?” Without waiting for an answer, he flicked open his Zippo and a big flame erupted. His left hand waved a cloud of smoke away.

“I asked when you took it in.”

“The Fairlane? Let me think.” Two puffs later he coughed out, “Maybe two weeks.”

“Mind if I see your sales records?”

“Officer, I handled the deal myself. Sure I got the sales records.” He motioned to Jake with his head to follow. “Everything’s done by the book with me.”

The hut was no more than twenty by twenty, just big enough for the brown-topped desk, a chair, and a four-drawer file. In the back corner was a coffee nook with a Bunn coffee maker on a small wooden table. The other back corner looked like it might hide a small restroom behind a door. Jake noticed two folding wooden chairs behind the office door, probably for customers. Ben pulled out a receipt book from the top drawer along with a black binder.

"Gotta keep good records for the state," he said as he flipped through the receipt book. He found what he wanted on the second page in. "Humph!" He licked a thumb, then went to the binder. "Took the Ford in a week and a half ago. A woman traded up to a '73 Pontiac. Transferred the plates and all." He pulled out a carbon copy from the binder and handed it to Jake.

Jake fired off one question: "Was it a dark blue 73 LeMans?"

"Yes, how'd you know?"

"I need to use your phone."

"I didn't do anything illegal, officer. The paperwork was done right."

Jake watched Ben light up another Lucky Strike from the one that was still burning. "Relax, Ben. You did just fine." Jake was wondering if Ben always did things by the book.

"Sergeant Garcia, this is Jake. Can you see if the Pontiac detective by the name of Morrow is in?" There was a slight pause. "Can you get me his number?"

It was near six in the evening when Detective George Morrow and FBI Agent Allen Jenkins met Deputy Jake Bush at the turn around at the end of Shag Bark Lane. Jake had already made sure the dark blue Pontiac LeMans was parked up near the old house that was tucked back in the woods. To be on the safe side, Morrow had requested and got a search warrant for the property on Shag Bark Lane deeded under the name L. Anderson. Two other cars were on the way for backup.

Jake was sitting in a waiting room at St. Joseph Mercy Hospital on Woodward in Pontiac. A little girl, soon to be eight in September, was cuddled up next to him, reading the fifth book on the pile of at least twenty that she had gathered up. They were waiting for the girl's mother, Madeline Richards. A preliminary check by the emergency room doctor said that Brianna appeared to be in good shape, but he needed the mother's permission to complete a more thorough examination.

Detective Morrow and Federal Agent Jenkins were at the department headquarters booking Joan Chapman on multiple charges, mainly kidnapping. A corporal, Jeremiah Schmidt, working the afternoon shift, had finally located Mrs. Richards at her place of employment, a small auto parts manufacturing plant on Mound Road. The corporal called the hospital to let Jake know they were on the way. It took *Smitty* an hour to find a neighbor who knew where the Richards woman worked. He was the one who delivered the good news to Mrs. Richards and was now escorting her to the hospital with his lights and siren.

All during the ride to the hospital, after leaving the old house in the middle of the woods, the little girl referred to the woman they arrested as, "the lady," never using a first name. "That lady wanted me to call her mommy, but she isn't my mommy." Jake heard that phrase no less than ten times. He just let the girl ramble on. God, he felt good.

This is one pissed off little girl with an attitude of a sixteen-year old. Jake smiled as he used his rear view mirror to look at her holding onto a doll with one leg. She was squirming around as she talked from the back seat of his unit. *Joan, you snatched the wrong kid.* Jake knew there was a lot Brianna would tell Jenkins and Morrow. But not today. Today was her day to see her mommy again.

Jake was glad she found a stack of books in the corner of the waiting room. He was enjoying the little girl, but she was a non-stop talking machine with dimples and a smile that disappeared into a stern look when she switched subjects, talking about "the lady."

"When will my mommy be here?" she asked for the tenth time. Jake told her she was coming. It had been almost three full months since the girl had last seen her mother. Brianna was anxious and Jake was too.

The little girl's smile and bounce brought back a painful reminder of his youngest, Jeanette. *She'd be about a year and a half older—if she were still alive.*

Jake felt his heart sink a bit at that thought, but Brianna's voice broke in: "Then farmer Brown tripped over his milking stool…" She started to laugh, showing Jake the picture in the book she was reading.

The name "Brianna" came out in a scream. A woman burst through the waiting room door. The book the girl was reading ended up on the floor. "My Brianna…" tears were flowing as the woman was on her knees hugging and kissing and crying all at the same time.

Tears were in Jake's eyes too as he took it all in. He didn't move, not wanting to interrupt something so warm and beautiful. Jake looked up and saw the corporal standing inside the door. A smile was on Schmidt's face. Jake thought he saw a tear on his left cheek. The corporal looked over at Jake, nodded, then gave him a thumbs up. It was only then that Jake thought about Jenkins and Morrow and the pats on the back from them back at the old house on Shag Bark Lane. After three long months, the girl was going home.

Chapter Thirteen

Father Stanislaus Wyda—pronounced Vida—taught chemistry and physics at St. Mary's of Orchard Lake. He had a PhD in both. One look at him might give you the impression that he was a diminutive mad scientist, being he was only five four, running around his laboratory or classroom in a knee length white lab coat, wearing his ever-present thick glasses with wild hair standing on angles protruding around a very high forehead. The Roman collar around his neck quickly erased the thought that he was mad—sometimes.

Beyond the classroom, Father Wyda was an ardent fisherman, targeting the slab-sized panfish the lake was noted for. Every morning, the good Father would get up before sunrise, read from his Breviary, and silently push out his 12-foot MirroCraft aluminum boat onto the lake to fish for an hour or more, depending on how much daylight he had before morning mass. Every evening was spent the same way, casting whatever he thought would tempt the big ones—crickets, mealworms, red worms, and on occasion something artificial. During the summer, everyone knew where Father Wyda was—in his boat on the water.

Across the back of his boat, in bold black letters, was the word *Pequod*, the name of the whaling ship in Melville's

Moby Dick. Some of his students five years before had painted the name on it as a joke. The priest liked the name and what it implied. He knew he was a little man in a little boat with big dreams—catching the state of Michigan's largest bluegill or crappie.

The old Polish priest rowed all over the 795-acre lake. He did not want to spoil the tranquility of the morning or evenings with even the hum of an electric motor. God help you if you and your motor boat came too close to him while he fished. Priest or not, he had some very choice words for you—in Polish of course.

Father Wyda used the bare minimum amount of equipment. He carried a light spinning rod, a net, a chain stringer and a nine-pound anchor—the kind with the two pointed prongs with about 200 feet of rope—and his bait, of course. He fished edges and drop-offs, and with the anchor he could find and stay over the schools of gills or crappies that thrived in Orchard Lake.

It was just after Labor Day and the start of the school year was three days away. Father Wyda was at his favorite ledge 100 yards from the north side of Apple Island. He had nearly a full stringer of fish, something the elderly Polish ladies who worked in the dining hall kitchen fried up for the priests every Friday evening. The only thing lacking was French fries. In the "old country" there was no such thing as French fries.

After a decent sized crappie was put on the stringer, he had his limit. The priest tugged on the anchor rope to bring it in and start his long trek back to the dock to the east. It did not want to budge. His tugs turned to yanks. He was hung up on something. He rowed left to change his angle and tugged again. Nothing. He rowed 180 degrees and yanked again. The anchor seemed to budge, just a little. Being a PhD in Physics, Father Wyda stopped to ponder. The bottom of Orchard Lake was a sand and stone mix, nothing that would feel like a log. Surely there weren't any stumps in this part of the lake. *Leverage* and *fulcrum* were words he drilled into the heads of his students in his classroom, so he rowed another 180 degrees.

Two tugs later the anchor was on the way up. He knew he was in about 50 to 60 feet of water and he strained as he went hand over hand, pulling up about two feet of rope with each tug. *This's got to be a sunken boat* was what was going through his head as he pulled and pulled. The water was clear enough where at about six feet under the boat he could see the anchor was caught on a mass of something. Not a log, not a part of an old boat, but something. Two tugs later he made out the top part of his anchor and some logging chain wrapped around a canvas tarp. Rather than pulling whatever it was onto the boat, he tied off the anchor rope to one of the stern handles. He knew it'd be easier rowing with whatever it was back to the dock. He was tired of tugging and lifting. Rowing was easier.

Jake was on his way to Saint Mary's of Orchard Lake, a boarding school on Old Pontiac Trail south of Commerce Road. His new boss, Lieutenant James Leicht, had said one of the priests thought he found a body. This was his first assignment as a detective. His sudden promotion by the sheriff made him the odd man in the detective bureau.

"Bush, go see if they really found a body. You won't need a partner for that." Leicht threw Jake the last set of keys hanging on the bureau's peg board. "Call for the ME if it is."

The Oakland County Sheriff's Department, at the insistence of Sheriff Johannes Spreen, broke with tradition and named John Anthony Bush a Detective Sergeant. The media coverage on the recovery of Brianna Richards, the kidnapped little girl, and the arrest of Joan Chapman earned Jake a promotion. When a deputy gets a lot of good ink in the papers, the sheriff looks good. Good publicity is always sought by those holding a political office and an election was coming up.

Today was Jake's first day wearing a suit and no cowboy hat. He felt naked. Jake's promotion increased his pay $152.00 a month and taxes took a big bite out of that. He also had a wardrobe problem. He hadn't owned a suit since his high school graduation and it became a gift to St. Vincent DePaul's as soon as he tried it on after his tour with the Marines. A little scrimping and some smart shopping with his wife on a trip to a wholesale clothing warehouse in Detroit's Second Precinct got him enough clothes to get by without resorting to seeing what Goodwill Industries or the Salvation Army had on their racks. Jake was thankful he remembered Jim Breedlove, a cop who knew how to shop for discounts for men with badges. The mint green sport coat, white shirt and green tie had Jake "looking like an Irishman." Those were his words to his wife as they shopped. She said he looked good in it. He gave in, thinking that it and the two other sport coats would help him fit in with the rest of the guys—the twelve-man detective bureau.

Orchard Lake was just across the blacktop from St. Mary's, the school that shared its 125 acre campus with Saints Cyril and Methodius Seminary. Jake had cruised past the site a few times when he had worked in the area in uniform, never stopping, but always wanting to. Jake thought of his one visit to the school in the 50s while on a grade-school outing, remembering one of the original Michigan Military Academy buildings built in the early 1800s had been converted into a gymnasium. The basement under it still had the stalls for the horses used at the academy. Jake wondered why he even thought of something like that as he headed to the school to see Father Wyda. *Maybe this horse thing with Edie's contagious?*

As Jake got near the school he looked to the left. There

was only one dock within sight of the campus. Five men were on it, all looking at something at their feet. Minutes later he was looking at what held their interest. It was a painter's white tarp that was about six feet long with logging chain spiraled from one end to another, held in place by duct tape. Protruding from one end was the toe of a shoe. Jake made a call on his radio to get the Medical Examiner and the department's forensic unit rolling.

A thin, elderly man wearing a gray short-sleeved shirt with an open collar, later introduced as the school's rector, was Monsignor Tadeusz Filipowicz. He expressed the consensus of the group, all whom were priests: "I think Father Wyda has landed the missing Jimmy Hoffa."

Jake did not comment on their speculation. *Everyone was finding Hoffa these days.*

He gathered their names, and specifically the general location where Father Wyda snagged the chain-laden tarp. Jake looked at the short priest. "Father, would you be able to go out on one of our boats to give them an approximate location of where you might have caught your anchor on this?" Jake looked down at the bundle on the dock.

"I can take them right to the spot," the priest said with a bit of a Polish accent. "Triangulation. That is how I have all my spots memorized." He smiled as another county car pulled up. Orchard Lake Saint Mary's was going to be famous for a day or two. Maybe even longer.

Jake knew other cars and trucks would follow. The "finding Jimmy Hoffa mania" would have every newspaper and television station represented in short order. The media monitored all police frequencies and the call for the medical examiner would have them arriving in droves.

It took two days for the ME to finish his work on the contents of the tarp. With all the media hype surrounding the body at the lake, the sheriff held a press conference. He got right to the point: "Though it was a body, it was not Jimmy Hoffa." There were a few groans heard among the reporters. "For one, what remained of the corpse was too tall. It has been determined that the victim was a male, at least 6-4, a lot taller than the missing union leader. The man died from two bullets to the back of the head. Most importantly, the deceased person was a male Negro."

Some of the media representatives had already left as Johannes Spreen, the Oakland County Sheriff, finished his brief statement to the press. "The Medical Examiner had estimated that the body had been in the lake for at least three months." The sheriff added that the deceased person's dental records might give them a lead on who this individual was and that he'd keep them informed. Nobody seemed to hear that last part since the body was not that of Jimmy Hoffa.

Jake was categorizing the evidence when Deputy John Kaminski stopped in to see him. Through a lot of canvassing, the deputy had the name of a fisherman who had seen a couple of guys loading a boat into the back of a van at the public launch earlier that summer. "The guy said they didn't look like fishermen. It was a couple of big guys wearing white painter's coveralls."

"Can you make some paper on it? I've got a lot to sort through," Jake waved his hand toward the pile on his desk.

"Yes sir." Kaminski looked over at the tagged heap of chain on the floor. "How much chain do you figure's in that pile?"

"Thirty-two pounds. The ME weighed it."

"Must have been enough to hold a body on the bottom of the lake."

"Especially when the body was sliced open from his nuts to the breastbone," Jake answered.

"Minimum bloat doesn't float," added Kaminski. He chuckled a bit at his ghoulish joke. Jake didn't. "Sorry sir."

Kaminski moved over to a vacant typewriter at an empty desk and slid in a blank four-copy Incident Report Form and started pounding away at the keyboard.

Jake asked the deputy to wait while he read the report. He didn't want to call him off of the road if he had any questions.

Jake read that the fisherman, Roscoe Koontz, had remembered a few specifics about the vehicle the two guys in painter's clothes were driving.

Kaminski quoted Koontz: "It was a 1969 GMC Handy-Van," saying the fisherman knew that for sure, being he owned 'one of those pieces of shit for eighteen months. And that was eighteen months too damn long.'"

Farther down the report it read that they had a small boat loaded in the back of the van with the nose sticking out. Koontz remembered that because they were tying the doors to the boat to keep them from flapping open.

A time or two Jake stopped reading to ask Kaminski a question. The responses were a curt "Yes sir," or "No sir."

There was something in the deputy's answers that caused Jake to stop. "John, is there a problem we should talk about?"

"No problem, sergeant."

Jake set the report down. "John, it's me Jake. The same guy who worked the Elvis detail the shift opposite of you. What's with the sergeant thing all of a sudden?"

"You want the truth?"

"Yes."

"Not too many people around here—the guys…" Kaminski was stumbling for words.

"It's about me making detective, isn't it?"

"Yeah, that's the short of it."

"Do you and the guys think I should have said no to the promotion?"

"No, but…"

"John, I didn't ask for this. You know that."

"Yeah." His head hung a bit.

"Hey, I'm not your boss, just another suit in the detective bureau. I'd like to be Jake to you, even a friend, if that's possible."

Kaminski shuffled around a bit, smiled and said, "Jake was that really a sister-in-law who showed up to see Elvis that one night?"

Jake smiled. "Thanks for the info on these two guys. With your help, maybe we can nail 'em." Jake put the report in his in-basket. "By the way, we've got a partial print or two on the tape."

It was Kaminski's turn to smile. "You'll get em." He left, giving Jake a half-assed salute before leaving, along with a big grin.

Jake finished reading. John Kaminski was pretty precise in his report: The van was one of those flat-nose types with the motor between the driver and passenger seat. It was white with the name of a painting company on its side. The report ended with the contact information for Roscoe Koontz.

Jake leaned back in his chair thinking about what Kaminski had said. *I wonder how many of the guys are pissed.*

It was mid-September and classes were in session at St. Mary's of Orchard Lake. Jake had called Monsignor Filipowicz's office. He had an update on Father Wyda's catch from a few weeks before. Jake was invited for lunch by the monsignor. At 11:45 a.m. he was shown to the faculty table at the high school's dining hall. Jake sat sandwiched between the Monsignor and Father Wyda at a table of at least ten other priests. The Monsignor introduced them all. The only thing Jake remembered was they all had the first name of "Father," and a Polish last name. He didn't try to remember any of them, most of which he'd never be able to pronounce.

Grace was said by the monsignor and bowls of Kielbasa, sauerkraut and boiled potatoes were passed around. The old Polish ladies who worked there were scurrying back and forth, pouring coffee and making sure the bread plate and the bowls stayed full for their guest and the priests.

The young men attending Saint Mary's that semester filled the rest of the tables in the room. The monsignor had said there were about two hundred students attending the high school. It was only then Jake remembered having a cousin who went there for four years—Uncle Stan's boy, Ron.

"You've already surmised that wasn't Jimmy Hoffa who Father Wyda pulled out of the lake, right?" Jake said as bowls were passed. He saw nods from those around him. The men were eating quietly as Jake talked. "The guy was a small-time dope dealer, who apparently moved into someone's territory uninvited." Forks moved slowly to mouths and the priests listened as Jake talked. "Two taps to the back of the head with a .22 caliber ended the man's life. A typical mob hit." Some forks stopped as most of the priests crossed themselves, no doubt offering a silent prayer.

"Do you know the man's name?" Father Wyda asked.

"Why do you ask?"

"Just so I can include him in my prayers."

"Charles Little," Jake answered. The priest crossed himself again when Jake said the name.

Monsignor Filipowicz changed the subject since he knew St. Mary's had their fifteen minutes of fame the month before. "Detective Bush, where did you go to school?"

"Notre Dame in Harper Woods." Jake saw a smile on the priests' faces, a Catholic boy among them. "I had a cousin who went to St. Mary's," he quickly added.

Monsignor Filipowicz looked around, "I don't remember anyone named Bush who attended our school." His eyes danced around the table toward the other priests, looking for someone to fill in the blanks.

"His name was Buszewski. Ronald Buszewski. My dad

Americanized our name."

The monsignor smiled, "Ronnie. I remember him well. A good basketball player, but a real cut-up. He was in my office for a number of things." The priest took a small bite of bread after soaking it in the juice on his plate. "And what is your cousin doing these days?" His eyebrows lifted with the question.

It was Jake's turn to smile. "He took over his dad's business, distributing the *Macomb Daily* and *The Detroit News* to paper boys and grocery stores the last I heard." Jake stopped there. He knew the priests did not need to know about his cousin's side job.

While some of the Fathers talked about having Ron in a class some twenty years before, Jake remembered dropping in unexpectedly on his cousin. It was a Sunday in early October, a week or two before he had met Edie. He was just driving around wasting time and somehow ended up in Mt. Clemens.

While he was having coffee with Ron and his wife, different phones started ringing and Ron's twin 13-year olds took turns answering them. One phone hung on the wall in the kitchen, the other was on the counter. Jake could see them from where he sat in the dining room. When the phones kept ringing and the kids kept answering, Jake started to put two and two together. Short phone calls and notes taken by the kids were easy clues to follow. His cousin was obviously a bookie and his kids were taking down the bets while their dad was busy having coffee with his cousin, a cop.

Jake remembered asking a question as he was leaving, "Ron, what's the spread on today's Lion's game?"

Ron just shrugged and smiled with a "You do what you gotta do" look on his face. Yeah, as the monsignor said, Ron was a real cut-up.

Jake thanked the priests for lunch and said he'd drop in to chat when back in the area. Now, being a part of a small detective squad, he doubted he'd have much time to do that.

"Officer Bush?" It was Father Wyda's voice. "Before you

go, can I show you around?" The priest especially wanted to show Jake his laboratory and boat. When Jake finally drove away he made a mental note to look up his cousin. Ron was always good for a laugh.

The visit at Orchard Lake took most of the afternoon. It was a Wednesday and Jake knew the west siders would be down at Nick's for a cup or two of rancid coffee and some of his famous chili. He thought he'd stop to join in on the weekly after-work bull session.

At Nick's, Coca-Cola was the only thing on tap in the way of soft drinks. Jake knew Nick kept a secret stash of Pepsi's somewhere on ice if he simply asked for it. It came in a Coke glass though. He asked Beatrice, the woman behind the cash register, for one as he headed for the table of cops in the back of the room.

Jake noticed that Mel Williams and John Kaminski weren't there, but Ben Squires and three other deputies he knew from his shift were sitting at the normal big round table, laughing and joking. Jake hesitated for a minute. He and Squires had some history, though they never really said more than hello to one another.

When Jake had first joined the county he thought he had seen Squires somewhere before. It took a while, but Jake finally recognized Ben as the one-time Inkster officer that beat him out of the Northville job. Now Ben Squires was working road patrol on the sheriff's department on his shift. Jake always meant to, but never asked Squires why he wasn't still working in Northville.

The man, baptized as Benedict Abel Squires, was a big, barrel-chested man with short arms and a booming voice. You always knew when he was in the room. Since the last time Jake saw him, nearly ten years before, the chest had started to ooze more toward his beltline and he had put on thirty or more pounds. As Jake grabbed a chair at the table the four deputies went silent. They got up, grabbed their checks and left. Not a word was spoken.

Beatrice came up with Jake's drink. "What'd you say to those guys? They're usually here a couple of hours." She started clearing the half-eaten bowls of chili. "Need any ice?"

"No thanks." Jake got the hint. These were some of the "guys" who might not be too happy about him being promoted to the "suit squad," as the detectives were sometimes referred to.

Chapter Fourteen

Sam was strutting around the house in the new pair of cowboy boots Jake and Edie had gotten for him. He was having a few friends over for some cake and ice cream because it was November 13th and his tenth birthday.

A much bigger surprise came after his friends were gone. That day it became official; Hank and Sam were adopted by John Anthony Bush. Edie and Jake had been planning this for the past year. She had finally located her ex-husband and he agreed to sign off on the boys if she dropped any claims for back child support. Jake didn't have a problem with letting Gary Douglas off the hook. Jake and Edie didn't need anything from Gary except his signature. Jake had already thought of Hank and Sam as "his boys," and now they were—officially.

Sam was also excited for another reason. He had picked out a house, one of the four on Edie's latest list, just west of Milford on Indian Hills Lane. He liked it because it had a small lake a quarter of a mile beyond the barn and a lake he could go fishing on. No more five-mile bike rides to throw a line in the water. Little did he know that Edie and Jake had already had put in a bid on it.

In 1972 Percy Cabala saw *The Godfather* five times in two weeks. That's when he decided he was going to be a mafia Don. At age twenty-five, he officially changed his name to Vito Calabrese at the Oakland County courthouse.

He was Italian and was born with a bit of a beak, sometimes referred to as a Roman nose. Then he dyed his hair jet black, combing it straight back using a bit more than the recommended "little dab" of Brylcreem. He shopped at Jack's Fifth Avenue, a nice men's shop at the Eastland Mall, and came away with the proper suits, shirts and ties. Marty, the tailor at Jack's, recommended a gray fedora with a wide hatband to top off his ensemble. Vito liked the aura it seemed to give him—the look of a mobster. He bought the whole package for just under a grand.

Vito was a short little shit, topping out at five eight, but there was nothing he could do about that, though he did try platform shoes for a month. He said he felt like he was walking in some broad's heels, so he pitched them and just made sure those around him were big. Mr. Coppola taught him well.

There was a rumor floating around that he killed a man, a panhandler in Pontiac behind the old downtown hotel, but that was just a rumor Vito started in order to get in close with Tony Macetti, a guy that was connected to a family in Detroit. Vito talked a lot and bragged even more. And no one knew what was truth or fiction.

The young Calabrese started out as just a street-corner hood, smalltime for the most part, making a buck here and there by running numbers for Macetti. The money wasn't all that good, but it was steady. Sometimes Macetti told him to rough up a couple of guys and it happened. Of course, Vito had his pals do it—that's what he hired the big guys for.

The years passed and Vito went from small-time hood to a bookie spending a lot of time at Northville Downs and the Hazel Park race tracks. Then Macetti disappeared. Vito figured someone pulled the pin on him. He was sure that in the mafia, things like that happened. He remembered losing count of the bodies while watching *The Godfather*. That movie was real life to him.

Vito had a couple of his boys answering the three phones he had going in the back room of a building he was renting while the races were going on at Hazel Park and Northville. He loved watching the horses live. The white cinder block building he was renting had an old sign over the opaque window that read: All-Around Painting. Vito kept the sign on the building even though the company went out of business ten years before. It was a good cover. He thought the name might come in handy someday.

In no time he moved up to pushing a little weed and a few pills between racing dates, but nothing hard. That was until his supplier tipped him off to the profit margin he could pocket if someone wanted to snort a line of cocaine. Business was so good, he had to take on two full-time associates, guys nicknamed Rhino and Hands.

Vito's main territory was along the I-96 corridor in Oakland County, places like Novi and Northville. There were new housing developments springing up, being bought by young urban professionals—dope smokers in their college days. He had a product and a market. His business grew. He didn't really need the bookie gig any longer, but it paid the rent.

For his thirty-eighth birthday Vito bought himself a four-door black BMW. He turned over his old white GMC Handi-van to Hands and Rhino after having it painted with his phony business name on the sides. Six months later it came in handy. Someone was trying to move in on him. Vito never knew the guy's name until after it came out in the papers.

Vito knew he had to protect his territory. There'd always be guys like Charles Little who'd try moving into his area. He vowed that any who did would go swimming in one of the many lakes in Oakland County, thanks to Rhino and Hands.

In 1972, at the age of 22, Abraham Vogtmann inherited 80 acres of cropland off of Sashabaw Road north of Sherwood. His dad had died in the arms of a whore while he was vacationing in Vegas with his wife, Hilde. His mom happened to be getting her hair done while Arnie, who happen to carry 350 sagging pounds on his 5 foot 8 frame and was just plain ugly, cruised the strip.

Young "Abie," as his father called him, was a graduate of Oakland University with a business degree. He inherited his smarts from his mother. Unfortunately, he acquired all his father's ugly genes. Abie started going bald before he turned twenty. The only hair he had on the top of his head sprouted in a single patch that looked like an unattended garden and only a few straw-colored weeds grew—and they were dying. His double chin rolled right into his shoulders. In short, he was not a man who drew looks from the opposite sex.

The Widow, Hilde Vogtmann, gave the kid the farm because she was heading back to Hornbach, a small village in Germany. She cursed the day she let a U.S. soldier steal her virginity and move her into the "Middle-of-Nowhere, Michigan." The good side of it was that the Prudential Insurance Company had sold her husband three policies when he was stationed in Germany. One was a $50,000 policy with double indemnity for accidental death.

The Las Vegas coroner had no trouble listing Arnie's death as accidental. The coroner knew it'd be bad for the city's image if the prostitute was mentioned, so the doctored police report read that Arnie was the victim of a hit-and-run driver. End of story. Hilde could live very well in the old country.

For four years, young Abie tried making a go of it by tilling the ground, but farming wasn't bringing in enough to pay for next year's seed. Abie started a small scam by cutting coupons out of newspapers and magazines for mail-in rebates, often bragging he cleared at least $200 a month using forged receipts he generated off of a cash register he had found at a garage sale. Abie always had his eyes open for another way to tuck a bit more under his mattress.

The Sunday edition of *The Detroit News* was filled with coupons and Abie thought he had hit the mother lode—a bonanza. It wasn't the fifteen coupons he had clipped; it was recognizing the picture of someone from high school on the front of the Sunday Society Section. The name under the picture confirmed it was a guy he knew who puffed on weed between classes at Pontiac Central High School—a real hippie who was definitely stoned on their graduation day.

"Johnnie Chesterfield," Abie said smiling to himself as he read the article. Somehow the guy had made the grade and was living in the affluent city of Novi, Michigan, with all its fancy houses, back-yard barbeques, and ladies' teas. Then and there, Abie decided to add one more crop to his rotation—Marijuana. Yesterday's hippie was today's affluent home owner and Abie was betting that guys like Johnnie Chesterfield still smoked a little dope. His four years of frustration were coming to an end.

Abie wasn't going to waste the time he had spent at the local university, especially when he recalled taking a class called "Advertising in Today's Marketplace." Even the casual observer knew the professor, Dudley Smith, was half-high most of the time. A phone call later, Abie had an appointment with his old teacher. He was looking for some guidance.

Smith steered Abie in the right direction to get started. It was surprising, even to Abie, the amount of information that was readily available at the university library. Two weeks later, Abie planted a few seeds, compliments of Mr. Smith, under some heat lamps. Abraham Vogtmann became a basement horticulturist.

During the summer of 1978, when his corn got to "knee high by the fourth of July," he hauled his dad's dusty Montgomery Ward rototiller to the middle of the corn patch. There he tilled up roughly an acre of half-grown stalks and replaced them with his basement crop. He stopped to think about what he'd do the next year when beans would be his normal crop. He shoved that thought aside. *Next year's a long way off.*

By moving his plants to the middle of the cornfield, he knew he was at the mercy of Mother Nature, but the cornfield would be a lot safer than growing pot in his house. He had no desire to spend time in a state institution. He just wanted to make money—lots of money.

A big bank account does not cure loneliness, but it helps and Abie was beyond lonely. Many years before, a quick look in a mirror had told him that his only recourse to finding a wife was in the monthly want ads in the back of *Hustler Magazine*. There were fifteen ads for European brides, and the one with pictures of blond Yugoslavian women in his recent October issue had caught his eye. One phone call gave him his answer: They were expensive. It was time to reap what he had sowed, and time for Abie to come up with a sales plan.

One of the drawbacks of the business he was getting into was that marijuana was not a product he could openly advertise. Then, he remembered reading about his old classmate, Johnnie Chesterfield, and joined the afternoon happy hour bar scene in the Novi area. Mingling with the crowds of young upcoming urban professionals, he searched for one man. It took three weeks before he found himself sharing martinis with Johnnie at the Les Chez, a new name given to the remodeled Novi Hotel.

Abie found out fast that some businesses do very well by word-of-mouth advertising. By the time his first plants were ready for harvest, he had a long list of buyers like the Chesterfields. Johnnie and his wife Morgana, put on some really big, rocking parties.

The farmer/entrepreneur was making a delivery for Johnnie and five of his friends. His new plants were doing well in his basement and he had harvested some of the earlier fruits of his labor. Abie's corn would bring in peanuts compared to what he had grown in the center of his eighty-acre field.

It had been a month and a half since Abie tracked down Johnnie and they were meeting for the delivery. He had chosen Les Chez, remembering the spread of food they put out for their after-work gatherings. It was as good as any place to meet and he could eat his fill and not have to throw a frozen pot pie in the oven for dinner.

He walked into the hotel making a beeline to the bar dressed to mingle with the after-business crowd. In reality he still looked like a balding, extra-large Bartlett pear stuffed into a dark green leisure suit. The wide-collar shirt that exposed a gaudy pendant of an eagle hanging on a gold chain and his shades did nothing to enhance his looks. Most of the male customers he had seen on his first visit wore suits and ties. He knew he wasn't going to go to those lengths. He hated neckties, and besides, leisure suits were in, even green ones.

He caught a glimpse of himself in one of the many mirrors on the walls and shuddered. He knew he looked better and more comfortable in coveralls and barn boots, but he was there on business and dressed to become part of the happy hour crowd.

Abie's eyes were immediately drawn to the waitresses scurrying back and forth. They were all wearing black, mini-length French-maid dresses, fish-net nylons, high heels topped off with a little black bow in their hair. The ladies went with the Parisian Les Chez theme.

Abie ordered a drink from the brunette that paused at his side as he slid into a back booth. He had to wait a few minutes for his erection to subside before he wandered over to check out the spread of food.

He chuckled to himself. *Hors d'oeuvres—just a fancy-assed name for chicken wings, nuts, cheese and crackers*. He filled two plates and slid back into the booth, eating and slowly sipping on his rum and Coke, waiting for Johnnie to show. He checked his watch as he went up for a second two-plate helping.

Back at his booth, as he was working on some chicken wings, Abie noticed movement close to his table. He looked up as two men slid into his booth, one on each side. His head bobbed from one to the other as he wiped his chicken-fat covered fingers with a napkin.

"Do I know you guys?"

The one to the right pushed the plate of chicken wings out of the way. "No, but we know you."

Abie looked to his right. The man had the shoulders of an ape, rounded and droopy, was at least a head taller than Abie while seated and hands as big as hams. The man on his left had rough, thick, wrinkled skin on the back of his neck like an African animal. He had a double chin. Both were bald as billiard balls.

The guy to his left squeezed in a little tighter while the man on his right had his big hand squeezing Abie's thigh. "Just order another drink while we talk."

The message was short and sweet. "You are dabbling into someone else's territory," the man to his left said.

"If you want to keep breathing, stay away from Vito's customers," the other said. End of conversation.

Abie's new drink hadn't yet arrived when his two new friends were walking out the door toward the hotel lobby. Walking side by side, they filled the eight foot wide opening.

Who in the fuck's Vito?

Eight minutes later Johnnie was ordering a drink over his shoulder from the waitress as he slid into Abie's booth. "Sorry I'm a little late, pal." He slid an envelope across the table as he talked. "One of the guys said he'd stick with his old contact."

A girl brought Johnnie's gin and tonic. He thanked her and threw a five on her tray, then continued his conversation with Abie. "I tried that sample you gave me. It's top of the line." Johnnie took a sip of his drink and grabbed one of the chicken wings off Abie's plate. "The envelope contains the agreed amount. We'll take what the one guy backed away from." Johnnie smiled, "His loss. Our gain."

Abie slipped the envelope into a pocket inside his jacket. The thickness of it erased the memory of his recent visitors. "On the way out I'll give you the stuff," Abie said as he looked around the bar and through the door to the hotel lobby. "You tell anyone where we were meeting?"

"Just the guys in the club." Johnnie had a question in his eyes as he spoke.

"Next delivery we'll meet somewhere else."

Abie fidgeted with the straw in his drink, his head spinning as if he was looking to see if they were being watched. He patted the envelope again to make sure it was there.

Five minutes later, Abie left a ten dollar bill on the table to cover his two drinks and a nice tip. At his car, he looked left, then right and popped the trunk. He handed a paper sack from Kroger's to Johnnie. Two king-sized boxes of Wheaties were in the bag.

"Wheaties?" Johnnie asked.

"Breakfast of Champions," answered Abie. "Ingenious packaging, don't you think?"

Johnnie smiled again, shook Abie's hand and walked to his Mercedes. Over his shoulder he yelled. "I'll call you when I need more cereal."

Abie waved and climbed into his 1968 Plymouth Valiant. He watched Johnnie's taillights leave the parking lot. "Next year, I'll have one of those fancy cars—and a woman to drive around with too," he whispered as he turned the key to start his car. The two other guys in the bar were forgotten. He had three thousand dollars in his pocket and more of his crop to package up when he got home. He thought about his new business venture, but knew any kind of farming had risks. The return on this crop was better.

Abie didn't notice the van following him as he took the ramp onto I-96 to head east toward I-75. The two men in it had gotten rid of their coats and ties and had slipped into white coveralls. The driver spoke. "Guess he didn't get the message."

"Vito ain't gonna like that," the passenger answered.

"Well, you know what Vito said to do if he didn't."

The passenger just smiled.

Vito's men, Rhino Bumgarden and Hands Kritchman, kept Abie Vogtmann's car in sight going north on Ortonville Road. They were biding their time, looking for the right place to make their move.

The two goons came by their names naturally. Ralph, alias Rhino, was big—six foot four topping two sixty—with thick skin that rolled where it should have creased.

Henry, alias Hands, was an inch shorter than his partner, but thirty pounds heavier with meat hooks for hands that took a size XXXL glove if one could find something that big. Both were equally incapable of smiling.

A black and white sheriff's car had Rhino back off on the gas. "Looks like that cop's gonna stop our guy," Rhino said.

The lights on the cop car went on and Rhino pulled over to the shoulder of the road. There was no need for Hands to answer. He just watched.

Chapter Fifteen

Deputy Mel Williams had been pulling to a stop on Rattalee Lake Road and caught sight of a dark Plymouth Valiant heading north. It was the only car he had to wait for before continuing with his afternoon shift working the northeast corner of the county. Mel caught sight of another set of headlights a quarter of a mile further down the road.

The Plymouth passed. The lack of taillights on the car had Mel pull onto Ortonville Road. It was a slow night in his corner of the county and he didn't have a good reason for not stopping the car.

Probably a blown fuse, Mel thought to himself as he flipped on his light bar.

"What the hell?" Abie mumbled as the flashing red lights lit up his night. He checked his speed. He was fine. *What's he want?*

He eased his car onto the shoulder of the road and stopped. The cop pulled in behind. Abie's mind was racing and his heart pounding. He rolled down his window, waiting.

"Sir, can I see your license and registration?"

Abie fumbled with his wallet. He found the license and leaned over to the glove box and hit the button dropping the door.

The beam of a flashlight shone through the opening to

Abie's left, followed by a voice. "Better be pulling out papers. Slowly."

Abie paused, turning to look over his shoulder. Under the head of the flashlight was the unmistakable muzzle of a pistol. He almost pissed his pants.

"I'm j-just getting the r-registration."

Abie dragged out a handful of papers, dropping them onto the seat next to him. He sorted through them, grabbing the one he wanted. His left hand was violently shaking as he handed the registration and license to the officer.

"Relax, buddy." Mel said as he looked at the license under the beam of his flashlight. "I stopped you because you have no taillights."

"I didn't know they were out."

"Probably just a fuse. Let's look in the trunk."

Abie closed his eyes, putting his head back. *Thank God this wasn't happening on my way to Novi.*

"Something wrong?" Mel asked.

"No, nothing officer. I just haven't been stopped before." Abie opened his door.

The deputy started to walk to the back of the car following the driver, noticing a set of headlights slowly making a U-turn to the south. Mel gave it no further thought.

Abie dropped his keys twice trying to find the lock to the trunk. "Sorry."

"You're a little nervous, Mr. Vogtmann."

"I'm new at this." The lid popped open revealing three bags of peat moss and a small spade, a few pounds of loose corn kernels and other pieces of trash.

A chipmunk jumped out of the trunk when Mel pulled one bag away from the left side, causing him to jump back into Abie. Mel looked at the man standing next to him, his flashlight combing the man's body from top to bottom. His clothes were ridiculous. "What're you growing besides chipmunks?"

"Growing? What d'ya mean?"

Mel pulled the bag further to the side. There was a nest of

bits of paper, leaves and miscellaneous debris just under the wiring harness. He aimed his light on the wires. "There's your problem." The rodent had gnawed away at the plastic around the wiring, using it in her nest. "What's the peat for?" Mel asked.

"I farm. I forgot I still had some in there."

Mel laughed. "You don't look like a farmer." He turned to head back to his car. "Be right back. I'll jot this info down and you can be on your way."

In five minutes the deputy was handing the license and registration back to Abie. "Get your wiring fixed." He smiled. "And you might want to clean out your trunk a bit. Make sure there's nothing else nesting in there."

Things were going great on the home front for Jake, but he sometimes felt the tension at work. The guys in the suit squad weren't the friendliest bunch and Jake had another brief encounter with Ben Squires. He was heading into the county courthouse just as Ben was leaving. Somehow a wad of spittle landed near Jake's shoes. He was running late for a court case, so all he did was turn and say, "Good morning to you too, asshole." He said it loud enough for Squires to hear.

Jake's answer to situations like that was to blow the shit out of a few targets so that's where he headed after a full day in court. He really didn't know the whole story with Squires, but he planned on dealing with that another day.

The sheriff's department had an up-to-date, five-lane pistol range. Jake used it often. The county had a monthly qualification requirement. He maintained his shooting regimen that had saved his life a time or two already. He knew there'd always be a guy named Theo Poet, or even a woman like Lynn Franks at some point in time, down some road, even in a place as tranquil as Oakland County. He knew this was a reality in life for any law enforcement officer, even a detective sergeant. Then too, a couple of scars seen in the mirror after a shower were also a constant reminder. Jake pulled into the lot at headquarters. He had a box of wad cutters he wanted to burn and the range was probably empty.

———

Jake was heading to the Northville Police station. Someone had phoned in a tip with the name of someone who might have some knowledge about a few B&Es that had been happening in the north end of the county. It was something Lieutenant Jim Leicht thought he could handle by himself.

The lieutenant had Jake doing little jobs while waiting for Detective Sergeant Don Yeaman to put in his papers. Until that happened, Jake was the extra man in the bureau doing odd legwork for the lieutenant.

Yeaman had thirty-nine years on the department and had been threatening to retire every time a new case was assigned to him. Leicht had included the retirement forms when he dropped three recent B&E reports on Don and his partner's desk. He hoped Don would get the hint.

It's not that Yeaman couldn't do the job. He had been the go-to detective in the bureau for the past twenty-five years, but a couple of off-the-job injuries had slowed him down. Don had a penchant for tempting fate with his new-found hobby: skydiving. His latest jump had him limping, and needing some surgery on his right knee.

Jake was following normal procedure by checking in with the local department when conducting a county investigation. The northern part of Northville fell within Oakland County and was one of the many municipalities within the county that had their own departments. Troy, Pontiac and Novi were some of the others. That's exactly what Jake was doing as he headed to the Northville police station—following protocol—but the trip brought back memories. The last time Jake had been there was November, 1967. He was to be interviewed by the chief about a job he never got.

Now, eleven years later, Jake walked toward the main desk and the sergeant sitting there. The name plate above the officer's badge read: Wilson. Jake flashed his badge, telling the desk sergeant that he was heading for an address in their town and told him the purpose of the visit.

"Do you know a Timothy Mott?" Jake was asking as he caught sight of a familiar picture on the back wall just over the clock.

"No, never heard of him. You sure he lives in town?"

"Whoever called it in said he does. I just want you to know I'll be knocking on his door."

The sergeant made a note in the log book, nodding, "Thanks for stopping and letting us know." He closed the book, an indication that no more conversation was necessary.

Jake turned to leave, but stopped. "I noticed the picture on the wall. Is John Horshig still the chief?"

"Yes. Did you want to see him?"

"If he's not busy."

The sergeant punched in three numbers on the phone.

"There's a county dick out here. Are you available?"

Wilson nodded his head and looked at Jake as he put the phone down. "First hallway to the left. Then first door on the right."

Jake gently rapped on the door jamb and entered. "Chief Horshig, I'm Jake Bush, Oakland County." Jake extended his hand, noticing another picture he had seen eleven years before, a younger John Horshig wearing a City of Inkster police uniform.

The chief rose, shaking Jake's hand. "Glad to meet you, detective." The chief still had the same firm grip Jake remembered from their first meeting.

"Uh-hem," the chief cleared his throat, a nervous habit Jake also remembered. "You look familiar. Have we met?"

The question took Jake aback a second. "We might have crossed paths over the years. Who knows?" Jake did not want to rehash how they met a long time ago.

"What can I do for you?"

Jake told him about being in town to interview Timothy Mott, a name that had been dropped in a burglary investigation and wondered if the chief had heard of him. He hadn't. Jake made a little small talk and thanked him for his time. Before leaving Jake raised the question he really wanted to see the chief about.

"Didn't one of our deputies, a guy named Ben Squires, work here at one time?"

The question had the chief lean back in his chair and Jake heard the familiar, "Uh-hem." There was a pause. "Yes he did. Why do you ask?"

"I heard him talking about it one day," Jake lied. "How long did he work here?"

The chief cleared his throat again before answering. "About two years."

"Only two years?" Jake looked around. "Seems like a nice town to work in. Why'd he leave?"

The chief seemed to sit a little straighter before he continued. "We decided it would be best if he left our department."

"We, as in you and him?"

"Yes." Jake waited to see if the chief had more to say. Horshig seemed to squirm a bit in his chair. "I was happy he found another job," the chief paused, then added. "Pretty quick if I remember right."

Jake smiled. He remembered a time or two that he had butted heads with a boss in Detroit. In a small town like Northville if someone had to leave, surely it wouldn't be the chief.

Horshig tilted his head to the left. "Anything else?"

"No. I was just curious. I'll just go see if Mr. Mott's at home." Jake started out the door. "Want me to stop by and check out as I leave?"

"No, that won't be necessary."

An hour and forty-five minutes later Jake was leaving Northville. Mott had given him two names who might be involved in some burglaries. The chief and his sergeant evidently weren't aware that the guy had been recently paroled and moved in with his parents. Jake was sure Mott dropped the names just to make sure the cops wouldn't find any reason to revoke his parole. He said he didn't want to go back to the state penitentiary. The prison in Jackson wasn't a vacation paradise.

As Jake was heading north on Novi Road, he saw a Northville black and white pulled over on the opposite shoulder taking an accident report. It looked like one car had rear-ended the other. Jake made a U-turn and pulled in behind the patrol car. He wanted to talk to the officer. It was a nice sunny day, so Jake just leaned against the hood of his unmarked county car and waited.

Ten minutes later the officer was returning licenses and registrations to the two drivers. He paused at his unit, then walked back toward Jake. "Waiting for me?"

Jake nodded, flashing his tin. The cop had more than a few gray hairs on his temples so Jake knew he had some years on the job. "Got time for a coffee?"

Jake followed the Northville car two blocks up the road and pulled in beside him in front of Maggie's Café. An hour later he was leaving. The copper, Gus Anderson, had been on the job for fifteen years, and knew all about Ben Squires—or at least the rumors about him. Gus said Ben was spending a lot of time hanging around a guy named Vito and spending way too much time at the race track.

"The chief thought this Vito guy had some mob ties and there was a lot of talk going around about the two of them." Gus took a few sips from his cup. "The race track has been bringing in a lot of people and money into the city for nearly 70 years. Any hint of a cop and a mobster hanging out together wasn't good, if you get my drift."

Before they parted Anderson mentioned that he was glad

to see Squires go. "I thought the guy was a jerk the one or two times we crossed paths. But who am I to judge? A couple of the other guys thought he got a raw deal."

Anderson went south while Jake continued north, feeling he had some insight now on Deputy Benedict Squires. Somehow guys like him always had a following.

Things'll catch up to him.

Jake didn't regret calling Squires an "asshole." He smiled all the way back to his office. He had two names to feed his boss and had learned a bit about his antagonist.

———

On January 15, 1979, Jake, Edie and the boys were loading a U-Haul truck, driving it just over forty-two miles, then unloading it. They closed on their new house two days before. Jake bribed Mel Williams and John Kaminski to help with the heavy lifting at both ends. The payoff was steak dinners at Carl's Chop House for them and their wives. With all the stuff they had to tug and lug through six inches of wet snow, Jake got off cheap.

That was the first time for Jake and Edie to visit the famous steak house. If truth be known, Jake would have rather gone to Shakers and see his old friends, but Edie overruled him. He forgot about where he would rather be once he started working on the medium-rare porterhouse the waiter placed in front of him.

Their new house was on Indian Hills Lane putting Jake closer to work. The location cut his drive time down to less than twenty minutes. The house was a three-bedroom ranch, built ten years before. There was a two-and-a-half car garage attached to the brick home. The only thing Edie had said was she wanted to change the carpeting immediately. A teal green with spirals in it just did not look good throughout the house. Jake had to agree, the color looked like dried puke.

The biggest selling point, in Edie's eyes, was the barn out back. It had three stalls, built three years before, but never housed a horse. The previous owners had wanted to get a couple to ride through the nearby woods, but the wife was diagnosed with leukemia and all plans were put on hold. Her death that fall caused the house to be put on the market.

Abie Vogtmann had an old-fashioned basement under his house. There was a double cellar door on the back, one he had used as a snow slide when he was a kid. He stopped using it as a way into the basement because it was built with oak planks, and he thought they weighed too damn much. Abie felt plenty secure with the big old rusty hasp and padlock in the middle of the doors. He had been using the inside stairwell for a while to get to his little subterranean garden.

Vito's men had been watching the house since the bar encounter, waiting for the right opportunity. A thaw got rid of most of the snow, and the two associates were told to see how big a threat the farmer was. Rhino and Hands had no trouble with the old padlock or the heavy doors. They figured the outside entrance was the best way in without the owner knowing someone had been there. Vito wasn't in any hurry. His men had tailed the last guy three months before popping him and slipping his body into Orchard Lake.

"He's purely small time," Rhino told Vito afterwards. "'bout a couple dozen plants is all he's got."

"Come spring, if he's growing more, the ice'll be off the lakes, and..." Vito stopped right there. Rhino and Hands knew what he meant. Abie just got a couple of months reprieve.

Chapter Sixteen

Ben Squires hated the name his mother had hung on him—Benedict. By the time he was ten, he was tired of his classmates saying he had the name of a traitor. The name calling stopped when he started kicking ass. Being the biggest kid in his class, he quickly became just Ben.

After high school he worked in construction, but spent too much time collecting unemployment checks during the winter months. He saw an ad in the paper and put in an application for the Inkster Police Department in 1964.

Becoming a cop could be likened to having a calling to the priesthood or the ministry. There really are those who want to serve humanity. It happens. Then too, some are just looking for a job and apply. There's a third group, those lured by the power you can wield when wearing a badge.

When Ben applied for an opening on the Inkster Police Department, he needed a job, but most of all he wanted some of the power a badge would give him. He had remembered being on the receiving end of a cop on a power trip when he was in high school. He was driving his Nash Rambler and got stopped on Michigan Avenue for doing what the cop said was ten over. Ben was sure he was only doing a couple miles over. He went to court to fight the ticket, but didn't even get a chance to tell his story when the judge chided him for wasting the court's time and fined him $30, twice what it would have cost if he had just paid the ticket.

Ben wanted some of that power. He was physically fit, an average student in high school, jobless, and was married with no children. Because of his marital status, he was not high on the draft board's list for a call up to Vietnam. Thus, he got the job. For three and-a-half years Ben worked the streets as a patrolman.

Inkster in the 70s was a small, predominantly black community west of Detroit that covered 6.25 square miles. Ben and his wife helped make up a part of the city's small, white minority. Back in the 1920s and 30s many blacks moved north to work for Henry Ford in his auto plants. Dearborn was a "whites only" community, so they settled in the next town west, one named after Robert Inkster, a Scot who ran a sawmill in the area during the 1860s.

As a cop, Ben thrived on writing a lot of tickets to any of the "black bastards," as he called them, who dared to drive through his city with a taillight broken, or a license plate not illuminated. Woe to any of them who happened to be doing five over. He or she might get two tickets if they didn't know enough to keep their mouths shut. Ben's twenty or more citations a day quickly became infamous within the department. Oh, some of his bosses loved him, but his fellow officers didn't. He thrived on the power his badge, gun and pen gave him.

Ben was a big man, bouncing somewhere in the neighborhood of 230 pounds. The furrows on his brow magnified the lack of a smile on his face. His size, booming voice and badge kept him from having too much trouble—other than one scuffle he had with someone who didn't like getting a chicken-shit ticket from the same "white honkey" two weeks in a row. That guy got fifteen days for drunk and disorderly, though stone sober.

At some point in time, he started signing all his tickets and reports with his initials: B. A. followed by his surname. This signature looked more official than his given name. If anyone would ask, he'd simply say the initials stood for "Bad Ass."

Ben finally got bored with his home town and started looking around. He had heard there was an opening in Northville, another small city a little north and west of Inkster. He felt he had an in there. The chief had been a one-time Inkster sergeant who loved Ben's traffic ticket production. He applied and got the job.

Northville promised a bit more pay because there was some overtime when the harness track was open. Within two years Ben had made the transition from just a ticket writer to someone with an in at the track. The overtime pay was for doing traffic and security beyond his normal shift. He made a few extra bucks on a horse every now and then, thanks to a new friend named Vito. Vito was a small-time bookie who said he would throw a tip his way when the odds were right. A horse going off at 12-1 paid pretty decent for the *C*-note Ben put on its nose.

The next thing Ben knew, for the price of saving the guy a parking spot near the track entrance, were a few more tips on horses, all eventual winners. That led to an occasional drink at a local watering hole with the guy, which ultimately earned him an invitation to see the police chief.

His meeting with the chief went something like: "Patrolman Squires, this is a small town. What you do on or off the job gets around."

That was his first warning from Chief Horshig. Ben just pooh-poohed the little "watch who you associate with" talk. He was making money thanks to Vito Calabrese. His next visit to the chief's office had him looking for another job. Within two months he resigned from the Northville Police Department and was wearing a tan uniform as a deputy on the Oakland County Sheriff's Department.

After of few years of working road patrol, Ben was assigned to Commerce Township and a substation temporarily set up in the township office. It was adjacent to the post office on Fisher Road. His small office had a desk, a phone and a radio, but not much more. It took two months for a file cabinet to show up for the miscellaneous paperwork he might generate. Ben put in for straight midnights when the department stopped rotating shifts. His boss, the shift sergeant at headquarters, was nine miles away, so he was basically on his own. Of course, he was always within reach by radio or telephone.

Things were so slow in Commerce Township he'd relieve the afternoon shift wearing civvies, sometimes never even bothering to put on his uniform. About twice a week he'd go out and write a few tickets, but often felt that was too much bother. He learned to sleep with an ear tuned to radio calls for "Three Thirty-four," his black and white. After midnight, radio calls for the deputy assigned to Commerce Township were fairly infrequent.

Once a week Ben would make a point to show up at one of the cop bars like Rotten Rob's or make the bull session at Nick's in Highland Township and that was just to catch up on the department scuttlebutt.

Nick's in Highland was where he first heard about Jake Bush making detective. He remembered seeing the guy, an ex-Detroit copper, a time or two, but wasn't impressed. He and a bunch of other deputies with more seniority on the department were leap-frogged "just because the sheriff liked getting his name in the papers," is what one of the deputies said to start the conversation. "Fuckin' politicians" and "kiss-ass cops" were phrases Ben added when it was his turn to say something in what seemed to be an ongoing bitch session. Ben did not like Jake Bush.

The Oakland County's detective bureau had a staff of twelve detective sergeants, and one lieutenant. Twice a week two of the lieutenant's men met as a part of the *Child Killer Task Force*, so Lieutenant James Leicht was happy when the sheriff had promoted Jake Bush.

The normal robberies, burglaries and an occasional murder were stretching the bureau's resources and Jake's promotion into the bureau slightly eased the overload. Leicht put Jake to work before he had even assigned a desk in the back of the DB at headquarters. The department maintenance crew did find an old oak one in storage for him to use until the next budget allowed the department to purchase something to replace it, or if Don Yeaman really retired.

Jake didn't complain about the desk, needing only a writing surface, but three out of the four drawers on the desk seemed to be welded shut with age. Then too, the Royal electric typewriter that was found with the desk barely worked. The Letter *d* had to be hit three times to print out on paper.

The detective team of Yeaman and Roberts had been assigned the folder on the recent string of B&Es in the county. They were busy in court; that's how Jake ended up making the trip to Northville.

Jake knocked on his lieutenant's door. "Boss, do you really want me to check out those two names I got in Northville?"

"Why not?" the lieutenant asked, motioning Jake to come in.

"I'm not too sure about Mott. He came up with the names pretty quick."

The lieutenant pointed to a chair. "You'll learn not to discount any fuckin' lead. Work on it a bit until Yeaman and Roberts finish their court case. If you eliminate the names, so much the better." The lieutenant moved toward the Bunn machine in his office. "Want some fuckin' coffee?"

"Sounds good." As Jake hung his sport coat over the back of a chair, he was chuckling to himself at his boss's term: *fuckin' coffee.* "I don't think I can put a face on Yeaman and Roberts."

Leicht was topping off his own cup after filling one for Jake. "Yeah, we've been so fuckin' busy I forgot." He paused, looking at Jake. "Cream or sugar?"

"Sugar, and I'll get it." Jake moved over next to his boss and started helping himself.

The lieutenant settled back in his chair. "The first morning I see Yeaman and Roberts' asses in the fuckin' office, I'll introduce you. As a matter of fact, our next NFB Session, you'll meet them all," he paused. "And you can buy the fuckin' donuts."

"Okay." Jake slowly stirred his coffee, moving toward his chair. "Right now, boss, I have to be honest. I do feel a bit out of place around here."

"I'll take the blame for that. And yes, I've heard some of the grumbling about your fuckin' promotion," Leicht put in a chew in his mouth. "It's my fault for not taking the time to introduce you to everyone before I put you to work."

The lieutenant waited until Jake took his seat. "With over 900 square miles under our jurisdiction and a ton of paperwork, it's good to have you help with the mundane bullshit that needs to be done around here, so don't fuckin' worry about what anyone thinks."

Jake just nodded. The conversation moved to talking about the six crews the LT had working in the DB and him tossing a few questions at Jake about his experiences in Detroit. Jake knew his boss was trying to put him at ease. Two cups of coffee and a half hour later the lieutenant brought the meeting to an end saying, "Check the records on the names that guy gave you. Maybe you'll come up with something, maybe not."

Jake's boss, Lieutenant James Leicht, had been running the DB for five years. He had attended West Point until a neck injury ended his football career. He had said: "Everything went fuckin' downhill from there." He said since he couldn't be the next General Patton, he decided to become a cop. He grew up the son of a Pontiac police officer. Somehow he chose to become a deputy on the Oakland County Sheriff's Department instead. He admitted his vocabulary was a direct result of spending too much time with the “fuckin’” football coaches and drill instructors at West Point.

Jim Leicht was a big man, standing six two, with a jut jaw that normally had a chew stuffed in it somewhere. The LT had a white porcelain pail behind his desk to spit in whenever he needed to get rid of his chew. It was said that when he worked the road in tans he used a bottle from Mountain Dew. A time or two his relief had to use rubber gloves to discard a scum-filled green bottle before leaving headquarters to start his shift.

Leicht was built like he belonged in an ad for a Charles Atlas protein drink. He maintained a daily regimen in the Pontiac YMCA’s weight room and had arms and shoulders that stretched the fabric of any shirt because of his Y time. He was forty-five, combed his dark wavy hair straight back and had an ever-present smile that looked more like a sneer.

Jake had been told that the LT earned the respect of the members of the OCSD when he was a rookie by throwing a nearly seven-foot tall drunk through the front door at Conni’s bar when the guy grabbed the barmaid by the tits without her permission. The barmaid was Conni.

Her bar was a shot and a beer kind of place that the cops working the eastside frequented. Leicht never had to pay for a drink at the place from then on.

One of the first things Leicht did when he took over the detective bureau was to start a Monday morning “No Fuckin’ Bull Session.” Leicht felt it was a good way to kick off the work week and to get his men’s minds back on the business at hand—solving criminal cases.

The LT had a grease board hung outside of his office with the heading: **NFB Session**. Underneath he would note the start time, the name of the detective whose responsibility it would be to bring the donuts and lead off that week’s session. Leicht would find a spot on one of the detective’s desk, park his butt and start the session off.

Jake had the clerk request the records for Anibal and Butler as his boss suggested. When he had them, he pulled out a pad of yellow-dog and started writing. On one sheet he put the name of Leon Anibal and flipped a page, writing down William Butler's.

Butler and Anibal had graduated from Pontiac Central ten years before, according to their records, but that seemed to be their only connection other than both being arrested for burglary. "Well, they're not virgins," Jake said to himself. He made two phone calls and set up appointments with Frank Richards and Bill Williams, the two men's parole officers.

The next morning he grabbed a Ford out of the pool and made his way to their office at the county building. An hour later he was adding to his notes, writing that they may have crossed paths in prison and adding their current addresses. He threw in a little side note after checking a map. Anibal and Butler lived thirty miles apart.

What puzzled Jake was that Mott had definitely said the two were working together. He was hoping to find a connection to confirm that Mott wasn't sending him or anybody else on a wild goose chase.

Jake knew that crime detection was not something he'd suddenly start doing. Most of the time on any department they'd team an old-timer with the new guy. Jake had been dropped into a situation where he was waiting for someone to retire to get a partner—someone who could point him in the right direction. Rather than do nothing, he pulled copies of the three burglary reports and started making notes on page three in his pad.

There were no prints found at any of the scenes and all three businesses were entered through the roof. The first burglary was at the Ace Hardware on M-59, the second was at a welding shop and the latest at an auto body shop. Power tools seemed to be the main focus at all three, along with some gauges and torches taken from the welding shop.

Jake was finding out that detective work required a lot of

reading. The arrest records of both men covered crimes in Oakland and Macomb counties, as well as the cities of Pontiac and Troy. He wanted to see the initial crime reports, hoping to find some similarities and maybe a clue that would say Anibal and Butler had teamed up.

He got more than he asked for when he contacted the detectives who handled their cases. There were a total of twenty-one burglaries cleared up by their arrests. Anibal was involved in seven and Butler admitted to fourteen. After ten phone calls and a trip to the various detective bureaus, he had plenty of reading material. He poured himself a coffee, leaned back in his chair and started. Jake's notes were growing.

It took Jake two days to go over all the reports on the old burglaries cleared up with the individual arrests of Anibal and Butler years before. They were similar to the three new cases he had on his desk in one way: All had taken place after the businesses were closed on a Saturday night and reopened on a Monday morning.

Jake drew a box in his notepad titling it: Approximate time of crime. In another box he made the note that they went to the same school and in another, may have crossed paths in Jackson. Jake remembered reading that one crime cleared in the arrest of Butler was a roof job and all his new cases the entry was made through the roof. He drew another box and put Butler's name in it, noting: *previous roof job.*

Jake didn't know it, but he was doing what detectives do—deducing and detecting.

Chapter Seventeen

Rhino and Hands had been watching the Vogtmann farm for three rainy evenings. Vito wanted an update on how the basement gardener was doing. A set of headlights bouncing on the dirt driveway had them slouch down in their seats.

" 'bout time he left the damn house," said Rhino.

"Yep," was all Hands said.

They gave Abie five minutes before pulling in behind the farmhouse. They went to the old cellar door and noticed the broken padlock was still in place. They entered and scanned Abie's plants. There were over 100 plants growing in different stages.

"Think the fat prick would mind me using his phone?" Rhino asked. Hands didn't answer. A minute and a half later, Rhino was back in the basement. Using his right hand, he mimed making a cut across his throat.

Hands just smiled, patted the .22 he carried for these special occasions and pulled the chain on the overhanging light fixture, following Rhino up the steps and into the night. Hands let down the cellar door, not bothering to put the broken padlock in place. "We gonna torch it?"

"Vito said after we pop him."

Hands smiled again, his jagged teeth glistening as the beam from Rhino's flashlight half-way illuminated the damp darkness. Rhino, with Hands in the jump seat, drove the white van back onto the road to wait. They knew the old Plymouth would be back. Abie never left the house for more than a couple of hours.

"Ever wonder where a dipshit like him goes on nights like this?" Rhino asked.

"Why should I?"

"Hell, I don't know. I'm just making conversation." Rhino poured some liquid from his thermos into its lid. "I forgot. You don't like to talk." He motioned the thermos toward Hands.

"I'll celebrate later." Hands had the cylinder open on his little Colt .22, spinning it twice, and snapping it closed. He pushed back in his seat, letting his legs stretch out in the van's passenger side.

Rhino was dozing with his head against the window, when Hands saw the headlights and the little yellow blinker light flashing in the night. He poked his partner's arm and grunted. Rhino knew the drill. They'd give Abie a half hour. He'd be asleep by then. They knew the house. Knew where he slept. They had even seen the foolish pajamas he wore.

Rhino smiled. "Think he'd look good, going for a swim in his silk Playboy bunny PJs?"

"He won't be able to swim," Hands answered.

As with others before, Vito's men would take Abie alive, gag and hogtie him. In the van they'd wrap him in a canvas drop cloth with some duct tape like he was a roll of carpeting. They'd pick up their boat on the way and find a deep lake before they put a bullet in the back of his head before letting him slip overboard. He'd be wearing enough logging chain to take him right to the bottom.

The lights were out in the house when they entered and in less than five minutes Hands and Rhino tossed their package in the back of the van through its side door. "Let's get the boat," Hands said as he slammed the door shut on their van.

The bound and gagged Abie Vogtmann was neatly wrapped in a white canvas drop cloth, writhing like a caterpillar trying to rid himself of his cocoon. All he could do was roll a foot one way, then a foot or so the other. He had never gotten a look at the men who had grabbed him. Everything, including the gag around his mouth, happened so fast he never had a chance to say a word.

He wanted to say, *I'll give you all my money,* if only he could. Minutes later, as the van bumped down whatever road they were on, a chilling thought crossed his mind. *They're gonna kill me.* Muffled moans through his gag were all he could muster.

Deputy John Kaminski caught a glimpse of a white van turning in front of him at the light on Bogie Lake Road. He caught the word "painting" next to a name. As he watched the van turn he remembered the report he had made months before. He pulled into a gas station on the corner, hoping the occupants of the van would forget about his black and white Chevrolet with a star on its door.

"You see that cop?" Hands asked.

"Got him in my mirror. He pulled into the Shell station." Rhino checked his speed. He was doing thirty. No reason for the cop to give him another look.

Kaminski grabbed his mic, watching the van's taillights fade in the distance. He was giving it some room. "Radio this is Three Thirty-two. Can I get an assist, Bogie Lake Road heading south from M-59?"

"Radio calling Three Thirty-four." There was a pause. "Three Thirty-four, you out there?" There was no answer.

"Squires where the fuck are you?" Kaminski was saying to the inside of his car as he pulled back onto Bogie Lake Road, trying to keep the van's taillights in sight. Kaminski knew the deputy assigned to Commerce Township, Squires, was the closest.

"John, this is Mel, what d'you have?"

"A white van. Might be involved with the body found in Orchard Lake a while back."

"Where you at, I'm heading your way," came Deputy Mel Williams' voice.

Kaminski gave his location. The radio operator cleared the air of all traffic. Minutes passed and Kaminski picked up his speed. Bogie Lake Road wove around small bodies of water, heading south and east. One minute Kaminski had thought he saw the taillights ahead, then lost them again.

"Lights are gaining on us."

"Think it's the cop?"

"He's closing in if it is."

"Fuck!" Hands pulled his bulk over the motor box that rested between the two front seats in their Handi-van. He flopped into the rear compartment.

"What're you going to do?" Rhino asked as he checked his mirrors.

"Get rid of our package," Hands answered as he opened the van's side door.

"Where?"

"Anywhere. Let me know when you don't see the lights behind us."

Seconds passed.

"Now!"

Hands opened the side door and grunted as he struggled with the man in the drop cloth, then booted it out into the night. He watched Abie bounce once and roll into a ditch. He tossed his .22 into the night before pulling the door shut.

"Now what?" Rhino asked.

"Now if it's a cop on our tail, we won't have anything to explain."

Kaminski's radio came alive. "I'm heading west on Cooley Lake Road." It was Williams.

"The taillights just passed Bogie Lake," Kaminski shouted into his mic.

Mel knew the van would be heading his way in seconds.

"Got 'em," Mel said into his mic as he hit the switch for his light bar. He saw Kaminski's light bar break the peaceful March night behind the vehicle between them. Williams slid his car sideways, blocking Bogie Lake Road. The vehicle between them had two choices, go in the water or stop.

"You son-of-a-bitch," Williams yelled when his spotlight fell on the truck between him and Kaminski. It was a silver Chevrolet pickup with a topper. Not a Van. Kaminski was running up the side of the pickup, glanced at the woman behind the wheel and put his pistol away.

"John, what happened to the van?"

"Too many turns. I must have lost it."

Williams moved his unit and motioned the woman to go on her way. "You sure it was a van you saw?"

"Positive. A white van. A GM product that has a sign on its side for some painting company." Kaminski kicked at a stone on the pavement between him and Williams. "Damn!"

"Sorry I took so long," Williams said.

"It's not your fault. Where in the fuck was Squires?"

"Don't know." Williams shrugged as the words came out. "What's next?"

"Me, I'm going to drive the road backwards—real slow. Just to look." Kaminski turned toward his unit.

"You need any help?" Williams asked.

"No. The van's gone. I'll be okay." Kaminski ducked in behind the wheel of his car and before he closed his door he spoke. "You're planning on paying Squires a visit, aren't you?"

"You're reading my mind," the corporal called back over his shoulder with a broad smile.

"There's no more headlights behind us," Rhino said as his eyes went from one mirror to the next. "We lost him." Rhino had grabbed a left onto the first road he saw in his headlights. They were on Pinecrest Drive heading around the top of Bogie Lake.

"Fuck!" As usual, Hands was brief.

"What?"

"I tossed my pop-gun with the package."

"Wanna go back?"

"No, stupid." Hands tried climbing over the motor box, but gave it up. "Stop a minute. I'm tired of bouncing around back here." Ten seconds later he was back in the passenger seat, lighting up a cigarette. Rhino had pulled into a darkened driveway, doused his lights and watched for traffic. His window was rolled down. The cool night was still.

"What cha think, Hands? Should we go back and find the farmer?"

"No. If that was a cop on our ass, there'll be more cops." He thought for a minute. "Let's go and torch the guy's place."

"What we gonna tell Vito?"

"The guy's gonna die in that ditch back there, so we tell Vito nothing. We torch the farmhouse and we're done."

"Good plan," said Rhino. He filled the top from the thermos he had sitting on the motor box between them. "Want a nip?"

"After I see the flames."

Deputy John Kaminski slowly drove north on Bogie Lake Road. At every curve and every driveway, he'd slow and scan the area with his spotlight. Two miles down the road at a sharp curve, his light caught a bundle of something in a ditch half-filled with water. He stopped. Five minutes later, he was on his radio, calling for an ambulance. Whatever was wrapped in the canvas was moving. Kaminski's pocket knife made short work of the duct tape and freed the half-conscious man.

"You need me back there?" It was Williams on the radio after hearing Kaminski's ambulance request.

"No, everything's under control," Kaminski answered. He had a guy in pajamas in his back seat shivering and he knew what Corporal Mel Williams was planning. While waiting for the ambulance, he took a couple of orange cones from his trunk and marked the spot. He'd want to come back in daylight.

Mel Williams pulled in behind the Commerce Township sub-station on Fisher Road. A black and white, Ben Squires' unit, was parked. Williams checked the hood for heat. It was wet and stone cold. He walked around and let himself in the small sheriff's department's mini-office. There, with his feet up on the desk, cranked back in the only chair in the office was a very sound-asleep deputy, Ben Squires. He wasn't wearing a uniform. WJR was playing on the radio in the background with the soothing voice of Jay Roberts, the captain of "Night Flight 760."

With a quick kick at the casters under the chair, a very big Ben Squires took a tumble to the floor. Ben's head clipped a drawer handle on the file cabinet on the way down, opening a gash on the side of his head. Ben's eyes flew open as he scrambled to right himself. Instead, he spent a few seconds on his hands and knees trying to come full awake.

"Morning, asshole."

Ben knew the voice of Corporal Mel Williams.

"I must have dozed off." Squires used the desk to pull himself onto his feet. Blood was dribbling down behind his ear and onto his shoulder. "What the hell you doin' here?"

"Just wondering why you didn't answer your radio?"

"I didn't hear no radio."

"How in the hell could you with Jay Roberts lulling you to sleep?" Mel touched the Bunn coffee pot. The burner wasn't on. He tossed the cold coffee into the sink, put a load of fresh grounds into the basket, poured a container of water into the machine and flipped on the burner switch.

"What are you doing here?" Squires asked again as he struggled to his feet.

"Kaminski needed back-up. You didn't answer. I came to see what the fuck you were doing." Mel opened cupboards, looking for a coffee cup. "You were sound asleep."

"Mel…"

"Look asshole, you don't even have your uniform on." He found a stack of cardboard cups. "Just curious, Ben. Ya ever think of turning in your badge?"

Squires looked away, running his finger over his right ear. "Where's this blood coming from?"

"Looks like you hit something as you fell out of your cradle," Mel said as he poured himself a cup of fresh coffee.

"How 'bout pouring me one?" Squires asked, putting his hanky against his head.

"Pour your own, you worthless fuck." Williams walked to the door, opened it and turned. "When one of us needs back up, we need it now."

Mel shook his head and started to leave, then stopped. "Look Squires, I'd think about finding another job if I were you." He opened the door. "And I wouldn't step outside for a while. I'd kick your ass in a heartbeat." Mel let the door slam behind him.

He slowly walked to his unit, hoping that Squires would come out. Squires was almost four inches taller than Williams, but he had the pissed-off factor going for him. He waited, then slowly dribbled his coffee onto the parking lot. He wasn't thirsty. He waited a good minute more, hoping the big man would come out. He didn't. Mel drove off, heading toward headquarters, wondering why Kaminski needed an ambulance.

Chapter Eighteen

Big John Kaminski, wearing jeans, a flannel shirt and a Carhart jacket, rode with Detective Jake Bush heading toward Bogie Lake Road. He was off duty, but wanted to see what else might be at the scene where he found the man taped within in a painter's drop cloth. Cops like Kaminski did not mind donating a little of their own time. Being a cop is not always an eight hour job. To some it's their life.

Kaminski had been relieved by the day shift and was waiting for Jake Bush visiting with the clerk behind the desk. "Bush's like clockwork. He makes the first pot of coffee in the DB every morning about seven." Mosely, the desk clerk, laughed as he said it. "And he'll be doing that for quite a while." Kaminski knew what he meant. Jake would be low man in the DB until someone died or retired.

Kaminski knew Jake would want to go out to the scene with him. He had been the one involved with the body found in Orchard Lake that was packaged the same way. Kaminski figured there had to be a connection. Jake would see it too.

It was a cloudy spring morning just itching to rain. Jake and John Kaminski were driving in as much daylight as they were going to get. Jake had left a note on Lieutenant Leicht's door before he left, just in case the boss would be looking for him.

"So who was the guy wrapped in the drop cloth?" Jake asked as he drove west on M-59.

"Nobody knows. He took a couple of good bumps on the head when he got tossed." Kaminski took a sip of the coffee Jake had given him. "No ID. All he had on was his pajamas." Kaminski laughed to himself, thinking of the silk Playboy PJs.

"I'll probably go to the hospital when we're done out here." Jake said as he took a left on Bogie Lake Road. "You're sure it was a white van?"

"Positive. Just like the one on my report in the Orchard Lake case."

"And it had something about a painting company on the side?"

"That's what caught my eye."

"Got any ideas where you lost it?"

"None. Too many curves and too many places for them to ditch me." Kaminski took another sip. "I know it had to be after they dumped their baggage."

"No doubt." Jake and John figured the van had to have at least two people in it. A driver and another that got rid of the guy in the drop cloth.

"Where was your back up?"

"None close."

Jake didn't press the issue. They had a lot of territory to cover in the county and sometimes help was at least ten or fifteen minutes away.

"You marked the spot?"

"Yep. With cones. Should be coming up pretty soon."

Kaminski's eyes caught the sight of an orange traffic cone ahead. "There, on the right." Jake glided to a stop and flipped on his hazard lights.

Kaminski had already taken the duct-taped tarp back to headquarters after the ambulance crew finished cutting the victim out of his cocoon. "I did a cursory check of the area, but we'll see more in daylight."

Bogie Lake Road was a blacktop with gravel shoulders

and ditches that meandered with the turns in the road for the most part. Where there were no ditches, the road touched the edges of small waterways and cuts off of Lake Neva, unnamed ponds and Bogie Lake itself.

The traffic cones were south of Ridgefield Court and Pinecrest Drive on the west side of the road. A three-foot-wide ditch had water moving slowly through it. The spring thaw along with the recent rains had everything wet and flowing.

Kaminski and Jake methodically checked the area for anything that might be connected with a man being dumped that was trussed up like an Egyptian mummy. A Cadillac that was heading north pulled to a stop. "Lose something?" the driver called out.

Jake flashed his badge at the man, not wanting a bunch of onlookers plugging up the road and maybe spoiling some evidence. "Sir, this is a crime scene. Mind moving along?"

The man turned off his car. "Something happen?"

"Please sir, we're looking for…"

"Strange. I had something happen in the middle of the night at my place too," the man interrupted.

Within a minute, Jake and Kaminski had the man in their car. Max Reeves said his dog woke him in the middle of the night, growling. He said there was a van in his driveway for about twenty minutes. "I thought it was some guy dipping his girlfriend."

"No one got out of the van?" Kaminski asked.

"No. It just sat there."

Reeves said that he watched the van and only saw the glow of a cigarette. The time fit with when Kaminski was trying to catch up to the white GMC van. "I had my dog, so I wasn't really worried about someone coming in," he laughed. "Oscar'd eat anyone alive."

"Who's Oscar," Jake asked.

"My ninety pound Rottweiler." Reeves sat in the back seat smiling. "Then, before you know it, they backed out of the driveway and took off."

"Did you see what kind of a van it was? Jake asked.

"No, they didn't turn their lights on 'til they were down the road heading northeast."

Jake got Max Reeves's address and phone number and asked him to take them back to his house. For one, he wanted to see where the van had been parked and secondly he wanted to borrow a rake. Kaminski had mentioned that they should check the murky water in the ditch around the area where the victim was found.

The radio in Jake's detective bureau plain-Jane Chevrolet came alive. Lieutenant Leicht had another team of detectives coming out to assist, Burrows and Lakatos. By the time they met on Bogie Lake Road, Jake and Kaminski had retrieved and bagged two cigarette butts from the side of the Reeves driveway, and had pulled out a Smith and Wesson .22 caliber nickel-plated revolver from the ditch twenty feet from where the man in the tarp was found. The pistol had a bit of mud caked around the cylinder. Kaminski had marked that spot with a hunk of wood.

Detective Ed Burrows was graying around the temples and had droopy cheeks. He was wearing a wrinkled suit under a trench coat. Jake had seen the partner, Jimmy Lakatos, around the bureau a time or two. Jimmy was the younger of the two, who Jake figured to be near forty. Jimmy, out of habit, always had an unlit cigar in his mouth. He didn't smoke them, just chewed it all the way down to a nub. They introduced themselves to Jake as he was bagging the .22.

"Just fished this out of the ditch," Jake said, holding the plastic bag high. "Couldn't have been there long."

"Humph!" was all Jake got out of Burrows as he eyed the gun. "Find anything else?" It was Burrows asking as he picked up the rake and started re-combing the ditch with it. Jake told him about the butts they found.

"What makes you think the butts have anything to do with this?"

Jake told them about the witness, and gave them the

address. "The guy stopped out of curiosity, and he told us about having a van in his driveway in the middle of the night."

"And you went over there?" Burrows asked.

"Yeah. And that's where we found the butts."

"Next time, wait until someone shows up who knows what they're doing," Lakatos said munching on his cigar.

Jake's eyes shot toward Lakatos. "Didn't know anyone was coming out."

"For your sake, I hope you didn't fuck anything up," Burrows butted in.

Jake's face started to turn a shade darker by the time Kaminski stepped in between the detective team and Jake.

"Jimmy, Ed—nothing's been screwed up." Kaminski knew the dicks from a couple of other cases. He motioned to Jake with his head toward their car. "Ed, between the two orange cones is where I found the guy in the tarp. Twenty feet up the ditch is where we fished out the gun. I stuck a hunk of wood in the mud. The scene is yours. Maybe you'll find something else." Kaminski turned, walking behind Jake. He turned back. "When you go see Reeves, give him his rake back. We borrowed it. Thank him for us."

Jake stopped and turned. "Are you going to the hospital to see the Vic?"

"The lieutenant hadn't said," Lakatos answered. "Hey, leave the butts and gun with us."

"Nope. Chain of custody. We found it, we tag it. The report'll be on the boss's desk." Jake smiled. He hated smart-ass cops—always had.

"It's good you went out there with Kaminski. Less chance of losing some fuckin' evidence." Lieutenant Leicht was talking as he read Jake's report. Kaminski had already gone home. Four hours of overtime was enough.

"Don't know how good the cigarette butts'll be." Jake

said, “They had soaked up some ground moisture before we found them.”

“All evidence is good. The lab might even be able to lift a print off of the pistol you pulled out of the water.”

“Think they can?”

“Sometimes. Now get over to the fuckin’ hospital and see who the victim is.”

“I thought Burrows and Lakatos caught the case?”

“They did, but you can help them on it. They need fresh eyes and ideas.”

“They didn’t sound too friendly. Like I was horning in on their turf.”

“Well they’ll just have to fuckin’ learn to live with it.” The lieutenant took out a folder to start a file and dropped in Jake’s report. “They work for me, and I’m glad you don’t sit around and wait for direction. By the time you get back from the hospital, they should be in and I will formally introduce you guys.” The LT had forgotten to introduce Jake at the last three NFB sessions. That was Jake’s prompt to leave. Saint Joseph Mercy Hospital was where John Doe had been taken.

———

The volunteer at St. Joe’s gave Jake the room number once he flashed his badge. He took the elevator to the third floor. He stopped at the nurses’ station and introduced himself.

“Yes, officer. Room 332, just down to the left,” a matronly middle-aged nurse had said.

“Did you get a name on him?”

“I don’t know if he’s even awake yet. A doctor is in with him now.”

Jake found the room just as the doctor was walking out. “How is he?”

Jake had slipped his leather badge holder in the left breast pocket of his sports coat. The doctor took a good look at the detective’s star before answering. “He’s suffered a concussion, but he's awake."

"Is he talking?"

"Not much. More scared than anything I would say."

"Got any problem with me asking him a few questions?"

"No, go ahead. I'm planning on keeping him overnight."

The man had his eyes closed as Jake came in. He took a quick glance at the chart hanging on the end of the bed. The John Doe had been scratched out and the name Abraham Vogtmann penciled in.

"Mister Vogtmann," Jake said in a low voice. He repeated it twice more, a little louder each time before he saw the eyes flutter open.

"Yes?"

"Detective Jake Bush, Oakland County. It was one of our guys who found you. I need to ask you a few questions."

The man nodded, fighting to keep his eyes open.

"Do you remember what happened?"

"Nothing."

Jake confirmed the man's name and got his address. "You never saw anyone?"

"No. It was dark."

"Can you think of any reason why someone would do this to you?"

"None."

Jake's questioning went on for the next twenty minutes. Vogtmann's answers were short. The man was not saying much. "The doctor said you'd probably be sent home tomorrow. You got someone to call, or someone I can call for you?"

"I live alone, so no."

Jake put his card in the man's hand. "Call me if you remember anything, or need a ride home."

Vogtmann nodded and looked away. Jake made a quiet exit.

Chapter Nineteen

A blue-gray haze hung over the ceiling of the detective bureau dimming the fluorescent lighting as Jake walked in the door. Thoughts about his hospital visit with Abie Vogtmann were shoved to the back burner. A party was in full swing. A large square sheet cake sat on one of the desks pulled out into the middle of the room. A deputy's badge had been designed with gold icing and placed in the center of the cake. Reproductions of handcuffs and a pistol made with black icing were fit into the top corners of the cake, while Donald Yeaman's name was scrolled beneath the badge.

As Don started to cut the cake, Burrows nudged Jake's arm with a Styrofoam cup filled with coffee. "Here kid, something to wash it down with."

Jake smiled at the "kid" remark. He was gramps in uniform, now he was a kid in the DB. "I take it that Yeaman put in his papers."

"It's about time. The old bastard's got more time than Noah on this boat."

A shrill whistle quieted the clamor and the lieutenant took center stage. "I'll make this fuckin' short and sweet. The oldest fuckin' dick still working," there was a pause, "or should I say, hanging around this shit hole, is finally hanging it up. Take a fuckin' bow, Don."

Applause and shouts echoed off the painted cement block

walls of the bureau. Jake took a sip of his coffee and shook his head. Yuck! He started looking for the sugar container.

Jake smiled to himself. He thought he was back in the corps with his old drill instructor. The word "fuck" was an adjective in both the lieutenant's and the DI's vocabulary. The word was again becoming common vernacular. Jake's only concern about being thrust into a group of guys full of salty language was he'd accidentally carry it home. *Edie wouldn't appreciate that.* He knew he'd have to make a conscious effort to watch what he said. He believed in leading by example, and Hank and Sam would never hear those words from him, or so he hoped.

"All right, let's move the party to more friendly confines," bellowed Yeaman. "Rotten Rob's and the LT's buying."

"Who said I'm fuckin' buying?"

"We did!" at least six different voices rang out.

Jake hesitated, wondering if he was invited. A meaty hand grabbed him by the elbow. "I'll ride with you, partner." The voice Jake heard was almost a whisper.

"I didn't think…"

"You're going." Roberts smiled. "I'm Cliff. The boss said you'll be taking Don's desk."

Jake looked at the man. A light brown fluff of hair centered the man's widow's peak. Cliff was 6 feet or a touch over, and a large chest filled his suit coat.

"The boss hadn't said anything to me—officially that is."

"How official do you want it? Don cut the cake. He's done today."

"I…"

"You talk too much. What're you driving?"

"A Ford pickup. Where's Rob's?"

"I'll show you."

Cliff and Jake walked out to the parking lot. A half dozen cars were already pouring out of the lot onto Telegraph Road. Jake led his new partner toward his Ford. "This is it," he said as he unlocked the passenger door. "Hop in."

Jake hit the starter and started toward the exit from the department's lot. "Where to?"

"Cesar Chavez Avenue in Pontiac. You'll see the cars stuffed around the bar."

Fifteen minutes later Jake found a place to park near Rob's. "Looks busy."

"Yeah. It's a watering hole for us and the Pontiac PD." Cliff led the way. "You've never been here?"

"I don't drink."

Cliff stopped in mid-stride. "Order orange juice then. I don't want anyone thinking my new partner's some non-drinking pussy." Cliff started walking again. "Hope the hell you can shoot straight."

Jake could read his partner's mind: *What kind of a guy have they stuck me with?*

"Maybe tomorrow we'll have to bust some caps on the range just to see."

"You're on." Cliff held the door for Jake.

The smoke and the wall of noise in the dimly lit bar had Jake stop for a minute. Cliff nudged him forward. "The corner over there. That's Sylvia's section."

"Who's Sylvia?"

"You'll see." A wide smile spread across Cliff's face as he grabbed a chair at a table for eight. "I hope seeing half-dressed women don't make you blush."

Burrows and Lakatos pulled up a couple of chairs. A pitcher of beer and frosted glasses slid from a small round tray and banged down on the table as a brunette wearing a skimpy white top that exposed a healthy cleavage asked, "What'll you boys have?" She put her left hand on her hip as she cocked it to the side. A pair of shapely legs was evident under her red micro-mini skirt. The tip of her tongue ran across her lips twice, as if to say—*quit wasting my time eyeing me up. Order a damn drink.*

The boisterous cops were filing in to the bar, so Cliff whispered in her ear. He sat and pulled a chair out for Jake. "Sit. The party's just starting." Jake grabbed the offered chair.

Four more from the DB came in and sat, two stopping to pull up another table. "Hey Don, over here," one yelled. Don grabbed the seat at the head of the table.

Sylvia reappeared with a larger tray. Four pitchers and a dozen frosted mugs hit the table. "Who's got the fuzzy navel?" she called out. Cliff motioned for her to put it in front of Jake.

The gang of cops roared and beer slopped while Lakatos was pouring from his pitcher. Cliff pulled Jake close and whispered in his ear. "It's straight OJ. At least they'll think it's got booze in it."

"What kinda fuckin' ex-Detroit cop drinks a fuzzy fuckin' navel?" It was Leicht asking the question. Another roar of laughter overwhelmed the amped-up juke box.

Jake saw Sylvia laughing with the rest of them. "The tough ones," Jake said, loud enough for all to hear. He tossed the straw and chugged down his drink. Another roar filled the bar and more beer was spilled.

"Good come-back, kid," yelled Burrows as he raised his glass in a mock toast. More laughter followed. Sylvia put another OJ in front of Jake without him asking. As with the last, he sniffed it before taking a sip. He was satisfied it didn't contain vodka or schnapps.

Two hours later, he wanted to make his exit. "You ready to go, Cliff?"

"Go ahead. Don'll give me a ride."

Jake made it to the head of the table to say good-bye to the retiree. Yeaman pulled him close. "Don't start anything Cliff can't finish." He laughed, spilling some of his beer on his shirt. "I'm busting your chops. There's not much Cliff can't finish." He tilted his head back and roared. Jake waved to the rest of the guys and headed out the door. Edie was no doubt keeping supper warm for him.

The bar crowd he left behind was made up of Pontiac cops and a dozen or more deputies that had been drifting in. They were mingling with the detectives and throwing friendly jabs at Yeaman. He had been around for more than thirty years. Everyone knew Don Yeaman—a cop's cop.

Jake was making coffee in the DB just after seven the following morning. The LT had been good on his word the day before. Jake had formally met with the whole bureau during the party at Rob's. Again, Jake found himself laughing within. Leicht had introduced him as fuckin' Jake Bush as he led him from one team of detectives to another. That was as formal an introduction to the Oakland County Sheriff Department's Detective Bureau as he was going to get. Now he was wondering if he'd be now known as "fuckin' Jake Bush" rather than just Jake.

As was his normal morning ritual, he poured the water into the Bunn machine's reservoir while holding his cup under the machine. He replaced his cup with the pot, added some sugar and headed to his desk.

There was an envelope in his *In Box*. It was the preliminary report from the lab on the gun and cigarette butts. Burrows came in and went straight to the coffee pot.

"Ed, I got a lab report on yesterday's evidence from where the guy was tossed." He held it out for the detective.

The old dick just lifted one eyebrow. "Hang onto it."

"Why?"

"The boss says it'll be you and Roberts's case."

Jake stood for a few seconds before Burrows continued, "We're up to our asses in alligators and one less case on our desk is good."

Jake just shrugged and started reading the report.

It said the brand of both cigarette butts was Camels, non-filtered, and a partial print was lifted off the pistol. They were running it through the system. There was a signature on the bottom of the report along with a phone number.

Lakatos stopped at Jake's desk. "You did good at the scene. Now all you got to do is nail the son-of-a-bitches for littering our roadways."

"You didn't find anything else?"

"Nothing. You gonna move your shit up to Yeaman's desk?"

"I'll wait to make sure it's all right with Roberts first."

Lakatos nodded. "Good idea."

Jake was stirring in his 249 granules of sugar in his cup of fresh-brewed coffee when saw the button on his phone flashing. He picked it up. "Detective Bush here."

"This is Abie Vogtmann. You said to call if I needed help."

"What can I do for you?"

"I need a ride home."

"Can you give me a half hour?"

"Yeah." There was a pause, but no disconnect. "Officer, I know this is a strange request, ah, er, do you have a coat or something I can wear?"

Jake remembered the guy had been snatched wearing his pajamas. "I'll bring something." As he hung up the phone, Roberts was pouring himself a coffee.

"Cliff, got a minute?"

Jake told his partner about the call and his offer to pick the guy up and take him home.

"Let me get a lid for my coffee."

"I can take care of it myself."

"Jake, we're partners. The boss said it's our case, we'll work it together."

Jake smiled as he grabbed someone's old coat that had been hanging on a rack in the back corner of the office since he moved his stuff into the bureau. Cliff was leading the way.

A half hour later, Cliff Roberts and Jake Bush were picking up Abie Vogtmann. On the way to the hospital, Jake had filled his partner in on what he knew so far, and how this case might tie in with a body taken out of Orchard Lake late the summer before.

Jake handed Vogtmann the coat. "Abie, this is my partner, Cliff Roberts. Cliff, meet Abraham Vogtmann."

"Hi." Vogtmann said as he shrugged his arms into the coat. "I really appreciate this."

"No problem. Where to?" Cliff asked.

"Do you know where Sashabaw Road is?

In a half hour the dull gray Chevy was passing Sherwood on Sashabaw. Cliff slowed as Abie said they were within a quarter mile. He turned at the mailbox Abie pointed out.

A red Independence Township fire department van was parked at the end of a 300 yard driveway and two men were walking around the remnants of what was once a two story farm house. It was reduced to charred bits and pieces, a far cry from what was once a house clad with green and white tarred shingles. Most of what remained had fallen into the cellar, including what was once the roof.

"Oh my God..." Abie moaned as his eyes took in the charred remains from the back seat of the detective's car. In silence Cliff, Jake and Abie Vogtmann climbed out of their car.

Cliff flashed his badge at the men. They identified themselves. One was the chief of the township's all-volunteer fire department and the other an officer with the Michigan State Police Fire Marshal's office.

The Fire Marshal spoke. "Arson, plain and simple. Gasoline was the accelerant. Two empty gas cans that were most likely used are over there."

"You taking them, or you want us to?" Cliff asked.

"We've got them. Give me your badge numbers and phone. I'll copy you on our findings."

"What happened to my car?" Abie cried out.

What was left of his 1968 Plymouth Valiant sat on its rims behind the burned out house. The house fire roasted anything within fifty yards of it, the car included.

Cliff opened the back door to his county car. "Mister

Vogtmann, have a seat. I think it's time you filled us in on why someone's so pissed at you that they try and kill you then torched your house."

Chapter Twenty

Abie was talking fast, at first trying to not say anything that might get him in trouble with the cops—until he realized he had nothing to protect. His house was gone and so was everything connected with it or to the life he had known. He stumbled over words as he talked, but in the end Detectives Cliff Roberts and Jake Bush heard the whole story about his illegal crop, the meetings with Johnny Chesterfield at the old Novi Hotel, the two visitors he had there and all he could remember about ending up in the ditch on Bogie Lake Road a couple of nights before.

"They said I was cutting into someone's territory. I don't have a clue as to who they were. All I know is they were big, bald and mean looking."

"Would you know them if you saw them again?" Roberts asked.

"Guys like that, you don't forget."

The Salvation Army came up with some clothes and a toothbrush for Vogtmann and the YMCA had a place for him to stay for a while. Abie's only hope for survival was in the hands of the Oakland County Sheriff's Department because he couldn't even touch the small bank account he had at the Detroit Bank and Trust. His identification had gone up in flames along with any dreams he might have had.

———

Cliff was driving toward headquarters. “So how many cases do we have going besides this fiasco?”

“The only thing the boss had me working on was some B&Es.” Jake thought for a minute. “He had me follow up a report on a body found in Orchard Lake, so we might catch that too.”

“Well partner, that’ll give us something to start on in the morning. Today we’ve got to take care of some other business.”

“And that is?”

A smile crossed his lips as he said, “The range. I need to see if you can shoot straight.”

Jake smiled too. “Care to make a little wager?” It had been a long time since he had a partner to shoot with. Now he did.

“Loser buys lunch tomorrow,” Cliff answered without hesitating.

“You’re on.”

———

The next morning, Jake filled Cliff Roberts in on all the information he gathered on the open B&E cases, the background on the two names he had that might be involved, and the file he had started on Abie Vogtmann.

“I threw in a copy of the report on a body fished out of Orchard Lake since Vogtmann and the dead guy both were wrapped in a painter’s drop cloth. There’s another report Kaminski wrote up on a possible witness in the Orchard Lake case about a couple of guys and a boat.”

Before noon, Leicht dropped three more files on their desk. “Fuckin’ vacation’s over Roberts.” He smiled as he said it. “Show the kid how we do things in the sticks while you’re at it.”

Demetrio's was Jake's favorite place for Coney dogs. The restaurant was on 10 Mile in Warren. That's where he often had lunch with his wife. He had won the bet at the range. Cliff thought it was a bit of a drive just for a hot dog, but that's where they went.

"How many of the damn things are you going to eat?" Cliff asked fifteen minutes after the pair sat down in a booth and ordered.

Jake was downing his second and had just ordered two more. "I usually stop at two, but since you're buying, four might do." He smiled while wiping a bit of mustard and chili off his lips. "I used to shoot once a week with some of my partners in Detroit. How about we make a habit of it?"

"No more bets though."

"No bets. Just practice."

"Tuesdays after work sound good to you?"

Jake nodded as the waitress dropped the second plate at the table. Pointing to the plate, he said, "Split those with you." Cliff didn't answer; he just pulled one of the dogs onto his plate.

After Cliff took two bites, he took a swallow from his Coke and said, "I'm just helping you out so we can get back to work."

Ten minutes passed and Cliff pulled out a ten to cover the bill.

"I'll get the tip." Jake threw a buck and a couple of quarters on the table.

Jake had given the fire chief and the state fire marshal all the information he had on the owner of the house. He got a phone number where he could reach them with anything else they might find out. He typed up an information report to add to the Vogtmann file. He and Cliff had concurred that the arson had to be related to Vogtmann being snatched.

"I see we caught the Orchard Lake case," Jake said. It was in one of the folders Leicht had thrown on their desk. He handed it to his partner. "I think we ought to treat this and the Vogtmann case as one."

Cliff just nodded and started reading.

The two detectives spent some time going over the file. Some prints were on the duct tape used to wrap the late Charles Little in a drop cloth before he was deposited in Orchard Lake. Those prints matched the ones on file for a Ralph, aka Rhino, Bumgarden. Bumgarden was a white male with a DOB of 2/18/42. The man's record showed arrests and convictions for assault, and attempted murder. He had served 6 1/2 years in Jackson and was paroled in 1973.

"Did the lab find any prints on the tape on the Vogtmann snatching?" Cliff asked.

"I'll give them a call."

Fifteen minutes later Jake was telling his partner that the lab was still working on the evidence. "I gave them our number. They said they'd know more in a day or two." Cliff was prioritizing the files as he read them. "How do we know where to start, or which one comes first?" Jake asked.

"Here we're jugglers. Right now we've got five balls in the air, but one is hotter than the other. Vogtmann gets the nod on that." Cliff stacked the files in the order he had decided. "Sometimes we may have to split up with you going one way and me another, but for the most part, we'll work them all at the same time together." He pulled the report on the possible witness to the Orchard Lake case. "Start checking the *Yellow Pages* on painting companies. Maybe this Rhino guy is working for one of them."

The bottom drawer in Yeaman's desk had an old copy of the *Yellow Pages*. He checked the date. "Cliff, you got a newer book? This one's from the mid-60s." Cliff found one in his drawer and tossed it onto Jake's desk without saying a word. It landed with a thud.

Cliff had a phone in his ear and started dialing while Jake

was making a list of painting companies. The book was for the Metro Detroit area, and Oakland and Macomb Counties so there was a bunch. He eliminated anything south of Eight Mile, trying to minimize his list. When he finished, he had 143 painting companies. It took most of three hours to list them all. Jake got himself a cup of coffee, figuring he'd find a map and start plotting where they were.

His desk was a cluttered mess, so he grabbed the old phone book to pitch it. Out of curiosity, he thumbed to the section on painting companies. He didn't know why he bothered, but he found four more addresses to add to his list before dropping it into his waste basket.

He pulled the reports out of the file that Kaminski had taken from the possible witness and the one on the van that disappeared on Bogie Lake Road and reread them. He went back to his list and highlighted in yellow those that had the word "painting" in its name. That cut his list down a third. He didn't plan on eliminating any; he just wanted to speed up the process.

The phone rang and Cliff picked it up. After a couple of uh-huhs and jotting down some notes he said, "That was the lab. They got a name to go with the partial print on the pistol. Some guy named Henry Kritchman. I'll get a record and photo on him." One of the wheels on his chair squeaked as he pushed from his desk. "One good print came off of the tape. Take a guess on whose it is?"

"Henry again?"

"No. A Ralph Bumgarden—Rhino." Cliff tossed his cup toward Jake. "Make a new pot an' pour me one while I get some records and photos pulled. Maybe we're making headway and Vogtmann can ID them.

Sylvia ran her tongue over her lips a third time as she waited for the customer in front of her. There was only one teller still open at The Detroit Bank and Trust. Sylvia's eyes darted to the two other cages where the tellers were counting their cash. It was near four and they were done for the day. Her hand gripped the Colt snub-nosed revolver in her right Carhart jacket pocket. She overheard the teller saying to the woman at the window, "Thanks for coming in, Mrs. Callou. See you next Friday."

She knew she was on. Sylvia tugged the brim of her hat to lower it over her eyes just a bit and moved toward the teller. "Good afternoon sir. Isn't a lovely fall day?" the teller said. Sylvia didn't answer, she just pushed a note toward the teller and placed the barrel of Colt on the window sill just enough so the woman could see it. The note was self-explanatory: *Push no buttons and empty your cash drawer or you won't see your kids tonight.*

It took exactly thirty seconds from when the note was passed for Sylvia to stuff the pile of bills into the empty pillowcase she pulled out of her coat pocket. She glanced to her left then to her right. The tellers closing out for the night were oblivious to what was happening in between them. In the seconds that ticked off she saw the stacks of money they were counting, but she and Grace had two strict rules: *Don't get greedy* and *Four minutes in and out.* Sylvia took one step backwards then turned and headed for the door. She saw Grace pull to the curb in her black Dodge Dart. Sylvia smiled as she slid in the passenger's seat.

———

Lieutenant Leicht stuck his head out of his office. "Roberts and Bush! The Bank at M-15 and Clarkston Road. It just happened. Get there before the fuckin' Feds do."

Cliff was driving as their radio blared. "All units stand by for information on a car and occupants wanted in a robbery armed at the Detroit Bank and Trust in Clarkston ten minutes ago." There was a pause. "The car is described as a black Dodge Dart, possibly a 1972 model. Partial license B as in Boy, R as in Robert, occupied by two males. Number one:

White, approximately forty-five years old, five eight, 160 pounds with a big-barreled chest, wearing a scruffy beard, a brown ball cap and a waist length matching coat. He showed a blue steel pistol to the teller. Number two, the driver of the car was described by a pedestrian as a smaller built white male wearing a hooded parka. The car was last seen in the vicinity of M-15 and Clarkston Road heading east."

"One of the files the boss tossed our way is on a couple of other bank jobs," Cliff said.

"What about Vogtmann?"

"Balls in the air, man. Balls in the air."

Jake had read the file that Cliff mentioned. Twice in the past month there were hold-ups at banks similar to where they were heading. They were branches of various banks serving smaller communities. He had made some notes from that file. They were still fresh in his mind. The first week of December a bank was hit in Milford. And two weeks prior to that another one was robbed in Walled Lake. The robber in Walled Lake was close enough to match today's gunman and a black car was seen leaving the scene. The gunman at the Milford bank was a slightly built man with a mustache and only around five foot tall. The car used in that robbery was a light blue Ford.

Grace and Sylvia were sharing an iced-down bottle of Cold Duck, using a couple of long-stemmed glasses they thought fit the occasion.

"Five thousand and change," Sylvia announced as she poured. "Not a bad take for a few minutes work." Her tongue traveled the oval of her mouth twice as she talked, a habit she had picked up somewhere, many years before.

Grace tipped her glass for a sip, the bubbles from her drink tickling her nose, causing her to sneeze. She pointed at the stack of bills in front of her. "I think it's time to quit Rotten Rob's. I'm tired of getting patted on the ass by all those cops."

Sylvia giggled, adding, "No, no. That's the beauty of working there. Show a little tit to get a bigger tip and keep an ear open to see if they got a line on the bank jobs we've been pulling."

Grace frowned, "I've never had any tits to show." She took another swallow. "Maybe I'll go see one of them boob doctors and finally get something I can brag about." She puffed out her chest, showing off the little she had.

"Make sure they're not too big, little girl. You'll fall on your nose," Sylvia said as she was dividing up the take. One pile was hers, the other for her partner. "Hey, here comes the news. Turn it up."

The six o'clock news was on WWJ-TV. The report was brief. No more than twenty seconds long. It named the bank and said that police were looking for two men in a black Dodge. It mentioned that the FBI said the robbery was done by what they called "a Mutt and Jeff team."

"Well," said Grace. "The disguises are still working. They lost me though on the Mutt and Jeff bullshit."

"They're old comic strip characters. A tall guy and a short guy." A wide smile crossed Sylvia's face as she said it. "Guys." She took another sip of champagne. "If only they knew."

And what the FBI and the police did not know was that two women from different backgrounds, a Sylvia Porter and Grace Buchner, ended up working at a bar in Pontiac, a cop bar no less.

Sylvia was born and raised on a ranch in North Dakota a few miles south of Rugby. Her husband was working in an oil field in Alaska—that is, her ex-husband as she explained to Grace. "The low-life found some Eskimo woman who chewed hides to tan them. There was no alimony. He left me high and dry. The damn bank repossessed the ranch."

Sylvia ended up in Pontiac, Michigan, when a sister invited her to come out and stay for a while until she found a place of her own. She had nowhere else to go. "I never will figure out how I went from riding horses one day to pushing drinks in a town named after an Indian."

Grace, on the other hand, was raised in Pontiac and studied to be a beautician after high school. Once she finished her schooling she ran off to Hollywood, taking a job working for a movie studio. From hair dressing she graduated to being a make-up artist and working for MGM. Two years later she was the wife of a doctor for nearly fifteen years.

"My husband was a chiropractor," she told Sylvia. "He got sued a couple of times for manipulating the wrong thing on a patient or two. The next thing I knew he was in Texas with one of the women who sued him and I was back in Pontiac and working at Rob's."

Both women, hurt, pissed off and broke, found an apartment together just to survive on the two dollars an hour plus tips, pushing drinks at a place called Rotten Rob's. After a year there and hearing all the cop stories, Sylvia came up with the plan to tap some banks. With Grace's experience at MGM's make-up department, some clothes from a Goodwill Store and a Colt pistol, the only thing her ex had left at the ranch, all they had to do was pick a target.

———

Jake dropped a copy of the report written by the first deputy responding to the bank in the file he was holding on the two previous hold-ups. Even though the FBI had the lead in the case, the bank robberies were still one of the active files assigned to him and Cliff. He called Agent Allen Jenkins to see if the feds had any leads. They didn't. *Just another ball in the air.*

Cliff pulled up his chair across from Jake. "Got some pics to go with the names. Let's go visit Mr. Vogtmann."

Chapter Twenty-one

Abie was going through the twelve-pack of photos that Cliff had brought. Jake was driving while Cliff did most of the talking. They were on their way to the Secretary of State's office so Abie could get a duplicate driver's license.

"I really appreciate all your help."

Jake adjusted his mirror so he could glance at their passenger in the back seat. "Maybe you can return the favor by helping us find the guys who grabbed you."

Cliff turned in his seat. "Take your time, Mr. Vogtmann. There's no rush. See if anyone in the photos look familiar."

Abraham Vogtmann was shuffling through the stack. He then went through them a second time and a third time, finally pulling a couple out.

"These two." He handed the pictures to Cliff. "These were the guys who threatened me at the old Novi Hotel."

"You're positive?"

"Yeah. There's no mistaking them."

"How about their voices? Would you say they were the same guys who were taking you for a ride?"

"I couldn't be sure." Abie looked out the back window on the detectives' car, then to each side. His eyes were darting all around as if he didn't feel safe even in the company of two cops. "When they had me bundled up, I was too scared to pay any attention to their voices."

"What are you looking for?" Cliff asked.

"Nothing," Vogtmann answered, but his eye movement was saying something else.

"I think you can stop your worrying. They think you're dead," Cliff said as he took the two pictures from Abie.

"They do?"

"Yeah. We fed the papers a story on finding a dead body on Bogie Lake Road." Cliff smiled. "We just gave the papers enough, hoping your kidnappers relax and make a mistake."

He flashed the two pictures towards Jake. They were copies of the Jackson Prison mug shots of Henry Kritchman and Ralph Bumgarden. Neither had a neck, their large bald heads grew right out of their shoulders. They weren't smiling. There was a set of numbers at the bottom of each—their prison IDs. These were the same two men identified through prints found on a .22 pistol and pieces of duct tape, one around the tarp binding a murder victim and the other in a kidnapping.

An hour later, Vogtmann was back at the Salvation Army and Jake and Cliff were on the way back to the bureau. "Well, we got names and faces," Jake said. "Now all we have to do is find them."

"How many businesses do you have on your list?"

" 'bout a hundred and fifty."

"That many?"

Jake just shrugged. "Give or take a couple."

"That's a lot of doors to knock on."

Jake told Cliff about highlighting just those businesses with the word *painting* in its name, but that still gave them a hundred or so to check. Then they talked about when they'd start trying to find the one business they were looking for; the one that employed Kritchman and Bumgarden, aka Hands and Rhino.

"It'll be a lot of leg work, but it's got to be done." Cliff said.

"You aren't thinking about knocking on doors and asking

for them, are you?"

"Actually we'll check with people around the businesses. The neighbors. Unless you got a better idea."

"I talked to a couple of parole officers when I got some information on the B&E file on our pile. If these guys are still in the system, maybe they've got a place of employment on one or both."

Cliff Roberts smiled. "Got their phone numbers?"

"Yup." Jake was pulling into the headquarters lot as he answered.

Hands and Rhino were relaxing in two overstuffed chairs that faced Vito's desk. "Now let me get this shit straight. You thought a cop might have been following you the other night?"

"Yeah, but it was too close to tell. That's why we tossed the guy." Hands got up as he talked, walking to the fridge in the back of his boss's office. "Okay to have a beer?"

Vito just waved him off. "Well, the paper said the guy's dead."

Hands had his head in the fridge. "You want one boss?" He already had grabbed one for Rhino.

"I'll pass." Vito was paging through that day's newspaper. "To be on the safe side, keep the van parked for a while." He tossed the paper aside. "Nothing. All we got is that one little item on them finding a body the other day."

He reached for his rolodex and flipped through the pages. "To be on the safe side, I'm going to call in a marker." He dialed a number. On the second ring a voice answered. "Yes, Mrs. Squires. Is your husband at home?" There was a pause. "Okay. Can you give him my number? I'm an old friend." Vito gave his phone number and just his first name. "Have him call me at his leisure, please."

Rhino popped the cap on his beer using his teeth. "You got some ideas?"

"Yeah. A deputy I know will be able to tell me if they're looking for the van, and find out if the body they found is our man."

Hands and Rhino smiled and tipped their bottles toward each other. Vito always had the inside info. If he didn't, he had ways of getting it.

Jake made a call. Frank Richards happened to be in the Region 10 office. He was one of the parole officers that covered Wayne, Oakland and Macomb Counties. He said it would take an hour or two, but he'd see what if anything they had on Ralph Bumgarden and Henry Kritchman. Jake gave Richards their DOBs and prison numbers from the files.

Jake looked up to see his boss standing and waiting for him to get off the phone. "Yes sir?"

Leicht dropped a couple of documents on Jake's desk. "Ballistics report is in on the .22 you found on Bogie Lake Road." He smiled. "It's a fuckin' match to the slug found in the vic's head in the Orchard Lake killing."

Jake grabbed the report and read it. Beneath that report was another on a B&E Roof Job that happened over the weekend. Butler and Anibal came to mind. They, or someone else, were back in business. He scanned it. *Same MO.* The burglary happened between closing on Saturday and Monday morning at a business that rented tools and equipment for the do-it-yourselfer. There was a long list of miscellaneous tools and some welding equipment missing. *One of the balls in the air.*

It was well after dark when Jake pulled into his garage. He noticed a light on in the basement. Edie greeted him with a short kiss. "I've kept dinner warm. Just hope it hasn't dried out."

"Where are the boys?"

"Downstairs. Pumping iron."

Jake wasn't all that happy about not being able to spend much time with the boys. "I'll go check on them before I sit down." His wife just smiled, knowing what was going on in his mind.

Hank was spotting for Sam who was doing bench presses. Jake's footfalls on the wooden stairs had the boys stop. "Hi guys," he said as Hank set the barbell on its stand.

The boys in unison yelled out, "Dad!"

"Got time to come up and visit while I grab some supper?" Sam beat Hank to the stairs, taking two at a time to the top.

Edie was dishing up some lasagna on a plate for Jake. "You guys ready for some pie?" Not waiting for the expected answer, she served up two pieces for the boys and another for her husband. "I'll be in watching 'I Love Lucy' while you guys talk."

Jake's supper and pie for the boys came before any talking.

"Dad, they're signing up for Little League, will you coach us again?" Sam asked as he pushed his empty plate aside.

"I wish I could." Jake saw the frowns on the boys' faces. "My new job has me working way more than I expected, and…"

"That's OK," Hank interrupted. "We understand."

"Speak for yourself," Sam chimed in. "It was better before." He started to leave, but Jake grabbed his arm.

Jake turned Sam's chin where he could look into his eyes. "Quit puffing up that lower lip, son. I'm sorry, but…"

"Dad, it was better before you made detective. Now you hardly spend any time with us."

"Yeah, I know. But I'm working on some really big cases. Maybe after I put some guys away, it'll slow down." Jake didn't know that for sure. His boss kept bringing in more files just when they were making headway on one.

"Tell you what, guys. I know a river that the crappies use this time of year for spawning. Saturday we'll load up the rods and catch some dinner. How's that sound?"

Hank beamed. "Maybe you can tell us about the bank robbers. I saw something about it on TV today."

"Maybe…"

"By Saturday, Dad'll have them two guys in jail. Right Dad?'

"Boy, you've got a lot of confidence in me, Sam."

"That's 'cause you're the best detective in the world. Better than Sam Spade."

The boys went back downstairs, looking for the cardboard box they had packed their fishing tackle in. Jake had already hung their rods on nails on the back wall in the basement.

Jake slid in next to Edie on the couch. "The boys miss you," she said.

"I miss them too." He wormed his arm around Edie's waist, pulling her closer. She put her head on his shoulder. "I just hope you're not sorry for marrying a cop."

"Not in the least."

Jake's phone rang. It was Richards. "I got an address on a place Bumgarden is supposed to be working. A body shop."

Within ten minutes, Jake and Cliff were on the road, heading for an address on Walton Boulevard. "That number should be east of Joslyn," Cliff said as Jake drove. A short time later they were parked in front of a boarded-up cement block building. The trees sprouting from the flat roof said the business had been closed for a long time. "I figured as much." Cliff looked at Jake. "Did you bring your list?"

"Yup." Jake dug it out of his coat pocket and handed it over to his partner.

Cliff ran his finger down it, looking for addresses close to where they were. There were three within a ten mile radius. "Hit Lapeer Road and go north."

By lunch time they had five addresses crossed off their list and by quitting time had checked out and eliminated seven more. The two detectives had a simple method. They'd drive by the address on their list, look it over, then find an open business in the neighborhood and ask some simple questions regarding the painting shop across the street or down the road. Most of the businesses knew their neighbors and the vehicles they used.

For the next three days they did the same: Look for a paint shop, then eliminate them one by one. They were doing the monotonous legwork that went with the job, but the list was getting shorter. It was a Thursday, a nice sunny day that was a sure sign of spring.

"Wanna go to Rob's once we check this last one out?" Cliff asked. Jake just shrugged, indicating he didn't care. "I'm sure they have Coke there."

"I drink Pepsi."

"Then have an orange juice. I'll buy."

Inside Rotten Rob's, Cliff grabbed a table. In a corner Jake saw Mel Williams and a couple of other deputies. He waved at Mel and grabbed a seat. Sylvia was passing with a tray full of glasses and a pitcher of beer. "Be right with you guys," she said as she passed.

Cliff smiled as the waitress walked by. She was wearing a black micro-mini skirt, fish-net nylons and a white sleeveless top that was cut nice and low.

"How do you always luck into picking her table?" Jake asked.

"You complaining?"

"Not really."

Sylvia reappeared. She put her tray on the table, bending a bit, just to show enough. She ran her tongue over her lips twice before talking. "Okay, you're the fuzzy navel guy, minus the fuzz." She laughed, running her tongue over her lips again. "How about you, big boy?" She was looking at Cliff as she asked.

Cliff pointed his finger towards his partner. "He'll have a Pepsi, if you have one, and I'll have a Schlitz in a frosted mug."

"Pepsi, we don't have."

"Make it an orange juice then," Jake answered.

Sylvia spun on her toes, heading for the bar. "Hey Grace, catch that table in the corner."

Jake's eyes found the other barmaid. "You ever have Grace wait on you?"

"She's nice, but let's face it Jake, the scenery isn't as good."

Sylvia appeared with their drinks, carefully giving the two detectives plenty to see. "You ought to switch to Coke. It's a quarter cheaper than OJ." Her tongue ran across her lips, moistening them as she winked.

"I prefer Pepsi," Jake answered.

"Suit yourself. Thought I'd save you some money." She moved to catch another table of cops. It was shift change time.

Jake noticed Cliff's eyes never left Sylvia. "You like what you see?"

"My wife was better looking and had more class."

"But your eyes say something else."

"We'll talk about this tomorrow." Cliff drained his mug of Schlitz, threw a five on the table and left. Jake waved a good-bye to Mel in the corner. He and his friends had just had another pitcher delivered.

Chapter Twenty-two

Jake was making coffee as Cliff came in the office. There was no good morning greeting from him. Nothing. Cliff started digging into the pile of files on their desk as Jake turned back to the pot. “Coffee partner?” he yelled back toward their desks.

“Black,” was Cliff’s response.

Jake put a coffee in front of his partner and moved to his desk. The bureau was set up where each detective crew faced one another. Jake and Cliff’s desks were mid-way from the Bunn machine in the back corner and the lieutenant’s office in the front of the DB.

“Morning,” Jake said as he slid into his chair.

“Humph!”

Cliff was busy reading the file in front of him. He opened a drawer, pulled out a rolodex, flipped through a couple of tabs, grabbed his phone and dialed. “Yeah Rob. Cliff Roberts here. Glad I caught you opening this morning.” There was a pause. “You guys still makin’ breakfast?” Another pause. “My partner and I’ll be in. Keep the griddle warm.” He hung up the phone.

“We’re going to breakfast, partner.” Cliff tossed the file he was reading toward Jake as he grabbed his coat off the back of his chair.

"I ate at home."

"Eat again."

Jake was reading the file on the bank robberies Cliff handed him. Cliff was driving. "Notice anything?" Cliff asked. "Pay attention to the physical descriptions, and then FBI follow-up."

Jake read them more carefully.

"One of the guys had a nervous habit," Cliff hinted.

"Uh-huh!"

At Rotten Rob's Cliff had Rob come join them while they ate. Rob was a retired Pontiac copper who took over the bar ten years before, cleaned it up and started to cook breakfasts. Rob specialized in three egg omelets. The afternoon menu only offered burgers, fries and deep fried mushrooms, something simple that the bartender could throw together.

Cliff was having his favorite, a Mexican Omelet with double salsa. The small talk was out of the way by the time Cliff and Jake had finished their meal. "Okay Roberts, I haven't seen you in here in six months. What's on your mind?"

"Gotta address on Sylvia?"

"No wonder I haven't seen you. Coming in after work, are you?" Rob rolled a toothpick around in his mouth. "She does have nice legs." He laughed a bit before continuing. "She don't like men much from what I heard."

"Who says I'm looking for a date?" Cliff pushed his empty cup towards Jake. "You know where the pot is?" Jake took the hint and went and got the pot. He topped off all three cups.

"Did you know she and Grace are sharing a place?" Rob asked as he poured some cream into his. The next twenty minutes Rob told Cliff and Jake all he knew about the two barmaids he had working for him.

Cliff took a sip of his coffee. "What hours do you have them working?"

"I close the joint on Sundays. My wife doesn't like me working on the Sabbath." Rob pushed his cup toward Jake and Jake obligingly went and got the pot again. "Monday through Thursday Grace and Sylvia work the two to ten shift. Fridays and Saturdays I got them working five 'til closing."

He mentioned he had one girl come in and cover the last four hours during the week. "She works the Big Boy on Van Dyke. Nothing to look at, but needs the extra hours. I'm a sucker for working mothers."

Rob thought for a while. "You know Cliff, maybe you could change Sylvia's mind about men. She spends a lot of time joking and talking with cops so I know she likes men with a badge."

Cliff was smiling as he slowly said, "I guess there's no fooling you, Rob. She did catch my eye."

"Figured so," Rob chuckled.

Cliff asked him not to start any rumors.

"My lips are sealed."

Cliff and Jake were back on the road. They had Sylvia's address. "You get where I'm going with this, Jake?"

"I think so. Sylvia's nervous habit."

"Exactly. And Friday afternoons. All the banks were hit on Fridays near four."

"And today is Friday." Jake knew they weren't going to be canvassing painting companies the rest of the day. Cliff had other plans.

The pair of detectives slowly drove by the address Rob had given them. It was an apartment building in downtown Pontiac at 1432 Baldwin Avenue. Two more trips around the block and Jake had written down seventeen license plate numbers. The cars used in the bank robberies were described as a light blue Ford and a black Dodge Dart. Anything near being light blue or any dark car within walking distance of the address made the list. They'd be able to get a registration check on all of them. They were looking for cars registered to either Grace Buchner or Sylvia Porter.

At two in the afternoon a non-descript Chevy belonging to the Oakland County Sheriff's Department was parked a block away and across the street from the apartment building where Sylvia and Grace lived. They had a straight line of vision to the main entrance. A 1974 black Dodge Dart, registered to Buchner, and a light blue 1971 Mercury, registered to Porter, were parked within ten cars of one another. Cliff had filled up a quart thermos at a 7-Eleven and was sipping on what he had poured into the cap from the thermos.

"Want some, partner?" Cliff waved an empty take-out cup he brought from the store.

"Got any sugar?"

"It's black."

"No thanks." Jake paused, then asked, "You mentioned your wife last night. I didn't know you were married."

"Was. She died a year ago. Cancer."

"Sorry. I hope I didn't…"

"You didn't," Cliff said, cutting him off mid-sentence.

Silence filled their car. It was obvious Cliff didn't want to talk about his wife. There was movement at the entrance to the apartment building and Jake quickly brought up his binoculars.

"Anything?"

"Just some black guy taking his dog out for a walk."

Both cops settled back in their seats. The plan was to watch and wait. Two and a half hours later, Grace came out and got in behind the wheel of the Dodge. Sylvia climbed in beside her. They were dressed for work with their legs sticking out from under their spring jackets.

Jake broke the silence. "What now?"

"You got the list?"

"Yep."

"Let's check out a couple more painting companies, then call it a night."

Saturday morning Jake got Hank and Sam up at 5 a.m. By 6 they finished breakfast at a Big Boy Restaurant on Van

Dyke and Big Beaver Road and were heading to the Clinton River. There was a small dam near the Fern Hill Golf Club where Jake had heard the crappies in the spring liked to congregate and cohabitate. He had made sure that he and the boys could cut across the course and throw some pinkies in the river for an hour or two. The golf course had not officially opened yet, and he got to know Justin Halverson, the groundskeeper, on a B&E report he had taken at the man's house when he still was wearing the department browns.

There was a tear in Jake's eye as memories flooded through his mind. Memories of him showing his son, Mike, how to tie on a pinky—a lead pink jig with a white feathery tail. The lure would be trailing about two feet behind a clear bobber. That's how Mike and he caught buckets full of near-ready to spawn crappies on the Tittabawassee River near the Edenville dam many years before.

"Hey Dad! I got one," Sam squealed.

"Me too," Hank yelled.

"Don't drop that rod tip," Jake instructed.

His thoughts of Mike vanished.

Two hours later, there was little room in their five-gallon pail. Jake had brought a rod, but it went unused. He had been kept busy showing his sons how to cast and how to unhook a flopping black crappie without getting stuck by the fish's back fins.

"You want to fish, you take them off," he had said when Sam got poked the first time. Jake had the boys throw back anything smaller than 5 inches. "You'll see why," he said when Sam complained, "when I teach you to filet them."

Hank and Sam conned Jake into taking them again Sunday morning. "Make sure you're back in time for church," Edie warned.

"You want to go with us?" Jake raised an eyebrow as he asked.

"I'd rather sleep in."

Jake really knew Edie would love to go and see all the

excitement the boys had spent an hour talking about, but knew what she loved more was having a dad for her sons. Fishing was good *Dad time*. His new job didn't give him much of that.

Jake had the boys home by nine so they could make the 10:30 service at Our Redeemer Lutheran Church. The town of Washington, Michigan, was a bit of a drive from their new home, but Edie was still singing in their choir and Jake liked being there for her and the boys.

———

Monday Jake and Cliff were back working on the list of painting companies after Leicht's NFB Session. It was slow work, but had to be done since the addresses from the parole officers on Kritchman and Bumgarden turned out to be dead ends.

"Did you see we had another B&E report lying on our desk this morning?" Jake asked.

Cliff was going over their county map compliments of AAA. "Uh-huh." He flipped the map over. "I think we're going to work a weekend or two and sit on some addresses."

"And see if Butler and Anibal are working together?"

"Exactly."

Jake crossed another painting company off the list. The phrase: *Balls in the air* echoed in his mind. He was glad he took the boys fishing both days the weekend before.

Tuesday and Wednesday had them knocking more painting companies off their list. By Thursday morning they had whittled it down to ten.

"Where'd you get this address from?" Cliff had his finger on the map stretched across his desk. "The one on Opdyke Road."

Jake looked at his list. The address on Opdyke was at the bottom. "Oh, that one was an address I got out of the old *Yellow Pages* you gave me."

"They still in business?"

Jake just shrugged as Cliff tossed him the car keys. "It's next."

The address had them going south off of Square Lake Road. They spotted a white flat-roofed building with double overhead doors facing Opdyke. Over an office window hung an old sign. The words were barely distinguishable: All-Around Painting.

Jake made a U-turn in the lot at Stoneycroft Hills Golf Club. "There's a lawn mower shop across the road." He headed toward it.

"You're learning."

They were in the lot for Ted's Lawn and Home Equipment. The separate sign read, "New and Used." Push mowers of all makes were on one side of the building while a new line-up of reddish-orange Ariens riding mowers were being driven into place facing Opdyke Road by a guy in oil-spotted work clothes.

Sitting in a plastic molded chair against the front of the brown-brick building was an older man. He had a coffee cup in one hand and a smile on his face. His near pure-white hair was combed, parted on the left. He wore a starched white open-collared shirt.

"Yes sir, you Ted?" asked Cliff.

"Ted Senior. If you are here to buy a mower, see my son, Junior. He's the salesman."

"And what's your job?" Jake asked.

"Retired."

"That a job?" Jake leaned against the building as he asked.

"That's the job Ted Junior gave me two weeks ago when I gave a guy too much for his old mower." He smiled. "As a retiree I drink coffee and sit, smiling. That's my only job."

"Why don't you just stay home then, mister…?" Jake asked.

"Easton's the name." He took a sip of his coffee. "Been coming here for forty-three years. Wife does the books." He took another sip. "If I stay home I'd go nuts." He looked into the bottom of his cup and tossed the last bit onto the concrete pad. "Now I just sit here and watch the traffic…of course, I could dress funny, dance around carrying a sign trying to lure in potential customers." Ted laughed at his own joke. "Junior would love that."

"What do you know about the painting company across the street?" Cliff asked, changing the subject.

"Hasn't been a painting company for…" He thought for a bit. "Fifteen or more years." He looked at Jake offering his empty cup, "Can you get me another shot of coffee, son?"

First Rob, now Ted thinks I'm the coffee gofer?

Before Jake could move, a woman about Ted's age came out with a pot and filled his empty cup. "Thanks. I was just going to have the boy fetch me some," he said.

"Young Ted is inside if you need some information on the tractors," she said before sliding back into the building.

Ted took a sip and looked at Jake. "You're cops. Right?"

Jake and Cliff nodded and flashed their badges.

"Who you lookin' for?"

"We're interested in the painting company," Cliff answered, thrusting his chin toward the building across the street.

"Old Ben Mueller died a long time ago. He had no kids to take over the business. It's no longer a paint shop. They pretend it is, but it's not."

"What do you mean, pretend?" Cliff wiggled his butt into a seat on a new tractor as he asked.

"Oh, they've got a white van with a sign on it, but they're not painters."

"What makes you say that?" Cliff tilted his head as he asked.

"No ladders on the top of the truck and two guys too big to climb them if they had any. They don't make ladders that strong."

Jake cut in. "What kind of hours do they keep?"

"Don't really have hours. Two skinny shits show up mostly around noon. Then a guy with a suit might show up in a big car. I think it's a Lincoln. Maybe a Caddy." Ted sampled his fresh coffee and blew on it a bit. "The two big guys show up whenever the short greaser is there."

"Short greaser?" Jake butted in.

"The guy in the suit. Short like me, no more than five six. Greased down black hair. A dago I'd say."

"Italian?"

"Something like that. Wears a fedora and has a coat draped over his shoulders like in the movies."

Ted looked around, like someone might be listening, finally lowering his voice. "I think it's a bookie joint or something."

"You're pretty observant," Jake said.

"That's my job. Ted Junior says to sit out here and watch the traffic. I'm retired."

"What about when it's raining?"

"They let me inside. I have a corner chair near the coffee pot." Ted smiled, took a sip, and added: "Can't sell anything though. Junior says so. I think retired means I'm fired." Ted shook his head. "Opened this place nearly forty-five years ago, and now they want me to just stay out of the way."

"Want another job?" Cliff asked.

"Doing what?"

Cliff handed Ted a card. "Call us when you see some activity over at the paint shop."

Ted smiled. He was back to work.

Chapter Twenty-three

Cliff had Jake park north of the old painting company after they picked up some burgers for the road. "The plan?" Jake asked.

"Sit and watch for the big guys. The boss said he'd have Burrows and Lakatos request a search warrant for the building while we keep an eye on it." Cliff bit into his hamburger. "Tomorrow we're sitting on it 'til one."

"What are we doing after one?"

"We check on Sylvia. It's Friday."

"Oh yeah, another one of our balls in the air." Jake opened his bag. "You really think she's involved?"

Cliff shrugged. "Just a hunch. Not too many people I know lick their lips like our bank bandit except her. I always follow my hunches."

"We'll have to catch her in the act."

"Yeah. I can't see either one of us requesting a search warrant based on lip licking. They'd laugh us right out of the prosecutor's office." Cliff slid down in his seat to relax.

"On the way to a bank or after?"

Cliff smiled. "After might be the smartest. We'll see."

"What about Rhino and Hands?"

"We'll get them eventually.

Jake sat back, slouching behind the wheel of their

Chevrolet. To make any headway on all the balls they had in the air, there was a lot of watching and waiting in the detective business. So he resigned himself to do just that.

He finished off his lunch while it was still reasonably warm. Jake was tickled the burger joint had Pepsi Colas to wash down his sandwich. He refused to drink a Coke like it was poison.

His mind flashed back to how he spent his first dime of paper route money at the old corner store on Eight Mile and Strasburg. *Twelve ounces of Pepsi versus six ounces.* He knew how to spend his money wisely. Coke lost a customer because of their small bottle.

Cliff drove as they headed out from headquarters the next day. As he parked to watch the paint shop he whispered, "Patience is a virtue." Jake had heard that phrase a few times already in the brief time they had been partners. Cliff always said it every time he pulled in somewhere to sit and watch.

Like old times, Jake thought, *working with Jesse Scott or Gunny Wynn in Detroit.* He liked not just having a partner again, but a good partner.

There was no activity at the paint shop. Cliff checked his watch and hit the ignition and headed for Pontiac.

Twenty minutes later, he slid their plain-Jane Chevrolet into position across the street and down the block again. The view to the apartment building was blurred by a steady rain. Two hours of silence was broken only by an occasional swish of the wipers on their Chevy. At four-thirty a pair of umbrellas appeared and walked toward Porter's light blue Mercury.

Jake lowered his binoculars. "They're dressed for work."

Cliff shrugged and cranked the Chevy to life. "Let's go talk to Ted Senior."

"You giving up on Sylvia and Grace?"

"'til next Friday."

Ted Easton Senior wasn't sitting in the rain when Cliff drove up. They expected him to be near the coffee pot inside. He was.

Ted smiled as the two detectives approached. "I was gonna call you."

"You see something?" Jake asked.

"That's just it. I haven't seen a thing going on over there for three or four days now." Ted got up and dumped the remnants of his cup in the nearby sink. "The last I saw anyone over there was the day before you guys showed up."

"Besides the van, did you figure out what kind of a car your Italian drove?"

"A Cadillac. A maroon one with a black vinyl top."

Five minutes later, Jake was on the radio calling for Burrows and Lakatos. "Did you get the search warrant for 23789 Opdyke?"

"It's in my hand," Lakatos answered.

"Can you bring it by? Cliff and I want to execute it now."

"Now?" Jake could hear the moan in Jimmy's voice. "It's quitting time."

It took twenty minutes for Burrows and Lakatos to show up. The first thing out of Jimmy's mouth was, "This'll cost you."

Burrows handed the warrant to Cliff. "What are we looking for?"

"Anything to tie this place in with a murder and a kidnapping. And maybe a couple of goons called Rhino and Hands."

A piece of concrete put a hole in the front door window big enough for Cliff to work the lock on the handle and throw the deadbolt. The front door opened up to an office with a desk, two couches, and a small refrigerator. The windows were painted over. Jake hit the switch to turn on the overhead fluorescent lights. The four officers proceeded to check out the building. A door in the back of the office led to the two garage bays. The first bay had remnants of newspapers, tape and paint cans and not much more. The second bay was another area that held two smaller desks and a small restroom in the back. No one was at work.

The next two hours occupied both crews of detectives as they bagged and tagged pieces of newspapers, masking tape, empty beer bottles and paint cans. Three cigarette butts were found clogging a small sewer grate under the bits of paper. It was apparent that the once white van was now navy blue and recently painted in the first garage stall. In that bay, Jake found something interesting: A corner from a plastic package and a piece of metal banding. He had seen something similar before. He bagged and tagged both.

Cliff saw what Jake put in the bag. “Why you baggin’ that?”

“I have hunches too.”

A few partial finger prints were lifted off the desk and refrigerator in the main office. Anything that might indicate who all used the building also made the evidence bags they were gathering. Dust marks remained on the desks where three telephones once were. There wasn’t much more to bag and tag. The ashtrays, the waste baskets, and all the drawers in the three desks were empty. There wasn’t even a notepad or a pencil around.

“Looks like someone knew you were coming,” Jimmy Lakatos said.

Cliff just grunted a response. He knew Michigan Bell, or whoever was the current phone provider, would have a list of the phone calls incoming and outgoing for the place.

Jake was packing the evidence bags in the trunk of their car. “How hard is it to work with the phone company?”

“It’ll take a warrant,” answered Cliff. “But it’s not that hard. Just more paperwork.”

Lakatos and Burrows were in their unit waiting for Jake and Cliff to finish loading the evidence. Lakatos rolled down his window. “On the way in, pull into Rob’s. A couple of burgers and beers will pay for our time and help.”

“Another day,” Cliff said. “We’ve got another couple hours of paperwork ahead of us.”

"We take rain checks," Lakatos said through their open window as Burrows drove off.

———

Saturday and Sunday evenings brought more sitting, watching and waiting, only this time Cliff was in one car and Jake in another. A coin flip had Jake watching Leon Anibal's house while Cliff got to watch Billy Butler. Saturday night was a bust.

Sunday morning came early for Jake. He had three hours sleep before Edie woke him for church. She had to nudge him three times during the Pastor's sermon. His head was dropping on his chest.

Nightfall on Sunday brought Jake another four hours of boredom until his radio came alive. Cliff said he had movement and was loosely following a black Dodge truck. "Not much traffic out here, so I'm trying not to get burned."

"Keep me posted." Jake leaned back in his seat. He already had too much coffee. A light came on in the house he was watching. Leon was starting to stir.

Fifteen minutes later Cliff reported that he had to give up on Butler. He had been driving down residential streets with his lights out to avoid being spotted and nearly hit a pedestrian.

The light went back out in Anibal's house. Jake just sat and watched. A set of headlights broke the emptiness of the night behind him. He scrunched down in his seat. The vehicle slowed, pulling to the curb at the driveway to the house he was watching.

"Cliff! Got your ears on?"

"Go Jake."

"Your package just arrived at my location."

"Heading your way."

A two car tail on the black Dodge pickup heading west out of Pontiac after midnight was much easier. Cliff leapfrogged the truck and when he got in place, Jake would peel off to do the same. The cat and mouse game slowed as the Dodge with Butler and Anibal pulled into the Big Boy Restaurant on M-59 just before US-23. Across the highway Cliff swung into the all-night Shell station while Jake, at a distance, followed the truck into the restaurant's lot. The two men were heading in to the building when Jake turned in and he got a good look at them.

A short radio conversation between the partners had Jake going in to get a couple of coffees to go. The restaurant was half-full with truckers and afternoon shift workers stopping in for an after-midnight meal or an early breakfast.

Jake saw the two men he was interested in being seated in a booth in the back corner as he walked in the door. They were reading menus by the time Jake had his two cups of coffee and had paid for them. He drove over to where Cliff was waiting.

"They're eating."

"Did you get me something?"

"Just coffee." Jake handed the cup to his partner. "Double cream, right?"

Cliff just snatched the cup from Jake, pried the lid off. "You're lucky." It was black, the way he took his coffee.

"Keep an eye on the truck while I grab something to munch on inside." Jake held out a hand. "Give me some cash if you want to eat."

Cliff's five dollar bill got Jake and him some Hostess Twinkies and chocolate cupcakes. When Cliff started to say something, Jake raised his hand. "That's all they had besides jerky."

"Shoulda went in across the street," Cliff lamented as he tore open one of the packages of Twinkies. "Who eats these fucking things?"

"We do when there's not too many options." Jake slid in the jump seat of Cliff's Pontiac. "So what's the plan?" He took a sip on his cup and opened a package of cupcakes.

"Well, they sure in the hell aren't just having breakfast to talk about old times in the middle of the night. We're going to stick with them."

Leon Anibal and Billy Butler worked nights, but only on an occasional weekend. Leon was a quiet, soft spoken man, no more than five feet eight with the arms and shoulders of a gorilla. He was a follower, letting his partner in their midnight enterprise pick the targets. He was there for the bull work. Leon flunked out of high school and tried his hand at a few snatch-and-grab B&Es that didn't quite pan out. He had met Billy Butler in Jackson prison.

Billy Butler's dad had said Billy would never make anything of himself when his son got a dishonorable discharge from the U.S. Navy. He had spent six months in the brig at Treasure Island for a burglary at the base PX on NAS Moffett Field in California prior to being booted by the Navy. Billy was proving his dad right when he ended up in Jackson prison for two years for a couple more B&Es.

Billy was tall and thin, that made him the perfect size for what he had been planning while in jail. When he was paroled he took on a partner and between the two men, had been quite successful going through a roof or two to make a living. Tonight they had stopped for breakfast on their way to a job.

"I'm not really hungry," Leon said as he tossed his menu aside. "You sure about this set up?"

"Relax, will ya?" Billy motioned the waitress over. "Two eggs over easy, toast and bacon. He'll have the same." The waitress topped off their cups and turned for the kitchen.

"I said I wasn't hungry."

"Food will settle your nerves."

"I'm not sure about doing a gun shop."

"A piece of cake." Billy stirred in some cream. "I scoped it out yesterday. It's in the middle of nowhere."

"Yeah, gun shops probably have alarms on everything."

"The windows and doors, yes. Not in the fuckin' roof."

The waitress dropped the food in front of Anibal and Butler, topping off their coffees again before heading to another table.

"Why in the hell did you pick a gun shop?"

"I told you. Sammy steered a guy onto me who wanted some guns. Sammy don't do guns. The guy called me. Twice. He has a buyer for all we bring in." Billy started salting his eggs. "I picked the place. Biggest in the area."

"Can you trust Sammy? Maybe our fence lined you up with a cop."

"Not a chance. The guy—Vito's his name—is legit." Billy took a swig of his coffee. "Eat, Leon." He pointed to the plate of food in front of his partner. "He's too damn short for a cop. Some big-deal Italian. He's the man behind the drugs floating around."

Leon lifted himself half way up. "No drugs. I'm not getting involved in that shit!"

"Relax, man. We're just doin' our normal stuff. No drugs."

Leon settled back down and started on his eggs. "You bring the grappling hook?"

"I tol' you, relax. Everything's in the two duffle bags in the back of the truck. Gloves, the rope ladder, even the new battery operated sawzall we picked up on our last job…" Billy shoved a triangle of toast into his yolks. "…and a couple of empty duffle bags for the loot."

"What about cops?"

"Jeez, man. It's a hick town. We hit it after three when even the law is sleeping. 'sides, in the middle of the night if we see headlights within a mile of us, we'll just pass on the job." Billy ran the last triangle of toast over his plate, and took a bite. "Leon buddy, I got it all figured out."

Forty-five minutes later, the Dodge with Leon Anibal and Billy Butler was taking the Owen Road exit off of US-23.

"I'll pass them by and make a U-turn up the road," Cliff said into his mic.

Jake double clicked his to acknowledge Cliff's transmission and loosely followed the Dodge. Anibal and Butler were heading east. Jake pulled into a Clark Station, paused, then dropped off the ramp. The mic's cord was strung across his lap. The taillights on the pickup were a quarter of a mile ahead. He was trying to keep the lights in view. Jake whispered under his breath: "Where you at, partner?"

Cliff must have read his mind as Jake's radio came alive. "I'm heading east on Silver Lake Road north of you. You going east?"

Jake double clicked his mic, but saw the road angled to the left. "They're heading into town," he paused. "What town we in anyway?"

"Fenton." Cliff was going about ninety as he said it.

"Going left. I've got to drop them or they'll burn me." Jake slowed, putting more distance between him and the Dodge. There was no one else on the road heading in either direction.

Luck was with Cliff as he hit Leroy Street. The Dodge pickup was passing the corner, still heading north. Cliff turned south very slowly as he spoke into his mic. "Go north on Leroy, Jake."

"Making the turn, heading north."

"Jake, I'm guessing. There's a big-time gun shop on the north end of town. That may be their target."

"You're guessing?"

"What the hell else can I do? You can shoot a cannon down these streets and not hit anything." Cliff made a U-turn and parked, waiting for Jake to catch up.

Thirty seconds later Jake saw taillights flash twice. He pulled in behind his partner, jumped out and ran up to the passenger's side and slid in. Cliff was on the radio, putting the car in drive and started to move.

"Station Three?"

"Three, go ahead."

"This is Bush and Roberts, the 300 detectives. Can you get ahold of whoever has the City of Fenton and tell them we're visiting?"

"That's Genesee County. What you doin' way up there?"

Two more radio transmissions had the Fenton City PD and the Genesee County Sheriff notified. As Cliff drove, he filled Jake in on the place just north of town called Guns Galore. He had been in there a few times looking for some wad-cutters for his .357. "Best prices in the area."

"And you think Anibal and Butler have it in their sights?"

"They're burglars. Yes, I'm guessing, but beyond us, there's nothing. Just lakes and woods." He took a left on a dirt road. "I think the place is just up the road. We'll walk."

It took Jake two minutes to catch up to his partner.

"Where've you been?"

"I called dispatch to let the locals know a couple of dicks would be at Guns Galore."

Jake and Cliff broke into a trot. The sign at Leroy said they were on Pineview.

"Smart move, but I never liked being called a 'dick,'" Cliff said.

"What are you?"

"A dick sergeant." Cliff pointed to the road. "Gun shop's on the other side."

"How far?"

Cliff didn't answer, just kept trotting.

It turned out that the building was at least a quarter of a mile up the road. There was a patch of woods before the parking lot for the gun store. A dim light illuminated the inside the shop and was showing through the barred windows on the front and side. The night was quiet except for the tree frogs singing at a distant swamp. Jake took the lead, inching along the edge of the lot toward the back of the building. They caught their breath as they picked their way keeping close to the trees. Jake stopped.

Cliff bumped into his partner. "What the fuck?"

"Listen." Jake put his arm out, holding Cliff in place. "You didn't hear it?"

"I hear frogs."

"Shh!" Jake took two steps. "Back of the building." He took another step. "Did you bring a flashlight?"

"No. You?"

Jake just shook his head. On the positive side, Guns Galore was a white cinder-block building and Jake and Cliff's eyes had adjusted to the darkness.

A beam of light spilled from the roof on the back of the building shining down on a figure climbing.

"Hurry Billy!"

Jake poked Cliff. "That's what I heard. Voices."

Screeching tires broke the quiet darkness. Two sets of headlights were swinging into the parking lot spraying gravel. Cops. One, a county car, the other, a city car. A uniformed officer jumped out of each.

"They're around back," yelled Cliff as he and Jake broke into a run with guns drawn.

Chapter Twenty-four

Monday morning had Jake making coffee. The NFB Session's grease board had Mangold and Brooks supplying the sweets that morning. Half of the guys complained when they brought in bagels and two spreads to go with them. That was until they tasted them. George Mangold was a good Jewish boy who had an in at Detroit's Eastern Market. His wife's mother ran the bakery.

Brooks talked about the string of lake-front home burglaries they were working on. The perpetrators would eat only certain kinds of food found in the house, like Ritz crackers, salami, and Budweiser.

"Must be Machelski and Popp pullin' your jobs," called out Burrows. "That's their standard every-day lunch."

Laughter filled the DB until the LT interrupted with, "What part of 'No Fuckin' Bullshit' don't you understand?"

Burrows shrugged as he blushed a bit. "Check the crumbs on the floor of their car. I rest my case."

"Lakatos, what do you and the comic have going?" Leicht asked.

"Nothing big, boss. Someone's stealing the mail out of the boxes on Old Pontiac Trail."

Roberts ended the session talking about the white van with the sign for the painting company possibly being navy blue and the sudden closure of the building on Opdyke Road.

Cliff and Jake also mentioned the arrests made on the attempt B&E at Guns Galore before the session broke up.

"Well, one less ball to juggle," Cliff said out as he walked with his empty cup toward the coffee pot.

"That's what you think. Leicht put two more beefs on our desks. He must have come in over the weekend."

"Just so you know, Jake, the first thing I'm going to do this morning is hit the prosecutor's office and get a warrant, then go see Ma Bell." He poured a coffee for himself. "How about you tying up any loose ends with Anibal and Butler?"

Cliff, sipping on his coffee, walked back to his desk and thumbed through the two folders Jake had mentioned. He dropped them back on Jake's desk. "These can wait. Small time shit. We have a murder to solve."

"Do you need me to go with you?"

"No. Hit the phones and see if the surrounding counties have any roof-job B&Es that we can link to those guys."

"I still can't figure out why the guy in Northville ratted them out."

"Might be a simple pay back." Cliff was putting on his sport coat, holding the file for the paint shop under an arm while he struggled getting in his other arm. "Lotta stuff goes on in prison. He might have owed them for something." Cliff took a couple of steps and turned. "Your man might have been their bitch."

"You think?"

Cliff shrugged his shoulders. "It'd be a damn good reason to drop a dime on someone."

Billy Butler and Leon Anibal were being held in the Genesee County Jail for the Fenton PD for the attempted B&E at Guns Galore and possession of burglar tools. Warrants were also being drawn up charging them for the six roof-top burglaries in Oakland County.

Jake was already on the phone as his partner left. It was common for one detective to go in one direction, while the other went a separate way as long as there'd be no apparent danger for either of them. Cliff could handle getting a warrant and Jake could handle the phone.

Three hours later his phone rang. "Sheriff's Department. Jake Bush here."

It was his partner. "Step outside; we're doin' lunch." Cliff was not one for long conversations.

They went to the old Pontiac Hotel. Cliff liked their pizza and dimly lit dining room. "Any luck on the phone?" He asked as they slid into a back booth.

Jake filled him in on two possible cases in Livingston County and another in Washtenaw. "Macomb County said they'd get back to me."

Cliff must have called ahead because a hot extra-large pie soon followed them to their table. The hotel only had Coke on tap, so Jake settled for water. "How'd you make out with the warrant?"

"I had to wait in line, then in and out. Michigan Bell's been served. They said they'd need at least a couple of days to pull the records together. The account for the paint shop was opened under a Percy Cabala's name." Cliff slid three slices of pizza onto a plate. "I'll run that name when we get back to the office."

The name, Percy Cabala, was a dead end. He had no record with the county or the state. Jake phoned the county clerk's office looking to see if a Percy Cabala owned property within the county. He was told they'd call back.

Fifteen minutes later, Jake's phone rang. It wasn't the county, it was the lab.

"This is Woods. I just wanted you to know in the folds of that bit of plastic package you sent over we hit pay dirt. There were minute traces of heroin."

"Anything else?"

"We're still running the partial prints. I'll get back to you.

I thought you'd want to know about the narcotics."

Jake thanked the lab man. Cliff was waiting to see if his partner got anything useful. "Well?"

"Looks like the paint shop was also dealing in drugs." Jake told him about the traces of heroin found in the folds of a piece of plastic he had tagged as evidence from there. "They cleaned the place up, but not good enough. I remembered some plastic packages that were similar to what I found at a drug bust in Detroit."

"I kinda figured as much when Vogtmann said the two goons threatened him at the Novi Hotel."

"All we have to do is find out who this Cabala guy is."

Cliff smiled. "A trip across the street to circuit court might give you that answer. They keep records on people changing their names."

Jake hadn't thought of that, but that's why he had a partner. "If it'd only be that easy." Jake put on his sport coat and headed out the door.

Two hours later, Jake had the name of Vito Calabrese. Percy Cabala had officially changed his name on August 14th, 1973. He ran the name through the Secretary of State's office, then through the state's criminal records division. Vito Calabrese had a clean driving record and one arrest in Novi on a bookmaking charge back in 1974. He hadn't been arrested since. The file showed that he had pled guilty and paid a fine. The arrest meant they had his prints on file.

Jake's phone rang just as he was taking off his coat the next morning. It was Cliff. He was at Michigan Bell. No sooner than he hung up, it rang again. This time it was the Fenton City PD. They wanted either him or his partner at the Genesee County Courthouse for a preliminary hearing on Leon Anibal and Billy Butler. He looked at his watch. He had a half hour to make the hearing. Jake threw a note on Cliff's desk and grabbed a set of keys for one of the pool cars.

Just as it had been in Detroit, Jake got to the court house

and waited. The wheels of justice were moving slowly in Genesee County; the presiding judge was an hour and a half late. Abel Brant, the county prosecutor, went over the arrest three different times with Jake. The prosecutor blushed a bit when Jake asked if the judge was even in the building. Jake knew, no matter what, the officers, the lawyers and everyone involved in a case had better be there at the assigned time or face contempt charges when the gavel sounded bringing court into session.

Jake knew judges set their own hours. He laughed to himself when he thought back to the many hours he had spent in Detroit Recorder's Court—waiting. He remembered a judge named Callahan spent Tuesday mornings playing a few games of euchre before starting on the day's cases. Jake hated Tuesday court dates in Detroit.

By 1 p.m., Jake was back in his office. He had picked up a sandwich at a Jewish deli just down the street from the courthouse. His desk was covered by stacks of bi-fold printed pages about eighteen inches wide with holes on both perforated edges. Cliff had his nose in one of their files at his desk.

"What's this?" Jake asked, pointing to the stack nearly a foot thick.

"Some new computer print-outs from Ma Bell. Three months of records for the phones at the paint shop." Cliff looked over the top of the file he was reading. "How'd things go up north?"

"Both bound over for trial and bail was set."

"Good." He leaned forward, looking at Jake's sandwich. "Did you get me something?"

Jake didn't answer, he just unwrapped the Pastrami and cheese on a huge rye Kaiser roll. It had been cut in two. "Get a paper towel or something. I'll share." Jake dug deep into his pocket for his Case knife and cut the accompanying six inch dill pickle in half. "You're on your own with a drink." He popped the cap on a sixteen ounce Pepsi. "I won't share this."

Cliff just shrugged as he bit into his half a sandwich. "What the hell you got in here?" He was holding a piece of a bell pepper between his fingers.

"Who knows? I just told the guy to make me a sandwich like he was making it for himself."

"Peppers don't agree with me."

"When you buy the sandwich, you can choose what's on it." Jake pointed to the stack of papers on his desk. "What we got here?"

"Records of the inbound and outbound calls at the paint shop. Then there's reverse directories on the numbers. One by address; the other by name."

Ten minutes later, Cliff started to wad up the brown paper towels he had been using for a plate. He must have decided the bell pepper wasn't going to hurt him since Jake saw only a few globs of mustard, mayo and crumbs on the make-shift plate. "By the way, I'm going out to talk to the complainants on our two new cases. See if you can find out anything useful to us in those records."

Jake thumbed the edges of the stack of paper. "You're not going to help?"

"Not today. That'd be like reading the white pages." Cliff smiled, put on his coat and grabbed the two new files off his desk. "I'll be back."

"You've got mustard on the side of your mouth." Jake tossed a wadded up napkin at his partner.

"Oh, I almost forgot. Thanks." The back door to the bureau parking lot was swinging closed as Cliff said it.

Jake went to work on the computer sheets from Michigan Bell. He pulled on the top one and found that they flowed continuously, folding out like an accordion. There were numerous pages for each of the three phone numbers assigned to All-American Painting Company.

At a glance, Jake could see that there were nine columns on each row indicating a time and the number and whether it was inbound or outbound. All the stacks started with the most recent date the phones were in use. The last activity listed for any of the numbers was dated June 4, 1979, at 0945 hours. The phone company was using military time. He glanced at the calendar on the wall, remembering that it was on the 5th they had first talked to Ted Easton at the lawn mower place. The print out confirmed what Ted Senior had said about not seeing any activity since the day before he and Cliff showed up at the mower shop.

Ninety-five percent of the calls were incoming on the first two numbers. The date logged for their last usage was June 3, a Sunday and the incoming calls ceased around 2000 hours or 8 p.m. Jake remembered his cousin's twins answering two phones on a Sunday morning. It was apparent that these two phones for the painting company were for a bookmaking operation. He knew his cousin was taking bets on football games, but people bet on everything. It was baseball season and most Sunday baseball games were day games. He thought that there might even be some horse tracks operating on Sundays. He wasn't sure on horse racing. That was something he'd have to check with Cliff on.

Jake had planned on starting with the pile for the number 517-855-1996. It was the last phone used. That number had an equal balance of incoming and outgoing calls, but his eyes moved to the stack he had not looked at sitting on the far edge of his desk. Jake pulled them over and noted that the pages were a reverse directory for outgoing and incoming calls. These pages were simpler; they were indexed by phone number with only four columns for each row. The first column listed the date, the second was the phone number; the third gave the address for that number, and the final column, a name assigned to the number.

Numbers, numbers and more numbers were rattling through Jake's brain for over two hours, trying to make heads or tails out of the computer print-outs. He needed to take a break and go for a walk. Cliff was right. It was like reading a phone book.

He flipped to the *out* sign next to his name on the board next to Leicht's office and walked to the 7-Eleven two blocks away. He grabbed a Pepsi out of one of the eight foot refrigerators lining the back wall. *No wonder Cliff left me with the paperwork.* He shrugged, grabbed a second bottle and carried both back to the bureau. They had a small college dorm fridge near the coffee pot for his back-up drink. It was time to get back to the real drudgery of detective work.

Jake's phone was ringing as he got to his desk. "Grab a car and meet me at Sylvia's place." It was Cliff.

"What's up?"

"It's Friday."

Jake ran to the row of pool cars. It was just after 4 p.m. He was at least ten minutes away from the women's apartment building.

On his first pass, Jake spotted Cliff sitting in their normal ride. He parked, walked and half block and slid in beside him. "What's up?"

"Another bank. This one in Troy. A black Dodge was seen picking up the robber."

"I saw the light blue Merc."

"Yeah. Grace's Dodge is gone."

"What time was the hold-up?"

"Three forty-five. If they're going to make it to work, they should show up anytime now."

They never showed. At five, Cliff gave it up. He told Jake he'd see him at the office after slipping by Rob's to see if they were at work.

Jake was at his desk working on the Ma Bell print-outs when Cliff came in. "Well?" Jake asked.

"Both at work. Miniskirts and wide smiles." He walked over to the coffee pot and filled his cup.

"The black Dodge Dart?"

"In Rob's lot."

"Maybe you're playing the wrong hunch?" Jake walked over and flipped the switches to turn the burners off under the coffee pots. "You know what you're drinking's gotta be a half day old."

"Tastes good to me." Cliff looked up at the clock. "I'm heading home."

"I'll be right behind you." Jake looked at the five piles of Ma Bell sheets. "I want to check one more thing on these." He pointed toward his desk.

"They'll keep 'til Monday," Cliff said.

"I know."

Jake pulled over the pile for the number 517-855-1996, then grabbed the one for the reverse directory. The last number called on June 4th was for a place called U-Store on Groesbeck Highway in Warren. He rummaged through his desk and found a yellow highlight marker and highlighted the entry. He couldn't wait until Monday, so he dialed the number.

On the third ring it was picked up. "U-Store-Em, can I help you?" It was a female voice.

Jake didn't identify himself as a police officer, wanting to remain anonymous for the time being. His main interest was what type of business he was calling. As he figured, it was a locked storage facility, and he asked questions about sizes, rates, etc.

"I'm sorry, sir. This is an answering service. Can you give me your name and number and I will have the owner call you on Monday morning?"

"Can I just call back Monday using this number and get the owner?"

"Yes sir, you can, but I can save you the trouble…"

"No trouble. I'll just call back on Monday," he interrupted and hung up.

Jake tossed the print-out on his desk. It could wait until Monday.

Chapter Twenty-five

Jake called Edie before leaving the bureau, telling her he was on his way. His mind was churning. Monday morning was a long way off. The highlighted address on Groesbeck Highway was stuck in his mind along with Cliff's words from the day before: "We've got a murder to solve."

Groesbeck Highway, more familiarly called M-97, was a road he had traveled many times. Jake's dad, Ted, worked just off M-97 on Nine Mile at Bundy Tubing and it bordered some swampy land just to the west where, as a kid, Jake had built rafts with his buddies and tried his first cigarette. Now all had changed. The swamps were filled and if there wasn't something already there, a new business was being built.

Instead of heading home, he headed southeast. *Edie'd understand.*

Cliff went in past the desk sergeant and waved as he headed toward the DB. He had stopped for gas a half mile down Telegraph and filled up at a self-serve station. He went in to pay and remembered he had taken out his wallet to add some of his business cards. "Shit!"

He had to leave his badge at the gas station to insure his return. "I'll be right back with my wallet," he told the clerk. "If I'm not, you can be a detective sergeant on the Oakland

County Sheriff's Department."

"You gotta be one hell of a detective," the young black station attendant said as he looked at the star on its leather badge holder that Cliff had pulled off of his belt before bolting out the door.

Back at his desk, Cliff went straight to his wallet and sheepishly looked around to make sure no one was watching. He caught the eye of the county worker mopping the floor, waved and said, "Later, Bill."

Bill didn't even look his way; he was swaying to the music that was being piped in through his earphones.

Jake's phone rang. Cliff hesitated, then on the fourth ring, picked it up. "Detective Bureau, this is Roberts."

"This is Jake's wife, Edie. Is he still there?"

"No, he left a while ago."

"That's strange. He called and said he was on his way home. He should have been here by now. I thought something might have come up."

"He probably stopped for milk or bread."

"Maybe, but… I shouldn't have bothered you." She clicked off.

Probably stopped for gas and forgot his wallet. Cliff chuckled to himself and started to leave, then walked back to Jake's desk. On the top of the stack of papers, he saw the yellow highlighted address. *Yeah, that'd be Jake.* He copied the address on a notebook he pulled from his breast pocket. It was a good thing that the Shell station was on the way he needed to go. Cliff wanted his badge back.

Jake was hitting the peak of rush hour traffic, but was in no hurry. He and Edie and the boys had a weekend planned visiting some of her family to the north in Hillman. He thought about calling but didn't. He just wanted to see the lay of the land around the storage place.

He was deep into Macomb County, jumping onto I-696 and getting off at the M-97 exit. M-97 was clogged with Detroiters heading northeast from the city and those working in the small shops up toward Mt. Clemens and those heading back toward Warren or even Detroit. He checked the gauge on his pickup, he needed to stop. At a Gulf station he filled up and checked his oil. His '69 Ford was starting to use a quart every now and then. *One of these days I'll have to replace the old girl.*

He spotted a pay phone and called home. Edie was not too happy. She had planned a nice pot roast and the boys were starting to get on each other's nerves. "Sorry, I'm getting too involved with a case. Feed the boys and I'll be home in an hour or so."

Jake caught an address and knew he was close. The storage place was on the east side of the highway. He slowed seeing three rows of long garage-like buildings behind a fenced-in area. They were white with dark brown overhead doors. On each side there were at least fifteen garage doors. He noticed the front gate was open as he went by. A yellow sign with black lettering read: U-Store-Em with a phone number underneath. There was a paved road between each of the long buildings. Jake passed the third and last building that was a part of the storage business and saw a dark blue van backed up to an open overhead door.

Fuck!

Jake kept driving until he could flip a U-turn in a dentist's office parking lot. With his left arm he unconsciously put a little pressure on the bulge of his shoulder holster. The Smith and Wesson .357 was resting comfortably in place. He knew he had two speed-loaders in a pouch on the right side of his belt. He didn't have time to go somewhere to call the Warren PD. He needed to check out the navy blue van that just happened to be at the storage place—the last phone number called from the paint shop—a van that might be involved in drugs, a kidnapping and possibly a murder.

Too many coincidences.

A pang of unease went through Jake for a second. He didn't know if there'd be two or more guys, but he had to check it out.

Cliff saw the long row of storage sheds, the yellow sign and the rusty quarter-panels on Jake's white 1969 Ford pickup as it turned into the open gate. Before he could make a U-turn, he spotted the navy blue van. *Fuckin' cowboy!* Cliff felt for his own magnum with his left elbow. He turned around at the first break in traffic and made a right into the storage business's lot. Jake was going across the front of the lot, heading to the end row and the blue van. Cliff drove between the first and second row separating the long storage building, hoping there was a driveway around the back end. There wasn't. The driveways were one-way in and the same way out. A two-foot wide gravel walkway separated the buildings from the twelve-foot cyclone fence that ran around the perimeter of the storage facility.

Cliff broke into a run along the fence, drawing his pistol. As he turned around the corner of the building, he spotted Jake talking to a man and a woman. He skidded to a halt and holstered his gun.

Jake looked up when he heard the crunch of gravel. "Cliff, what are you doing here?"

Cliff slowly walked toward Jake, the blue van and the couple. "I could ask you the same question." He started to turn back toward his car and stopped, pointing at his partner. "Jake, meet me at the first coffee shop you see as you head for home. We need to talk." Cliff was pointing his right index finger with the thumb erect. That was a habit Jake noticed his partner having when he was doing some serious talking to someone; just like he was pointing a make-believe gun.

"There's a Biff's that I passed."

"Then see you there." Again, the finger point, thumb erect.

What the next half hour amounted to was a good old-fashioned ass chewing. Jake had no recourse, but to take it all in. It was not just that Clifford Roberts was senior detective, but that he was right. Had Jake run into Rhino and

Hands in a van at the storage place, all hell would have broken loose. Two ex-cons, who may have killed one man and dumped his body in Orchard Lake would not have simply raised their hands when Jake flashed his badge.

"I'd be going to your funeral," Cliff had said for the third time. "And I hate funerals, especially when they tell me to put on my uniform for the fuckin' service."

Cliff was right. Luck had been on his side when he approached the navy blue van and found Mr. and Mrs. Anderson putting some of their furniture in storage while they looked for another apartment to rent.

Jake tried to make light of the discussion. "You're sounding like Leicht using 'fuck' as an adjective."

"No! I'm using it 'cause I'm pissed. From now on, no more playing Lone Ranger. It's me and you. We are partners. Somebody shoots at you, I want to be there shooting back."

"I was just going to look at the place…"

"Then why did you go talk to the people with the blue van?"

"Because…"

"Because you are a cop. You were playing a hunch and it could have cost you," Cliff's right index finger shot out with the thumb up, "and I'd be watching your ass being zipped up in a body bag."

Jake checked his watch. "Your verbal reprimand is duly noted. Can I go now? My wife is expecting me."

"She's the reason I showed up."

"She is?"

"Yes. She called looking for you. I saw the highlighted address. The rest is history."

"Looks like I'm in for another ass chewing when I get home." Jake stood to leave. He paused, looking into his partner's eyes. "Thanks for backing me up, partner. I was a bit concerned when I saw the blue van."

"I figured as much. Go home and don't let her beat on you too much." Cliff threw a five on the table to cover the booth rental. They never ordered anything. "Hey Jake…"

"Yeah?"

"Just so you know, I'd a done the same thing." Again, the make-believe gun pointing toward Jake. Jake thought he saw a slight smile, but knew Cliff never smiled.

Edie had kept Jake's supper warm in the oven. She didn't say a thing. The silence was deafening. "Talk to me," Jake said as he pushed out her chair with his foot.

Edie sat, not saying a thing. A tear slowly descended down her right cheek. She reached for Jake's hand.

"I know I should have called."

"I was worried. That's why I called your office." She started to get up. Jake grabbed her hand. "I'll make us some tea."

"I'll try not to worry you again."

"As long as you're wearing a badge, I'll worry."

"You'll get gray hair."

A tear stopped in the middle of her left cheek as she smiled. "I already have gray hair."

"No you don't." He turned her chin with his finger, looking at each side.

"It's on the top where I part it. The stuff in a bottle covers a lot."

"How long have you been hiding the gray?"

"Since I fell in love with you." Edie stood on her toes, pulling his face close to hers. She kissed him.

"Where are the boys?"

"At the movies with the neighbor and his kids." She glanced at the clock over the stove. "You've got about a half hour."

Jake smiled. His supper was getting cold, but his wife wanted a thorough apology and he wanted to thank her for loving him.

Chapter Twenty-six

Sylvia talked as Grace stuffed a suitcase. "That was a hell of an idea, Squeak, us getting another apartment.

"Don't call me Squeak!" She latched the suitcase after putting in the last of the men's clothing they had picked up at the Goodwill Store a couple of months before. "I don't like it."

"Well, you are just a little squeak of a thing." She gave Grace a little poke with her index finger. "Don't take things so serious all the time. Laugh. Have fun."

"I get enough of the snide remarks at Rob's, like 'when you gonna grow some tits little girl?' or, 'you sure you're old enough to work in a bar?' "

"Forget it," Sylvia sighed. "All I'm trying to say is you had a great idea with the other place. A basement apartment. No stairs. In and out with no prying eyes."

"We had to come up with something. That old drunk in number four asked me which one of the guys I was screwing, the broad chested one or the skinny guy."

Sylvia laughed. "Yeah, two chicks renting a place and strange men coming and going. We've got too many nosey neighbors here." She grabbed the full suitcase. "Let me get this, Squ… Grace. Would ya get the door for me?"

It had been two weeks since Grace came up with the

basement apartment on Dixie Highway near Silver Lake Road. She found it a week before they had hit their last bank. That was the fourth bank they held up and were talking about maybe pushing their luck. Sylvia missed North Dakota and had half talked Grace into going in on a ranch with her—after Grace had a little silicon surgery of course. They had already accumulated over thirty-five thousand dollars. Their goal was a hundred.

———

Jake could smell coffee as he pushed through the door to the DB. Cliff was back at his desk that faced the coffee pot and the door. Jake noticed the pot was half empty, poured a cup for himself and called to his partner. “Need a warm up?”

“I’m good.” The answer came without Cliff looking up from what he was engrossed in.

“Two questions. Are you trying to take over my coffee job?” Jake placed his cup on his desk and slipped out of his sport coat. “And what brought you in so early?”

“You can start getting here a little earlier so I won’t have to do your job.”

Jake checked his watch, then the clock on the back wall. It was 7:06. “I know; your girlfriend kicked you outta bed.”

“Wrong.” Cliff nudged the papers he had been looking over toward his partner. “Did you see this phone number?” Cliff had done his own highlighting on one of the sheets of out-going calls made from the former paint shop.

Jake pulled the page a little closer and the date of the call. “I never got that far.” He looked a question at Cliff.

Cliff slid out of his chair and sauntered up toward the Bunn machine. He half-turned, giving his finger point. “Check a page or two up from that call. The number is listed three times. The first time outgoing, and twice incoming. The name tied to that number is someone named Benedict Squires.”

The only thing heard was the clock ticking for a few

seconds. "Our Ben Squires?" Jake asked as he pushed the print-out file back onto Cliff's desk.

Cliff shrugged, moving toward the coffee machine. "The clerk's getting me the department roster. This guy might have been calling other deputies too." He returned with a fresh cup of coffee and told Jake about coming in early because he thought the lists were the key to making some progress on the guys in the van and whoever was behind what looked like a pretty big operation.

"The bookmaking might have been a start to something that grew into whatever it is." Cliff took his chair, leaning back and taking a swig from his cup. "When I was checking the list of outgoing calls against the reverse directory the Squires name came up. I went to the incoming calls and see he called the paint shop back after his house got a call—twice. The second call from him was a day before they shut it down."

Jake reached for the list, but Cliff had already picked it up. "Do you know Squires? I can barely put a face on him."

"Somewhat." Jake proceeded to tell Cliff what he knew about the one-time Inkster and Northville Police officer who was now one of them. "Kaminski and Williams know a bit about him too. You might want to talk to them since I'm biased."

Cliff smiled, remembering a guy or two he did not like working with. "You mentioned a bookie that he was friends with in Northville. Got a name?"

Jake pondered a minute, trying to remember his conversation with the Northville cop. "Vito, if I remember right."

"Bingo!" Cliff started dialing his phone. "There's a guy who owns some storage sheds that we need to talk to." Minutes later, he stuck his head in the LT's office to beg off of the NFB Session. He and Jake had work to do.

Bill Smillie, the owner of U-Store-Em said he'd meet the officers at his facility. He worked out of his home on Federal in Warren, “Just down from the Catholic church,” Bill had said. Cliff told him to bring the keys and books for his storage units. Cliff told Jake that he thought Smillie mentioned the church to sound upstanding or righteous.

“The name, Smillie, rings a bell.” Cliff was thinking as he drove, heading toward the City of Warren and M-97. Ten minutes of silence followed. “Now I remember. There was a string of burglaries we made a bust on in early ‘67.” He paused. “Don’t hold me to the year. A guy named Smillie, pronounced like a smiley face. He was their fence. You can’t forget a last name like that. They were trying to cut a deal.”

“Did you check him out?”

“We were too late. He ran a pawn shop in your old bailiwick—Detroit. It was torched during the riot.”

“If it’s the same guy, maybe he wasn’t totally put out of business.”

“Yeah, if it’s the same guy.”

“If he demands to see our warrant, he might be.” Jake added.

“Good point. One of us can sit with him while we get the Warren PD involved and get a warrant.” Cliff made a turn, heading southwest down M-97. “The reality is we do need a warrant to make this all nice and legal.”

“I was thinking the same thing.” Jake snickered a bit. “By the way, I took the liberty of calling a buddy of mine who works in Warren.”

“You did? When?”

“This morning before I left for work. He’s a detective. He and his partner will meet us there at ten. He said he’d have a warrant with him.”

“How in the hell’s he going to do that?”

“His older brother is the Prosecuting Attorney in Macomb County. I gave him what info we had and told him there’s probable cause to link it to a murder, kidnapping and drugs.” Jake smiled. “We worked together in Number Thirteen way back when. Said he could pull some strings for us.”

Cliff’s hand became his make-believe gun and pointed it

at Jake. "Smart thinking."

Jake thought he heard a chuckle and leaned forward to see if Cliff was smiling. He wasn't.

Cliff continued. "Maybe that's why I made the coffee this morning—other than you make it too damn weak. Coffee should wake you up, not put you to sleep." Cliff took his foot of the gas and coasted for the changing light at Ten Mile. "What made you call your buddy?"

"Knew we'd need a warrant, and knew damn well you and I don't want these guys walking on some bullshit technicality."

Jake watched Bill Smillie slowly unfold his body out of a red Chevy pickup as they drove into the storage facility. He was all of forty-five, maybe even fifty, 250 pounds, well over six feet tall with about a 54 inch chest. The man reached back into his truck and pulled out a cane. Smillie wore a white tee shirt and well-worn dark blue bib overalls, but no hat. As he approached their plain-wrapped Chevrolet, Jake could see he needed the cane to walk. The detectives slid out of their car.

Cliff badged him as he started to talk. "You Mr. Smillie?"

"Yup."

Cliff said that they were with the Oakland County Sheriff's Department.

"Oakland County, eh. What brings you here?"

"We're following up on someone who left our place in a hurry." Cliff reached into his coat pocket, pulling out his small spiral notebook and leafed through it. "You rent one of your units to someone named Cabala or Calabrese?"

Smillie was carrying a three-ring binder. Before he opened it, he asked, "On what date?"

Jake looked at his partner. Bill Smillie wasn't so much worried about a warrant, just wanted a place to start looking.

"Around the first of the month," Jake answered as he flipped through his own notebook and found the page with the lawn tractor guy's name on it. "The fourth, to be more specific."

Smillie handed Jake his cane to hold. "Got it right here." He pulled a sheet out of the back of the binder. "Vito Calabrese, in on the fourth of June. Rented two units. 229 and 230." He closed his book and took out a stub of a cigar from the big pocket in the middle of the bib on his coveralls. "They came in early afternoon. Two vehicles. One fancy high-dollar outfit and a dark van." Smillie started going through his pockets, looking for a light. Cliff tossed him a matchbook. "Thanks." He puffed the stub to life. "The one guy, Vito, or whatever you said his name was, paid for six months in hundred dollar bills. He stuck around and shot the shit with me while the two apes in the van made a couple of more runs."

"Can we have a quick look in the units you rented?" Cliff asked.

"Can't—unless you have a warrant." Smillie's eyebrows lifted, as if hoping the detectives did. "I signed a contract with the guy. Here, I'll show it to you." He showed the paper he pulled from behind a flap in the back of the book. It was made out to Vito Calabrese. "I promise complete security when I rent a place out. All my customers get a key to the gate and a key to what they rent."

"The warrant's on the way." Jake said. He checked his watch. "It'll be here in a half hour or so."

"So we wait. I don't mean to be uncooperative, but…" He looked around at his units. "I have rules, both for those who rent from me and things I can guarantee, like their privacy."

"I can understand that," Cliff said. "So we wait."

"One of these days I'll learn. A cup of coffee would be nice about now." Smille flicked the hot ash off his cigar and put it back in his pocket. "Maybe I should turn Unit 101 into an office."

Jake offered to go for a ride up the road to Biff's. Both Smillie and Cliff liked that idea. He got coffees to go and some cinnamon rolls that were strategically placed by the register. *Bait.* Jake loved cinnamon rolls, so he grabbed three.

Over coffee and rolls on the hood of the red pickup Cliff asked about whether Bill owned a pawn shop in Detroit at one time. Bill said it was a cousin; one that was doing three years for reopening another on Van Dyke and taking in more than what was legal.

Jake smiled at the man's story. He too had a cousin who dabbled in some shady deals. It hadn't yet gotten through the family grape-vine via any of his aunts that Ron had been caught, so he might still be running his bookmaking operation. He understood. *You can't pick your relatives.*

At 10:16 a plain-wrapped Chrysler pulled into the storage lot. Jake spotted the toothy smile on Jimmy Mulligan's face behind the wheel, one he hadn't seen since 1965. The car barely came to a stop when Jimmy jumped out. "Yep, the Polack needs my help again."

Jake noticed Jim's red hair had turned light gray, but the smile was the same. His freckles had faded over time and the crow's feet next to his eyes were more distinct. "Save your Irish blarney for another day. Did you bring the warrant?" Mulligan was wearing a dark green blazer with his family coat of arms on the left breast pocket.

"Jake, have I ever let you down?"

"Once. When you wouldn't move to TMU with me."

"Ah, the lad missed me." Mulligan looked around at the rest of the group, smiling broadly, as if he was there to entertain them.

Jake introduced Detective James Mulligan to Cliff and Bill Smillie while Mulligan nodded toward his partner. "This is Koz."

"The name's Bill Kozelczewski," said the cop in the passenger seat.

"See why I call him Koz?"

"Right this way guys," Smillie waved his head, indicating where he was leading the four officers. "Last two on the left." They walked toward the south side and far end of the second row in the storage yard. They took their time.

Smillie was struggling. He needed the cane. That was for sure. He mentioned Korea and a bit of shrapnel in his lower back as they followed behind.

Smillie hadn't spent more than a second glancing at the court order Mulligan had unfolded and flashed as they walked. He was too busy fumbling through a big ring of keys. The Macomb County logo and seal was all he seemed interested in.

He put the key into the first overhead door he stopped at, turned the handle and lifted. The spring-loaded door screeched on its rails as it rose. The concrete floor was bare. "What the hell?" He repeated unlocking the second door and pulled. The second bay, a twin 15 by 15 foot room with a 10 foot ceiling was empty too.

Bill Smillie backed up, looked at the numbers over the doors to make sure and rechecked the rental papers. "These are the two he rented. And like I said, he paid for 6 months." He scratched his head. "I know I watched them unload some stuff in the first one, and saw the van come back with a couple more loads."

Cliff peered in both openings. "What did you see them unload?"

"Boxes. Big cardboard boxes and some stuff wrapped in plastic."

Jake moved into the first bay. He pointed with his toe at a cigarette butt in a corner. "It's not totally empty."

Mulligan's voice rang out. "Jezus Christ, Jake. It cost me breakfast to get my brother up early to get you the warrant. All for a cigarette butt?" He turned. "Come on, Koz. We've got work to do." He handed Jake the paper. Jake just shrugged.

"Call me if you need anything else." Mulligan winked and walked back to his car. Koz followed.

Jake and Cliff spent the next hour going over the empty storage bays. The only thing that Vito and his men left undone was to sweep the bays after moving what had been there at one time. Jake collected five smashed cigarette butts; three in 229 and two in 230. They were bagged and tagged. Jake spotted an empty package of *Camels* lodged in the base of the cyclone fence that ran next to the last bay. He picked it up with his pen through the torn off end. "Never know if there are prints on cellophane," he said.

Cliff just nodded.

They had high hopes of a bay or two holding some dope and maybe something else that would lead them to Hands, Rhino and Vito. They essentially had nothing.

Jake thanked Bill Smillie for his time and cooperation. Cliff gave him his card. "Call me if you hear from Vito or anyone else about these two units."

The three of them were walking back to where they parked their vehicles. "He gave me three hundred dollars. Now I can't rent them for 6 months," Smillie mumbled.

Jake stopped walking. "Do you still have those hundred dollar bills?"

"They're in the truck." He looked dismayed. "You're not going to take them, are you?"

"I'll give you a receipt. You'll get them back after we run them for prints."

The ride back to Oakland County was quiet. Jake finally broke the silence. "You know, the only thing we are going to find out with the butts and the prints is that we were on the right trail."

"Yep."

"We're still going to have to track them down."

"Uh-huh."

"Well, at least we won't have to do a boring stakeout for days on end." Jake was driving, heading up Telegraph Road. "Where do we wanna do lunch?"

"Pete's Coney's is up ahead."

That's where Jake headed. Next to cinnamon rolls, he liked his Coney dogs.

Chapter Twenty-seven

"We'll have to check the times and dates that Squires called and when he got called," Jake said as he pulled out of Pete's lot and turned toward headquarters. "The fourth was a Monday and that was the last day the phones were used."

"Uh-huh." Cliff answered as he rolled down his window. The sun was shining and the June temperatures made the past winter and wet spring just a bad memory. "We need to see if there were any other names of guys from our department on the printout."

"That'll be next once we get the department roster from the clerk."

Jake thought about Vito Calabrese and his connection to their department. If they hadn't had the Michigan Bell printouts, they wouldn't have stumbled upon it. They were no closer to making an arrest, but he knew they were closing in on Vito Calabrese and a couple of guys called Hands and Rhino.

He wondered aloud. "Three calls between the paint shop and Squires just before they folded their tent and took off. Got any ideas on that?"

"You said they knew each other back during Ben's days in Northville."

"Rumors, but nothing concrete."

"It's time to get Leicht involved on this."

Jake let what Cliff said sink in. "Three calls does eliminate any chance of a wrong number."

"Uh-huh. Let's get a time-line on paper before we talk to the boss."

Jake and Cliff pulled the reverse directories out, one grabbing the outgoing, the other the incoming calls. Jake carefully went over the outgoing calls and found the first to the Squires residence was on May 31st at 1400 hours. Jake used the blackboard on the side wall next to their desk to start their notes.

Cliff worked on the stack of incoming calls to the paint shop and took the yellow highlighter and made a couple marks. "Looks like Squires, or someone from his house, called the paint shop on June 1st at 0915 hours and then again on June 3rd at 1522 hours." He transferred those dates and times to the blackboard.

Jake looked up when he heard Lakatos' booming voice from the front of the office. "Hey Bob, still on light duty eh?" Lakatos was talking to Deputy Bob Marlowe who worked road patrol. He had twisted an ankle chasing a couple of runaway calves on Pontiac Trail.

"Just for two more weeks." Marlowe was walking gingerly between the desks in the DB. "Roberts and Bush, I've got a copy of the roster you asked for."

Jake stuck out his hand to take it as Marlowe continued. "Did Squires find you the other night?"

"When?" Jake asked.

Marlowe paused a minute. "Friday night. I was working the afternoon shift on the desk. He came in looking for the crew who was looking for the white van on the kidnapping."

Roberts stood. "And?"

"The sergeant told him you two were. Squires said he had some info for you. I told him where your desk was."

Jake looked at his partner, then back to Marlowe. "You sure it was Friday night?"

"Yep. About seven." Marlowe looked puzzled. "I told him you had probably gone home and he said he'd leave you a note. Any problems?"

Jake said there were no problems. Cliff added another note to the blackboard: June 15th Squires in our office.

Jake brought back two cups of coffee. "I didn't see any note. You?"

"No."

Jake looked at his desk calendar. "That was the same night you followed me to the storage place."

"Yep. And the address was on your desk, highlighted in yellow. That's how I knew where you were."

"You're thinking what I'm thinking." Jake stirred his coffee with a pencil and flicked it dry. "Maybe another phone call was made. Probably right from here."

"That'd be my guess. Now we know why on Monday the storage bays were empty." Cliff plopped down in his chair. "Let's run the phone numbers off of the roster Marlowe gave you again. I want to be sure there's no other cops getting calls from Vito or calling him."

"Leicht isn't going to be too happy about this." Jake pulled the roster closer and started checking for phone numbers on the Ma Bell printouts that matched their department roster. "You know, this is going to take a while."

All Jake heard was a grunt from his partner.

It took two full days to go over the reverse directories with Cliff helping. Each number had to be checked and rechecked. There were no short cuts.

Near the end of that second day, a typed report was handed to Lieutenant James Leicht that gave the time-line of the calls between the paint shop, the Squires residence and Marlowe's mention of Ben's visit to the detective bureau on Friday the 15th. The Squires number was the only one they had found that belonged to a member of the Oakland County

Sheriff's Department, but one call had been placed from Jake's phone to the paint shop. The time corresponded with Ben Squires' visit on June 15th.

Roberts summed up their report to their boss. "Then we got a search warrant for the storage bays on Monday the 18th and they were empty. It's not a big stretch. We think another phone call was made to Calabrese from Jake's phone."

"If this is true…" Leicht threw the report down on his desk as he got to his feet. "I'll personally tear the fuckin' badge off his shirt."

Jake and Cliff sat still while the LT paced around his office. "The fuckin' Sheriff is going to be livid." Leicht looked into the half-filled cup of coffee that sat on his desk. Old stains covered the inside. The LT never washed or rinsed his coffee cup. He had said the stains gave his coffee flavor.

It was as if Leicht could read their minds when he said, "If you think this cup is stained..." He slowly sat back in his chair, tilting it back. "...not half as stained as our department is with a bad cop in our midst."

In a much more subdued tone, Leicht said he'd be talking to the Sheriff, Johannes Spreen, and to the Under-Sheriff, Harry Jones. "I'm not sure, but I think Jones is the one who hired Squires when he was a captain."

The silence that took over the room told Jake and Cliff their meeting was over.

Back at their desk, Jake told Cliff about working some bar holdups in Detroit that were pulled by an off duty cop. "It wasn't fun—finding out it was a cop."

"I need a beer. How 'bout stopping at Rob's with me?"

"I'll meet you there."

Cliff and Jake didn't have any reason to celebrate at Rob's. No one liked finding some dirt on a fellow police officer and having to do something about it.

Sylvia brightened the inside of the dimly-lit bar as she waltzed from table to table. She tossed a couple of bar napkins in front of the two detectives.

"A Schlitz in a frosted mug for you," she said as the first napkin landed in front of Cliff, purposely bending, showing off her cleavage. "And you, you're the fuzzy navel guy…without the fuzz or is it without the navel?" She smiled, running her tongue over her lips.

"Ah, you remember me," Jake said as he smiled back. He was used to the verbal barbs that accompanied his non-alcoholic drinks.

"I remember the Schlitz guy better." She canted her head, eying up Cliff. "Hope you like your women without frost." She winked and spun, her mini-skirt drawing the eyes of everyone in the bar.

Jake watched Cliff's eyes follow her to the bar. "You know, partner, I think she's hitting on you." Jake could see the redness cover Cliff's face, even in the low neon glow at Rob's.

"You jealous?"

"No, I'm happy at home."

Sylvia arrived with the drinks interrupting the banter—a beer for Cliff in a frosty mug and a straight orange juice for Jake. She pursed her lips throwing a silent kiss toward Cliff as she put the beer down and headed to another table.

"Got to admit, she's got nice legs." Jake said, watching her leave.

"Uh-huh."

Jake lifted his drink. "Don't look now, partner, but she's licking her lips again." There was a pause. "While she's staring at you."

"Maybe I ought to ask her out to see when she and her partner are going to hit another bank."

"I think she'd only say so much, even in the throes of passion." Jake smiled and swirled around his drink, its tiny ice cubes clinking.

"Maybe I'm wrong about her dressing like a guy." Cliff whispered as he emptied his mug.

"No, I think you're right." Jake finished his OJ and

looked at his partner. “I know it’d be kinda hard arresting someone you’re banging.”

“I’m not banging her.”

“I saw your eyes. Mentally you are.”

“Fuck you!”

“Next Friday, let’s watch her place all day.”

“Why?”

“I got my own hunches.” Jake left a five to cover the drinks and a tip. Cliff tossed two more ones onto the pile. He liked Sylvia’s smile and the little peek at her cleavage.

Chapter Twenty-eight

On Thursday, June 24th Sergeant Ron Vanderhyde pulled into the Commerce Township substation. Two days had passed since the meeting between Roberts, Bush and Lieutenant Leicht. Earlier that afternoon, Leicht had met with Sheriff Johannes Spreen and his Under-sheriff, Harry Jones and presented them with the report from his detectives and copies of the Michigan Bell phone records.

Ben Squires had just relieved the afternoon shift at the substation. Vanderhyde carried a letter from Sheriff Spreen. The sergeant handed it to Squires.

The letter read: "Deputy Benedict Abel Squires you are hereby ordered to report to the office of Sheriff Johannes Spreen at 1 p.m., Friday, June 22, 1979 for a preliminary inquiry. If necessary, a formal hearing will be held on Wednesday, June 27th at 1 p.m."

The letter went on to say that it was the deputy's prerogative if he desired legal representation he should call his union representative. The rep's name and number was listed.

Squires read the letter. "What's this?"

"As of now, you are being placed on administration leave—with pay," The sergeant added. "Kaminski is outside and he'll cover your shift until further notice."

Squires reread the letter. "What's this shit about calling my rep or bringing a lawyer?"

The sergeant shrugged. "I don't know what they want to talk to you about, but it might be sound advice."

"Kinda short notice."

The sergeant held out his hand. "Can I read the letter?" Squires handed it to him and Vanderhyde read it. "If your union rep can't find a lawyer for tomorrow, make sure you have one for Wednesday. I'd at least ask someone from the union to be with you."

The visit from Corporal Mel Williams popped into Ben's head. *So I wasn't in uniform and missed a radio call. That was what? April?* That was the only thing he thought that would warrant a meeting with the Sheriff. *No, too much time had passed.*

He smiled. "No, I won't need anybody with me."

"Your choice. I'll tell them you'll be there."

At 1 p.m. the next day, the secretary, Mary Farnsworth, led Deputy Benedict Squires into Sheriff Johannes Spreen's office. A polished redwood oval table stood off to the side ten feet from the sheriff's desk. On the far side of the table, near the wall, were three chairs. To Squires' left sat the Sheriff, next to him was the Under-sheriff and the third chair was occupied by Detective Lieutenant James Leicht. There were two empty chairs facing them.

Spreen stood. "Deputy Squires, have a seat." He paused. "You alone?"

There were no formal introductions. Spreen was known for getting straight to the point. He had been the commissioner of the NYPD and retired before being elected the sheriff of Oakland County.

"Yes sir, just me," Squires answered as he put his summer straw Stetson Lawman hat on the empty chair.

Spreen looked at his secretary. "Thank you Mary, would you please hold my calls for an hour or so?"

It didn't take an hour for Lieutenant Leicht to outline the

report he had received from Roberts and Bush. The computer printouts from Michigan Bell were presented with the numbers called, the times, and who the numbers belonged to.

"This Vito Calabrese who called your house, who is he?" Spreen asked as soon as Leicht finished.

Squires paused a few beats before answering, "I don't think I want to answer that without an attorney."

Leicht read more, giving the dates and times that calls were made to the paint shop from the Squires home.

Spreen took the floor, asking, "Did you, Deputy Squires, make those calls?"

Squires answered, "Sir, I, er, um, think I should have brought someone, an attorney maybe." He looked down at the floor.

Spreen and Jones jotted a few notes on the pads in front of them. Lieutenant Leicht continued: "On the 15th of June, a Friday evening, you stopped by the detective bureau to see Bush and Roberts, supposedly to pass them some information…"

Before he could continue, Squires interrupted. "I want a lawyer."

Sheriff Johannes Spreen stood. "Deputy Squires, I want your badge and sidearm. You are hereby suspended until we have some satisfactory answers to your obvious connections with a person we are interested in finding—Vito Calabrese."

Leicht got up and relieved Squires of his Colt .357 magnum and his star.

"My advice to you," the Sheriff continued, "is to return on Wednesday with an attorney for a formal hearing." Spreen walked around the end of the table, "And before you leave today, if I were you, I'd give Lieutenant Leicht the address and/or the contact number you have for Mr. Calabrese."

Squires stood, bent over and grabbed his hat. "I have nothing further to say, sir."

Sunday morning, Alice Squires woke and wandered into the kitchen. The coffee was made and an empty cup sat on the kitchen table. There was some coffee residue at the bottom of it so she knew her husband was near. Ben had been silent since he came home late Thursday, other than saying he was ill and had taken the night off. She went to work as usual Friday morning at the Mound Stamping Plant. Her husband appeared to be all right, though quiet, when she got home and fixed dinner. He didn't go to work that night either. He had spent most of Friday evening and all day Saturday down in his wood shop, something that was not all that unusual. He had always said he liked his alone time and she just let him be.

Ben and Alice had no children. He had said kids would just get in the way. While Alice's friends at work talked about what they did with their husbands, Alice didn't have much to say. Ben Squires had been working straight midnights and she the day shift for the past two years. If anything, theirs was a strange marriage and not much conversation passed between them. Ben normally spent his Sunday mornings reading the paper and not much else while she went to the Saint John United Methodist Church in Pontiac. Ben had not been inside a church since their wedding fifteen years before.

"Ben, how about going out for breakfast in the morning?" she had said as she stuck her head in his shop on Saturday night.

He waved his hand as if shooing her off, "If that'll keep you from hounding my ass," he had said.

"You all right, Ben?"

"I said I'd go. Now leave me alone."

She got up Sunday morning and dressed for church. Outside she could see Ben's old, go-to-work Ford Falcon in the driveway. Their newer Buick sat next to it. She called out. "Ben, are we still going to breakfast?"

There was no answer. She checked the spare bedroom, the back office, then went out on the deck to see if he was in the back yard. Nothing. She let the screen door slam behind her as she came back into the house. "Ben, are you in here?"

Silence filled the house. She went to the back landing and noticed the light was on over the stairway. She figured Ben was in his shop again. He carved and chiseled decoys, figurines and all kinds of things that mostly collected dust on shelves down there. She slowly descended, calling out, "Ben are you down here?" She pushed open the door that separated the laundry room from Ben's woodshop and peered in.

The fluorescent lights that lined the back wall over the tool bench were on. In the middle of the room was a rough-hewn oak table that Ben did most of his work on. As Alice's eyes searched the room, she saw Ben's feet under the oak table. One was bare and the other had on a house slipper. She recognized his pajamas. There was a small stream of blood working its way toward the drain just beyond the bare foot. Alice let out a scream, turned and ran.

She stumbled climbing up the stairs to the phone and knocked the receiver off the wall. She pulled on the curled cord, got control of herself and dialed one of the emergency numbers Ben had posted on the side of the refrigerator.

Her voice cracked when she heard a voice on the other end. "Please help. My husband is hurt…"

She rapidly answered the questions as they were asked, giving her name, address and husband's name.

Ten minutes later, she heard a siren in the distance. She sat and waited, not wanting to go back downstairs. She had gotten a glimpse of her husband. His head was wrapped in his work raincoat and that's where the rivulet of blood was coming from.

While she waited, she remembered Ben getting out of bed about 6 a.m. as she rolled over and glanced at the clock on the dresser. It was too early to go for breakfast. She slept until 7:30.

If only I had gotten up with him. The tears were flowing as thoughts danced in her mind. *He never said anything.* There was a pounding at the door as the siren waned in her driveway.

The medical examiner had ruled that Benedict Abel Squires, age 44, had died of a self-inflicted gunshot from his off-duty .38 caliber Colt Detective Special. It was in his hand. He had wrapped his head in a sleeping bag with a sash from his robe and topped it off with a raincoat. He apparently did not want to leave his wife with a big mess.

———

Monday morning Jake walked into the normally empty bureau. The lights were on. Leicht was sitting on the desk closest to the Bunn machine. The lieutenant was looking into his empty stained cup. "How do you get a fuckin' cup of coffee outta this thing? I poured in a thing of water and it's not brewing."

"We turn off the power for the weekend. You gotta plug it in and wait for ten minutes or so while it heats the water in the reservoir."

"That's too fuckin' complicated. You'll have to get in a little earlier."

Jake plugged in the machine, pulled the basket out and tossed the wet grounds away. Cold water will not brew coffee. He checked his watch. "What're you doing in so early?"

"Your pal offed himself?"

"Who?"

"Squires. He ate his gun."

"When?"

"Yesterday morning. Don't you watch the news?"

"No." Jake paused. "I guess your meeting with him and Spreen didn't go too well."

"It evidently didn't." The LT stood and shuffled toward his office. "Bring the pot in when it's ready." He waved his empty cup at the Bunn machine as he walked.

Roberts, Lakatos and Burrows banged in the DB's swinging door.

"Can you believe it? We got the call from Leicht just as the wife and I were heading out for brunch." It was Lakatos talking, his unlit cigar flipping in his mouth with each word. "It cost me the whole day and more."

Burrows was following his partner and Roberts alongside him, just listening. Burrows took his coffee cup off his desk and propped his ass in the same place Leicht had been sitting. He lifted his eyes toward Jake. "You heard, right?"

"The LT just told me." Jake grabbed the full pot when it stopped dripping. "You guys catch the case?"

"Yeah. We left his house at one this morning. Hey, where are you going with the pot?"

"Leicht was first and he carries more weight than you."

"He can have the second one." Burrows held out his cup for Jake to fill. "The boss said you and Roberts had something on him."

Jake poured, shrugged and walked into the LT's office, pot in hand. He was still trying to digest what he had just been told.

The 6 O'clock news on WJBK Sunday evening had mentioned an apparent suicide at a lakeside home in Commerce Township, saying, "Details at Eleven." Jake hadn't seen either broadcast. The boys had talked Jake and Edie into going out to Buddy's in Detroit for pizza after a full day of hitting them fly balls at Hoyt Park. He was too tired to stay up and watch the news.

Jake poured himself a coffee and went to his desk. His biggest challenge was how he was going to find Vito Calabrese. His eyes went to Leicht's NFB Session board. Popp and Machelski had the lead that morning. That meant apple fritters would be in the bags they'd be carrying. Jake knew Detective Machelski's weakness.

There'd be no bullshit for sure. The dead deputy would be the subject of the session. Jake couldn't understand why a man would kill himself, but then, he did not know how deeply involved Ben Squires had been with Vito Calabrese.

Chapter Twenty-nine

"I'll get right to what's no doubt on your fuckin' minds." The bulge of chew in the LT's cheek moved as he talked. "One of our deputies blew his brains out. He somehow was involved with a guy we've been looking for in connection with a murder and a kidnapping. End of fuckin' story. Read the rest in today's paper." The LT spit out his chew into his half-filled coffee cup. "Popp and Machelski, where's the fuckin' donuts?"

Johnny Popp shrugged his shoulders as he looked toward his partner.

Jim Machelski smiled, pulling out a bag from under his desk. "It was John's turn, but I knew he'd forget so..." He walked the bag from Sanders Bakery up to the desk Leicht was sitting on. Machelski grabbed the biggest fritter he could find, fingering three or four to get to it before handing the bag to the lieutenant. "Here you go, boss."

"And what's on your agenda besides eating?"

Machelski moved back to his desk and fumbled through some papers. "Troy PD asked us for some help. There are two old ladies cashing social security checks operating in and around their town."

The LT looked over at Burrows and Lakatos and nodded. "What's been stolen by your mail thief?"

"Mainly social security checks," answered Burrows.

"You guys need to talk to Popp and the guy eating his second fritter. This is the reason we have these fuckin' sessions."

Leicht grabbed a bag of Redman out of his back pocket and stuffed another chew in his mouth. "Roberts and Bush. There any progress on the bank robberies?"

"I've got some hunches we're working on," Roberts answered.

"Work a little harder. I want to beat the feds on this." The boss was looking at Jake as he said it. Leicht had been turned down by the FBI fifteen years before, so there was some serious competition when the two agencies were working the same case.

"We're looking at a couple of women that may be involved," Cliff said, and went silent. He didn't want to say too much.

"Fuck the women. I want you to nail the bad guys," Leicht said.

A gravelly voice shouted out, "My thoughts exactly. Fuck the women." A few snickers arose from the detectives sitting around the front of the bureau. The voice was that of Johnny Popp.

The LT waited for the back and forth chatter to stop. The four other teams gave a brief report on their pressing cases. He looked around the room, then said, "If there's nothing else, let's get to work."

The men started to stir. "Hold it! One more thing. The cop that ate his gun saved us some bad press. He did us a favor." Leicht stood, dumped his spent chew from his cup into the nearest waste basket then poured himself some fresh coffee.

Jake noticed the LT didn't even rinse it and just shook his head as he went to his desk. The rest of the six teams of dicks floated back to theirs. One yelled, "Jim, there any fritters left?"

Popp answered for his partner who had his mouth full. "Evidently you've never seen my partner eat."

Jake pulled out his chair and sat. "Where do we go to next with Calabrese?"

"Back to the list. There has to be a number that was called from the shop. Maybe we'll find Vito through a girlfriend or a wife—if he has one."

Jake grabbed the stack of printouts. He knew going through the numbers would be his job. Cliff didn't like reading the *White Pages* as he called the computer generated numbers. "What you got going?"

"I got six reports on small-time complaints to check out." Cliff grabbed his sport coat off the back of his chair. "Remember, balls in the air. You do the reading and I'll do the visiting." He was smiling as he walked out the door.

By Wednesday Jake had leads on three numbers that were called more than any others and the names and addresses that went with them.

Cliff picked the first one on Jake's list to sit on and watch. They were hoping to find the maroon Cadillac with a black vinyl top that Ted from the lawn mower shop had seen. Cliff said they had to start somewhere.

They first drove by the two-story colonial that sat on a cul-de-sac. On the north side was a two-car garage attached. Jake picked a spot between some cars parked on the street to blend in a hundred yards past the house.

Cliff took the first turn on their Bushnell binoculars. "You gotta name that goes with this place?"

"Grammatico. And before you ask, nothing on the name. Might be a phony. The records show the number was called twice and this house called the paint shop four times."

Five hours went by before one of the garage doors lifted. A blue Chrysler backed out. Cliff made out a mint green car occupying the second slot in the garage. He put the glasses down on the seat. "No Cadillac in there. Maybe we'll have to get some surveillance help from the boss once we check all three places."

"Where to next?"

"Let's grab something to eat and find the next place."

"Where do you want to eat?"

"Someplace where we can grab it and go. We're wasting a lot of time."

The second address on Jake's list was in Novi. There was a new development of upscale houses on Mandalay Circle. Only five houses were occupied, three more were just being framed in and it looked like at least another ten lots were available. The address they were looking for was the only house with a full lawn and landscaping.

"Holy shit, Cliff, look at that layout."

The house that Jake was talking about sat on what looked like a curved lot. The three door garage angled forward closer to the road. Cliff drove slowly as they looked at the two-story brick colonial. The address matched the reverse directory.

"Swanky place," whispered Cliff. "Anything on the name?"

"Phone's got just the initial 'I' and the last name Herwitz that goes with it. No record. No background info." He flipped through his notebook. "Might be a lawyer. I found an ad in the Yellow Pages for an Isaac Herwitz. He's a CPA too."

"Probably doing Calabrese's books. Vito doesn't want to get nailed like Capone."

"Maybe, if we're lucky, he's putting Vito up for a while," Jake said.

The garage was only one story high and connected to the east side of the house. The lack of a house on either side made blending in impossible. Cliff drove around the circle at the end and was able to park amongst three trucks. The trucks belonged to a crew of carpenters framing in a new house. From there Jake had a straight-line view of their target from about 250 yards away. "Watch while I go and talk to some guys."

Jake picked up the glasses and adjusted them. In ten minutes Cliff slid in back behind the wheel. "Tomorrow we're pounding nails."

"What?"

"We'll drive your bucket of rust and hang out with the crew. That'll give us a good eye on the place." He looked at his watch. "That is if we don't see any movement in the next hour and a half."

"What, no overtime tonight?"

"No. Ed and his crew leave at 4:30. We're blending in."

"Ed?"

"Yeah. Ed Peters. He's the boss. I said we'd bring lunch tomorrow."

Jake glassed the big colonial house until Ed and his crew packed up their gear to leave. "Guess you're driving tomorrow," Cliff said as he hit the ignition.

"Then you're making the sandwiches."

"A deli is. Novi has to have one. Lots of Jewish people moved here. They moved their delis with them."

"What time we starting?"

"Pick me up at 5:30. Ed's crew starts at 7:00 and I gotta get the sandwiches."

At 6:45 a.m. Jake's white Ford pickup was turning onto Mandalay Circle. He and Cliff were wearing jeans and T-shirts. Ed was there looking at a blueprint. He nodded at the two detectives. "Got tool belts?"

Cliff shook his head. Ed tossed them two from the box on the back of his truck. "There's two hammers in the back." Jake and Cliff put on the belts. Instead of nails in the pouch, each had their snub nosed .38. Jake's was a Colt, Cliff's a Smith and Wesson. They hung a hammer in the loop on their belts.

Jake and Cliff took turns straddling the trusses in the upper level and glassing number 833 Mandalay Circle hoping for a visit from a maroon Cadillac or to see one coming or going.

At noon a white Lincoln pulled out of one side of the garage. Three hours later, a black Mercedes drove into the second side. Jake saw the third garage had a boat parked in it. It was another dead end.

"Bet the lawyer knows where he lives," Jake said as he climbed down a ladder.

"Well, you know we're not going to ask him." Cliff helped store the ladder on Ed's truck. "At least, not yet."

Ed named a bar in Novi where they'd be having a beer and Cliff said they'd try to catch up with them there. Both left the tool belts minus their pistols with the crew leader.

Cliff slid behind the wheel. "Let's take a look at where we'll be tomorrow."

"I thought you were buying beer for Ed and his guys?"

"I gave him a five spot in case we didn't make it. What's the address?"

Jake flipped open his notebook and grabbed the map. "We need to head up Telegraph to Hickory Grove."

The AAA map was taking up Jake's side of the dash. "The address we want is on Chestnut Run Drive." As he followed his finger across the map, he added. "Looks like whoever lives there has a lake in his backyard. Ever hear of Orange Lake?"

"That's Bloomfield Hills. Now that's the real-high rent district."

Jake was studying the map of Southern Oakland County. "It's another cul-de-sac."

Cliff nodded his head slowly. "I've got a feeling on this one." He smiled—just barely. "There a name that goes with this one?"

"A woman. Nancy Grasso." Jake was looking for the next turn.

"Maybe a girlfriend?"

"We hope." Jake folded the map and tucked it away.

Cliff made a run up Chestnut Run Drive, slow and easy like he was lost. The house sat on the turn-around loop at the end of the road. "That lake's probably off the back of this place."

"Uh-huh."

Cliff drove around the area checking out Chickering Lane then around the football field behind Lahser High School, trying to see if they could get a good angle to glass the place.

Two hours later, Jake and Cliff were having a coffee. "We've got a dilemma," Jake said as he stirred in his 249 granules of sugar in his cup. "Tomorrow is Friday and we need more recon on that house back there."

Cliff flipped a coin. "Tails. We'll do the bank robbers first. That'll make Leicht happy." Cliff drained his cup and stood. Jake checked his watch. It was near seven. Edie would be keeping his dinner warm again, or so he hoped.

The next morning, Jake and Cliff were sitting on Sylvia's apartment. After an hour Jake got out of the car. "I'm going for a walk. I didn't see either of their cars. Maybe they're parked around the block or in the alley."

Cliff nodded as he poured a fresh coffee for himself from Jake's thermos.

Fifteen minutes later Jake slipped in the passenger seat. "The Dodge Dart and the Merc are gone."

"I don't like that." Cliff tossed the last of his coffee out his window. "One of their cars is always near."

"Let's take a run over to Rob's for breakfast. Maybe he knows something."

Cliff nodded. "Maybe they got lucky and are getting laid somewhere."

"That's a thought." Jake looked at his partner. "Jealous?"

"Fuck you. They're bank robbers."

"You doubted your hunch the other day. What happened?"

"I changed my mind."

Rob wasn't at the bar. Reggie, the night bartender, was.

"Two Mexican omelets and home-made toast," Cliff called out as he slid into a booth near the bar.

"You're outta luck. I don't do omelets. Only Rob does. I

can do burgers."

Cliff looked at the time. It was eleven. Jake shrugged. "Two burgers then—with everything."

"Beers?"

"Root beers," Cliff answered. He looked at Jake. "Can you handle a root beer?"

Jake nodded. The burgers came with fries and the root beers in frosted mugs. "Rob take the day off?" Jake asked.

"He's working nights. Two of his girls quit at the end of the shift on Wednesday. He's going to be on nights 'til he finds some new help."

"Let me guess. Sylvia and Grace?" Jake took a bite of one of his fries.

"Yep. No notice. Sylvia just told me to tell Rob they won't be back."

Cliff jumped in. "They say where to send their pay?"

"Said for me to tell Rob to keep it. Shit, they only get a couple a bucks an hour. They make their money in tips."

"Lot of cops here that night?"

"The normal Wednesday night bunch. Some of your dicks. Some of the Pontiac uniforms."

Back in their car, Cliff was driving down Telegraph. "They got spooked."

"Think they spotted us last Friday?"

"No. Maybe they heard something."

"How?"

"Cops talk shop. If you worked at Rob's and it was full of cops, you'd hear shit." Cliff went silent for a minute. "I shoulda never mentioned anything about us looking at a couple of women."

"Let's go back to their apartment," Jake said, changing the subject.

"Without a warrant?"

"Let's see if the manager is friendly."

Cliff made a U-turn to head back to Sylvia's.

Chapter Thirty

Sam's day had started like most since his summer vacation began. His dad was at work and so was his mom. He and his brother were old enough to take care of themselves.

His chores were out of the way and his front pockets were bulging with two potatoes wrapped in tin foil. They were his lunch. He stopped to grab the cottage cheese container from the refrigerator filled with bits of newspaper and worms as he jumped on his bike for his secret place. His fishing rod was tied to his back fender with bits of binder twine and stood erect like a whip antenna on a police car.

Sam loved the house his mom and Jake had bought. It was on Indian Hills Lane, a road that went a mile into a woodsy area west of Milford, a perfect place for him. He didn't care much for the horses. That was his mom and Hank's thing. Begrudgingly he mucked out the stalls and fed them when it was his turn, but his summer day didn't really start until he could grab his fishing gear, jump on his bike and make it down to the far end of the lane to a pond with no name.

Hank had been busy currying out Duke, a jet-black quarter horse his mom has just bought when Sam dashed out the barn door yelling to his brother, "I'm going for a bike ride."

Hank knew Sam wouldn't be home until about the time their mom would be pulling into the driveway. She always got home before his dad and Sam always beat her home.

The pond, which Sam thought he should name Bluegill Lake, was something he had found as he wandered the woods once summer vacation started. He was an explorer, so while his mom and dad worked and Hank played with the horses, he'd be in the woods building a fort and fishing.

The navy blue van was tucked back off of the road down an overgrown two track. Rhino has his head leaning against the window on his side. He had his seat behind the steering wheel back as far back as it would go. He checked his watch. "Pretty soon," he said.

Hands sat the other side of the motor hump, scrunched down just so he could see over the dash. He rolled down his window just enough to toss what was left of a cigarette into the woods.

"Hope you don't start a fuckin' forest fire."

"Up your ass," Hands said as he rolled up the window to keep the mosquitoes out. "I don't like this shit."

"What don't you like?"

"This. Snatching a kid."

"You getting soft?"

Hands lit another cigarette and didn't answer.

"Have you ever made the money Vito pays?" Rhino asked. No response. "Boy, you sure have changed in just the last couple of days. You were the one who got us lined up with Vito. Now I don't know."

The buzz of a mosquito broke the silence. Hands caught it mid-air and crushed it. Then he flipped a second butt out the window. "Fuck the money. I'm not into snatching a kid."

Rhino shrugged. "What's so different about this?"

"Lots."

"When he had us ice someone we did it. When he said to

pick up a kilo of coke, we picked up the dope."

"This is different."

"I don't see it that way." Rhino checked his watch again. They had been watching the kid for two days already. "You know Vito's got it all worked out. We hold the kid for a while, then cut him loose."

"And the Feds'll be after our ass. That ain't very smart. And it's a kid."

"I'm telling you, Vito's got it covered."

Hands had been arguing with his partner since Vito Calabrese came up with the plan to snatch one of Jake Bush's kids. Vito thought the cops were getting too close and he was tired of running. His inside man came up with the detective's address and told him about his family.

Vito's idea was to put the area into a panic as it had been before when the cops were looking for someone dubbed by the press as *The Oakland County Child Killer.* He said that would give him enough time to find another building and "...get back to business as usual." He was losing a lot of money playing hide-and-seek with the cops.

Sam always hid his bike inside the woods, carefully covering it with a couple of sumac branches cut from a small growth with his dad's axe. He didn't want anyone to know about *his* private fishing hole.

About a quarter of a mile inside the woods he came to his camp. Under a make-shift lean-to he had built, Sam had his cache of essentials: the axe, a small shovel, Jake's old hunting knife, a box of wooden matches, a can of charcoal lighter fluid and whatever he thought he could take from the pantry shelves without his mom noticing—like a box of raisins and a half bag of marshmallows that had been on the shelves since they moved in.

His first order of business today was to salvage some half-burned logs from the day before. Jake had taught the boys how to cover a campfire with dirt to smother it, and Sam did not want to give away his secret spot because he was too lazy to make sure his fire was out.

He put the two potatoes inside the rock ring and added the half-used logs topped with a couple more from his stash of dead limbs he had dragged into his camp from around his lake. A few squirts of the fluid and one match got the potatoes baking. It was time to fish.

Sam didn't hear the twig snap. He was busy reeling in something bigger than the normal bluegill he had been catching when a musty smelling cloth bag covered his head and a set of huge hands grabbed his arms. He twisted and kicked backwards at his unseen attacker. He knew he hit something when he heard a yelp.

"Help me hold the little bastard."

"I'm trying to keep his head covered," a second voice answered.

Sam went limp when it felt like a tree fell on him. He lost all the wind from his lungs.

"Tape the little bastard up while I make sure he can't see us."

Minutes later, Rhino and Hands slid their package into the back of their van and slammed the doors.

The kid in the back was screaming for his dad and his mom as they drove off.

"He's gonna hurt himself," Hands said.

"Maybe he'll shut the fuck up if he does."

Rhino knew where he was going and was driving the speed limit, not wanting to attract any attention. He looked over at his partner.

"You are going soft." He laughed. "Never thought that would happen."

The yelling from the back started again.

"My dad's a detective and he's going to shoot you dead." Sam kept repeating it while he bounced around as the two guys drove somewhere. It was dark. *No it couldn't be.* But it was inside whatever they put over his head.

A while later, the engine quit and Sam heard doors open. He kicked and twisted as the two men pulled on his legs then lifted him from the truck—at least he thought it was a truck. Sam tried remembering everything so he could tell his dad. He heard two doors slam as they tried to stand him up. *A van or a suburban.* Another thing to remember. He was sure it was two men. Their voices were different.

Sam shouted out, "My dad's gonna get you. The both of you. He will."

"Stand and shut the fuck up, kid." A set of hands held his arms. Another hand was pushing him.

"Open the fuckin' door." The fat guy said. At least Sam thought he was a fat guy. He sounded fat, so Sam imagined him that way.

Sam heard a garage door go up as he was pulled by his arms until he felt he was on solid ground. Whoever the guys were had taped his hands together as they zipped him in that smelly bag. His feet were loose, so he kicked as he walked and screamed. "You guys are going to get it. Wait and see."

"Just walk kid and settle down," a second voice said. It was a kinder voice.

"Walk or we'll drag your ass." The fat guy again. He was mean.

"Lock him in the john."

Wait. That was a third voice. Sam was making mental notes. It had a different tone to it. He tried to remember each voice so he could tell his dad.

It was dark. The bag was still over his head and he knew he was on a floor. He felt the tape being cut from his wrists only to be replaced by what felt like his dad's handcuffs. He heard the door slam.

Sam twisted around, finding a wall or the door with his feet. He only had one shoe on, but he could kick. So he kicked and kicked and yelled and yelled. "My dad's a policeman. He'll get you." He tried sitting up and banged his head on something.

Sam stopped to listen. Nothing. So he kicked and yelled all the more, "You son-of-a-bitches. You son-of-a-bitches." Those were the only words he seemed to remember. He yelled for what seemed like hours until he could yell no more. His feet were numb and his throat was sore. He didn't know how long he'd been on the floor. It was hot, even hotter wrapped in whatever it was and now he only had the strength to kick once in a while. No one cared how loud he screamed or how hard he banged on the wall. He started to cry.

"Mom. Dad. Please come get me."

Sylvia Porter's manager, Gerry Evans, answered the knock on his door. He lived on the lower floor of 1432 Baldwin Avenue. Evans had a three day growth of graying stubble, was wearing a stained tee shirt, and wide red suspenders were holding up his crumpled tan slacks. The knocking came from a pair of cops holding out badges.

He had no problem letting Cliff and Jake into the apartment rented under Sylvia Porter's name. He let out a burp as he said, "They're gone."

He led them to the apartment saying, "Paid in cash for next month too." His keys jingled as he found the right one and opened the door. "They said a family accident and had to leave." He moved out of the way to let Cliff and Jake in. "Even said I could have the furniture."

"They mention where they were going?"

"Wherever it was, they were in a hell of a hurry."

A phone call to headquarters had Lieutenant Leicht sending a team to get a warrant for the place. Jake and Cliff stood by to keep it secure until the lab tech arrived.

John Woods was the tech and he went right to work, dusting the light switch plates. "Don't be touching and adding to my work load as you snoop around," he said as Jake and Cliff looked for anything the women might have left behind.

Cliff laughed as he motioned with his head toward Woods. "They always send me the grumpy bastard."

Two boxes of Chinese take-out, a half bottle of catchup and some mayo were left in the refrigerator. The cupboards to the right of the sink had some canned goods and a box of Cheerios. Part of a four-piece set of dishes and some pots and pans sat dirty in the sink, the rest were in another metal cupboard.

Jake rummaged around the bedroom and found nothing besides empty coat hangers in the closet and dust bunnies under the beds—except for a crumpled up piece of paper. It was under the dresser. He straightened the paper out. It was a rent receipt for an address on Dixie Highway. Jake used the phone to call the clerk asking him if he could type up a request to secure another search warrant for that address.

"I'll have it ready by the time you guys get back to headquarters," came the reply. Jake didn't want to waste time even though the prints at both places might even be a dead end. Prints meant absolutely nothing if Sylvia and Grace had never been arrested.

"Sounds like they're long gone," said Cliff as Jake showed him the receipt. Jake just nodded.

The second address turned out to be a basement apartment with an entrance from the alley. Men's clothing and a suitcase-sized make-up kit were tagged and bagged. Evidently the girls didn't take the time to cover their tracks.

"Well, you were right about them, partner," Jake said as he banged out the report on his typewriter.

"Being right didn't put them in jail though, did it?"

"They'll pop up somewhere."

A phone call later, Allen Jenkins, the lead FBI agent, admitted they had been looking in the wrong direction. Neither the FBI nor the Oakland County Sheriff's Department had a clue as to where to start looking for Grace and Sylvia.

"Well, at least their prints will now be in the system,"

Jake said as he pulled his report out of the typewriter.

Cliff just shook his head. "If they're smart, they'll never see the inside of a jail."

"They're not that smart. They'll get greedy."

Jake's phone rang. He picked it up as he heard his partner say, "Bet you five on that."

Jake nodded and spoke into the phone, "OCSD, Detective Bush."

"Jake, Sam's gone..." Edie's voice trailed off and she started crying.

"Edie! What do you mean 'gone?'" Jake's heart started pounding.

The next voice he heard was Hank's.

"Dad. Something happened to Sam."

"What do you mean?"

"We found one of his tennis shoes by his secret lake." Jake heard the catch in Hank's voice. "And his bike's still there."

"Tell your mom I'm on my way." Jake dropped the phone into its cradle, grabbed his coat and started to the door.

Cliff was grabbing his coat too. "Jake, where you goin'?"

"Something's happened to Sam."

Cliff caught up to Jake by the back door leading to the parking lot. "Jump in our car."

"No, I can handle this."

Cliff grabbed Jake by the shoulder. His grip said more than the words. "We're partners. I'm driving." Jake didn't argue. He slid in the jump seat of their Chevy.

On the ride toward his house, Jake told about his youngest son's secret lake that everyone knew about. "He's a spunky kid that loves to explore. Edie and I found his foot path to a pond one evening when we were out for a walk." Jake stopped talking for a few beats. "Hank found his little fort another day and told me about it. I told Hank to not let Sam know we knew." Jake sat there shaking his head. "Hell, I used to do stuff like that when I was his age, so we didn't say anything to him. We let it be his little secret place."

"How old is he?"

"Eleven."

"Jake, he's probably off exploring somewhere else."

"No. Hank and Edie found one of his shoes and his bike."

It had been over two weeks since Vito had Hands and Rhino empty the storage sheds. Vito paced the floor of the old warehouse building that had part of the floor filled with the contents from the sheds.

The two goons were sitting on a stack of wood pallets at the closed-down auto parts supply house on Alpha Drive near Wixom Road. Their navy blue van was parked inside next to a maroon Cadillac with a black vinyl top. Hands and Rhino had been sleeping in the back of the van.

Hands pulled out a pack of Camels and offered his partner one even though he knew the guy didn't smoke. Rhino just raised the palm of his hand to say as much.

"Now what? We got the kid tucked away," Rhino said.

Vito paced the floor. "Let me think."

A cloud of smoke went into the air as Hands said, "Now ain't the time to be making a damn plan."

"Let Vito do the talking," Rhino barked at Hands. His voice softened. "Boss, anybody beside us know about this place?"

"I borrowed it for a couple of days."

Hands lifted his head, slowly blowing out another layer of smoke. "A couple of days?" He stood, towering over his boss. "You have us snatch a kid. A cop's kid no less and we're moving again?"

"My friend said some new tenants are coming in next week. We got a couple of days."

Hands looked over to Rhino who was half lying on the stack of pallets. "You said Vito had everything covered. Bullshit!"

Rhino sat up, reached in his pocket and flicked open a

switchblade. He started cleaning his fingernails while his eyes shifted to Vito. "Why did we do this, boss?"

"You remember all the press a year or so ago? Four kids were snatched."

"The ones found dead?" Rhino asked.

"Yeah, them."

Hands walked toward Rhino on the pallets. "I'm not killing a kid." He felt for his pistol tucked in the back of his pants, a mental reassurance.

"Hear me out." Vito turned his back on his men. "A lot of press and no arrests. We grab a kid and all of a sudden every cop is looking for an AMC Gremlin again. Not us." Vito walked in a tighter circle.

"What do you mean looking for a Gremlin?" Hands asked.

"That's the car they were looking for when the kids went missing."

Hands pulled out another cigarette and lit it. "This ain't gonna work, boss."

"And why not?"

Vito spent the next half hour telling them about the detective team that was causing all their problems. "An old pal was filling me in on them." He pulled a handkerchief out of his pocket and wiped his brow. "I told you early on. There's money to be made and I won't let anyone get in my way. Not even the cops."

Vito continued, telling them about what Squires had fed him about the warrants for Henry Kritchman and Ralph Bumgarden for murder and attempted kidnapping. "No doubt they have prints and who knows what else. So you are in it up to your asses. Me too." Vito's usual smile was gone. He started heading to his car. "If you go down, so do I."

Vito slid into the seat in the Cadillac. Before turning the key he said, "I'll find us a place. Keep the kid under wraps 'til I get back."

Chapter Thirty-one

Leicht had sent Lakatos and Burrows along with a team from their lab to the scene as soon as he got the call from Cliff Roberts. Before Roberts hung up, the LT said, "Make sure Jake stays with his wife. We'll take care of the scene."

It was Cliff Robert's brute strength that kept Jake from running out the door as Edie and Hank related what they found by Sam's little fort near the end of Indian Hills Lane. Jake wanted to go there.

Thirteen minutes after Roberts got off the phone Lieutenant James Leicht's tires were throwing gravel in Jake's driveway. The LT had pulled in behind Jake's department car and two black and whites. Cliff had heard the gravel flying and stepped onto the porch to greet his boss. He had left Jake and his family in the care of deputies Williams and Kaminski.

"The lab guys are with Jimmy and Ed up the road working the scene," Cliff said as he pushed his way into the house with Leicht following. "Jake's wife brought back the tennis shoe they found. I have it in our car. It's a black canvas U.S. Ked tennis shoe. Jake and Edie said it belonged to their youngest son."

Leicht saw Edie's head buried in Jake's chest. Her body shuddered as she quietly cried. Jake just nodded toward his boss acknowledging his presence.

Edie heard the door close and turned her head and glared at the new cop in the room. "I want my son back! I want him back right fucking now!" She buried her head back in Jake's chest as her cries turned into wails. Jake just closed his red, puffed-up eyes. It was plain to Leicht that he had been crying too.

"We'll find him," Leicht whispered. "You'll have to trust me on that." There was a pause. "Jake, can you step outside for a minute?"

The lieutenant stood on the gravel driveway, pushing a stone with his toe. "How are you doing?"

Jake just shrugged.

"I want you to stay with your wife. Let us handle this."

"Boss, Cliff and I need to be working on this. Sam's my son."

"Think about it, you're too close to this and your wife needs you."

"She'll be all right. My son needs me more."

The lieutenant looked around, as if mulling over what he wanted to say. "Jake, listen to me. Stay home for a couple of days." The LT's voice remained soft. His right hand rested on Jake's left shoulder.

Jake looked into his boss's eyes as his voice cracked, "I'll give you a day, that's all."

Leicht nodded. "Jake..." The lieutenant had kids and knew just how Jake felt. "Oh what the fuck." The LT started to move toward his car. "Listen to me. You have a wife and another son who need you..." His voice trailed off as he climbed in his car and rolled down his window. "Give us some time." He hit the ignition. "I'm going to run up the road and see how things are going."

"Please boss, stop and let me know what you find out."

The lieutenant put the car in gear, then flipped it back into park and let out a sigh. "Tell Roberts to come with me. He can fill you in."

Indian Hills Lane ran to the north off of Commerce Road, three miles west of Milford. It meandered through woodsy terrain for three quarters of a mile ending at a circular turnaround. The road was one way in, one way out. Jake's house sat on the west side and was one of only three homes on the lane.

Lakatos figured someone wanted to talk to him when he heard the tap of a horn. Department protocol dictated the less cops tramping over a scene, the better. He was the closest to the road and came out to find Leicht's car. He didn't smile as he approached.

"Boss, we haven't found anything beyond what looks like something the boy brought out, but we're far from done."

The LT tilted his head as he said, "Turn over every fuckin' leaf if you have to.

Lakatos nodded.

"Work it like it's your own kid that's missing."

Lakatos slowly nodded again and turned to go back into the woods when Leicht started his car. There was no need to say anything else.

Burrows and Lakatos had to call it quits five hours later when darkness set in. Neither they or the lab techs found anything significant to that point. They requested a black and white to sit on the scene through the night and they had been turning over every leaf, hoping to find something to help them find Jake's son.

The Detroit Free Press, The News, the *Oakland Press* and the *Macomb Daily* resurrected the fears from the past the next morning as they replayed articles of the four children that were thought to be killed by a serial killer, the last of which had happened two and a half years before Sam disappeared.

Jake did not let Edie see the paper he retrieved from the box at the end of his driveway. He read it in the barn and hid it in between the hay bales. The reporters seemed to be more interested in rewriting about crimes of the past rather than what was happening with eleven-year-old Sam Bush.

Things were very quiet in the house. Edie seemed to be in a trance, not eating or talking, but her crying seemed to have subsided. Jake went out with Hank to take care of the horses.

"I'm worried about both Mom as well as Sam," Hank said as he forked in some clean straw into the stalls.

"Uh-huh," is all Jake could muster for an answer. He had filled the wheelbarrow with old straw and horseshit and was taking it outside to dump.

For the next half hour, Jake and Hank sat on the hay bales and just talked. Hank mainly said he did not understand what made people do such bad things. Jake had to admit he didn't either. They sat in silence for a while with Jake having his arm draped over Hank's shoulder as the boy silently cried.

"Dad, Sam once said you were the best detective in the world. He meant it and..." More tears flowed. Jake waited and pulled his son close. Hank's tears finally stopped. "Dad, we need you to find Sam 'cause I know you are the best."

Jake nodded and stood. He put his hands on his son's shoulders. "I can't unless you help me by taking care of your mom." Jake lifted his son's chin. "You're only thirteen, but..."

"Dad," Hank interrupted, "you go find Sam and don't worry about us. I can take care of Mom."

The next morning, the team of Popp and Machelski joined the first team of detectives and the lab people searching the area. Leicht wanted the second team going door-to-door and walking the road, looking for anything that might be connected to Sam's disappearance. The FBI sent Allen Jenkins to Leicht's office to keep abreast of OCSD's progress.

Burrows and Lakatos took the lead at Sam's campsite again while Popp and Machelski started knocking on the doors of the only two homes on the lane besides Jake's. That didn't take more than fifteen minutes. Both homes were set back in the woods and no one saw or heard anything.

"Anything?" Machelski asked as he saw Popp at their car.

"Nothing. The man of the house leaves at 6 a.m. and Mrs. Franks spent most of the day in her garden."

"I had basically the same at the other place. What's next?" Machelski asked as he slid in the jump seat.

Popp hit the ignition. "I'll take you to the turn-around and you work the east side, I'll take the car and work the west side. When you get back to the car, come back and pick me up."

The day was starting to heat up. The morning weather forecast was predicting temps near ninety. Jim Machelski already had shed his rumpled khaki sport coat and tossed it in the back seat.

"We got any mosquito dope in the car?" Jim asked as Johnny drove.

"You're the outdoorsman. You bring any?"

"No. I didn't plan on spending the day in the woods and getting eaten alive." Jim wiped the sweat off his brow. "How deep in are we going?"

"Ten to fifteen yards should cover anything that someone might have tossed."

It was 9:30 when Jim started zigzagging through the bracken from the turn-around. He knew his partner would be doing the same working his way north. The ferns were just below his knees, so he pushed them to the side with his toe to see if anything was tossed and hidden beneath the leaves. Immediately at the turn-around most of the ferns were trampled. From the signs, Jim determined this area was a favorite place for kids to park. Spent prophylactics, beer cans and tissues dominated the ground litter until he was more than twenty yards back down the road as it snaked south.

It took him a half hour before he was directly across the yellow tape marking the trail to Sam's secret spot. Because of the winding road, he had no idea how close he was to his partner. The gnats and mosquitoes were giving him fits as he slowly canvased the ground from the edge of the road to fifteen yards in. An odd beer can is all he found. Anything that looked to be a recent discard was put in a plastic bag, tagged and placed on the roadside for later retrieval.

Jim Machelski was working around the top of a fallen birch tree and noticed an old two-track heading back into the woods. The soil was sandy and ferns flourished, almost erasing traces of the old pull-off that petered out fifty yards in. As he straddled the dead tree, he noticed some ferns were broken. If he hadn't gone around the tree, he would have never seen them. He got on his knees and saw tire tracks in the dense sandy soil. He looked back over his shoulder at the tree, nodding to himself. There were fresh scuff marks and some footprints.

Yes, a man could move the tree out of the way, then pull it back to hide things.

Jim walked to the road and yelled to see how far away Johnny was.

"I'm almost to you," came Johnny Popp's raspy voice.

"Come here, I want to show you something."

With very little effort they pulled the birch tree off the trail. It was plain that a vehicle had used it recently at least once, maybe more. It hadn't rained, but some tire tracks were lightly visible, showing someone had backed into the trail and pulled out. The broken ferns stopped about thirty five yards off the road. Autumn Olive and high-bush cranberry bushes growing near the road would have hid any vehicle parked there.

"How far south is Jake's house?" Jim asked.

"No more than a hundred yards."

"You think someone could have parked in here to watch for the kid?"

"Yes. They'd only see what passed on the road, but..." Johnny started moving ferns out of his way with his toe, inching his way to the east. "...if you find any rubbers or Kleenex, we'll know it's just kids."

The two detectives reached the end of the broken ferns. Jim and Johnny moved back to where they thought the front of the vehicle would be. Johnny was teetering on a downed aspen tree on his side. "I can see about fifty yards of the road."

"Enough if you're waiting for someone to pass," Jim said as he moved to his right, pushing more ferns out of the way. "Hey Popp, see if there's anything on your side like candy wrappers, trash, or butts."

Jim had been Johnny's partner for four years. "You're talking to the guy who broke you in," he croaked.

Machelski stopped as he moved some the brush out of the way. Something white caught his eye. "Johnny, got any more baggies in your pocket?"

"What you got?"

"A fresh butt. Whoever parked here smokes."

Two unfiltered cigarette butts were retrieved. On the other side of the track Johnny found the signs in the sand of someone urinating and nothing else. The sand was too dense to get a plaster cast of the prints. They yellow taped the two-track at the road in case the lab thought different.

Johnny moved to finish his side of the road, stopping to let the lab crew know about the spot so they could recheck the area. Machelski pocketed the bag with the two butts. He'd make the report on it later.

Day three started early. The lab was working with the bits and pieces they and the two crews of detectives had put into evidence. Beside the cigarette butts, they had seventeen beer cans to fingerprint.

Leicht was in his office when Jake came in. The coffee was already dripping down into the pot. The LT could see the Bunn machine from his desk and saw Jake place one cup to catch the drippings as he poured himself another.

"Bush, what the hell you doing here?"

"I said I'd give you a day." Jake was bringing the pot into the LT's office. "Where we at?"

"Me first," the lieutenant interrupted. "How is your wife?"

"Like a zombie. She's not talking. Not eating. She's more

in a trance than anything."

"You should be with her."

"There's not much I can do. If I say anything to comfort her, she starts crying. If I touch her, she pulls away. I believe in her mind, she thinks Sam's already dead, or maybe she's somehow blaming me for what's going on."

"Through the department I can hook you two up with some counseling."

"If we get Sam back unharmed, maybe this will all go away." Jake stirred in some sugar. "Now where we at with the case?"

The lieutenant told Jake about the cans, the recently used two-track and a couple of cigarette butts they found. "We bagged a lot of stuff. Most of it could be just old trash. The lab's been working on it all night."

Jake's phone rang back at his desk. He left the lieutenant to answer it.

"This is Bush."

He could hear someone breathing on the other end of the line. Jake repeated: "Detective Bush, Oakland County."

"I don't want no part of this." The line went silent, but the breathing was still there.

Jake waited. He could hear the man light a match or a lighter, then a long exhale. Jake could picture the man lighting a cigarette, then blowing out a big puff of smoke.

"No part of what?"

Jake heard the man cough a few times and he waited. The line was still open.

"Snatching a kid. Somewhere in this world I've got one of my own."

Silence. Then more coughing and hacking.

Jake remembered his dad coughing in the mornings. It was a heavy smoker's cough. Jake waited. Another cigarette was lit. Another big puff of smoke exhaled.

Jake pictured the man. Cigarette butts that he put into evidence bags in the recent past came to mind. He broke the silence. "You smoke Camels." It wasn't a question.

Jake heard more coughing on the other end followed by more silence. Jake could still hear the man breathing and his own heart pounding.

"No matter what I've done in my life, I'd never fuck with someone's kid," the voice said.

Jake waited. He knew he was talking to either Henry Kritchman or Ralph Bumgarden. He had read their files at least four times. Hands or Rhino? The puzzle was coming together.

The guy called him. Jake waited and listened. Twice he wanted to say something, but he didn't. A third match was lit. Jake could almost smell the smoke.

Silence.

Then suddenly Jake heard another coughing fit mixed in with the words "Warehouse" and "Alpha" something followed by an unmistakable click as the line went dead.

"Wait! Don't hang up!"

Jake was talking to someone that was no longer there.

Chapter Thirty-two

Leicht had been watching Jake from his office door. He saw his man go pale as he yelled into his phone. The lieutenant walked toward the back of the bureau to Jake's desk.

"What was that?"

"Someone who said he didn't want any part of something. I'm sure he was talking about Sam."

Leicht bent over the desk closest to him, grabbed the phone and hit zero. "Bill, did you just switch a call to the DB?"

"Yes sir. Someone called for Detective Bush," the clerk replied. "I saw him come in." The LT replaced the receiver in the cradle. The room was silent.

Jake looked over his boss's shoulder. The clock was reading 7:15 a.m. The second hand slowly moved around the dial.

Leicht broke the silence. "Maybe he'll call back."

"It was the guy who smokes."

"Who smokes?"

"The guy who called me." Jake walked toward the coffee pot. The contents of his cup had gone cold.

"You're not making sense, Jake. Spell it out for me."

"I think this all goes back to the white van that went

missing on that attempted kidnapping of a guy named Vogtmann. I tagged some butts found in a driveway that night.

"Then we ended up getting a search warrant for a paint shop we thought was connected to the kidnapping and found some butts there. And then we searched some storage sheds and found more cigarette butts."

The LT propped his ass on the corner of the closest desk. He let Jake talk.

"In all three, the lab came back with the same results: non-filtered Camels. One of the guys we're looking for smokes Camels."

Jake rinsed his cup out in the sink. "Those paint shop phone records put Ben Squires in the loop. And what happens next? Squires was called in to explain and he blows his brains out before anyone finds out anything."

He poured himself a fresh cup. "Next my son is grabbed. Things are adding up and somehow I think there's a guy named Vito pulling the strings on all of this."

"Who's Vito?"

"A name Cliff and I came up with through the phone company. Percy Cabala was the name on the phone account and it just so happens this Cabala guy officially changed his name to Vito Calabrese a few years back."

Leicht joined Jake at the coffee pot. "Camels, eh?" He emptied his cup in the sink. "The guys bagged some butts out by your place yesterday." The LT filled his cup. "I'll tell them to put a rush on the cigarettes. In the meantime, go home. Take care of your wife."

"I'm not going home."

"I know it's your son, but let us do our job, Jake."

"And I'm going to do what I can. Somewhere, someone has my son."

"We'll find him," the lieutenant interrupted.

"Alive?"

The lieutenant stood there looking at Jake. He didn't have an answer.

“Here’s something I know for sure, boss.”

“What’s that?”

“The papers are resurrecting the Oakland County Child Killer. It’s not him.”

“We don’t know that for sure.”

“I do. It’s summer. The wrong time of the year. I’ve read everything the task force had on those killings. Sam’s kidnapping is something completely different.”

The doors to the bureau repeatedly banged open as Roberts, Lakatos along with the rest of the detectives straggled in. There was no banter between them. Everyone went to their desks and started shuffling papers or making phone calls. No one looked toward Jake. They had kids.

“I’m going to put a trace on all calls coming in to your phone. If you get another, try to keep them on the line.” Leicht turned and went back to his office. He needed to call the FBI and get the wiretaps set up.

“I’m not sitting around waiting for my fuckin’ phone to ring.” Jake said to no one. He had something to work on: The last words he heard on the phone. “Warehouse” and “Alpha” something.

———

“Where in the hell’ve you been, Hands?”

“Getting some smokes.”

Rhino watched his partner nonchalantly climb out of their van. He was juggling two coffees in his hands so he nudged the door closed with a knee. His boss had said the night before to keep an eye on Hands.

“Vito said to make sure we fed the kid. We’re outta milk,” Rhino said as he grabbed a coffee from Hands.

“You were asleep.” He put his coffee down on the dusty desk Rhino was sitting at. “I can go back.”

This was the start of the third day in the debris-filled warehouse. Sam Bush had been handcuffed with his hands behind his back to the sink in the bathroom with a canvass sack over his head, the drawstring just tight enough so he couldn't work it back over his head. He was fed twice a day by the same guy. The old army-issue sleeping bag lay underneath him. It was all the kid had to sleep on.

Sam got a look at the guy who always fed him the first day when he came in and took the cuffs off so he could eat. Sam jerked the mask off the guy. One big hand grabbed his wrist while the other covered his mouth.

"Shhh!" The man's huge hand stayed in place while he talked. "Okay, I know you're a tough little shit, but trust me. You're not supposed to see any of us so we can let you go." Sam stopped struggling. "They'll probably kill you if they know you saw my face. Understand?" Sam nodded.

The man put the handcuffs back on. There was a long chain between each cuff and he looped it around the base of the wash basin before fastening the second cuff. "I'll try to make you comfortable." The big man slid the sleeping bag under the boy. He opened the door slightly and took a peek out.

"Don't get stupid and you'll stay alive." Hands said as he closed the door.

The ritual was always the same. The man wearing a rubber mask would take the sack off and move the cuffs to the front so the boy could eat. He'd give Sam fifteen minutes for a bowl of Cheerios in the morning and some lukewarm slices of pizza in the evening. Those were the only times they let him go to the toilet. Twice the soft-spoken giant snuck Sam a candy bar, but words were kept to a minimum after that first day. Water was the only thing they gave him to drink.

"The kid behaving himself?" Hands asked as he took a sip of his coffee.

"I haven't heard him kicking on the wall. I think he finally figured it doesn't do any good." Rhino stood, stretched and rubbed his crotch. "I'll ask him when I go take a piss."

Hands let himself down into one of the chairs. "Vito coming by this morning?"

"He said he'd be here. Why?"

"Just wondering." He lit a cigarette.

———

Jake had his county map spread out on his desk. There was an Alpha Parkway, an Alpha Street, then a Lane and a Court. Jake was somewhat familiar with the area Alpha Parkway was in. A warehouse just wouldn't be in that neighborhood. It was too upscale.

The map showed Alpha Street on a little peninsula jutting out into Union Lake. That didn't fit either. Alpha Court and Alpha Drive ran off of one another. They were in the southwest part of the county. Jake thought the guy could have said either. The coughing made it hard to understand.

Roberts was flipping through his notes as he threw his sport coat over the back of his chair. "You know, we've never checked out that last house from the phone records." He flipped a few more pages. "The one on Chestnut Run Drive. The possible girlfriend. Nancy Whats-her-name."

Cliff looked up from his notebook. "What are you looking for?"

"A street."

Jake folded up the map and tucked it into his sport coat's breast pocket. He slid open his bottom drawer and pulled out the box of Remington ammo he kept in there, dumping them into his right coat pocket. He had two speed clips already loaded in the pouch on his belt.

"You sure you got enough ammo?" Cliff asked as he watched.

Jake just shrugged and walked toward the back of the bureau, grabbing the keys for their unit.

"Where you going?"

"Out."

"Not without me." Cliff grabbed two radios out of the charging rack, tossing one to Jake. "Here. We'll need more than bullets to do this right."

Jake started the engine while Cliff slipped into the seat beside him. "Remember? No Lone Ranger shit."

"You may not want to be a part of this."

"Why not?"

"Because nobody fucks with my family."

Jake was burning rubber as he roared out of the lot. "What's the quickest way to Wixom Road and I-96?"

"Orchard Lake Road. It becomes Pontiac Trail."

"Too many lights."

"Run the fuckers. You're a cop."

Cliff pulled the portable red light out of the glove box and let the magnetic base slam onto the roof. He pulled the lighter and plugged in the flashing light.

"Can I ask what's going on?"

Jake told him about the call. "All I know is the guy said he didn't want any part of whatever they were doing. I think he was talking about grabbing Sam."

"You're guessing."

"At least I am doing something."

The nose of their Chevrolet dipped as Jake had to stand on his brakes as he tried blowing the light on Old Telegraph Road. "Come on lady; get out of the fuckin' way." Jake wormed his way around the Ford with an old lady behind the wheel. She was yelling and pointing to the green light over her head. Jake just waved at her as he floored the Chev.

"How about letting me drive?"

"Just let me know if I need to make a turn."

"You're gonna get us killed."

Jake drove onto the shoulder of the road to get around someone who was too slow turning onto Commerce Road; Cliff put his hands on the dashboard to keep in his seat as Jake swerved back onto the blacktop. The speedometer said Jake was going seventy as he went across the back of Saint

Mary's. He remembered the boarding school, the body and the van—where all this seemed to have started.

"Where we headed?"

"The guy just said, 'warehouse' and 'alpha' something. I'm thinking it's either Alpha Court or Drive."

"Jake, I know the area. It's near the Ford Wixom Plant. There's all kinds of tool and die shops and warehouses that support the plant."

"All we gotta do is find the right one."

"How?"

Jake just shrugged as he took to the shoulder of the road again to get around a John Deere tractor pulling a wheeled grain bin. It was wheat harvest time.

"The ammo you dumped in your pocket. You planning a war?"

"I told you that you might not want to be with me."

"Why wouldn't I?"

"I might have to kill someone."

Haggerty Road's light was changing as Jake hit the gas. A Dodge pickup jack-rabbiting from the light had Jake swing hard right, then back left. He barely missed the front of the Dodge.

"Promise it won't be me." Cliff looked back to make sure the Dodge was all right. "Never did want to die in a car wreck."

Cliff righted himself in his seat. "Tell me why you might have to kill someone."

"If anyone hurts Sam, they die. Simple enough."

Cliff pointed ahead. "The road turns west just up there. Take it to Wixom, then south."

"You sure?"

"You told me to get you there. Listen to me and I'll get you there."

Rhino heard a tap on a horn. He pulled himself out of his

chair and walked across the warehouse floor looking through the dirty window next to the overhead door. It was Vito sitting in his maroon Cadillac. Rhino grabbed the handle and jerked the door up. Once the Cadillac was inside, Rhino pulled the rope to close the door.

"Did you guys feed the kid?" Vito asked as he worked his way out from behind the wheel.

"Not yet," Rhino answered. "Me and Hands was just talking about that."

Hands lumbered toward the Cadillac. "Boss, we need to talk." He closed the door on his boss's car as Vito let himself down into one of the chairs by the desk.

"What about?"

"The kid."

"What about him?"

Hands leaned against the side of the Cadillac. "I told Rhino I didn't like grabbin' a kid."

"Well, your job is to do what I say."

"The drugs or popping a guy; I can go along with, but I ain't into hurting a kid."

"You will if I say so."

"No I'm not. I'm getting out."

"What do you mean, 'you're getting out?'" Vito leaned forward in his chair. "You're already in it as deep as we are. There ain't no getting out."

Hands slowly dug into his shirt pocket and pulled out a pack of smokes. He pulled one out with his lips and flicked his lighter with his left hand. Rhino never saw it happen, but Hands also had his pistol in his right hand, hanging down against his leg.

"But I am. I'll just take the van. It'll be at my place. You and Rhino can pick it up there."

Hands was sucking in a long drag as Rhino's blade found home angled up just under the left rib cage. He turned, his eyes rolling as he grabbed Rhino's arm. A puff of smoke and two short coughs were all he could muster as he twisted and collapsed.

"I told you when you called last night he was up to something." Vito leaned back in his chair.

"Now I know how Judas felt," Rhino whispered. He bent over, wiped the six inch blade off on Hands' shirt and folded the knife closed. He paused looking over the body. "We've been together since '73 in Nam."

"Well, we couldn't let him fuck things up now after we've gone this far." Vito walked over, looking at the man on the floor. "You know, I kinda liked the big bastard myself."

There was a blank stare coming up from the floor. Vito took the tip of his shoe and pushed against the man's jaw so the eyes looked away from him.

"Four years with me and what, all of a sudden he has ethics?" Vito bent down and grabbed the small Browning automatic that Hands had dropped; putting it in his pocket He turned his back to the body. "You say he went out this morning?"

"Yeah. For some smokes and a couple of coffees."

Vito's thumb and forefinger smoothed his mustache as he thought. "Think he'd drop a dime on us?"

"I don't know." Rhino raised his hands and shrugged. "I'd say no, but since the kid, he's changed."

Vito looked at the cardboard cups. *7-Eleven.*

"How close is this place?" pointing to the cups.

"Three blocks. Maybe four."

"Go see if your friend used their phone."

Chapter Thirty-three

Vito paced the floor. *Sure as shit he made a call.* He stopped and looked at the body. *Who?* He knew he had to do something as he looked toward the bathroom door. On a small chain hanging from a nail was the key to the handcuffs securing the boy. He didn't have time to wait for Rhino.

Vito worked the key in one cuff and brought it around the basin leg and relocked it on Sam's wrist. He tightened the drawstring on the canvass bag over the boy's head and tugged at his arm.

"Come on. We're going for a ride."

Sam had been wondering why he hadn't been fed when he heard the different voice, the one he hadn't heard since the first day—the third guy.

"Leave me alone," he yelled, kicking his right leg toward the voice. His own was muffled by the bag. He kicked again and screamed.

Sam was hoping the one who had been feeding him would come to his rescue.

"Just shut the fuck up you little bastard or I'll blow your brains out right now."

"Lemme go! Lemme go!"

Sam fell as the man pulled on him. He felt his arms going up behind his back as Vito pulled on the handcuffs. The pain shot through his shoulders.

"Ow! Ow!"

"On your feet or I drag you, you little shit."

The man started hoisting him up into something. The bag was thick and tight. Only faint gray shapes filtered in. He realized he was being put in the trunk of a car when he smelled rubber and heard it bang shut over the top of him.

Sam listened. He knew he had to remember everything so he could tell his dad. He wanted to be tough, but tears started flowing.

"Dad? Dad help me!"

Jake and Cliff had crawled up and down Alpha Court then Alpha Drive and noted five "For Lease" signs. The area was neatly laid out with all the same type of one-story buildings: dark brown brick with whitish-gray concrete around the doors and windows. If Jake were to guess, they were all at least three hundred feet long and seventy feet deep with a neatly trimmed lawn and bushes in the front. All had the same designed sign planted in the middle of the lawn near the office area entrance made of brick and glass. Each sign announced the type of shop or business inside. No doubt, all the buildings were constructed by the same company over the past twenty years.

There were tool and die shops, machine shops and assorted warehouses; some were off-site connections to the Wixom Ford Plant that was just down I-96.

The backs of these buildings were mostly filled with windows and overhead doors surrounded by a black-topped lot, most of which was marked off for parking with faded yellow lines. Small signs hung above the roll-up doors indicating "Shipping" or "Receiving."

"They've gotta be in one of those," Jake said.

"Yep." Cliff shot out a finger. "Pull into that lot."

"They've got Sam in an empty building. The guy

definitely said 'warehouse' not an open shop."

"Slow down and think." Cliff paused, waiting for Jake to make the turn. He didn't. "Leicht was right," he said. "You're too close to this."

"It's my son they've got."

"We'll find your son if you'd just listen to me."

Jake made a U-turn and eased into the parking lot Cliff had pointed out then into open spot.

"Now what?"

"There's two places on Alpha Court and three on Drive. Which way do you want to go first?" Cliff was easing out his door as he talked. "And pocket that radio."

"Let's split up. You take the Court; I'll take the ones on Drive."

"No," Cliff quickly said. "There're at least two of them holding Sam. We'll work each building together."

Jake headed out of the lot toward the first building on Alpha Court.

"I'll take the street side. You take the back," Cliff said. "See if there's a window you can see in. I'll do the same. If you see movement, hit the radio."

Jake grunted and checked his S&W .357 as he walked. His elbow touched the pouch with the two speed loaders for reassurance. His right coat pocket bulged with the extra ammo.

Cliff saw his partner's subtle moves. "As good as you shoot you don't need all that weight you're carrying."

Jake just shrugged as he started to trot.

"Partner, walk casually," Cliff said. "Look like someone looking to lease the place."

"We don't have time to walk."

Rhino poured himself a cup of coffee in a medium sized cardboard cup and looked at the clerk behind the counter. "You been here all morning?"

The man at the cash register looked up. “I opened at six, why?”

“Friend of mine was in here. A guy ‘bout my size. Said he might have dropped something on the floor.”

“I’ve had a lot of customers coming and going. How would I remember just one?”

“He bought two coffees and a pack of Camels.”

The clerk shrugged.

“He said he tried calling me. Did he use your phone?”

The clerk looked toward the back where the phone and the restrooms were. “Hell, a lot of guys came in this morning buying newspapers, lunches and coffee.”

Rhino threw a twenty on the counter. “For the coffee and to kick-start your memory.”

“Your friend cough a lot?”

Rhino nodded.

The clerk pocketed the twenty. “Yeah, he used the phone.”

“You sure?”

“The only thing he dropped was his cigarette butts.”

Rhino banged out the door leaving his coffee behind.

———

1655 Alpha Court was a one-story dark brown brick building, typical of others in the area. An entrance was centered among what looked like offices that fronted the rest of the building. Windows were slung low with an occasional silent window air conditioner in the bottom near the ground. To the west were taller windows letting light into the shop or warehouse. To Cliff, the building looked recently vacated. None of the glass had yet succumbed to rocks thrown by bored kids walking by.

Jake went around the back and tried the first overhead door he came to. He expected to find it locked. It was. He peeked into the window of the entry door next to it. The inside was too dark to see anything. He moved along the paved ramp behind the building toward the taller windows. He peered in seeing nothing but dust-covered tables and cabinets.

This is stupid. He knew he had to be inside to really search the place. The lower end of the windows had a smaller pane two feet high and about three and a half feet wide. Each had a simple latch that would open toward him. A boxy dumpster with side doors stood between two windows. He looked inside it. A few boxes were littered on its floor. His eyes checked the windows. There were no alarm strips that he could see.

Jake used the dumpster's metal lift tabs to climb up to the window ledge. A sharp tap with the butt of his S&W punched a hole just above the latch. He reached in and turned the handle so he could pull the bottom of the window toward himself.

Jake grabbed his radio. "Cliff, I'm going inside." He bent down and slid sideways into the opening extending his feet to the floor and let himself down.

The morning's sunlight filtering in the dusty windows gave him enough light to scan the vacant shop floor that extended to his left. To his right were doors to an office area. In his left hand was the small Motorola radio, in his right, his Smith and Wesson. He inched toward the offices, noticing his own tracks in the dust as he glanced back to the windows.

The first door he tried squeaked as he eased it open. All he saw was more dust and no signs of any recent use.

"Cliff, we're wasting time here," he said into his radio as he walked to the front door and flipped the two dead bolt locks that secured it. The bright sunlight had him wincing as he looked for his partner. He wasn't going to worry about locking it behind him.

Cliff was walking on the sidewalk heading for the next "For Lease" sign. Jake ran to catch up.

"You know B&E is a crime, don't you?" Cliff said as Jake fell in alongside.

Jake noticed a slight smile as his partner talked. He knew

Cliff was trying to ease the tension in the air. The next building with a sign was three buildings up.

"I'll take the back again," Jake said.

Two overhead doors and windows went the length of the building in front of Jake. A few windows were busted out as were some smaller ones on the doors. Jake reached down grabbing the first door's handle.

"Jake?" It was his radio.

"Go."

"A dark blue van just went past. It's turning onto Alpha Drive."

Jake turned to look across the abandoned parking lot behind him. He spotted the van traveling between two buildings on the next block. It was at least 200 hundred yards away disappearing behind the next building.

The van reappeared in a driveway and turned toward the rear of a building in plain sight of Jake, 300 hundred yards off. He tucked himself between a power pole and the building to watch.

The driver stopped the van at an overhead door, got out, pulled the door up and entered. It was a big man wearing a white T-shirt and dark pants. Jake grabbed his radio.

"Cliff, he went inside a building off the back of Alpha Drive. I'm heading that way." Jake broke into a run.

"Wait for me."

Cliff's radio transmission went unanswered.

The first thing Rhino saw when he lifted the door was that the Cadillac was gone. He ran to where they were keeping the boy. *Shit!* The only thing left was an empty sleeping bag with a tennis shoe lying next to it.

Rhino's quick scan of the inside of the warehouse filled in the blanks. Vito booked it with the kid. Hands' body was on the floor right where he fell. The boxes from the storage unit were still stacked against the far wall. Rhino knew he had to get the hell out of there. He didn't bother pulling the door down as he ran to the van and jumped in.

Movement in the distance got his attention; a man running toward him. A man with a gun in his hand.

Rhino cranked the engine and threw it into reverse and did a donut on the blacktopped lot. He threw his left hand out the window and his Browning .45 automatic barked twice. Rhino had never seen Jake Bush, but now he knew who Hands had called.

Who else?

Jake was running at an angle 100 yards from the van when two shots rang out. He slowed to a walk—a calculated walk. The Smith came up and he carefully put the front blade in the center of the back sight.

The van cut to the right giving Jake a look at its back doors. Jake took a two-handed stance, his right fist and the butt of his .357 resting in his left. He wasn't looking at a silhouette target now as he emptied his pistol at the fleeing truck. He was focusing on the left rear window—the one on the driver's side.

Even though the van was at least fifty yards away and getting further with each second, he knew he hit it at least twice. He watched the van rock and almost tip over as it made a left on Alpha Court toward Wixom Road.

Cliff had caught up to where Jake was standing as the van disappeared in the distance. Jake hadn't heard Cliff screaming just seconds before. "Gun! Gun!"

"Hands or Rhino?" Jake asked.

His hands were moving as he hit the ejection rod dumping six spent shells. One of his speed loaders put six fresh rounds in the cylinder before he snapped it shut.

"One of them for sure." Cliff said holstering his gun.

Jake turned toward where their car was parked. His first instinct was to go after the van.

"Whoa Jake!" Cliff tipped his head toward the open overhead door. "Sam might be in there."

Jake stopped in his tracks. He took a deep breath,

knowing his partner was right. Fear gripped his heart as he walked to the warehouse. His shoes felt like they were concrete blocks.

He knew it had been a long time since he had really prayed, but he started.

Please God. Please! More words just wouldn't come to him.

Chapter Thirty-four

Jake only paused for a second when he saw the body lying in a pool of blood. It was in the middle of an abandoned warehouse littered with trash, small cartons and old wooden pallets. He saw two doors to his right; one to an obvious office cubical, the other had a tin sign reading: Restroom.

He quickly checked the small office. It contained two desks, no chairs, no phones and a couple of months of dust.

His feet stopped moving a couple seconds before easing open the bathroom door. He could hear his heart beating.

Please God help me...

He pushed the prayer aside. He didn't want to find another body—his son's.

A slim window at the top of the back wall gave off just enough light to reveal an olive drab sleeping bag and an empty black sneaker just off its edge.

Sam? Sam, where are you?

Jake's thoughts were interrupted by Cliff's voice on the radio calling for assistance.

He held tight to the proof his son had been there.

Where is he now? The van?

Two units manned by deputies Kaminski and Williams

were the first to arrive, followed by a crew of detectives. The deputies secured the outside area, while detectives Lakatos and Burrows came inside.

"Leicht and the ME are on the way," Lakatos said as he looked up from the body in the middle of the floor. He was talking to Cliff Roberts who was making a rough-sketch of the scene. Lakatos pointed out an open pack of Camels near the body on the floor as he asked, "Know him?"

"Never been introduced, but I'll bet he's one of the guys we've been looking for." Cliff looked at Jake for confirmation. He didn't get a response.

Lakatos moved around the body, avoiding stepping in the blood seeping from under it. He took an unlit cigar out of his mouth. "Hey Ed, come look at this." With the cigar clenched between his index and middle finger, he was pointing out a slight thin slit in the white t-shirt the man was wearing.

Ed Burrows hunched down next to Lakatos as he eyed up the blood soaked hole. "Knife wound."

"Yeah, that's what I was thinking."

Jake got up off the pallet he had been sitting on and walked over to his partner nudging him. "Meet me at the car."

Jake was behind the wheel of their Chevrolet waiting when Cliff got there.

"Jake, we can't leave. Leicht's on his way."

"We need to find that van."

Cliff reached in the open window and took the keys from the ignition. "The van can wait."

Jake picked up the tennis shoe he had put on the seat. "See this? It's Sam's. He was here."

"I know. But..."

"He might be in the fuckin' van." A tear streaked down his left cheek as he said it. "The van I shot at."

Cliff opened the driver's door, his finger waggling, inviting Jake out of the car. "He's not in that van."

"How the hell do you know?"

"I just know." Cliff sighed. "If we went driving around, where would we start looking?"

Jake shrugged. Another tear made a path down Jake's right cheek. He immediately flicked it away. "At least we'd be looking and..."

"Jake, listen to me." Cliff had his hand on his partner's shoulder. "I figure the dead guy in there was the one who called you. Maybe there's something in there that'll tell us where to start."

Jake slowly nodded as he climbed out from behind the wheel. He looked over the parking lot as flashing lights sitting atop the two black and white units dissolved within the day's bright sunlight. Another tear worked its way down his cheek.

The ME's wagon pulled up behind the plain-wrapped Pontiac, the ride Lakatos and Burrows had come in. Another Chevy screeched into the lot behind the ME's wagon. It was Leicht.

"Watch what you say, partner," Cliff said. "I want you with me. At least act like you've got it all together. If you don't, the boss'll take you off the street for sure." Cliff was talking as they walked back to the warehouse.

Jake rubbed his cheeks with a sleeve. "Somewhere out there's a blue van with some bullet holes in the back of it. Find it and..."

"Shh!" Cliff cut him off as Leicht walked up.

It took Cliff no more than a few minutes to fill his boss in on the call Jake had gotten earlier and how they ended up coming to the Alpha Court area.

"We had just finished searching one building and were heading for the next when I saw a blue van. Jake was in the rear of the next place. I called him, remembering we'd been looking for a blue van since we searched the old paint shop. We think it's tied in somehow to all this shit including grabbing Sam."

Leicht nodded.

"The driver went to that door," Jake was pointing to the

open overhead door. "In seconds he came out and jumped into the van. He started tearing out of the lot. When he saw me he started shooting."

"That in itself proves we were right on the van," added Cliff.

Leicht nodded again as he looked at Jake. "Was he alone?"

"I don't know." Jake's head dropped, remembering emptying his pistol at the van.

Cliff knew what was going through his partner's head. "There's a dead guy in the warehouse that I figure was the partner to the guy in the van."

"He kill him?"

Jake shrugged. "All I know is my kid had been in there." He held out the shoe he'd been carrying. "This is the match of the one they found by Sam's fort."

The LT nodded, watching Jake talk.

Cliff was watching the LT's eyes. "Looks like something went down before we got here and they grabbed the boy and booked it," he said. "The van coming back and then taking off doesn't make any sense." He paused.

"Because his partner was dead and Sam was gone," Jake added.

Cliff nodded. "Yeah. Why else would the guy show up, then cut and run?"

"Let's take a good look in there. See if there's anything they left besides a body," Leicht said.

"Besides the van, we need to be looking for a guy named Vito Calabrese and his maroon Cadillac," Jake said. He flipped through his notebook looking for the information they had gotten from the secretary of state's office two weeks before. "This asshole is behind all this shit. I'd bet on it."

"Get it on the air and then check out the place. Let's quit wasting time," the LT said.

Every fifteen minutes all the law enforcement radios in

Southeast Michigan repeated an *All-Points-Bulletin*:

"Attention all units; wanted for questioning in connection with the kidnapping of 11-year-old Sam Bush, the son of a detective with the Oakland County Sheriff's Department, is a dark blue General Motors van. The back windows may be shot out.

Also wanted is a 1978 maroon Cadillac Coupe Deville with a black vinyl top bearing Michigan license number B-Boy W-William 3257. It is possibly driven by a white male named Vito Calabrese. Both should be considered armed and dangerous. Approach with caution."

The dispatcher added the line about the boy being the son of a police officer. He knew cops took care of their own and would look harder and longer.

It was ninety-five degrees and a clear day. The sun seemed to be directly beating down on one particular trunk lid belonging to a maroon Cadillac parked in row C at the new Twelve Oaks Mall in Novi.

Sam hadn't felt the car move for what seemed like an hour. He was having a difficult time breathing with the canvas bag over his head. He was soaking wet from sweat and weakening with every passing minute. Somehow he managed to roll from this stomach to his back. Something caught the chain on the cuffs holding his arms behind him, but was able to work it loose. His hands reached and felt the pointy tip of what he thought was the jack handle. He remembered helping his dad rotate tires on his mother's car using a handle like that. He wanted to remember everything he could for his dad.

Dad? Mom? God? Anyone? Please help.

Sam couldn't cry. Not that he didn't want to. His throat felt like it was full of sand as he yelled, "Help me! Help me!" He started kicking at whatever was over him with his stocking feet. Two kicks were all he could muster.

Water. Just a sip.

Just beyond the food court, down the hallway that led to the restrooms and rows of quarter-operated security lockers stood three pay phones. Vito paced back and forth. Two women and one teen were using them. Twice he leaned in close enough so they could smell the garlic-laced sausage he had with his eggs that morning.

"Mama, what kind of a dress should I buy for Sherri?" The woman at the first phone asked. She waited for a response.

"No I want to get her a dress, not a skirt and blouse. I think she'd look good in pink."

He looked at the next woman, her thighs bulging, trying to escape from under her much too-tight shorts. "Look, Nathan, I don't give a rat's ass what your mama told you." Her eyes caught Vito looking at her and her hand covered the mouthpiece. "Mind your own business, asshole."

The other phone had a kid cooing, "No. You looked really cool yesterday. I liked how you filled out your sweater." There was a pause. "No really." The kid looked over his shoulder at Vito as he said, "Think I could ride my bike over?" He turned away from Vito's glare.

Vito ducked into the john. He had to piss. As he got back into the hallway the phones were now in use by two other women, but the kid was still there. Vito leaned against the wall across from them. One was checking on her kids, the other obviously talking to a boyfriend. The kid was whispering to whoever was on the other end as he fondled an obvious rise in his jeans.

"Okay jackoff, get off the fuckin' phone," Vito barked.

The two women looked toward the voice, wondering who the man was talking to. Then Vito ended the kid's call with his left hand slamming down the cradle while his right snatched the receiver from his ear. "Time's up lover boy.

Scram!"

Vito wasn't a big man, but his snarl had the acne-faced kid cowering.

"Screw you, mister," the kid said moving off.

Vito dropped a coin in the slot and dialed. It took three rings for someone to pick up. His voice went to a whisper. "Mom, I need to use the garage..."

Vito was cut off. He listened for all of five seconds when he raised his voice. "Yes, I know it's Thursday. That's why I'm calling. Call him and cancel."

He listened to the reply.

"No it can't wait 'til later, Ma, get him the fuck outta there!" He slammed the receiver into its cradle. The two women had stopped talking and were looking at Vito as soon as he raised his voice.

"Who in the fuck you lookin' at?"

He turned and scurried down the hall.

Acne Face had gotten to the desk under the sign reading *Mall Security*. A woman was already talking to the guard.

"Officer, I know I heard a voice coming from the trunk of a car, then a couple of thumps. It's a maroon Cadillac."

"Lady, look..."

"You gotta come. I know someone's in that trunk."

The overweight security guard looked past the woman's shoulder. It was cool in the mall and sweltering outside. "Whatcha need, Kid?"

"There's a guy by the phones who grabbed mine. I was still talking." Acne Face looked toward the hallway. Vito came into view. "That's him right there. The guy in the suit."

"Hey, I was first." The woman pushed the kid aside.

"Lady, I'll call the police. You can tell them your crazy story."

"You won't come out and check?"

"As you can see, I'm busy." We waved her off to the side. "Kid, what was happening back there?"

Five minutes later a car from the OCSD showed up.

Deputy Mel Williams answered the call after clearing the warehouse. The woman with the information was happy to wait until the deputy arrived. The Cadillac had left, but she knew what she heard and remembered all too well the kids that were kidnapped a couple of years before. One was her nephew.

———

Vito motored toward his house. He was mumbling as he drove, checking his mirrors. "Fuckin' bitch. I buy the place and she says she's got company."

Every Thursday his mom would have the priest from Saint Williams over for lunch.

Just my luck.

Vito had bought the house using his mother's maiden name five years before. He didn't want the name Calabrese or Cabala attached to any real property just in case the federal government in the form of the IRS came nosing around. Then too, he didn't like the Detroit neighborhood she and he lived in. Everything south of Eight Mile was turning black.

He knew he had to hide the kid somewhere until he could figure how to dump him. *Fuckin' Hands and his scruples!*

The cops probably found the warehouse and were no doubt after him. He needed to get his car off the street. The drugs left back at the warehouse were the least of his worries. Vito was out of options and running scared.

———

Leicht was driving back to headquarters haunted by the vision of Jake rolling his son's sneaker in his hands. He was wondering what he'd do if someone snatched his kid. He was counting on his men finding something that'd put them back in the hunt for the boy.

The deputy listened to the information the retired school

teacher was telling him—the voice she thought she heard and the thumping from within the trunk. She had been loading her own car with things she had bought and the Cadillac happened to be parked next to her.

"You said it was maroon. Did it have a black vinyl top?"

"Yes."

Within minutes the radios in Oakland County were blaring again.

"All units. We have an update on the maroon Cadillac possibly wanted in connection with the kidnapping of an 11-year-old boy. A car fitting that description was reported in the area of the Twelve Oaks Mall. A witness reported hearing sounds coming from the trunk."

Cliff and Jake had just put the ME wagon in their rearview mirror. They left Burrows and Lakatos handling the murder scene and Machelski and Popp came by to assist with the drugs Cliff had found. Leicht called in the second crew to handle the narcotics found at the scene. He knew Jake shouldn't be boggled down bagging and tagging evidence. The LT knew his man wanted to be out there looking for the blue van or Vito and his Cadillac.

A half block after leaving the warehouse, Cliff and Jake heard the radio update. Cliff reached into the inside pocket on his coat and grabbed the small notebook he kept there. He tossed it to his partner.

"Flip through the pages, Jake. I got that address in there on the place on Chestnut Run Drive."

Jake was half in a daze still fiddling with the tennis shoe when he heard the radio squawking about a maroon Cadillac. He dropped the shoe on the floor and found the address, remembering them checking out the place a few days before. He was back in the hunt and fully alert.

"The girlfriend?" Jake asked as he looked at the woman's name they had gotten off the phone records.

"I'd put money on it," Cliff said as he buried his foot in the carburetor.

Jake had his pistol out; spinning the cylinder to make sure the speed loader had done its job earlier. It had. Six mag loads were waiting to be used. He snapped it shut.

Chapter Thirty-five

Rhino stayed off the freeway knowing the police would be watching I-96 from the overpasses. Sometimes it took a while for him to figure things out, but it was obvious Vito had grabbed the kid and took off leaving their last shipment of dope behind. He remembered Vito saying it was worth a quarter million dollars. *He's got to be running scared.*

Rhino drove the blue van staying on country roads working his way north from the warehouse. He needed time to think. *Where in the hell would he go? Home?*

He remembered he and Hands had helped Vito move into a house once, but that was at least four years before. *Where was that?* That house was for Vito and his mom. He remembered Hands laughing about their self-proclaimed Mafia Don being a "Mama's boy." The house wasn't that far from the old paint shop; just west of it a few miles. That was the only day he had ever been there.

Vito had made a habit of meeting his men at a place he'd choose. Nothing he couldn't walk away from. He said it was in case the cops were breathing down their necks. For more than three years it had been the old paint shop. Then, if he had any pressing matters he'd call Rhino or Hands at either of their apartments.

Since they shut down the paint shop, Vito would call

them to say where he'd be. Like the storage units, or for the last couple of days, the warehouse.

Rhino wished he had Hands with him now. He was the brains, but it was too late. For five grand he had turned on the only man he had ever trusted. Vito had insisted they had to get rid of Hands. "He's going to cause some problems over the boy. It's him or us."

Rhino was suddenly overcome by a wave of remorse. *I did it for the fuckin' money.* He braked hard, avoiding a car that turned in front of him. *Ol' Judas Iscariot has nothing on me.*

His mind continued to wander as he drove. He was the one who put the nickname "Hands" on the guy back in Vietnam. *Boy the guy had big hands.*

He and Hands were in the same platoon in the Army. They shared more than a few reefers together, even got blown out of their minds a time or two dropping some acid. Many times they were in the same foxhole when *Charlie* started lobbing a few mortar rounds their way. *God, we were close.*

And yet, he was the one who ran the knife up under Hands' rib cage. *Stupid, Ralph. Plain fuckin' stupid.*

It was Hands who stuck the name *Rhino* on him. "It's perfect," Hands had said laughing. "Ever see the way your skin rolls on the back of your neck? It's like a rhinoceros." So Ralph became Rhino.

Rhino thought back to how they became partners. A corporal named Cheavers suggested someone needed to frag the little pip-squeak lieutenant they had for a platoon leader. He took up a collection. Like a bounty. "Just need someone with enough balls to step up and do it," Cheavers had said. Rhino didn't remember whether it was marijuana or the LSD that had him and Hands do the deed. The man wearing gold bars was history.

He thought for a second. *Nah, it was the money.*

At their court martial they were found not guilty for the fragging due to lack of evidence, but received Bad Conduct

Discharges after serving six months in the stockade for the cache of drugs he and Hands had thought was well-hidden under the floor of their hooch.

It was a few years after Nam that he and Hands had run across Vito. They were small-time street hoods and he was looking for some heavy hitters—muscle. He paid well and on time. Neither he nor Hands had a problem working for Vito—until the boy.

First he has me eliminate Hands, then the son-of-a-bitch leaves me for the cops at the warehouse. Fuck you Vito.

Rhino worked his way onto Pontiac Trail, blending the van in with the traffic. *Hands was right. We shudda never grabbed the kid.* Rhino had his fully loaded M1911 Colt .45, something he smuggled out of Nam, lying on the passenger's seat as he drove.

He mumbled to himself as he turned onto Orchard Lake Road. "Mister Big Shot, I've got a bullet with Hands' name on it just for you."

Woodland Estates. The name just popped into his head. That's where he and Hands had moved Vito. He remembered looking out an upstairs back window and seeing a small lake as they were bringing in the beds and dressers into two rooms. One was Vito's, one was hers.

Rhino drove toward the paint shop, thinking he could find the house from there.

———

The traffic on Lahser Road didn't slow their Chevrolet a bit as Cliff weaved around one truck then another. The first was pulling a trailer full of mowers and rakes. The second was an old farmer, driving about 30, looking at the crops in a small cornfield. The way houses were going up cornfields and farmers would soon be in the past. Five acre ranchettes and housing developments were taking over land that only a short time before had cattle grazing, or crops like wheat, beans and corn growing.

"Just past the high school then left on Hickory Grove," Jake said, interrupting Cliff's thoughts. He had the county map unfolded across his lap.

"How we gonna play this?" Cliff asked as he passed the school.

"Kick in the fuckin' door. Either the Cadillac is there or the girlfriend will know where it is."

"Make sure it's the right address. This isn't Detroit. We get the wrong house they'll have our badges."

The sign for *Woodland Estates* was easy enough to find. Rhino knew he just had to work his way up the maze of streets to find the right house. He took a left on Chestnut Run Drive then a right on Stoneridge. New homes were going up on both sides of the street. *No this isn't it.*

He pulled into a driveway, backed out and went back to Chestnut Run. A woman was retrieving mail from the box at the road. He stopped and stuck his head out his window.

"Lady, is there some houses up this way backed up to a lake?"

"Yes, up the road a piece."

Rhino waved and motored on. *Up the road a piece?*

He slowed to a stop when he saw a man sitting on a riding mower. He was in his mid-fifties, wearing a starched short-sleeved khaki shirt, matching pants and a pith helmet. He had what looked like a martini in his hand while his tractor idled; two green olives were in the bottom of the glass. *Tough life.*

Rhino climbed out of the van and walked up to him. "I'm looking for a buddy of mine. Drives a maroon Cadillac. I lost the address."

The guy cut the motor and looked first at the poorly painted blue van, then at Rhino. Rhino hadn't shaved in four days and was wearing baggy dungarees and a ragged tee shirt.

"You're bullshittin' me." He waved his arm toward the nearby houses. All were of a neocolonial design—two story, having three distinct sections with attached three-car garages. Each was sitting on two to three acres. All were a part of *Woodland Estates*. "You don't have a friend living around here."

Rhino's first instinct was to kick the uppity bastard's ass, but he wanted Vito. "I meant I work for him. I'm here to pick up some things for the dump."

The lawn guy took a swallow of his drink while he thought. Rhino looked for the maid or butler who might have brought out the drink. It was almost that kind of a neighborhood, but then, this guy wouldn't be mowing his own lawn if he had either.

"Second place down. The one with the red shutters." He pointed to the van. "If you got room in there, stop back. I got some things I'd like to get rid of—like my wife," he chuckled.

"Thanks." Rhino got in the van and looked for a big house with red shutters.

———

"Percy, don't you dare interrupt my Thursdays again," Nancy Cabala said. She was talking through clenched teeth and waving a crooked finger at Vito. The woman was dressed in a light tan linen pant suit and wearing a bit more rouge on her cheeks than normal. Her silver hair was pinned up in a bun. "Father Murphy's already here."

"Ma, it is Vito, remember? There's no more Percy."

He grabbed her by the elbow. "Why don't you and Father Murphy go somewhere for lunch?"

"Why are you home in the middle of the day?"

"Where's his car?" Vito interrupted.

"I picked him up."

Vito stood there, his arms folded across his chest. "Ma, you're not screwing the priest, are you?"

She reached back and slapped him. “Don’t be absurd.” Her heavily rouged cheeks got a brighter shade of red. “Father Murphy is in the sunroom waiting for me. We’re having iced tea and talking about us making a donation to build a new rectory.”

“I had to ask.” Vito smiled. “A donation I can handle, but knowing my mom was fucking the priest...”

She didn’t put much behind the second slap. Nancy spun on her toes and turned toward the sunroom and said over her shoulder, “You’ve got a filthy mind, son.”

In the garage Vito listened at the trunk for a few minutes. He heard nothing. *Good.* He didn’t care if the kid was dead or alive. He’d find a place to ditch him later. *Maybe in one of canals around Forest Lake?* The lake was just a few minutes from his house.

Rhino didn’t bother ringing the bell; he just put his 260 pounds behind a size 15 shoe and followed it in the shattered door.

Vito heard the crash. He opened the hallway door from the garage and came face-to-face with Rhino.

“What the fuck you doin’ here?”

“Looking for you. I want the money. The five grand.”

“Later.”

“There ain’t no later. You left me high and dry at the warehouse. I want the money, NOW!” Rhino had the Colt Automatic in his hand. The big muzzle pointed at Vito’s chest.

Vito’s hands were up. “All right! All right! The safe’s in the garage.” He turned, reopening the door as his other hand went to his right coat pocket, grabbing the pistol Hands had dropped in the warehouse. Vito spun.

Rhino saw the move. At first he didn’t believe his eyes until the little gun came up. Rhino’s Colt barked just once. The .45 caliber ACP hollow point 230 grain *Man Stopper* bullet with a muzzle velocity of 1080 feet per second knocked Vito off his feet and back through the doorway. Blood, flesh and bits of clothing spattered the walls and the hood of the maroon Cadillac.

Rhino stepped to the fallen body, rolled it over and dug into Vito's pockets. He found the car keys and the ring with the key to the cuffs. In the hallway behind him a woman started screaming.

Two seconds later he was in the trunk unfastening the cuffs and taking the canvas bag off the boy's head. He felt for a pulse. There was a slight one. He pulled the boy out of the trunk.

———

"It was the last place on the left if I remember right," Jake said as Cliff turned onto Chestnut Run.

"Uh-huh." He slowed, looking past a guy sitting on a riding mower. "There's a blue van up ahead."

The front door of the house was wide open. They heard a woman screaming and turned toward the screams. Near the end of a hallway, a man wearing a clergyman's collar and black suit was holding the woman.

Jake pushed past the pair and saw the body on the garage floor. He knew he was looking at Vito. The man's eyes were rolled back and lifeless. The mouth beneath the thin mustache was agape. The maroon Cadillac was just inside; beyond it, a Buick.

The trunk. Jake moved to the back of the Cadillac. The trunk was open. Sam was on the floor, wet towels on his forehead.

"Sam! Sam!" Jake knelt down next to his son, half picking him up.

"Call an ambulance," Cliff shouted toward the priest. The man in black moved down the hallway.

Cliff pushed Jake aside. "Go get some more wet towels." He started unbuttoning the boy's shirt, fanning him with the towel he'd removed from the boy's head. His eyes caught the movement of the entry door in the back of the garage. A slight summer breeze in the back yard had pushed it open.

Jake moved around the woman kneeling over Vito's body. She kept repeating the same mournful words. "My son! My baby!" Her hands were covering her eyes and tears were streaming from underneath them.

Seconds later, the priest and Jake had cleaned out the linen closet and were taking turns bringing Cliff cold, wet towels to put on Sam while waiting for the ambulance.

Since 1972, one of the prime-time TV shows was *Emergency*. It featured paramedics in action. Within a few years, there were Paramedic Units operating across the country. Pontiac had one unit in 1979 and it was dispatched to 1355 Chestnut Run Drive.

Becky Long and Marvin Lashway checked Sam's vitals as they listened to Cliff relating how the boy had probably been confined in the trunk of the car most of the day.

"You did the right thing," the woman paramedic said. "His temp is off the charts and we've got to bring it down. It's heatstroke." The boy wasn't moving as they put an oxygen mask on him and strapped him to a stretcher.

"We're going to St. Joe's," the woman said as they wheeled him away.

"You ride with them," Cliff said. "Leicht's got a couple of crews on the way."

"What about the other guy, Bumgarden?"

"Our guys will be combing the whole area and the K-9 Unit has a dog already working the track." Cliff wrapped an arm around his partner and gave him a little nudge. "Get going. Sam needs you a hell of a lot more than we do."

Chapter Thirty-six

Once the ambulance was on its way, Detectives Roberts, Lakatos and Burrows worked the scene. Leicht had Popp and Machelski going door-to-door looking for anyone who might have seen an unshaven man wearing baggy dungarees and a ragged tee shirt. Uniforms flooded the area.

For two days the OCSD and the State Police scoured the area of Chestnut Run Drive and all the surrounding streets. The driver of the blue van had evaporated. Oscar, the furry member of the OCSD's canine unit, had lost the scent at the edge of Orange Lake less than two hundred yards behind the Calabrese house. The State Police brought in a second dog and it too lost the scent at the edge of the lake. The door-to-door search was expanded to include the homes within a mile of Woodland Estates.

Nancy Cabala, Vito's mother, was unable to give any information to the detective team of Lakatos and Burrows. Between uncontrollable sobs and tears, she couldn't vocalize anything since seeing her son lying on the floor in a pool of blood.

Father Timothy Murphy was just the opposite. He had a clear picture of everything that happened. He heard a loud bang while in the company of Mrs. Cabala, followed by what sounded like a gunshot. He went with her to investigate. This led them to the garage where he saw Vito Calabrese dead on the floor and a man by the Cadillac's open trunk. The man was pulling a young boy from the trunk. This man then ordered the priest to bring him some wet towels, which he began putting on the boy.

"I was just getting more wet towels when you guys came in." Father Murphy wiped some sweat beads off of his forehead. "I take it he wasn't in the garage when you went in."

"No. Can you describe him?" Lakatos asked.

"Sure."

The priest's description, combined with descriptions by two other neighbors, put the same man behind the wheel of the blue van abandoned at the scene. This man was positively identified through latent prints found in the van and on the Cadillac's trunk as belonging to Ralph Bumgarden. One of the hardest things for the detectives working the scene to grasp was that Bumgarden did not immediately flee; instead he took the time to tend to Sam Bush.

"The wet towels and all," Cliff said to Burrows, "might just have saved the kid's life."

Sam Bush arrived at St. Joseph's with a temperature of 104.3 degrees. The attending physician's biggest fear was that the boy would suffer brain or organ damage. He was hooked up to IVs to replace lost fluids and ice packs were used to slowly reduce his core body temperature. Jake stayed at his son's side.

Leicht had already dispatched a deputy to bring Edie and Hank Bush to the hospital and stopped by to see how the boy was doing. Sam was unconscious as Hank and his mom came into the room. Hank was the first to speak.

"Dad? Will he be all right?"

"We hope so," Jake answered, pulling Hank in closer to

him.

The LT excused himself so the family could be alone.

Hank was happy his brother was safe, even though all the tubes and machinery had him concerned. Before long his fears were set aside as the nurses showed him how to read the equipment and understand what the readings and beeps meant.

"It means he's getting better," one nurse said.

Edie on the other hand remained silent. She sat in a chair next to Sam's bed, holding his hand and softly crying. Jake tried talking to her, but her full attention was on her youngest, running her fingers through his dark brown hair, making sure his blankets were just so, or adjusting his oxygen tube. A day later, when the hospital staff tried to reassure her that Sam was improving every hour, she never as much as acknowledged their presence.

By the third day, while Sam was improving and talking, Edie sat unresponsive, almost in a stupor. She ate very little and slept even less. An easy chair had been brought into the room the first day for her when she refused to leave her son's side. Day and night she sat there, holding Sam's hand while an occasional tear worked its way down her cheek.

Sam spent four days in the hospital's Intensive Care Unit. He seemed to be recovering rapidly. By the fourth day he was already talking his dad through each stage of his kidnapping. Sam's naps became shorter each day and his energy was returning.

Jake heard Sam say for the third time, "Dad, there was one of them that was real good to me. He snuck me some candy bars and I even saw his face once." Jake thought that might have been Bumgarden because he took the time to tend to the boy.

He had Cliff bring their file to the hospital. Through a short deck of pictures, the one Sam picked out was Henry, alias Hands, Kritchman, the body found at the warehouse.

"I think I can even remember the other voices," he said.

"There's only one voice left now." Jake said.

A broad grin swept across Sam's face. "I told them my dad was a detective and you'd shoot 'em."

"Well, just so you know, I didn't."

"Did Mr. Roberts?"

"No, Cliff and I had nothing to do with it. They were weeding themselves out." Sam had a puzzled look on his face. "I'll explain another time." Jake thought the sooner he stopped talking about the kidnapping and the men behind it the better, mainly for Edie's sake. She was there, hearing what was said, but staying silent.

By the end of Sam's stay in the hospital, he had told his dad all he could remember. "I knew you'd come to get me, Dad. I just knew." Sam looked at his mom. "You did too, didn't you Mom?"

The only response was a half-smile. Not a nod, not a word.

Many times Sam would say how he wished he'd grow up faster so he could be on the sheriff's department. "That'd be cool, eh Mom?"

A frown replaced the half-smile. "If that's your choice." She busied herself straightening Sam's blankets and refilling his water glass.

Jake was no longer concerned about Sam, but Edie. She started talking to some extent. Short phrases, seemingly angry phrases started coming out of her, but she never really engaged in the conversations. Jake knew she wasn't getting any better. Jake had used the phone in the lobby to call his boss the day they moved Sam out of ICU so Edie wouldn't hear.

"Boss, do you remember what you said about hooking us up with some counseling?"

Jake listened to the answer.

"No, it's my wife. I thought this would all go away when we got Sam back. It's not. In fact I think it's getting worse."

Dr. Emanuel Beyer stopped by under the pretext of seeing Sam. He was a psychiatrist who did *Pro Bono* work for the

Oakland County Sheriff's Department. The boy was bright and cheery and said he was ready to go home. Dr. Beyer concurred.

After observing Sam's mom while he was in the room, the doctor slipped his card to Jake. Edie had not spoken or moved the entire time. The card had the number for his office. "Call for a date and time after you have your son settled at home," he whispered.

———

After two weeks of dead-ends, the OCSD began concentrating on Orange Lake, more because of Lieutenant Leicht's persistence than anything else. "Two dogs can't be fuckin' wrong," he barked.

Three dive teams combed the lake. One of the problems with many lakes in the county is most were being overtaken by Eurasian Milfoil, a type of weed that forms in large masses, sometimes choking off small lakes. Orange Lake was not a large body of water.

Mid-day on the twentieth day of the search, the body of Ralph Bumgarden was found tangled in a mass of the invasive weed in ten feet of water. He evidently tried swimming across the lake to escape. It looked like he had tied his work boots around his neck; they ultimately contributed to his drowning. The Medical Examiner had said that from the condition of the body the lake's snapping turtle population had been feasting on it, but death by drowning was the official cause on the death certificate.

———

Jake made an appointment for Edie with Dr. Beyer before Sam was released from the hospital. His wife had changed from a bubbly, talkative woman, a partner in a two-way relationship to someone withdrawn and responding only when spoken to. It was as if she was angry at the world.

Doctor Emanuel Beyer fit the picture Jake thought a

shrink would look like. He was a bit on the chunky side, mid-thirties, thin disheveled hair and wearing wire rim glasses. He had a brown briar pipe clenched between his teeth on the left side of his mouth that was never lit and was mainly used it to point at the words dangling in the space between him and the person he was talking to. His voice was soft and he had a gentle smile, nothing that would throw you off guard. Edie had just shrugged when Jake told her he planned on both of them meeting with the doctor for the first visit.

After two sessions alone with Edie, Doctor Beyer started calling every colleague he could think of for their opinions. The most repeated phrase he had heard was that Edith Bush was suffering from psychotic depression or in layman's terms: a nervous breakdown. Dr. Beyer thought that was an easy cop-out. Somehow he remembered a paper he had read by a fellow psychiatrist named Jeanette Segal. She had been working with veterans from Vietnam and came up with a new term in the mental health world: Post Traumatic Stress Disorder. He found and studied Doctor Segal's paper with renewed interest.

Through three sessions and hypnosis, Dr. Beyer had determined that Edie, by day three of the kidnapping, had already accepted the fact that her son would be sexually assaulted and killed—yet another victim of the Oakland Child Killer. He then called Dr. Segal for a consultation.

Doctor Beyer was interested in Segal's suggested treatment. That being, dealing with the trauma she's experienced, rather than avoiding it or any reminder of it. That's why he recommended sending Edie to the Newberry State Hospital where Doctor Segal worked.

"I'm open to anything," Jake said. "I want my wife back."

Detective Mel Williams had the coffee running through the Bunn machine, the traditional morning ritual for the junior detective in the bureau. The corporal was upgraded to the suit squad when Jake Bush had taken a three month leave of absence to be with his wife.

Williams also inherited Jake's partner, though he couldn't move his stuff into Jake's desk. Cliff was hoping Jake would only be gone the three months.

"Mel," Roberts called out. "You might as well move your shit up here." He was pointing at Jake's old desk.

"Why the change of heart?"

"Because I helped him move this past weekend." Cliff looked through the drawers in Jake's desk to see if he had left anything behind. He didn't. "He put in his papers. He's gone."

"Where'd he move to?"

"Newberry. In the upper peninsula."

"What for?"

"For him and his sons to be near Edie. They say it'll help with her treatment."

"What's he gonna do for a living?" Mel asked as he brought an armload of books toward the front of the bureau.

"Cut down trees for all I know." Cliff thumbed through the stack of pistol magazines Williams put on Jake's old desk and thought better of taking on his new partner in the basement range—for money at least.

Mel dropped his second load on the desk. "My money's on him joining the local PD or getting on the county department up there. He's a cop and always will be."

Cliff Roberts spent the next half hour telling his new partner about Jake's wife, Edie. "Doc Beyer has some ideas and is working with another shrink up there. The doc said they hoped within six months she'd be back to her old self."

"What brought that on? The kidnapping?"

"I guess."

"But the kid made it, and other than the heat stroke, was unharmed."

"The psychiatrists are saying it'll take some time for her to realize that—mentally."

Cliff started leafing through his in-basket. Mel filled a cup of coffee for himself and asked, “You want some?” raising the glass pot.

Cliff raised a finger, “Hold on.” He was reading a FBI bulletin. “I guess I owe Jake five bucks.”

“For what?”

“We were working a string of bank hold-ups and had a line on a couple of women posing as men.” Cliff paused then looked at Mel. “Remember Sylvia and Grace, the two girls who worked at Rotten Rob’s?”

Mel nodded. “Sylvia for sure.” His smile broadened. “Nice legs. Nicer rack.”

“Well, two banks have been hit in North Dakota. One in McClusky, the other in Velva. Same M.O. as the ones back here.”

He flipped through his *Rolodex,* found the number for FBI Agent Allen Jenkin, and dialed. While waiting for the call to go through, he added, “I bet Jake we’d never hear from them again. Well, I was wrong.”

About the Author

Your author is a 75-year-old retiree that winters in Arizona and spends his summers in Michigan. His wife's subtle suggestions resulted in his first novel, *Among the Tin Cans and Broken Glass.* It is based on his personal experiences in the 1960s as a police officer in Detroit as seen through the eyes of Patrolman Jake Bush.

Alley Justice and his latest work, *The County,* are novels with more exciting street cop adventures of Jake Bush in Detroit and Oakland County during the 1970s.

The author's life-long love of bird dogs led to a work of non-fiction, *Good Ones and Scallywags.* This is a collection of short stories about dogs, birds and people he encountered across the country, thus the thought-provoking title.

The Author and children

Made in the USA
Columbia, SC
15 June 2018